Immortality 101: The Intro Course

SASHA'S GAMBLE

Clash of the Queens

J. X. Danforth

Copyright © 2012 by J. X. Danforth

All rights reserved. No part of this book may be used or reproduced in any manner whatsoever without written permission, except in the case of brief quotations embodied in critical articles or reviews. Please do not participate in or encourage the piracy of copyrighted materials in violation of the author's rights. Purchase only authorized editions.

a goodlife guide
www.goodlifeguide.com

TABLE OF CONTENTS

INTRODUCTION: THE SAFFRON STALLION 3
CHAPTER 1: THE PARTY FROM HACK 11
CHAPTER 2: M.V.P. 21
CHAPTER 3: QUO 29
CHAPTER 4: SMALL FAVORS 39
CHAPTER 5: ONE HUNDRED AND TWENTY 49
CHAPTER 6: SOMEONE ELSE'S BLOOD 59
CHAPTER 7: THE PINK PONY 67
CHAPTER 8: THE RIGHT TIME 73
CHAPTER 9: CALISA AND RO 83
CHAPTER 10: BLACK AND WHITE 95
CHAPTER 11: THE SISTERS 111
CHAPTER 12: UNKEMPT REDEMPTION 123
CHAPTER 13: THE TRICK SPIN 141
CHAPTER 14: GO FISH 153
CHAPTER 15: IMMORTALITY 101 167
CHAPTER 16: THE SNYPERX 183
CHAPTER 17: NEESE HIGHWATERS 197
CHAPTER 18: MISTER JEAN-LUC 215
CHAPTER 19: THE THING THAT HELPS 229
CHAPTER 20: TITI CHANG AND THE CRESCENT 239
CHAPTER 21: FORTUNE 257
CHAPTER 22: LADY LUCK 265
CHAPTER 23: THE HEAD TABLE 269
CHAPTER 24: PRESCOTT'S BRAND 281
CHAPTER 25: REBECCA 293
CHAPTER 26: THE ODDS 301
CHAPTER 27: THE WHITE POCKETS 309
CHAPTER 28: SNITCH 319
CHAPTER 29: DUELISTS 333
CHAPTER 30: ERIC 345
CHAPTER 31: KAMELEON 353
CHAPTER 32: MIRACLE 365
CHAPTER 33: STOPPER 371
CHAPTER 34: ONE HUNDRED AND TWENTY 379
CHAPTER 35: ROLL 389
EPILOGUE 397
APPENDIX I 403

For Jason

SASHA'S GAMBLE | *Clash of the Queens*

CUT

You don't gamble to win. You gamble so you can gamble the next day

– Bert Ambrose

IMMORTALITY 101: The Intro Course

THE SAFFRON STALLION

It was a bar.

No matter where it was, no matter who ran it, no matter what the customers called it, it was still a bar, and an old bar nonetheless. Even with all of its post-modern conveniences, the Saffron Stallion was nothing but a bar, complete with the scent of alcohol and desperation, with a hint of hope, usually provided by those who very stubbornly believe that, with enough beer down one's throat, all of one's problems became just another good show.

The patron sitting alone on his red vinyl stool spun in a slow circle, taking in the superficiality of it all. It was not an unattractive superficiality. After all, every soul is superficial at some point in its existence. A little pretense never hurt anyone. By the same token, if a person could make his or herself up, prepared to be judged by appearance alone, so could a bar. With its endlessly tacky name and massive rows of flashing neon, the Saffron Stallion flaunted its goods like the cheap hooker it was built to imitate.

It wasn't all bad though. The patron signaled for service from the bartender. He had to wave extra hard, as the man had little depth perception, what with one bad eye and the other blind. He was missing a finger, too, the middle digit from his left hand, so that it always looked like he was giving someone the bird in reverse.

IMMORTALITY 101: The Intro Course

"What can I do you for?" he shouted to the patron, not bothering to move down from his spot at the end of the bar. With his good hand he grabbed the next shot glass in a long line and began to wipe it with a dishtowel that had never made acquaintance with soap in its entire existence.

The patron wrung his hands. He hated it when the bartender, whose name was Geoffy, cleaned his wares in front of the customers. Not that sanitation was an issue. Not here. No, he just wanted Geoffy's full attention when he ordered his drinks. "You see the menu?" he asked, pointing at the lit board above the bar, colored suspiciously like those seen at popular fast-food joints.

Geoffy didn't look up. It wouldn't have done any good anyway. "Yeah."

"That'd be my order."

Geoffy let out a sound that was a cross between a snort and a short laugh. He'd lost one eye in the Crazy Bets, and none of the Saffron Stallion's regulars would be surprised if he traded in his voice box one of these days, just for some Luck. That was the way old Geoffy was. He denied having lost that finger in a Bet, though. No one knew where that one went. Possibly one day old Geoffy woke up and it had walked off on its own.

"Yer drinking too much, V.P.," he grunted to the patron, simultaneously hauling his own massive, three hundred and fifty-pound bulk to the neat line of bottles against the back wall. His stubby hands worked with a dexterity that seemed unnatural to the rest of him as he began to mix drinks as bright as the bar's neon-pasted walls.

"So what?" said the patron, watching the swirls of alcohol dance their way into a martini glass. "What's it gonna do to me? Kill me? Gut my liver? Don't give me that crap. And don't call me V.P. either. It's a shitty nickname."

"Yer mouth is as dirty as ever."

"And yours is minding my business again, as usual." The patron, the man who hated to be called "V.P.", searched his pockets and swore. "Never a cigarette around when you need one."

Geoffy put the first drink in front of the patron, a dirty martini. The man downed it in one gulp and pushed the glass back. "Keep'em coming."

Old Geoffy mixed up a pink Cosmopolitan, a woman's drink refused by most men as it posed a threat to their masculinity, but alcohol was alcohol, and the patron downed it without a pause, already drumming his fingers impatiently for the next. Geoffy arched a brow slightly, but made no comment. He kept the drinks coming, and his customer drank them one after another.

"You know," he said after the man's fifth drink, a somewhat lame attempt at making conversation, "there was that news about B.C., and I hear…"

"Screw B.C.!" shouted his patron with a sudden burst of anger. Two well-dressed women who had just approached the bar decided it was a bad time and changed their course, steering toward the nearest booth instead. The man did not notice. His eyes were getting just a bit red, which, in Geoffy's experience, was the only sign that the alcohol was taking its toll. "Screw B.C. and her stupid games! She can go f…"

"None of that!" said Geoffy sternly. Despite his occupation pleasing the sleazy and the loose of morals, the bartender considered himself rather conservative, aside from his admitted addiction to the Crazy Bets. "I won't have you running your foul mouth in my bar. I know yer frustrated, V.P., but I *will* toss you out until you decide to cool down."

The patron glared, but said nothing. With one hand he nudged his empty glass, a gesture equivalent of "fill 'er up". Geoffy did, a scotch on the rocks this time. "She's got ya down, hasn't she?"

"Believe it."

"B.C.'s crazy, alright." Blinking his bad eye, Geoffy patted the patron's arm sympathetically, or as sympathetically as he could manage. "Tell you what, ya wanna bum a little Luck off me? Take a turn at the Timetables? Speed things up at least."

The man shook his head solemnly. "Not worth it. I'll just wait."

"And drink yourself into a coma in the meantime?"

"Give me ten reasons why not."

"Awfully demanding of you."

"Just get me another damn drink."

Geoffy shook his broad, lumpy head but said nothing. Instead, he did as he was told. He was, after all, a bartender, and the job of a bartender was to fill his customer to the brim with the toxin of their

5

choice. This particular patron was something of a friend, and he personally liked the guy, despite the man's faults and quirks. He mixed up a gin and tonic, sliding it across the bar to the patron's waiting hand the way those cowboy bartenders would in old western movies. The patron drank it in silence, slowly this time, with his eyes – dark as the stubborn grease stains on the bar floor – downcast. He swallowed one gulp at a time, as if the very act hurt him. Geoffy wondered how much the guy really enjoyed his drinks.

"They're not bad words, you know," the man muttered after two gulps, speaking in a low voice as if intending to hold a conversation with himself.

Geoffy went back to cleaning his row of glasses. "I know," he said lightly.

"They're just words. We made them up. Well, I mean, other people made them up, then gave them meaning, and somehow it's bad now."

"Finish your drink, V.P."

"Stop calling me that," said the patron, but there was a smile on his face this time around. Whether it was the alcohol finally taking effect or his mood picking up in spite of the circumstances, Geoffy didn't know. He took a tiny sip from his drink and said to himself, "Always hated that bloody nickname."

"Why is that?" asked Geoffy, rolling his finger around the inside of the shot glass he was currently cleaning, pressing the dirty dishtowel against its increasingly smudged surface. "Everybody calls you that, you know. You don't ever correct them. Except me. You always correct me."

The man scoffed. "Who knows?" he shrugged. The alcohol was indeed beginning to get to him. He hunched over the bar, struggling to either stay awake or upright, perhaps both. "Maybe I like you."

"Flattering."

"Or maybe I hate you. Hate you like I hate that bitch."

Geoffy scowled, but decided to ignore the profanity. "B.C.?"

"Who else?"

The neon lights of the Saffron Stallion flashed in unison just as Geoffy opened his mouth. He stopped in mid-sentence as the entire bar plunged into darkness then lit up once more before any of the barflies had had a chance to react. The split-second process made him think of what it must be like to be inside a giant's blinking eyelid. His patron did not trouble himself to look up.

"Looks like someone's got a message."

The patron called V.P. downed what was left of his drink and said nothing. He was definitely swiveling a bit now, even sitting still in his seat. Every few seconds he would lean unconsciously to one side, but always managed to pull himself back up again. Geoffy wondered how long it would be before he made acquaintance with the floor, and whether he would be dead to the world before he'd fully left his stool.

The lights flashed again. The patron tried to signal for another drink, only to slump forward onto the bar from lack of support as soon as he raised his hand. Geoffy chuckled and pretended not to see.

Another flash, lasting nearly a full second this time. The portly bartender gazed upward with kneaded brow. Three flashes for one message were rare. Not unheard of but rare. Someone wasn't picking up their message. Usually when a message was important enough to warrant flash signals, the receiver dashed out of his seat to find out what it was.

Unless the receiver was much too drunk.

Setting down his dishtowel, Geoffy nudged his patron's arm with one stubby hand. The man looked up with bloodshot eyes.

"What?" he said, trying to sound menacing and failing.

"You expecting a message?"

For a moment his words didn't seem to register. Then, in an expected drunken stumble, the patron got to his feet, lurched in one direction, and nearly fell. Geoffy reached over the bar and attempted to steady him, but someone had already beaten him to the task.

Standing with her head barely over the top of the far, with five perfectly manicured fingers wrapped around the drunken man's arm, was a young girl, about ten or eleven years of age, dressed up like a perfect dolly in a violet ruffled dress. Though much shorter than the grown man, she managed to keep him from falling. With both hands, she pushed him back onto the stool.

The patron shook his head, attempting to clear it. The girl waited patiently. Geoffy regarded her in surprise.

"It's not every day the Queen herself comes down to my little abode," he said. The girl turned to him and smiled sweetly, playing with her golden curls.

"It's an important message this man is waiting for," she said. "I thought I'd come down here and deliver it myself." She turned to the drunken man. "Isn't that right, Mich?"

The man called V.P., and now "Mich", blinked in confusion. The girl reached into the ruffles of her dress and produced a piece of paper, which she handed to him. It took him two tries to grab hold of it.

"The bet has rolled over," she said. "Do with it what you will." With that, she walked away without another word. The man looked at the slip of paper for a long moment, perhaps trying to focus his eyes for the most of it, and then burst out laughing. Geoffy sighed.

"Another drink?"

"I'm good," said the man, which was exactly what the bartender expected. He got to his feet again and turned to the girl's retreating silhouette, her back painted a strange shade of orange by the flashing neon. "Hey B.C.!" he shouted. "Fuck you!"

Geoffy rolled his eyes and picked up his dishtowel again.

DRAW

If you ain't just a little scared when you enter a casino, you are either very rich or you haven't studied the games enough.

— *VP Pappy*

IMMORTALITY 101: The Intro Course

1
THE PARTY FROM HACK

There was nothing exciting in her life until the red truck.

She was cruising along, listening to a pop radio station when the rain started to fall. Rain was a rare thing in the area, especially this time of year. Texas was a dry state, with dry humor and more than its share of dry personalities. But to Beki Tempest, as well as a few million others, it was home, a pleasant enough place to live. People said "howdy" and drove SUVs. What it lacked in rain it made up in long summers when the smell of sweat and barbecue filled the air.

They were playing one of her favorite songs, one by a solid-bodied young black singer. Though not a die-hard fan, Beki enjoyed the music of this generation. It spoke to a part of her that would always be an angry teenager, one of the many contemplating an escape plan from the drab adulthood that they all wound up in inevitably. She sang along with the tune, though unable to pick up more than half the words clearly.

"*All right, radio listeners!*" chirped the DJ. "*This is the Evening Tune-In with Lindsay K. Shall we play today's round of Take a Guess?*"

This was followed by a round of canned applause.

"*Okay then!*" said Lindsay K., as Beki pictured the DJ absently in her mind, probably a girl at least ten years her junior, wearing something three sizes too small, with a pinstripe tattoo peeking out just over her belt. Tattoos were still hip these days. "*Here comes our first question. Are you ready? Ok. Which well-known celebrity recently spent several million dollars to have a habitat constructed for their pet Siberian tigers?*"

She didn't know.

"*Wow, some people have all the luxury, don't they? Do we have a first caller? Oh! There it is!*" – the faint sound of fumbling – "*You're on the air!*"

"*Elvis!*"

Beki snorted and held on to the wheel.

"*No!*" the young, probably-bubble-platinum-blond DJ cried indignantly and hung up. "*God! Some people! Elvis is dead, get a clue! Ok, next caller. You're on the air!*"

"*Hello?*" came a confused, nasal voice. "Am I speaking to the operator?"

"*Yes, you're on the air, hello? What's your answer?*"

"*Yes, I need to order item number 354 on catalog...*"

The DJ hung up with a click. A rumble of conversation came from the background, obviously the young woman yelling at someone to "get those phone numbers sorted out already! This is the third time this week!"

"*Ok, sorry about that!*" said the chirpy voice again. "*We had some technical difficulties, but that shouldn't happen again. All right, let's do that again. The question is... oh wait, we have a caller.*"

The sky was turning a swimmy gray, as if someone had spilled gray watercolor. Leaning forward to examine the gathering clouds, Beki briefly wondered whether she was going to make it inside before the rain came down. She had not brought an umbrella with her and, with the heat wave, hadn't even thought about a jacket. But if luck held out, she should arrive just before it really came down.

"*I hope you have an answer for me, caller,*" said the DJ, a hint of irritation under her voice.

"*Yes, I do!*" replied a loud, slightly hoarse voice on the other end. It sounded like a middle-aged woman just beginning to get up in her years who had shouted orders to her children or husband one time too many.

"*That is absolutely correct!*" The DJ cried after the caller gave a name that Beki had never heard of. "*That is the celebrity who just last week spent 4.6 million dollars to have a one-square mile playground built for his pet tigers. Congratulation! You win our prize for the week, a...*"

"Oh, miss?"

The DJ paused, not used to being interrupted. "*Yes?*"

"Elvis ain't dead. I saw 'im at the gas station the other day."

Beki could almost see the DJ's wide-eyed, blank stare. "*Oh, um... that's nice. I mean, really?*"

"Yeah, he was driving a blue Mercedes Benz."

She turned the radio off.

Her destination was a party. Or that was what the invitation called it. Although there were more places than she could count that she would have rather gone at the moment.

The host was someone she did not wish to offend, more from wanting to save herself from a hissy fit than out of any sort of respect or affection. The dress was supposed to be casual but neat, which was code for "primp but don't look like you're primping". After procrastinating until five minutes before absolutely having to leave, Beki applied whatever makeup was nearest to her hand, pulled her hair back into a ponytail, and put on the cleanest blouse she could find. Her eleven year-old son had raised his head from the Gameboy in his hand long enough to give her a strange look as she stepped into her rarely-worn strappy dress sandals.

"What?"

"Nothing." He went back to his game, but one of his eyebrows was still suspiciously arched. She clicked her tongue and ruffled his hair, one of those things that kids hate but will miss when they grow up. "You just look weird all made up."

She glared in mock anger. "I do not."

"Yes you do," he insisted. He had thick, shiny brown hair like his father. For a boy his age, he was smart, but not smart enough to be labeled 'genius' or even 'gifted'. For that, Beki was grateful. She never was one for labels. "It doesn't look like you. You know, not like you normally."

"What do I look like normally."

Her son shrugged. "Messy."

"Messy?"

"But in a good way."

"Messy's good?"

"Sometimes."

"Is that why your room is the way it is?"

She saw the mischievous smile curl even though he didn't look up. "Maybe."

"Clean your room."

"No."

It had become a game at this point. Truth be told, she had long given up trying to force or coax him into the task. When he's older, Beki figured, he'd have to clean it, especially if he didn't want his girlfriends to see his Spiderman underpants with a giant hole on one butt cheek. The crunching of tires on gravel came from the driveway.

"Your father's home," she said, leaning down toward her son, who tore his eyes away long enough to kiss her on the cheek. "I'm off. Keep the junk food to a minimum. Tell him to make you some real food, and fix your bicycle while he's at it."

"Ok, mom," replied the boy in a tone that indicated the old 'in one ear, out the other'. But that was all right. If he didn't care about his bike, she didn't. It kept him out of the streets during the day at least.

She met her husband on the driveway as he got out of his car. He opened his arms and she dove into them. He kissed her, then looked her up and down.

"Don't you look fine," he whispered into her ear. "Too bad you have to waste it." His hands moved upward toward her breasts. "Forget the party. Stay here and play with me."

She pushed him off teasingly and kissed him again. "No honey. I have to go. I'm late. Make some dinner for yourself and Eric, OK?"

"Ok," he mumbled from the groove in her neck.

"I'm serious. There's chicken in the fridge."

"Uh-huh."

"You won't take him to a fast food joint like last time?"

"Uh-uh."

He wasn't listening. Sighing, she gripped his chin with one hand and looked him in the eye. "Repeat what I said."

"Chicken, no fast food."

"Good. I'm off." She took the car keys from his hand.

"Looks like rain," he called after her.

"No it doesn't."

"Suit yourself. And watch those sharp curves," he added, watching her walk away. "I know I am."

Gilligan Milani's house was as perfect as they came, if one's definition of perfection just happened to coincide with every popular fashion, interior decorating, and/or Hollywood fad magazine ever printed. From the manicured lawn punctuated with roses in all the right places, to the paved sidewalk leading up to the house made with stones that just happened to match the awning over the front door, to the name-brand kitchen toys, to the bedroom draped in purple silks that Gilligan coyly called her 'playroom' then brayed with laughter as if it was the most hilarious thing in the world; all the perfection ground on Beki's nerves exactly the wrong way. In this, she supposed, the house was still fulfilling its duty as something perfect—nothing else offended her senses quite so perfectly as Gilligan Milani's house.

From the moment she set foot in the house, Beki found herself drowning in two things. One was the heavy scent of incense, as mismatched and overwhelming as one could imagine. Gilligan always fancied herself an 'appreciator' of exotic things such as incense, or perhaps just exotic-smelling things. But the truth, as far as Beki herself could tell, was that the incense, as well as the French coffee press, the Indian throw, and the Chinese fans hanging on the walls, was merely another attempt by Gilligan to make herself appear as sophisticated as possible without cracking a book.

The other was regret. She berated herself severely for not staying home and curling up in a bathrobe with her husband. Even cleaning up her son's room sounded very appealing at the moment.

Gilligan herself was nowhere to be seen at the moment, neither was anyone else she knew. Beki did not know Gilligan's friends, nor did she care for them. Over the years, though, she did hear quite a bit about them, as Gilligan was quite the chatty one, especially when it came to her painted life. By the same note, hearing about it was like listening to paint peel. Beki knew enough at the moment to identify one particularly portly (and somewhat unattractive) man with a unibrow in the corner. According to Gilligan, he had had a fling with her, or rather wanted to, while dating another woman who, again according to Gilligan, was completely wrong for him.

The house was one-story with three bedrooms, and professionally decorated to the last detail. By the door was a small, delicate end table with a pile of nametags that read "Hi, my name is ___, let's be friends". At the end of the front hall was the vast living room, adorned with various expensive furniture that looked almost too kempt to touch. To the left was the hall leading to the bedrooms, where, again according to Gilligan, many wild, drunken romps had taken place over the years. To the right was the kitchen, which for the evening was an open bar. Beki considered helping herself to a drink just as a shrill greeting invaded her ears.

"Beckster!"

She grimaced, plastered a smile over it, and turned around as Gilligan maneuvered her purple-draped bulk through the partygoers. Though not an enormously overweight woman, Gilligan did not carry her weight well. She walked awkwardly and moved her bulging rear from side to side just a tad too much. Her passion for purple was evident in her floor-length sundress, which would have been flattering had her massive chest not been in danger of breaking free. Beki kept her smile steady as the woman wrapped two thick arms around her.

"How are you, Beckster?"

She hated being called Beckster. It was a nickname she had picked up in high school, and was kept going only by Gilligan's persistence. Still, it could be worse, she supposed.

"Fabulous," she replied, returning the hug. "Great party. Just like you to have an open bar."

Gilligan grinned, her whole face wrinkling up like a peach left in the sun too long. "Of course!" she said proudly. "A party is not a party without alcohol. Remember that time I got drunk in the Bahamas with Wendy, and Mark, and Ethan? Oh, it was so wild…"

Beki didn't remember. She had not been there. However, she did remember the story, as she has heard it at least a dozen times, all within the space of Gilligan's last three parties. Still, she kept quiet and nodded along as the woman told it.

"Where's Jonathan?" Gillian suddenly asked with a scowl. "Don't tell me he's left you to come out here alone."

Beki shook her head quickly. "No, no. He had to stay at work. Believe me, he'd never want to miss one of your parties."

There was not a word of truth in her answer, but Gilligan did not suspect. Jonathan had accompanied her to many of Gilligan's parties in their fifteen years of marriage, but this time she had declined when he offered to come. Jonathan had no love for the woman, and being here tonight would only result in him being grumpy and irritable later. In the interest of her marriage, she had let him stay home to drink beer and watch old movies.

Gilligan poured herself a drink. "I tell you, if I'm crazy enough to get married again, I'd want someone who goes everywhere with me. And won't forget birthdays, anniversaries, and all the other gift-giving holidays. It's just a rule, you know? And I'd have my wedding in the Bahamas. Gosh I do love the Bahamas. And the rehearsal dinner…"

Beki listened. It was what she was most accustomed to doing. Of course only one insignificant part of her brain was concentrating on the conversation. The rest was frantically trying to keep her body from making a dive for the bar.

"How's work going?" she asked as Gilligan took a breather to drink from her glass.

"Dull," replied the friend she hadn't quite considered a friend in over a decade. "Except there is this one cute guy who keeps hitting on me. I'm not interested right now, of course, but it's always nice to have the option."

"Wasn't your boss interested in you?"

"Oh that. Yes, I suppose. I do like him. He tried to kiss me once – did I tell you that?"

"Yes."

"Well, I might let him one of these days. The poor guy's got it bad."

Gilligan was, in politically acceptable terms, an administrative assistant – in layman's terms, a secretary. Her job mostly consisted, as far as Beki could tell, of sitting at a desk, wearing too much makeup,

17

answering phones, and flirting with everything that moved past her desk. Due to some cosmic phenomenon Beki could not comprehend, Gilligan was extremely popular with the gentlemen. Again, according to Gilligan herself.

"I may have him over one of these nights," the woman was saying, "and let him have a little romp in my playroom."

Her fingers crept toward the nearest bottle of Vodka. Beki quickly stopped herself and asked, "Do you still talk to Herb?"

"Not if I can help it. But he was at this other party last week, did I tell you? He was with that little bitch of his. But not for much longer, I can tell. Serves him right for cheating on me."

On her salary, Gilligan could not have afforded such a house, nor to throw the parties she adored. Her ex-husband Herbert had been a nice man if Beki ever saw one. After the divorce he had let Gilligan keep the house, and still gave her a fair share of spousal support. As far as Beki was concerned, Herb did not cheat. The woman he was with was sane and nice, if a bit bland like Herb himself. After his marriage to Gilligan collapsed after two years and he had moved out for six months, Herb met his new mate at a support group for survivors of troubled relationships. He claimed they did not hook up until the divorce was final and Beki believed him wholeheartedly.

"Yeah," she said absently. "Serves him right."

"Oh, there's Marcus!" Gilligan exclaimed, waving across the room to more people Beki didn't know. "I'm gonna go say 'hi'. He has such a crush on me, you know."

"Isn't your boss jealous?"

"He doesn't have to know." Giggling ecstatically, Gilligan set her empty glass aside, a sign that she was about to go mingle and enjoy her party and leave Beki on her own for the rest of the night. "Have fun. Have a drink."

"I have to drive tonight."

"Oh, hack!" Gilligan had an accent. Beki never figured out what it was aside from the fact that it made her "*heck*"*s* sound like "*hack*". "Relax! You're always so tense. And put on a nametag. That way people will know you."

"Yeah, I will." Beki said, allowing her voice to drift off since Gilligan was already nearly out of hearing range. A few moments later a burst of laughter erupted from across the room, followed by the sound of a familiar "Oh to hack with it!"

"To hack with it," Beki muttered to herself, and settled into a lone, secluded chair with a diet soda.

After an hour or two the party didn't seem so bad. While everyone else was busy pouring alcohol down their throats and copping a feel here and there, Beki found herself in sole control of the TV remote. She flipped the channels until she found a good movie and sank comfortably into a corner of the couch. Though she had picked up a nametag, nothing gave her the motive to fill it out. It sat empty on the nearest end table under a lavender-topped lamp. As the party guests became increasingly drunk, the noise level also rose, but it didn't bother Beki because no one bothered her. Gilligan's friends stuck to themselves and no one made an attempt to speak to her. Gilligan herself was nowhere to be seen, probably entertaining one of her male guests in her 'playroom'.

The movie was *Charlie and the Chocolate Factory*, a kids' movie but quite a classic in her book. There was something about children and candy, a sweet innocence that seemed lost in today's society. Sometimes Beki missed the simpler times, when kids played with friends and not computers, and learned about sex at seventeen instead of eight. Even her son, a good boy in every way, spoke with a general knowledge of the world that she did not gain until she was nearly twice his age. Children who grew up too much too fast were frightening.

Then again, some may argue that Willy Wonka was quite frightening himself. What kind of man wore purple suits and invited children, hopped up on sugar, to watch dancing midgets?

Thunder rumbled outside. The party guests roared with drunken excitement. Violet chewed on a piece of gum and blew up into a blueberry.

At some point someone sat down on the other end of the couch. Beki did not notice right away. Just another guest who had drunk too much. Though a bit underdressed compared to the rest in his wrinkled button-up shirt and dark slacks, he was as wasted as the rest of them. His eyes were bloodshot and his face puffy. He ran a hand over his face and through his dark hair, as if attempting to clear his mind. She sipped her soda and paid him no mind.

He watched the movie with her without a word, nodding off every now and then but always waking himself up instead. It was really somewhat entertaining to watch. Beki expected him to fall asleep at any second and slide right off the couch.

No such luck though. The movie rolled to an end on its usual happy note. Charlie flew off in the glass elevator. Beki reached for the remote. The newcomer beat her to it.

"Can we go now?" he asked her, and straightened a bit.

She blinked. "Excuse me?"

"Can we go now?" he repeated.

She chuckled. Obviously the man was so drunk he had mistaken her for his wife or girlfriend. "You shouldn't be asking me that," she said. "Want me to go find your wife? What's her name?"

The man burst out laughing, so hard that tears came out of his eyes. "You're funny," he said, then suddenly turned serious again, and, amazing as it was, sober. "Let's go. You don't belong here anymore. We can start another Round."

"No more drinks for you, buddy." Beki stood. "I'll go get you some coffee."

"Don't need any damned coffee," the man said stubbornly. "I'm sober enough to collect."

Thunder boomed once more outside.

2
M.V.P.

If she had to estimate, Beki would guess that the man was anywhere from thirty to forty-five years old. He was one of those people who could easily pass for a wide range of ages and look good doing it, though at the moment he looked a bit less than fine. In fact, he looked less than conscious. His eyes were red and his pupils dilated. His hair, which was thick and brown, spotted here and there with highlights, would probably be the envy of every middle-aged man in the room had he taken a second to comb it. At the moment, it was half-hiding his unfocused eyes. He smelled of alcohol, perhaps of drinks much heavier than those actually being provided at the party. Perhaps he wasn't even a guest, more likely a crasher who got his kicks making moves at unsuspecting partygoers.

As she watched, the man tried to push himself off the sofa with some effort. He was quite tall, with a dry face and tight skin. After the first attempt failed him, he cleared his throat as if a bit embarrassed and tried again. This time his effort yielded result as he got to his feet shakily, wobbled as if experiencing a bout of vertigo, and managed to remain upright to Beki's surprise.

"Alright," he said in a hoarse voice, then coughed and cleared his throat again. "Let's get going. We'll figure something out on the way."

If there was a man more desperately in need of coffee and/or a good slap on the head, Beki didn't know where to find him. Instead of sticking around to watch the man make a bigger fool out of himself, she decided the better course of action was to find someone who knew his name to take care of him. But just as she began to turn, five clammy fingers wrapped themselves around her arm.

"Come on," the man said persistently. "There is no point for you to stick around here. There's nothing here for you anymore."

He was even drunker than she thought. Beki pulled her arm out of his grasp. "Please don't touch me," she said as politely as one could to a drunk. "You have the wrong person."

He sighed. It was an exasperated sound. Raising a hand, he rubbed his face, hard. When he dropped it, he suddenly looked like a different person. Though his eyes were still red, next to all other traces of drunkenness seemed to have vanished. He stared at her with his dark eyes.

"Your name is Rebecca Tempest," he said.

She blinked. "What?"

"You are married to Jonathan Haden Tempest. Your son is eleven years old. You graduated college at twenty-two and have been working as a CPA. You live in a two-story house that you bought from your grandmother, decorated with furniture your aunt gave you as a wedding present." A fit of coughs seized him and he covered his mouth until it passed. "Was any of that off?"

She didn't know how to answer. As part of her mind searched for a way to slip out of the party to the safety of her car, the other parts fought to come up with a response that did not betray her sudden fear. She smiled. It felt like a shield.

"Did Gilligan tell you about me?" she asked, taking a tone of making casual conversation. "She's such an interesting person, isn't she? I remember when we met in school…"

"Don't know her," the man cut in, and coughed again. "Is she the fat chick in the purple dress? Someone should tell her she looks like an eggplant." Though looking much more composed now, his skin still had a slightly green hue that made Beki suspect he may vomit on her any second, which would provide her with a chance to escape even if it might cost her the blouse and expensive sandals. "But you've known her since high school. You don't like her because she's shallow and obnoxious and won't stop flirting with your husband. You secretly wish her the plague and feel guilty about it. Last year you bought her birthday gift from a rummage sale and told her it cost a fortune. Is all of that correct?"

It had to be a joke, her mind argued. Gilligan must have put this guy up to something. She always thought her jokes were funny, unable to comprehend the fact that a thirty-eight-year-old woman making prank calls and using novelty gags was just a bit on the pathetic side. But then again, Beki decided, what did she know? Maybe all of the gentlemen callers Gilligan claimed to have thought her silly tricks were cute.

But what about the gift she had bought? No one knew about it. She had picked out a sweater in Gilligan's size. It was a knock-off name brand, but very hard to tell apart from the real thing without a trained eye. Gilligan had always been the one to obsess about the value of gift giving, and it had seemed perfectly ironic for her to coo over a five-dollar sweater as if it had cost seventy-five-fifty.

The man was still looking at her, and she couldn't look away, for fear that he might pull a knife on her, even in this crowded party. And why not? He had obviously spent enough time stalking her.

"I'm leaving," she said firmly.

The man gave a sigh of relief and ran a hand through his hair. "Thank goodness," he said. "Come on, let's go."

"I'm not leaving with you," she told him, taking a step back. Her purse was at the foot of the sofa. She grabbed it and kept it between her and the persistent stranger. "I'm going to get in my car and go home. If you follow me, I will call the police."

"You can't hold on to this life forever."

He really was planning to kill her. Aside from the obvious problems with that, Beki found herself cursing her decision to even step out the door today. This just went to prove nothing good ever came from one of Gilligan's parties.

Without another word, she turned away and forced herself into the crowd. Few people looked up as she pushed herself through, putting as much distance between herself and the man as possible. She was nervous. She couldn't remember the last time she was this nervous. Was the man on her tail? Beki didn't turn around to look.

23

IMMORTALITY 101: The Intro Course

A few feet away from the door she stopped. Her car was outside, where darkness reigned and no one would hear her scream over the music and conversation inside should he decide to take her out before she could make it to the curb. Pivoting suddenly, she turned to the left, to the nearest washroom. It was the ideal place to hide while she called the police on her cell phone.

The man had to still be around. She did not have the kind of luck that would result in him giving up and disappearing just because she seemed unwilling to cater to his sick obsessions. However, she was lucky enough for the washroom to be empty. Walking inside quickly, she closed the door and fumbled with the lock.

It was broken.

With a cry of frustration she yanked on the knob.

And he was there. She was trapped. He was looking at her as if scolding her for running. She took a step backwards as he walked inside and closed the door behind him. Her hands felt around every surface she could find, looking for anything to use as a weapon.

"You don't have to do that," he told her, a little too calmly as the door shut with a light click. "There is nothing I can do to you at this point. No matter what happens, you'll be back at the Wheel soon."

The wheel? He meant her car. What else could it be?

"You must know why I'm here," he continued. "Your bet rolled over. Not too long ago. And…" – he sighed – "it did not end in your favor. I'm sorry."

He was crazy. But Beki kept quiet.

"So now you have to go back. I'm sure you know that. There's no point in sticking around, playing these little games with me. You and I both know Rebecca Tempest no longer exists. Her family will only suffer if you continue to stay here. Your Round has ended. Let the others get on with their game."

She took a deep breath. "Do you think this is a game?" she asked him. "You stalking and scaring me like this?"

He studied her. "Are you serious?"

"What's wrong with you?!" she shouted at him. Fear was slowly shaping into rage. "I don't even know you. And what do you know about my family?"

Shock washed over the man's face. It seemed to be working. Her legs felt like limp noodles, but at last she was getting a reaction out of him. But the danger had not passed. For all she knew, she had just enraged him into dispatching her on the spot. There was a hairbrush by the sink. She wondered if she could throw it at him as a momentary distraction.

"Wow," he breathed. Hands on his hips, he looked around, as if thinking things over. "It seems I've made some sort of mistake." He trailed his eyes on her again. "Can I ask you something?"

"What?"

"When was the last time you had a traffic accident?"

It was such a ridiculous question that she wanted to laugh in spite of the situation. But Beki kept a straight face. "High school," she replied coldly.

"Really?"

"Yes." She didn't know why he wanted to know, nor did she care.

The man nodded. "Alright then," he said. Something about his demeanor had changed. He was looking around, fidgeting with his hands as if distracted. "I'm sorry to bother you, Mrs. Tempest." He started to turn away, but paused and faced her again. This time he did not meet her eyes, but kept this gaze low.

"I know what I've being saying probably doesn't make sense right now," he said, almost shyly. "I don't want you to worry about any of it. It's not really the time or the place to worry about it."

She looked him up and down as he tucked his hands into his pockets. Now that she wasn't quite as frightened, Beki noticed that the man in front of her was actually somewhat attractive, in a weathered, worn sort of way. "Then why did you say them?" she asked.

"Because I made a mistake," he answered. "My name is Michigan Von Phant. There's a chance that will become important to you in the near future. And I must say" – he winked in a way that made her skin crawl – "for a second there you really sounded like yourself."

Then he was gone, disappearing as unexpectedly as he had appeared in her life. Beki stood in the washroom for a long moment after he left, until an inebriated blond woman stumbled inside and threw up all over her expensive sandals.

IMMORTALITY 101: The Intro Course

More likely than not, Beki Tempest was more aware of life in general as she left the party that night. There was no way to tell for sure since, after all, how could anyone be certain of these things? But that was what she felt in the depth of her mind as she emerged from Gilligan Milani's over-decorated house that night. The rain was just beginning to fall from the dark heavens and she could feel the cold pre-storm breeze tickle every hair on her bare arms.

It was often when one was deprived of something that one gained an increased appreciation for it. In this case it was a near-loss that triggered Beki's sensitivity to life. Had she come close to becoming the six-o'clock news? Were they going to bring in a camera to film her mutilated body on the floor of Gilligan's gold-tiled bathroom? Gilligan would probably love that. She'd probably give a tear-filled interview on how she lost a "dear friend" who "meant everything", then let the handsome, single cameraman comfort her by playing peek-a-boo between her breasts. Somehow, in Gilligan's mind, this would all be in loving memory of Beki, because that was just the kind of friend she was.

Beki reached the car just in time. The clouds parted and rain drummed against the roof of her car. She didn't start the engine, or even take out her keys. Instead, she sat there in the darkness listening to the rain.

You can't hold on to this life forever.

Had he been a normal dinner guest, she might have found the comment to be of philosophical value, worthy of an interesting conversation. But no such luck. Of course not. She wasn't the sort of person to have that kind of luck. No small favors in this life.

But then again, up until tonight, she had also never imagined herself to have the bad sort of luck, the sort that led her to meet a man who was obviously obsessed with her, watched her every move over the years, and knew far too much about her for comfort. It frightened her that he knew about Gilligan's gift, much more than the fact that he knew about her husband and son. After all, if one could not hide little secrets, one could hide nothing.

The thing to do, she decided, the reasonable thing, was to file a police report in the morning. Though she was inclined to believe the local police was less than helpful on most everyday matters, it couldn't hurt to do so. The man had been rather helpful in providing her with his name, even if it might be false.

Michigan Von Phant. It sounded like some sort of over-stylized num de plume.

With that, she fished the car key out of her purse and stuck it into the ignition, giving it an extra hard shove with a sense of resolve. The car hummed to life and she pulled away from Gilligan's curb.

To say the rain was pouring would be an understatement. It was as if some greater being above was emptying a gigantic ladleful of murky soup onto the earth. Even as the windshield wipers worked like crazy, doing their best to keep her line of sight clean, she couldn't help but feel annoyed that they could not turn faster than they were. The world drowned in itself as she drove twenty miles below the speed limit, merging as carefully as she could onto the near-deserted highway.

Though she could see no more than twenty feet in front of her, she did not fear getting into a traffic accident. For one thing, there were few cars on the road, and the ones she could see were moving just as slowly and tentatively as she was. As the car crawled forward, Beki began to wonder whether it was a good idea to leave the party early after all. She could've hid in the crowd for another hour or so until the rain let up. The incomprehensible Mister Michigan Von Phant couldn't possibly do anything to her with so many witnesses.

Or could he? She didn't want to think about it. The sooner she was home, the better. She wanted more than anything to be wrapped in the arms of her husband, to feel protected.

Perhaps it was Von Phant's question about traffic accidents that made her more aware of the red truck when it came barreling down on her from behind.

It was in the start of a tailspin, its front wheels just beginning to skid when its hulking shape appeared in her rear-view mirror. She happened to glance up at the right instant to spot it, and under normal circumstances would have held her position, assuming the truck was merely speeding and planning to pass her.

But it was in the last split second that she remembered his question, and thus remembered the last traffic accident she had being involved in, one that was less than half her fault and more than half the fault of an elderly gentleman who made a right turn too quickly. It had resulted in a bent bumper on her first hand-me-down car and an hour's lecture from her father, who thought it a great crime that she did not call to notify him right away.

And it was this thought that made her turn her wheel at the last second, out of the truck's way as it sped past her, missing her side view mirror by less than two inches and disappearing into the rain. She would continue along her way, driving as carefully as she could. She would pass the truck again in twenty minutes, but she would not notice. By then the red truck would have stopped, its custom-fitted rims spinning in futility as the tires sat silently in the mud. Its painstakingly polished grill would be bent, its hood arched upward like a misshapen tent, and its driver, a middle-aged man with a bald spot, a wife, two young children, a mortgage, and a mistress, would be leaning forward, his arms limp along his sides and his head against the cracked windshield, making a nice, big splatter like a ripe melon.

3
QUO

Stat hated his job.

It wasn't about pay, since it wasn't a paid job. No one was paid in his line of work, or rather that was the assumption. He was the only one in his line of work as far as he and everybody else was concerned. No one was sure how that happened. Hell, he had no idea how it turned out that way. He didn't know why he was at this job, and barely remembered what its purpose was.

To put it simply, he was a peacekeeper. That concept in and of itself was a hazy one. What was peace really? Did he stop the bar fights at the Saffron Stallion? Did he keep the black market Luck from circulating? Did he even try to enforce the rules of the games? The answer to the first question was usually 'no one cares', and for the last three, both 'yes' and 'no'.

His goal, overall, was to maintain. To keep things running the way they were supposed to run for as long as possible. There were no manuals, no rules, no guidelines, and no examples of how this was to be done, and not a single person knew what would happen if things stopped running the way they should. They just knew it was better to keep things the same, to keep the Wheel spinning and the dice rolling.

Stat lit a cigarette as he sat at the bar. Geoffy, who usually made an attempt to be friendly to all patrons, was making an extraordinary effort to ignore his existence at the other end of the bar. The whole place smelled of sweat. Sweat indicated heat, excitement, and fear.

Fear was what ran this place. These people existed on fear. Fear was what kept him busy. Fear was what gave him the power and authority that he did not want. Fear was the adrenaline that fed the brain of this whole operation. Everyone was so afraid. Afraid of him, afraid of the Wheel, afraid of living. And yet, they are drawn to it, every single one of them, himself included.

Eyeing the nervous Geoffy in amusement, he put out the cigarette on the surface of the bar. Geoffy seemed to contemplate raising a stink about it, but thought better of it and kept his head low, pretending to be occupied with cleaning the glass mug in his hand for the third time. Stat flicked the cigarette butt behind the bar with his fingers. Geoffy frowned but still said nothing.

"Aren't you going to say anything?" Stat asked, drumming his fingers on the bar. "Last week a guy spilled a shot and you yelled until you turned purple."

Geoffy grunted and kept cleaning the glass. He did not move to approach Stat, nor look up. "You do whatever you want, Stat," he said. "Ain't that the way it's been?"

"Maybe I like to be challenged once in a while."

"That so?"

"Must you assume everything I say is a trap?"

"Ain't it?"

"Only slightly more than half the time."

Two women approached the bar. They were both young, both beautiful, and both decided simultaneously, in some unspoken way, to sit as far away from Stat as possible. That was the usual way of things. He made people uncomfortable. One did not become a peacekeeper to socialize, or at least that's what his predecessor would've told him if he had one. He might have had a predecessor once upon a time. Truth be told, he couldn't remember. "You gonna offer me a drink or what?"

"What do you want?"

"Water."

"Don't got none of that."

"Then a wine spritzer."

Geoffy muttered under his breath, a comment that was either unintentionally overheard by Stat, or was spoken just loud enough so that his ear would catch it. It was something about a wine spritzer being a girly drink. Stat allowed himself a low smirk. After all, if he was stuck with this job, he was going to enjoy what little perks it had, one of which was to get under people's skins without really trying. Geoffy slid the drink across the bar clumsily, most likely on purpose. It wobbled a bit, threatening to tip over before Stat caught it. He didn't have to look up to know Geoffy was disappointed that it didn't spill onto his clean white shirt.

"I meant a white wine spritzer, Geoffy," he said, clinking his nails against the glass. "This is red."

That earned him a slanted glare from Geoffy. The bartender proceeded to clean the mug in his hand with more vigor than before. "Red only," he said in a huff.

"Now, now. That attitude won't get you back into Gypsy's bed any time soon."

The mug in Geoffy's hand slammed down on the bar. Geoffy's bad eye fixated on him in a manner that told him in no uncertain terms that he'd gone too far. Taking his red wine spritzer in one hand, Stat leapt off the stool and tipped an invisible hat at the bartender.

"Here's wishing you a good evening," he said.

Geoffy did not reply, nor did he attempt to enforce the usual rule of 'no glasses leave the bar'. And usually, Geoffy was quite a stickler about the rules of his bar.

Stat didn't care.

As soon as he was out of Geoffy's sight, which was actually a pretty short distance, he dumped the drink in the pot of the nearest plastic plant. A party of three was chatting away at a nearby table. Stat strolled by, left his glass in the table's center, and kept walking. The three looked up at him, at the glass, and went back to the conversation. One of them absently nudged the glass aside to the lonely, unoccupied side of the table as if it carried some sort of disease.

His watch said midnight when he entered the gates of the suburban community. It was called Edge Wood, a pretentious name for mostly pretentious people. The rows of small, quaint houses made him think of

IMMORTALITY 101: The Intro Course

dollhouses, filled with little plastic people, pretending to go on with their pretend lives. Some part of him envied them, because they had something he could never hope for, something called normality, even if it was all just pretend.

They pretend to live, pretend to love, and pretend to have something to work for in this realm. Little white houses as protective barriers, away from the fear, away from the paranoia, away from what they themselves could do with a pair of dice in their hands.

Still, even if it was all just a game, part of him yearned for it. He felt like the child everyone excluded from their playtime because he had a crooked nose or a clubfoot, despite the fact that he did not remember ever being a child. Was it really that long ago? Had he not played a Round in so long?

Stat slowed his footstep in front of one of the community's smallest houses. Its front was almost a perfect square, painted a light grassy green with white trims. The door was red and a black grate covered the sole visible window. Hanging above the door was a single lonesome lamp. Some may call such a house unique, or quaint, or some other awkwardly flattering word, but Stat preferred to call things as they were: the house was just plain ugly.

A dim light could be seen through the window, which was covered on the inside by lacy blue curtains. It might be too late to visit right now, but then the house's occupants kept an unusual schedule as it was. Every hour was just as perfect and inconvenient as the next. Stat looked up at the ceiling of the dome. It was black at the moment, a mock, starless sky. Here and there it had fallen into disrepair, exposing bits of wire and electrodes. He could pretend they were stars, he supposed. Not that it mattered. No one remembered what the real sky looked like anymore anyway. It was just another shield they had made for themselves, to keep the occupants safe and ignorant should the real sky ever come crashing down.

He ascended the faded stairs and knocked, then waited. It usually took quite a long time for the house's master to answer the door, and this time was no exception. So he waited, rocking back and forth on the porch and humming an unnamed tune. A shadow briefly appeared in the window of the house next door, and then just as quickly disappeared. They'd seen him. Usually they drew the drapes after they saw him.

He waited. Yes, there went the drapes.

Finally, a little less than an eternity later, the red door opened a smidgen and a pale hand appeared, followed by half a face, hidden by a dark hood. Grimm Sullivan liked his privacy, which apparently extended to showing his eyes and nose. A second later, another hand appeared, this one holding tightly on to a crooked cane. Stat smiled.

"Evening, Grimm," he said.

Grimm gave a slow nod, an acknowledgement and return of the greeting.

"Is it a bad time?"

Grimm turned his hooded head to one side, then to the other. *No, it's all right.*

"Can I come in?"

There was a momentary pause as Grimm maneuvered his cane so he could turn aside, clearing a path for Stat to enter. He did, and closed the door behind him. Grimm led him, walking with the weary dignity of a weathered man, to the small kitchen. With one pale hand, Grimm pointed at the old, chipped breakfast table. Its best days were behind it. Paint had fallen here and there, some of it almost looked like it had been chipped off on purpose. There were two chairs on either side of it, in spite of the fact that the house rarely had visitors. Stat sat down in one of them. Grimm raised a hand and made a gesture as if pouring from a pot. Stat nodded.

"Yes, tea would be fine."

With obvious effort, Grimm dragged himself to the kitchen using his staff. A series of awkward noises ensued as he began the difficult process of making tea using one skeletal hand. Stat didn't offer to help, nor did he wonder how his host was managing the task. Grimm wouldn't have it – it was routine.

The simple kitchen overlooked the living room, which was as just simply arranged, with only a couch, a bookcase, and a wooden stool in front of a fireplace that had not seen a flame in many moons. In front of the fireplace, on the stool, sat the most beautiful accessory in the entire house, her hands folded and knees together, the frills of her dress tumbling down along her legs like white, lacy waves of the tide. The ribbons in her hair were coming undone, but she didn't notice. She was facing the wall, her eyes were closed as usual, and she did not stand to

IMMORTALITY 101: The Intro Course

acknowledge the guest. Her skin was fair, her hair was like a waterfall of caramel and honey, and her lips begged to be tasted.

It was rather sad that, despite all her beauty, she was little more than a marionette. Stat forced himself to tear his eyes away from her. Grimm did not like it when others stared at her.

Though he wouldn't exactly consider their relationship close or special, Stat felt comfortable enough calling Grimm a friend, despite the fact that he had never gotten a clear look at the man's face. Grimm wore a hooded robe at all times, concealing his face from both friend and foe. The only parts of his body visible were his hands, which were thin as twigs and covered with pasty white skin. The joints of his fingers sometimes creaked as he wrapped them around his long cane, which was the only means he had of standing upright with his lame leg. Although Stat never figured out which of his legs was lame – it seemed to switch from day to day. Grimm never told and he never asked.

The cane was as curious as Grimm himself, long and knobby like the broken branch of an ancient tree. It was black as the night, though upon close inspection it did not appear to be painted. Stat knew no tree that grew so dark naturally. But that was another curiosity he never bothered to satisfy.

Fifteen minutes later, the marionette still had not moved.

Another ten minutes later, Grimm reappeared, balancing a hot pot of tea and two cups miraculously in one hand. A stranger might rush to help, fearing an impending accident, but in all the years Stat had known Grimm, he had never dropped a pot of tea.

Stat waited patiently as Grimm poured the tea and then settled himself into the other chair. He took his own cup and raised it.

"Cheers."

If Grimm was amused, he gave no sign. Leaning his cane against the wall, he brought his tea up to his lips. His chin and mouth was as much as Stat had ever seen of him. And judging by that, his face was as sunken and thin as the rest of him.

Stat set down his cup. "So, how's work, Grimm?"

At first it seemed the other had not heard. But, after a moment of silence, Grimm shook his head slowly, turned first to one side then the other.

"Dull and depressing as usual?"

A nod, just as slow.

"Do you want me to stop coming here, Grimm?"

Grimm looked up, then tilted his head slightly, a quizzical pose.

"You know what I mean. Does it hurt you to see me? To see her, I mean." Stat tossed a glance at the marionette in the corner. "I know it's her face you see on me, every time I'm here. Does it hurt?"

Grimm lowered his head. Then, his shoulders shook a bit, and Stat heard a soft, somewhat gurgling sound. At first he thought his friend was crying, but then, upon closer inspection, it seemed that Grimm was laughing.

"Something funny?"

Grimm sipped his tea. He looked at Stat, or at least that was what Stat assumed, given he couldn't see the man's eyes. Then he turned to the girl in the corner. She, of course, had not moved. His sunken mouth bent a bit, into a sad, crooked smile. It was a rare sight. Then, with a bit of difficulty, he lifted the teapot and poured Stat some more tea.

"I get it."

Steam rose from their cups and danced in the air like lost fairies. The marionette sat in her silence, living her blank existence in her colorful dress. Her beauty would never fade, not in this forsaken world.

"You're pretending, too."

Grimm nodded.

"You look across the table and pretend she's here. Isn't that right?"

Grimm looked down a bit, as if embarrassed.

"It's alright," Stat said with a wave. "If I'm fine with it, why shouldn't you be? That's my job isn't it? To keep the peace. If there's one person whose peace and sanity I don't mind keeping, my friend, it's yours."

It was an hour later that he exited Grimm's ugly little house, which made the visit much shorter than his usual stops. Under ordinary circumstances he would stay longer, sit at Grimm's chipped breakfast table, drink hot tea, and talk for several hours straight. Grimm would always sit there, listening patiently, never speaking a word. Stat had never heard Grimm's voice, and knew he most likely never would. Maybe that's why he appreciated the man's company so much. No one else was willing to listen to what he had to say. He was an anomaly.

IMMORTALITY 101: The Intro Course

Two steps off the curb, however, he stopped, suddenly regretting having left so soon. There, across the way, standing under a long-dead oak tree with claw-like branches, was a small figure, no more than four and a half feet tall. Most people actively avoided Stat, and he only purposefully avoided one himself. He'd gone quite a long time without seeing her, so long in fact that he was just beginning to forget her face.

As the artificial night surrounded them, Stat stood by the curb, contemplating whether to turn around and seek asylum in Grimm's house. The little girl with pink ribbons in her hair did not move either. Instead, she linked her hands behind her back and rocked on her heels, front and back, front and back. And she was smiling, which unnerved him even more. He hated it when she smiled, it usually meant she had cheated someone or something, or perhaps someone had cheated her and was about to pay the price. It had been a long time since someone tried to cheat Sasha.

It took nearly four minutes of stony silence before he made his decision. There was no point in hiding. Even if he turned around and headed back inside, she would wait – wait however long it took, like a panther stalking its prey. Instead of running, he took a deep breath and walked to the center of the street, his shoes clicking against the hard concrete.

She did the same, except her footfalls were light as a cat's. She stopped a few feet short of him, looked him up and down, and grinned. She was missing one of her front teeth, and her golden hair was tied up in pigtails.

"You look good," she said to him. "Very good, if I do say so myself."

"Vanity is a sin."

"Quite a word you picked up." She clicked her tongue cutely. "Sin. Did you learn that in a Round?"

"What do you want?"

Sasha twirled one slender finger in her hair, playing with it with more relish than Stat was comfortable with. The streets were too quiet and it was making the hair on the back of his neck stand. He wasn't sure what he was afraid of. Not this child, certainly. Or at least that was what he kept telling himself.

"Do you always assume I come bearing bad news?"

"Is that not your specialty?"

"Maybe this time I bring good tidings."

Stat rolled his eyes. Sasha probably saw it, but said nothing. "Do you?"

"No." She grinned, a wide, childish grin. "Only a warning. Well, no. Not so much. A heads-up if you will."

"About what?"

"An upcoming disturbance. It *is* your job to quiet those, is it not?"

She was playing games. He hated that. He hated it when she hinted at things instead of saying them, laying out puzzles for others to figure out. "Get to the point," he said sharply.

"There is nothing else to it." She spread her little hands innocently. "I'm just letting you know that something is going to happen, and it's going to be very, very… interesting."

"Is it your doing?"

"You can hardly blame me for it, if that's what you mean." As if timid, which he knew she was not, she took a step closer to him. He wanted to back away, but pride and stubbornness refused to allow him to show any sign of agitation in front of her. "Why do you dislike me so much, Stat?"

He stood his ground as she got closer to him, still playing with her hair. Was anyone watching this exchange? No, probably not. Only Sasha would seek him out like this. No one else wanted to lay an eye on him. They all drew their curtains as soon as he set foot in the neighborhood.

Something touched his waist. Stat started and stumbled backward. Sasha withdrew her hand, her large, innocent eyes bearing the look of a wounded bird.

"Why did you do that?" she asked softly, as if he had hurt her. He cleared his throat. She giggled. "Always so on guard. Have you always been like this?"

"As long as you've been around."

"How hurtful." She laid her hand on his waist again, caressing the fabric of his shirt. He could feel her warmth, so close, so unsettlingly soft. She leaned forward again, and this time he didn't move as she laid her cheek against his chest. His heart was pounding, he was sure of it, pounding like a jungle drum. "I like you, Quo," she whispered. "Why is it so hard for you to accept that?"

IMMORTALITY 101: The Intro Course

No one else called him Quo, and very few touched him willingly. She was the only one. As she stood there, touching him gently, her body so close, he felt a sense of self-loathing. Was it wrong for him to enjoy her touch? She was so small, so young in appearance, despite the fact that, for all he knew, she was his senior. In the Round this kind of thing was forbidden, taboo, but here, it was different. Just like no one cared much for him aside from the silent Grimm Sullivan, none of them would care much if he carried on with her. No, no one would mind that she was small.

What they would whisper about was that he was carrying on with Sasha. Sasha B. C.

The Sasha B. C.

He pushed her away, forcing himself not to notice those wounded eyes as their bodies parted. It wasn't wrong because she was young, or at least appeared so. It was wrong because she was Sasha.

And he hated Sasha.

Hated her no matter what the rest of his body wanted. He did not want her touching him, caressing him, kissing him…

"Go away," he said, much more firmly than he felt inside. "You've delivered your message. I don't know what game you're playing this time, and I don't care. Just go away."

For a moment he thought she would argue, but she simply nodded, stepped back, and curtseyed like a good little girl would. Her bare knees peeked out momentarily underneath the lacey hem of her dress.

"Then I'll bid you good evening," she said in all politeness, though an edge had returned to her eyes. "If you ever change your mind, Quo, you know where to find me. I know you haven't forgotten. It'll be just like last time."

Stat shuddered as Sasha's retreating figure disappeared into the night. Seeing her always reminded him why others viewed him as such a plague to their existence. He was a plague to himself, a bitter pill he had to swallow on a daily basis. But he was determined not to repeat past mistakes, not to give in again to those eyes.

For Sasha loved no one but herself.

4
SMALL FAVORS

Luck never gives; it only lends. – Swedish proverb

One phrase often uttered is "thank God for small favors". The truth was, no one ever thanked God enough for small favors. Rebecca Tempest was one of millions upon millions of people who took small favors for granted. And why not? No one ever noticed the small favors. It's the big favors that prove the universe turned the right way every once in a while.

Beki was a woman blessed with small favors, though she never realized it. As a person who'd never experienced anything exciting, she was also a person who'd never experienced anything dangerous or life-threatening or extremely inconvenient. She went to a good college fairly close to home, met her husband through friends and never had a cross word between them, had a relatively easy pregnancy and birth, and her son was normal and healthy. She had never been robbed, cheated or being cheated on, made the subject of any malicious rumors, and never had a flat tire during rush hour.

But these were small things. Few people knelt before their bed and thanked a faceless deity for *not* letting anything happen to them on a given day.

IMMORTALITY 101: The Intro Course

And it was because of this that Beki drove home that day not a bit worried about running into another car, or vice versa. It was because of this same pampered state of mind that she did not notice the red truck as she passed it. If some part of her did, her mind automatically reasoned that the driver had simply decided to park by the road to wait out a rain. She didn't think it was an accident, didn't think anyone died, and most of all didn't think that it was somehow completely her fault.

The red truck was but a single gear that set a series of unfortunately events in motion, much like the tragic tales of Lemony Snicket.

Three miles from her exit off the highway, her left rear hubcap began to make a small, soft, clanking sound that was easily masked by the thunder and rain. With two miles to go, it shook loose of the wheel and slid onto the road, gliding along and finally settling in the dead center. In exactly six and a half minutes, another unsuspecting car would drive over it, one of its slightly ragged edges would slice through the car's front tire just right, and send a grandmother and her two young grandchildren careening off the road to their deaths.

In the next five days, Beki Tempest would become indirectly responsible for the death of nineteen people. Of course, none of this could be blamed on her, not really. No court in this world would condemn her. Still, there's a lesson to be learned here, albeit a small one – always be thankful for small favors.

Beki met her husband during her first year in college. She was studying business and he was studying science. It wasn't until the second year that they realized their mutual attraction and began the usual steps of human courtship, which eventually led to a shared apartment, a small wedding, their first house, and their son, Eric, who was a spitting image of his father.

Their relationship wasn't what one would call perfect, for there was no such thing, but it was pretty damn close. In modern society, where there was a divorce for every two marriages, they had managed to stay close and faithful, hardly fighting, seldom arguing. Their jobs were far from glamorous, but with unemployment rising slowly in recent years, they'd managed to hold on to their jobs and provide for the family without trouble. Neither had major issues with their respective in-laws, nor were there awkward family gatherings with their extended family spread throughout the country.

They shared in their son's first words, first steps, first baseball game, and first awkward moment with the pretty girl next door, although that last one was much to the boy's embarrassment.

They spent their weekdays working and their weekends and evenings quietly at home, planning their future, which involved a bigger house, a college fund for Eric, and perhaps a second child and a dog.

Small favors. Lucky, some would say.

With the rain pouring, she certainly counted herself lucky to get home unharmed. Unfortunately, her husband's car had taken up the driveway, as their garage was, like those of most families in the neighborhood, stockpiled with things they did not use and thought it a waste to throw away.

She parked by the curb. The lights in her house were still on, indicating her husband and son were still awake. Turning around, she fished for the umbrella she usually left in the back seat and came up empty. She must have taken it inside the house unwittingly. Quite the wrong day for it. She would have to run to the house in those uncomfortable heeled sandals.

Clutching her purse close to her, Beki opened the car door and made a mad dash for the front door. When she managed to make it before the rain soaked through her blouse, she was so glad to be dry that it never occurred to her to make sure her headlights were turned off.

Around five a.m. they would turn off, having drained the car's battery.

Around four-fifty-eight a.m. another car would return to the neighborhood in the rain, mistake her headlights for those of an oncoming car, swerve, skip, and plunge headfirst into the house across the street.

Not long after that, the police and paramedics would arrive. They would sift through the crushed corner of the house, where the car was still embedded. They would remove the unconscious driver, who had taken a bad blow to the head and would not remember the accident when she awakened two days later. They would also move the rubble and retrieve from it the body of the pretty, redheaded twelve-year-old girl whose attention Eric had sought just a few days before, and her two friends, who were sleeping over. She had been wearing strawberry-patterned pajamas. The little painted fruits matched the color of her blood, which soaked through the starch-white sheet they threw over her, forming patterns here and there like roses on a field of snow.

Beki and her husband, along with half the neighborhood, would be out on the curb. She would stand under her umbrella, comforting the girl's devastated mother, whose hair was once as brilliantly red as her daughter's. As they all stood in the rain under the gray sky, no one knew that this was Beki's fault.

It was all her fault.

Suzy the secretary gave her a strange look when she entered the office on Monday. Beki didn't know the woman's last name, only that everyone else called her Suzy and so merely followed suit. Suzy was a large woman, easily over two hundred pounds, and never wore any makeup because it concealed her 'natural beauty'. Not that she was totally lacking in looks. In fact, she carried her weight rather well and had wonderful skin. Still, some people needed a little help with their 'naturalness' and Suzy was definitely a candidate of the kind.

She nodded at the woman. "Good morning, Suzy."

Suzy only gazed at her. Her usually cold eyes almost betrayed a trace of concern. "Mr. Peterson is looking for you."

There was a pot of coffee in the lobby, nearly empty, either a fresh pot that's already been frequented or a leftover pot. Beki didn't care. She poured herself a cup and took a sip. It was bitter, a little too strong, and tasted burnt, almost as if someone had neglected to clean off the blackened crust from the last pot. "What for?"

Two of her co-workers entered the front door. Juggling her briefcase and the cup of coffee, Beki tried to wave to them. To her surprise, like Suzy, they also gave her a strange look and quickly hurried away.

Suzy tapped the counter to get her attention. Beki turned around, perplexed as the secretary handed her a sheet of paper.

"Just go see Mr. Peterson," she said, almost snidely.

Beki nodded. She tried to take the piece of paper in her hand without putting down the coffee and wound up knocking the cup over. Embarrassed, she tossed the cup in the nearest trashcan, grabbed the paper, and headed for the elevator. The janitor would soon come by to mop up the mess, but he would use a slippery cleaning fluid that, when mixed with coffee, did not dry immediately. One of the firm's eldest members would come in a few minutes late that morning due to traffic, during the ten minutes Suzy wandered off to make a fresh pot of coffee.

He would slip on the spot, hit his head on the sharp edge of the receptionist desk, and his hip would shatter like glass as it struck the marble floor.

Had Suzy been around, she would have immediately called for help and the man might've made it home in a few weeks with new pins in his hip, but in those ten minutes, he lay helpless on the ground, unable to utter a word, and slipped slowly into unconsciousness. By the time his body reached the hospital, it was nearly cold.

Mr. Roger Peterson was a small, unaccommodating man. His office was large and furnished in black leather, a look straight out of Forbes magazine. He was about five and a half feet tall, approximately two feet wide, wore Gator loafers, Armani suits, and a perpetual frown. The most distinguishing feature about him, however, was his head of unrelenting dark brown hair. The officer workers have put together several secret pools, betting amongst one another on whether their superior's hair was a toupee or a natural blessing. Beki herself had taken part in the fun, though so far they had failed to determine one way or the other.

As she entered his office this morning, however, Beki had a sense of foreboding. Something obviously wasn't right. It was like being a kid called into the principal's office when they had no idea what was wrong. Had she unwittingly broken some new rule? Or broken an old one without realizing? Did someone die? Did someone tattle? If so, on what? The office and its big, imposing furniture made her feel very small. Perhaps that was the effect Mr. Peterson was hoping for. He didn't acknowledge her at first, his sunken eyes buried in a stack of papers. It wasn't until she cleared her throat that he looked up.

IMMORTALITY 101: The Intro Course

"Ms. Tempest," he said, removing his thick glasses and gesturing at the chair across from his massive oak desk. "Please have a seat."

It was like being called "young lady" by the principal. Beki sat down in front of him, making as little noise as possible and fighting every instinct to ask the obvious question: "am I in trouble?" Adults didn't ask that question, did they?

Mr. Peterson was silent for a moment. He tapped his glasses lightly against the papers in front of him, perhaps for dramatic effect. If that was the case, then it certainly was working. Beki felt like she was in some low-budget office training video.

"Now Ms. Tempest," he said at last, "Rebecca. You've being here for how long now?"

No good conversation ever began with that question. Beki sat up straight like a good little schoolgirl, however ridiculous it was, considering she was a professional in her mid-thirties. "Eight years, sir."

"Yes, that's right. Tell me, Rebecca, are you familiar with the firm's independence policies?"

If the accounting profession had a bible, the first verse would be the independence policies. Beki didn't have to be reminded of such a thing. It had already been drilled into dark corners of her brain that she herself didn't even know existed by the third day on the job.

"I am, sir," she said obediently, again like a good girl. She was nothing if not a good girl. It was a role molded into her being by a normal, tight-knit family upbringing.

"Are you aware of the rules regarding business gifts?"

She could think of no reason for the way he was looking at her, as if she ought to know her own crime. Strangely, it gave her confidence. Never in her life had she accepted an inappropriate business gift.

"I am."

Mr. Peterson nodded and tried to crack a smile. It came out just a little creepy. "Good," he said. "Good."

"May I ask how this concerns me?"

"Absolutely." Mr. Peterson put his glasses back on his near-nonexistent nose and linked his hands in front of him. "You see, for a while there it seemed that you weren't aware of that rule. Now it's not a big deal, but if necessary, we can re-train you…"

"Sir," Beki cut in firmly. She didn't want to interrupt him, but what he was accusing her of, or rather about to accuse her of, was utter nonsense. Plus, as much as she respected the man, which wasn't a whole lot, she hated his patronizing tone. "I assure you I have not broken the rule in any way. I am aware of how heavily this firm emphasizes independence from our clients and I would never jeopardize that."

Mr. Peterson nodded slowly. "That's very good to know," he said, in a tone that was unreadable. "It's good to know that you hold the firm's principles at heart. But you see..." he paused. Beki drew a deep breath as impatience gnawed at her ribcage. "A situation was brought to my attention last week, regarding a gift you accepted from a certain client. Now I can't say for sure..."

"Mr. Peterson."

"...whether this will affect your future here..."

"Sir."

"...but I think if we work through this..."

Beki slapped her hand on his desk. It seemed rude and wasn't something she wanted to do, but his incessant droning was taking years off her life. It seemed to get his attention at last. Mr. Peterson stopped talking and looked at her in mild surprise.

"Sir," she said firmly. "Please. I would feel much better if you could just tell me what this is about."

And he did. The sheer ridiculousness of it nearly caused her to storm out of his office, ranting at the top of her lungs about the idiocy of him, this whole firm, and its "principles". But she didn't. Because she was a good girl, and one that followed the rules at that. And so it was, she had broken the rules. As they would call it on daytime TV, it was a 'technicality'.

She walked out of his office quietly, with as much dignity as she could muster, which wasn't a whole lot. Her colleagues looked at her with sympathy, concern, and just a bit of smugness. She knew what they were thinking. She had thought similar things when others emerged from Peterson's office.

Poor thing. But it was her own fault. Her own fault that something went wrong, and her own fault that the rules got broken. And now she might be fired, because it was her own fault she made a mistake.

IMMORTALITY 101: The Intro Course

Mr. Peterson, unaware of this, would go on his day smoothly without incident. In less than twenty-four hours, he would be lying dead in the middle of Main Street, a horrified taxi driver who spoke less than a hundred words of English sobbing and attempting to give him CPR.

This was, of course, Beki's fault. She didn't realize it. Didn't realize that, as she left work for the day and stormed across the parking lot, her actions, in particular one of kicking aside a loose screw in the parking lot, would set off a chain of most unfortunate reactions that would lead to the death of smug, boring, well-meaning Mr. Peterson.

"A jar of pickles."

She nodded as they stood in line at the concession stand. Her husband had picked a good movie for once, but as luck would have it, it was sold out, so they had to settle for a less popular title that neither of them was too excited about. But a night out was a night out. Eric was home alone. Usually they were less than inclined to leave him by himself, but recently he'd been more quiet and subdued than usual and had asked that they go out without him. Beki secretly suspected that it was because he was still in mourning for the redheaded girl next door.

"That's what it came down to. A woman at one of the clients handed out jars of homemade pickles to everyone."

"You took one?"

"She left one on the corner of my desk." The pimply-faced teen at the counter gestured for them to come forward. She was about seventeen and smelled of sugar and pizza grease. "Medium popcorn, please. I don't think she was even aware that I didn't work with her. It seemed rude not to take it."

Jonathan shook his head. "It seems awfully nitpicky of them to blame you for this."

"They don't 'blame' me for it." The girl filled a brightly colored paper bag with popcorn and held it under the fake butter dispenser. "No butter please" – the teen rolled her eyes, which Beki didn't notice – "Mr. Peterson gave me a fifteen minute talk about how I was expected to observe independence rules and such. I *know* I should observe independence rules. But I don't even think this gift was one over the threshold limit."

"Know what this sounds like?" He slid his arm around her waist as they headed for the theater.

"What?"

"Just a bout of bad luck."

They went to see their movie. It wasn't great, but not terrible either. Someone came in late and spilled half his drink on Jonathan's pants maneuvering around in the dark. But overall it was still a pleasant evening.

Half way through their movie, the manager of the theater approached the teen who had served them, berated her for rolling her eyes at Beki earlier, and fired her. The girl, who was living on her own after escaping from a dysfunctional family, had nowhere to go and more debt than she could handle. She drove her half-paid off junky Gremlin to her father and stepmother's house, parked in the garage while they slept, lowered the gate, and turned on the engine.

IMMORTALITY 101: The Intro Course

5
ONE HUNDRED AND TWENTY

Sasha laid on her back on top of the green felt, the frills of her dress gathered in a bunch at her crotch, her legs bent upward. Her hair, usually neat and tied with ribbons in pigtails, was splayed outward like a golden fan. If anyone were to enter through the double doors right now, they would get quite the excellent view of her white cotton panties.

The pool table was regulation size, four by eight feet. Aside from the bookshelves, it was the only piece of furniture in Sasha's study. It had never seen a cue ball, or been scratched by a pool stick. Instead, it was a place where she lay when she wanted to think, with the felt beneath her, and the crystal chandelier above.

She let her eyes trail over the chandelier, over its millions of reflective surfaces, and the fractured light that fell over it. It was mesmerizing.

In her left hand was the object that was the cause of her frustration. It was the bane of her existence, her greatest treasure, and one of the best-kept secrets of the games. Only a select few had had the chance to see it, and even fewer had the privilege of touching it. It was rarer than rare. Her own special toy.

Sasha rolled onto her stomach, her legs raised in the air. The ribbons on her white socks had come undone. She made a mental note to tie them up later. A proper lady must always look her best. She was very talented when it came to looking good. Ribbons and frills were an extension of her being. At the moment, though, she was a bit unkempt, but as no one was around to see, it didn't matter as much. Unkemptness was allowed when she spent time alone with her treasure.

She turned it over in her hands, rolled it here and there on the felt. It was perfect, perfect and beautiful and mysterious all at the same time. Every now and then she would raise it to eyelevel and study it closely, touching its many sides, caressing them like a lover.

The dark study provided little light. The artificial dawn was rearing its head outside the only window. She had lit a candle earlier, upon her return from visiting Stat. It was nearly burned to the base, white wax rolling out of the candleholder like melted fat. The entire room was coated in the scent of books and incense, which was strange considering she was not so fond of the latter. It was most likely brought in by her last visitor. Although it had been many long days since his visit, his scent lingered stubbornly, that annoying man who could not take a loss like a proper gentleman. He had had the gall to curse at her, to call her a cheater and a liar and many other improper things. She *had* cheated him — cheated him with utmost skill and style. He was most ungrateful not to appreciate it, the bothersome man.

To disperse his stench, all she had to do was open the window, but she did not. It was already a bother to let outsiders into her asylum, but to open a window seemed to be an invitation for trouble. Not that there was much trouble around that she couldn't handle, or didn't cause; she simply did not want the rest of the world to invade her privacy. Her own little bubble.

She rolled her treasure around with her finger. It always rolled in a perfect circle, and only deviated from its path when she tried to put her hand in its way, as if eluding her. She grabbed it and attempted to roll it along the back of her left hand, a party trick that had never seen any parties. But it immediately fell off, despite her best efforts to balance it. As it hit the green felt, it rolled once more in its perfect circle, round and round, as if taunting her.

Finally, it came to a stop. She nudged it with her finger. It rolled no more, as if having decided to rest for the day. Sasha sighed and rested her cheek against the felt. It scratched her tender skin but she didn't care. Her treasure also lay there, silent, still. She imagined that it was staring back at her, and thinking, perhaps even making judgments. She had no doubt that it had a will of its own, and a strong one at that.

The double doors opened behind her. She didn't lift her head to greet the visitor, only said, "Close the door."

A soft wooden click. Everyone else's world was once again cut off from hers, which was how she liked it. Pushing herself off the surface of the pool table, she wrapped one hand around her treasure and used the other to turn herself around as she sat up, legs propped up in front of her.

The man standing with his back to the doors was tall and slim, his face hidden by the shadows of the dark room, though she knew who he was just by his silhouette. The way he stood formed a slanted curve, his right hand at his waist and the other running through his well-combed hair as usual. There was probably a snide look in his eyes, as was usual, and he was probably going to chide her for letting her undergarments show.

"Have I had no influence on you?" he asked, fanning himself with his left hand as he did. "I don't care how many lovers you've had, you ought to keep your goodies private. Good heavens, it is a sauna in here. How do you think in all this stuffiness?"

Sasha allowed a small smirk to creep to her face, but did not pull her dress over her legs. Her golden locks fell over her shoulders, perfect and beautiful despite the little attention she'd spared them.

"Good evening, Jean-Luc."

"It's morning."

"What difference does it make?"

"About three shades." Rounding the pool table, Jean-Luc strolled to her bookshelves and caressed the spines of her ancient books with his perfectly manicured fingers. "Evening wear is three shades darker than day wear." He glanced at her. "Although for one as adorable as yourself, it really does make no difference. You make everything look good, doll."

"What do you want, Jean-Luc?" Sasha scooted to the edge of the pool table and dangled her legs over it. "If you've come to bet again, I will gladly indulge you. But the stakes have been raised since our last game."

IMMORTALITY 101: The Intro Course

Jean-Luc chuckled. Actually, it was more of a shrill giggle. He pulled out a bound copy of *Kama Sutra* from the shelf and flipped through it, arching his brow every now and then. "No," he said. "I'm not going to bet against you for a while. It is simply not good for my poor heart. Besides," he snapped the book close, "I am not about to risk the measly little bit of Luck you left me with last time. But out of curiosity, what is the new minimum?"

"More than you can afford."

"That I certainly don't doubt." Turning around, he leaned against the pool table, his elbows resting on its side. The artificial dawn finally brought enough light through the window to light up his face. He had deep, dark eyes, taut lips, and a pale complexion. His nose was perhaps his most distinguishing feature. It was sharp, long, with a high bridge, very delicate and thin like a woman's. From the side it almost resembled a beak, or would if the rest of his face didn't look as if it was carved with the gentle, skilled hands of an artist. In a word, Jean-Luc was beautiful, the same way a slimy, sticky substance regurgitated by an acrophobic rainbow was probably beautiful.

"What if I want to play a Round against that little toy of yours?" he asked, eyeing her closed fist and inching closer to her. She tightened her grip around it. "Protective, aren't we? I'll put up some of my Luck, and you can even roll for me. I know you can't cheat on this one."

"Cheat?" She tossed the treasure into the air and caught it again. "Me? You must be mistaken."

"Don't bullshit me, Sasha. Everyone knows you cheat; they just can't prove it or are afraid to. You have everyone in this place under your pretty little thumb."

"Do you find it despicable?"

"I find it admirable."

"Now you're the one bullshitting."

He was sucking up to her, but even though she could see through him like a paper-thin piece of glass, it still got to her a little that he took the time to come to her abode just to flatter her into betting another round. In a world filled with fear, Jean-Luc was a rare soul, one who seemed to live to the fullest, unafraid of Rounds, unworried about the inevitable collapse of the dome, and, most importantly, undaunted in her presence. She liked that. Liked it more than she usually let on.

She also liked him, more than the common masses at least, as both an acquaintance and a lover.

"Does it matter that I am?"

"About as much as the difference between evening and morning."

"Touché, honey." Straightening, he walked around the pool table in small, calculated steps, fixed his hair as he did. His gait was a slightly unbalanced one, as he moved his hips more than most men and tended to sway just a bit as if wearing high heels. "I guess it takes more than a little flattery to get to Miss B. C.'s treasure. Unless, of course, I was Status Quo."

She felt herself stiffen a bit, but did not let it show.

"Who does the great Sasha B.C. see in Status Quo, I wonder, that makes her love him so much?" He smirked at her, apparently noticing her discomfort. "Did you think I wouldn't notice? It's actually quite obvious. I'm sure I'm not the only one. I'm just the only one willing to use it to my advantage." He stopped, this time leaning against the window with his legs crossed. "How about a bet on the house?"

Sasha laughed. Her treasure went from one hand to the other. "There is no such thing," she said.

"Reserving it for Stat, are you?"

"I reserve nothing for him."

"Don't lie to me. Your eyes go murky when you lie. It's not attractive on a pretty lady, almost as unattractive as letting her panties show."

She leveled her gaze on him. "Do you know why I tolerate you, Jean-Luc?"

"No, why do you like me?"

"I said tolerate."

"And I said what you actually meant."

"And there's why." She tried to roll her treasure on the back of her hand again, failed, and caught it in her other hand as it fell. "I'm not in the mood to bet."

"Visited Stat, did you?"

"That's none of your business."

"Too bad it's already been made into my business."

"What else do you want?"

"Do you want me to shut up that badly?"

"Anything short of betting." She held her treasure over one of the center pockets on the table and dropped it inside with a dull clunk. "Especially against that. That is a privilege to be earned."

"How about a b.j.?"

Sasha shrugged as he made his way to her side of the table. "Fine."

After Jean-Luc left, the study no longer smelled like incense. Instead, the scent of his aftershave and fluids fill the air. Jean-Luc's scent was always pleasant. Sasha enjoyed it, though not as much as she would have, had he been Stat instead.

She lay on the pool table again, her hands turned her treasure over and over, touching each of its perfectly symmetrical sides. All one hundred and twenty of them. She had counted them over and over. One hundred and twenty, each exactly like the other save for the small number carved in its center. How many times has she counted it now? More than a hundred and twenty times, surely. She rose from the pool table again. Noon was approaching and she had to make a quick visit to the Saffron Stallion. It wasn't a place she was particularly fond of, but when it came to information, there was no other place where it festered like the swamp that was the Saffron Stallion, its patrons merely flies and dung beetles that rolled in its pool of alcohol and vinyl.

Afterwards, she decided, after she found out what she needed to know, she would head to the Pink Pony, a place more fitting of someone of her stature. Perhaps one of these days, she would finally convince Stat to squire her.

There was never a bad time to drink.

That seemed to be the philosophy of the Stallion's patrons. Even at high noon, with the domed "sky" lit bright as can be and its painted clouds brimming with mock misty light, nearly every stool supported the slouching form of a drunk or half-drunk. Geoffy was serving up drinks and chatting with whoever happened to be nearest. It made no difference to him. For one who could barely see, he poured drinks with deadly precision. Either he was inhumanly skilled or he was most reluctant to give his customers even a drop more than they paid for.

Sasha counted the butts atop the candy-red stools. There were twelve, three of which were young women with painted lips and black fishnet hose; one of them, who was more heavy-set than the others, had chipped nails, possibly bitten out of envy for her friends' perfect figures. Two middle-aged couples sat next to each other; none were talking as they buried their heads in their drinks. Indeed, they appeared to be bored with each other. Chances were, they would soon go their separate ways to seek a momentary buzz in the arms of another. The rest of the customers seem to be uninvolved, each drowning their respective thoughts and problems in martinis, margaritas, and shots. All except one, that was – the woman at the end of the bar, who was sipping on a glass of transparent dark orange liquid and earning an appreciative glance from Geoffy's bad eye every few moments.

Sasha approached the bar, steering clear of its foul-smelling occupants. The bar was always jammed pack. Sometimes it seemed rather implausible that the Saffron Stallion was the only establishment that served any form of alcohol. With gambling engorging every corner, one would think liquor flowed more freely than water. Then again, perhaps it was for that very reason that the Stallion monopolized the liquor business – those who bet wanted to keep their minds clear. Luck was expensive.

The woman at the end of the bar noticed Sasha before she could get too close. With a deliberate twist of her long neck, she turned her face away from the girl and raised one thin, almost skeletal hand. Geoffy immediately answered to her beckon and came forward, his feet thumping against the floor like a limping elephant and his wide mouth cracked over in a grin.

"More tea for you, Gypsy?"

"Just one more, dah-ling, if you would."

"Of course he would," Sasha quipped.

The woman named Gypsy turned to Sasha and smiled, though her hazel eyes were burning venomously. Sasha was not deterred. Not a bit. This was, after all, nothing new. There hadn't been anything new in this world for a very, very long time.

"Geoffy would do anything for you, Gypsy. He would lick the floor gladly if it meant he could use that same tongue to lick your tits later. Isn't that right, Geoffy?"

Geoffy blushed. It was a very rare sight, and usually would be unnoticeable against his midnight-black skin, but this time his round cheek lit up like two Christmas treetops. Gypsy, however, only let out a soft chuckle.

"Uncouth as usual, Sasha. To what do I owe the displeasure?"

"I was about to ask you the same thing."

"Am I mistaken in the fact that you are the one who sought me out?"

The man in the stool next to Gypsy turned slightly, took sight of Sasha, and rose from his seat. He owed her, as many in this place did. It was always like that; the problem half these customers were trying to drink away was how to repay Sasha. Everyone knew this. Geoffy knew this and again didn't concern himself with it. Business was business.

Sasha turned up her nose and climbed onto the newly emptied stool, rather gracefully considering its size compared to hers. Resting her hands in her lap like a good little lady, she grinned at Gypsy. "Who said I came to look for you?" pulling her eyes away from the woman as if losing interest, she addressed Geoffy. "Has my dear Mich been around?"

Geoffy cleared his throat. His face was slowly returning to normal as he grunted. "No."

"For now long?"

"Not since you delivered your message."

Sasha clicked her tongue. "Incredible. Who would have thought Mich, of all people, could tear himself away from his beloved drinks for so long?" She looked at Gypsy, her face suddenly morphing into one of an innocent child. She smiled, a bright, kind, friendly smile. "You still look ugly today, Gypsy."

Gypsy scoffed and sipped her tea. "You still look like a twelve-year-old whore, Sasha."

"Do not deride that which you envy, Miss Hoss."

"When the day comes that I should envy you, I will burn down my Table."

"I will hold you to that promise."

Swallowing hard, Geoffy wisely kept to himself. He picked up the nearest empty mug and began to clean it, turning the dirty dishrag round and round in it, scrubbing as hard as he could while the two carried on. He had learned, somewhere along the way, repeatedly, that it was best to let women alone in these cases. Especially with these two.

Gypsy Hoss and Sasha B.C. were like oil and water – mix, light a match, and watch the flames.

Old was a concept and a state of mind, just like youth. Gypsy was not young by any standards, not in appearance or mind. Her body was attractively skinny, almost skeletal like her hands, but not quite. She looked like a steel spike planted to the ground – thin as a pin but unmovable by the strongest gust. Her silver bodice, lined with heavy black denim, further strengthened the illusion. It pushed her sagging, veined breasts much too high and flattened them like two half-cooked pancakes. The skin on her face and neck would sag were she a bit meatier. As it was, it simply drooped a bit, leaving her chin and neck to appear as if they had lost a tiff with gravity. Her hands were dry and wrinkled, like the claws of a vulture.

But, by Luck or by irony or by a joke of nature, her scorching red hair never faded. It blazed atop her head as if her scalp was the way station for the setting sun. Instead of growing, Gypsy's red mane exploded from her head, leaving in its path a crimson flood. Perhaps it was because of this that her hazel eyes maintained a constant energy. The energy displayed by her hair somehow wormed its way into her heart. She walked with confidence, spoke loud and proud, and took her lovers with a kind of cool, collected demeanor that kept them guessing and craving for more.

Many of these characteristics, unfortunately, made her too much like Sasha, who, despite being petite and youthful in appearance, spoke and acted as if she had been around for much too long, which she probably has. Her tight, fiercely golden curls, impossibly tamed down to the last hair, was the opposite of Gypsy's mane. Her blue eyes were freezing cold like a pool gathering at the base of a melting glacier. She moved like a Victorian lady, spoke softly with calculated shrewdness, and her own lovers were usually left a steaming mess, broken and bent, begging to serve her in exchange for another taste.

They were mirror images and yet polar opposites. No one dared to suggest the former in their presence.

Sasha hopped off the stool. She straightened the ruffles of her baby blue dress and fixed the ribbons in her hair. "As pleasant as this has been," she said to Gypsy, "I must be going now. I have what I needed and to stay in your presence any longer may be hazardous to my skin."

Gypsy had already turned her attention back to Geoffy as he filled her glass with more iced tea. It was really rather amusing. Gypsy was the only sober customer in the entire bar. Geoffy only served iced tea when she was around.

Sasha curtseyed. A short, quick, almost sarcastic movement. It wasn't necessary, and she was certain Gypsy didn't appreciate it, but she was somehow obligated. Ladies curtseyed when they left their present company. A lowly woman such as Gypsy Hoss would never understand. Pity.

Gypsy did not acknowledge her as she left the bar through the nearest exit. Sasha didn't mind. The stench of the Stallion was getting to her, and she couldn't wait to get to the Pink Pony, where she would be treated as she ought to be. She was a princess, a queen even, in this world. She was entitled to respect.

Besides, she needed a buzz, and the Pink Pony was definitely the place for it. Soon she would be home again, her head swimming but her senses heightened, and she would play with her treasure again. This time, she was sure, it would not dare elude her, not once the gears begin to turn.

6
SOMEONE ELSE'S BLOOD

Three days after Gilligan Milani's party, Beki drove her car to the shop for a regular inspection. On the way, its left front wheel knocked a loose piece of gravel off the road. It flew toward the sidewalk, wedged itself in the wheel of a ten-year-old's bicycle, and caused it to careen into the road, directly in front of a Greyhound bus.

Four days after the party, she entered a fast food restaurant for lunch. The young man who serves her would lose most of the skin on his face a few hours later to a vat of boiling hot French fry oil. Later that afternoon she would suggest a shortcut to an old man, who would follow it, become lost, and go on to be mugged and stabbed twice in an alley, his body later found in a dumpster.

Five days later, she attended the funeral of Mr. Peterson. It was a moderately lavish ceremony, with a quiet, classy jazz band, catered food, and a funeral party in designer clothes. The ceremony was closed-casket, and for good reasons.

Mrs. Peterson, whose name Beki was pretty sure was Grace, sat in the front row. Upon initial introduction, Beki had mistaken the woman for Mr. Peterson's daughter or niece, though after closer inspection, it seemed that her apparent youth was due more the grace of plastic surgery than God. The widow was wearing a red flower upon her breast and a skirt six inches too short for church. Her enormous breasts, though well covered, might as well have been hanging out for

IMMORTALITY 101: The Intro Course

all to see, as her top was much too thin and the buttons were in danger of popping at any second.

The young men in attendance, unsurprisingly, were focusing most of their attention on her. However, it was more out of curiosity than lust, for from the neck up and the waist down, Mrs. Grace Peterson was actually a skinny woman with bad complexion and thinning hair. Her legs resembled a pair of old matchsticks, so dry and hard that Beki almost expected a small flame to burst out when they rubbed together.

As the priest droned on about the life lost, Beki stifled a yawn and felt just a twinge of guilt for doing so. As discreetly as possible, she scanned the room. Two seats down from her sat Suzy, who had nodded off five minutes after the ceremony started. Five or six of her co-workers sat near the back. A few were trying to look as polite as possible, while others were obviously bored and weren't shy to let on. Beki sympathized. As much as she hated to admit it, she was bored.

The problem was, she realized, that she could think of no reason for her presence here. What was it? Sympathy? Sadness? Guilt? She had no love for Mr. Peterson, but it was not out of malice or anything against the man, not even after the ridiculous incident earlier in the week. He was just another salary man doing his job and she didn't fault him for it. Her general apathy toward him stemmed mostly from lack of direct contact. In fact, the words they exchanged about her "putting the firm's principles in jeopardy" were the most words they'd exchanged in a year.

Still, the man was dead. A life had ended. She wanted to feel something about it. Sorrow, empathy, anything. But nothing came and she continued her task of being bored. When the priest asked if anyone would like to say something special about the departed, she was almost motivated to leave her seat, take the stand, and give a nice, generic, moving speech, just to make up for the four cucumber sandwiches she ate. But as her legs had fallen asleep, it proved rather difficult to muster the strength, so she simply waited as others came and went on the stand, making their speech. The widow herself said a few words, but they were mostly incoherent and the attendees applauded her for effort.

After the ceremony, the casket was carried to the cemetery. Beki hung back in the procession and, despite the circumstances, couldn't help but notice what a beautiful day it was. The sky was vast and blue, not a cloud in sight. A pair of songbirds sang away in the cool shadows of a patch of weeping willows. This brought on further guilt. But, she rationalized, why shouldn't she be grateful for a beautiful day? A dreary day would only bring everyone down further. At least this way Mr. Peterson's last day above the earth was a beautiful one.

Grace was weeping quietly; her skinny shoulders and disproportionately large breasts jerked with each sob. Stepping a bit closer to the woman, Beki laid a comforting hand on her arm, partly as a gesture of sympathy, and partly to keep the woman from toppling forward into her husband's grave.

"I'm sorry for your loss," she whispered.

Grace looked up briefly with her puffy eyes. "Thank you," she said in a voice as mousy as her looks. "Thanks for coming. How did you know my husband?"

"We worked together." She paused, then added for good measure, "he'll be dearly missed."

There was no way to prove that, but at least it made the widow smile. "He was a good man."

"And he's in a better place now."

"Don't be so sure."

The voice came out of nowhere and for a moment she thought she'd imagined it, but there was a cool puff of air by her right ear that came with the words and she spun around.

He looked completely different from their last encounter. Gone were the wrinkled shirt and trousers. In their place was a black suit, cut to impress, a dark blue shirt sans tie, and shoes she could eat off. Instead of puffy and red, his eyes were now clear and shining with subtle intelligence. His hair was parted on the left, combed neatly and curled slightly just below his ears. As she watched, he favored her with a gentleman's smile and turned to the widow.

"This is a lovely day," he said. "I'm sure you husband would be pleased were he able to see it."

It was a strange thing to say, but Grace seemed not to notice. She turned to this new stranger and seemed charmed by his appearance. "Oh, thank you," she breathed. "Thank you so much for coming."

"It was my pleasure."

IMMORTALITY 101: The Intro Course

Beki took a step back. Her car was parked outside the cemetery. Could she make it before he noticed her departure? Why was he always around when her husband wasn't? As Grace carried on the conversation, she turned slowly and began to walk away.

"How did you know my husband?" the widow was saying, her fingers intertwined in a peach-pink handkerchief.

Michigan Von Phant wasn't listening to her, however. Beki could feel his eyes on her back as she quickened her step. The tall grass made it rather hard to walk in dress heels but she picked up her pace anyway.

"Sir? Did you hear me? How did you know..."

"I didn't," he said abruptly. "Please, excuse me."

She kept walking. Faster. Faster. Why was she running away from him again? More importantly, why haven't the police done anything after her last report? Anger brimmed in her as she remembered the fat police officer who came to her house, reeking of sweat and sugar and mumbling about how he'd "file a report" on the matter.

Her car was in the parking lot just outside. If she could make it to the gate at least the guard would notice them. If she could just...

Strong fingers wrapped themselves around her arm firmly. Her heart skipped a beat as he spun her around and she yelled out the first thing that came to mind.

"*I have mace!*"

At the same time he said, "You're being set up."

He stared at her. A long moment passed as they stood there in silence, his hand around her arm. Then, he chortled, snickered, and burst out laughing as she looked at him incredulously.

"Mace?" he gasped between chortles. "*Mace?* Are you serious?"

Feeling angry and suddenly embarrassed, Beki pulled her arm out of his grasp and kept walking, only to be stopped again. He was stronger than he looked, and she, in all honesty, was not in the best shape. His hand was tight as a steel vice.

He cleared his throat and brushed a lock of brown hair out of his eyes. He had very warm eyes that sparked underneath the sunlight and his features were more than fair. But it made no difference, she reminded herself. Plenty of serial killers were good-looking. He probably was lovesick and wanted her heart – in a little glass jar by his nightstand.

Blood pounded in her ears as he held her in place, seriousness suddenly returning to his face. She felt like his eyes were drilling down into her, keeping her paralyzed in place.

"Just listen," he said, enunciating as if speaking to a child. "I'm not trying to do anything to you, but it's in your best interest to listen to me. We've both been set up. This is all someone else's plan that's taking place. If you want to keep your loved ones in this life safe from *you*, you need to come with me."

Beki tried to pull her arm out again, but he held tight.

"Are you listening?" he pressed. "Just come with me right now and I'll explain on the way."

"Let go." He held her down even tighter. She felt the blood in her arms slowing as he squeezed it.

"Not until you agree to come with me."

"Let go or I'll scream."

"You can scream now but I'll find you again later, and by then it'll probably be too late."

She slapped him. He looked at her in shock as the side of his face slowly turned tomato red. Then, he let go.

"Alright," he said slowly, touching his face gingerly as if in disbelief. "Alright then. I'll go away now."

Then he started to walk past her. Beki's heart was still pounding away, both from apprehension and the disbelief that this was so easy. But as he stepped to her side, he slowed.

"Do you know why he died, Rebecca?" he whispered in her ear. "You killed him. This funeral, and that widow over there, is all because of you."

When she drove home that afternoon, Beki sped. As far as she could remember, she had never once sped in her life. She always drove at the speed limit or a few miles below. Let the others race, she often said, they just had to do it going around her.

But on the day of Mr. Peterson's funeral, she drove home fifteen miles above the speed limit. On her way, she unwittingly caused the death of two more people. All she wanted was to be as far away from the cemetery as possible. It was a lesson, she thought dimly as she drove, that she was supposed to learn: never take the day off work to go

IMMORTALITY 101: The Intro Course

to a funeral. The dead don't appreciate it and the universe punishes you accordingly with crazy stalkers.

At a red light, she screeched to a stop, nearly rear-ending the van in front of her. There were several young boys in the van, all of whom were joking and wrestling with each other. Two turned around and waved at her. She didn't wave back. Instead, she fished a compact out of her purse and looked into the small mirror.

She was shaking. She hated to feel this way but her limbs felt weak and loose, and her thoughts were racing a mile a minute as adrenaline was force-fed into her brain. To think that a stranger would have such an impact on her was almost humiliating. But then again, perhaps it was because he was a stranger that she was so afraid. Friends and family could say anything they want and our nature would tell us they were biased, or didn't mean it, or were merely joking. But a stranger was different, especially one that looked her in the eye and accused her of murder.

The person in the mirror was almost hard to recognize, as her mirror image looked much calmer than she felt inside. The car behind her honked in impatience as the light changed and she quickly tossed the compact aside and sped off again.

She drove down the highway, slowly easing her speed to twenty miles above the speed limit, with her mind racing even faster. There was something very unsettling about the situation and it had hooked its claws into her thoughts, refusing to let go. What was it? Was it that the stranger named Michigan Von Phant had implied that she killed Mr. Peterson? Was it his constant appearance wherever she went?

No, it was none of those. What really bothered her was that she believed him, believed those last cold words that he spoke.

Her bustling mind didn't hear the siren behind her, nor did it notice the police car with its flashing lights until she saw them in the rear-view mirror, and even then she immediately rationalized that they were trying to catch up with someone else. It wasn't until it followed her for another three to four miles did she finally pull over.

The policeman, unlike the man to whom she reported Von Phant, was tall, young, and alert. Unfortunately, he also seemed to be on the job for the first day and didn't have a clue how to do it. It took nearly five minutes of stammering and fidgeting for him to finally ask for her license and registration number. When she provided it, he glanced at them briefly and proceeded to lean on her window and toss flirtatious glances at her, her driver's license between his fingers. Normally she would be annoyed but just a bit flattered; today she only clenched her teeth, smiling forcedly and waited for him to shut up.

Luckily, he let her off with a warning ten minutes later.

Unluckily, he would become her victim within forty-eight hours. His body would not be found until a week later, floating face down in the dirty ravine. The mystery of his death would become a media darling.

Rebecca Tempest drove on.

It took nearly an hour to reach her street, despite the fact that the cemetery was less than twenty minutes' drive away. In her flustered state she had missed two exits and was forced to turn back and make a detour around a road that had been under construction for the previous two years.

However, as she neared the house she calmed a bit. Her foot tapped the brake lightly, bringing the car down to the local speed limit. One brush with the law was enough for the day. She was a good, law-abiding citizen, and thus showed restraint despite her mental state. She took a deep breath.

As she turned into her street, she spotted a familiar shape a few hundred feet up ahead. Her son was riding his bike. It seems her husband had fixed it up after all. It was wobbling a bit, though holding up just fine. It would be a nice break from the awful day, she decided, to drive up to his side and surprise him.

Had she kept driving slowly, nothing would have happened. Had she driven faster, she would have beaten him to the house.

As Luck would have it, she stepped on the gas to catch up to him just as the bike's right pedal fell loose. The boy stepped on air, lost his balance, and fell to the side.

The bike was not fixed. Both pedals were loose. It easily could have been the left pedal, which would have sent him falling onto the neighbor's lawn with a scraped knee. Instead, he toppled to the right, and for a moment was airborne. The first split second was almost fun, and the last thing he remembered was the bumper of his mother's car, bearing down on him with surprising speed.

IMMORTALITY 101: The Intro Course

7
THE PINK PONY

If the Saffron Stallion was man's short, sweaty best friend who always smelled of alcohol and was willing to lend an ear, the Pink Pony was his flimsy yet striking concubine who wore only the priciest fur, drank only the most expensive champagne, could care less for his troubles, and yet still kept him coming for more. Where the Stallion offered a warm, comfortable place to wallow in one's trouble, the Pony was the place to go if a man wanted to have trouble forcefully removed by a cold scalpel.

It was a lovely place, in the same way an oil puddle under the sun was lovely. True to its name, everything inside was pink, from the velvet bar stools to the ceiling trim to the dance floor. Tulip-shaped ceiling lights hung over pink tables, each presenting a thin light inner bulb that made one think of a woman presenting hers. The bar was long, rimmed with pink neon, and the tall drink glasses were a smoky pink. Even the small fountain surrounded by a circle of four sofas was lit pink by six lights at its base. The pink waterfall spilled over its three carved layers all day and night. The only thing that wasn't pink, in the entire club, was the onyx ceiling, which was dark as the artificial night.

Now it was true that only the Saffron Stallion served alcohol. No alcohol was served at the pink bar. In fact, the Pink Pony served only cold water and an assortment of iced sodas. And, of course, its specialty, the Pink Pony.

IMMORTALITY 101: The Intro Course

The drink, served in a tall opaque shot glass, was ridiculously popular. The base mixture contained a careful blend of peach tea, cherry juice, and a few other ingredients the general public didn't know nor care about. The bar tender, in presenting the Pink Pony to the customer, would place the glass down on the bar before adding the last two ingredients in full view of the buyer. The first was a small piece of solid carbon dioxide, which immediately chilled the drink and left a thin mist on the surface of the glass. Thin tendrils of smoke would waft up from the drink and spill over the side, as if the entire glass had being filled with pink fog. Then, the bar tender would lean over, wink at the patron, and drop in the two little objects that were the heart and soul of the Pink Pony. They were for taste as much as for decoration, two round little pills in a variety of colors, a mixture of caffeine and methamphetamine.

Unlike the Saffron Stallion, which was almost exclusively maintained by Geoffy, the Pink Pony had six bartenders, five female and one questionable. On most days they wore a wide range of pink outfits, including overalls, shorts and T-shirts, mini-dresses, skirts, and suits. On special days, which only came about because the pink-clad women said so, at least one of them would be nude. The six, who called themselves sisters, were the definitive element of the club. As they had been part of the bar as long as anyone could remember, their names were long forgotten, and the club's visitors only knew them collectively as the "Ponies".

When Sasha stepped into Pink Pony, the sofa nearest to the bubbling fountain immediately emptied. Its occupants stood up, casting curious glances at her as they did. They whispered and tittered to each other as they passed her, whispering words of envy, admiration, disgust, and gossip. Sasha made her way to the sofa and sat down, smoothing the wrinkles out of her dress as she did. Pink light from the lewd-shaped fountain reflected off her smooth cheek and shiny curls. She did not move from her seat, nor speak, but one of the Ponies, who was commonly acknowledged as the "den mother", came to her.

"Drink?" she said shortly, wasting no words.

"Yes," Sasha said, equally simply, to the Sequined Pony, who turned and gestured to the Blond Pony at the bar.

"Two?"

"Four, please."

Another gesture and the Blond Pony fished out an additional two pills from behind the bar and dropped them into the drink.

"What will you be paying with?"

"Luck."

Three Pink Ponies later, the world began to swim. But Sasha, collected as she always was, sat as primly and properly as she always did. The club began to melt before her eyes, sinking into a muddled pool of pink and black, here and there spotted with the fleshy bodies of its patrons. On the dance floor, a couple dressed in gold-beaded evening gowns was dancing, grinding against each other in the wash of the pink lights. The woman on the left, in a spaghetti-strap gown, licked her partner's ear seductively. She had a diamond tongue piercing in the shape of a teardrop. Her partner, who had significantly larger breasts, cracked a smile, exposing two fillings the exact shade of her dress. They seemed to move in slow motion, rubbing their bodies together to the music, which to Sasha's ears sounded more like rhythmic noise than anything else. She watched them through the watery curtain pouring from the fountain. Their bodies seemed distorted and obscure, like that of ghosts in heat.

Sequined Pony stripped off her top and climbed onto the bar, where she proceeded to engage in a slow, graceful routine that caught the attention of almost every eye in the bar. As several more customers made their way to the bar for a closer look, Blond Pony gestured for Jasmine Pony to join her and help in the making of a few more dozen Pink Ponies.

The disco ball spun like a demented moon, throwing fractured light onto the half-dazed faces of dancers, drinkers, and servers alike. Two of the remaining ponies made their rounds from table to table, offering drinks and other favors, which were usually performed on their knees. The last played DJ at the booth. She had put on a rocky tune, the kind loud enough to kill any coherent thought and dark enough to match the ambience of the club. It was she, the Mystik Pony, that Sasha focused her attention on.

As the club spun around her, she found herself thinking of her treasure again. But then, when did she not think of that thing? That wonderful, dreaded, awful, awful thing that captured her attention in such a way, wrapping its tentacles around her mind like no other? Granted, Status Quo also occupied her mind quite a bit, but he was merely an amusement, one that held more interest to her than most. Her treasure was something else. It was the single most valuable thing she owned.

Or perhaps it owned her. On some days it was so darned hard to tell.

The Mystik Pony put on a jazzy tune – "Stardust", one of the many products of the Round. Sasha personally didn't like music from the Round, or *anything* from the Round for that matter. To bring things from the Round into this place seemed a heresy, a wrongdoing of immeasurable extent. But she said nothing, only sat there, her emptied pink glass in hand as the Mystik Pony left the DJ booth and made her way over to the fountain.

She was the tallest of the Ponies, with strong arms and muscular legs. Her breasts were small and her hair was navy-blue, cut to an even length just below the chin. Just above the right corner of her lip was a beauty mark that seemed to migrate from day to day. She wore black lipstick, blue eye shadow, an eggplant-colored g-string, and a five-o'clock shadow that could almost be hidden by flashing lights and a thick layer of foundation. Sasha briefly wondered whether her rear end was cold as she sat down on the fountain's chilly stone base and crossed her long legs.

"I haven't got your chips," she said shortly, without so much as a greeting. Normally Sasha would feel rather upset about this, but the drinks had elevated her mood to a rather heightened state of euphoria, so she smiled instead.

"I'm not here for your chips."

"Just here to gloat then?"

"Perhaps. Besides," – she lifted the glass, nearly dropping it as a light wave of dizziness hit her – "I like the drinks."

The Mystik Pony scoffed. "So good at pretending, are we not?"

In her lightheaded state, Sasha somehow managed to be a little hurt, just a little, since the Mystik Pony would ordinarily be very accurate in her assumption. For there was no one in the world who loved to be owed more than Sasha B. C. There had been many trips prior to this one where she simply sat at the bar and watched the Ponies at work, as if she owned them. It put a little pressure in the air, added a little intensity, and made the Ponies sweat in their silk panties. Usually during these times, as now, they would pretend she didn't exist, or occasionally addressed her shortly and coldly. It was a sign of fear, which was richer than usual around these parts. And why not? Soon she might own them completely, whenever their Luck ran out.

That time could be very, very soon.

In the meantime, Sasha kept on smiling as she held her glass closer to the Mystik Pony, who was giving her a glare that could cut glass.

Just like her tits, Sasha thought. Out loud, she said, "refill, if you please?"

The Mystik Pony scowled, but took her glass. She sashayed to the bar, handed the glass to the Blond Pony, who filled it once more with tea and juices, and four little round pills. Most guests were charged extra for such a service, especially one accompanied by a drink with twice the potency, but for Sasha, the Mystik Pony merely brought the drink back and headed back to her station at the DJ booth. She put on another piece from the Round, perhaps just to annoy Sasha. *Symphony No. 5* by someone who once used the name Ludwig van Beethoven for one Round.

Sasha sipped her drink slowly and leaned back on the sofa, watching the dancers and drinks go about their business. Faintly aware of her surroundings, she wished for two things — one was Stat. In spite of the Ponies' general coldness toward her, she was quite fond of the club itself and still yearned for Stat to sit here by her side at the fountain one day. It might happen. There was plenty of time, as always.

The other was her treasure. She considered bringing it with her for the next visit. Perhaps a glass of Pink Pony would help her decipher its mysteries. But she decided against that idea.

It was, after all, too precious.

IMMORTALITY 101: The Intro Course

8
THE RIGHT TIME

The hospital smelled of disinfectants and death.

Until this day she had never realized death had a smell, and yet there it was, and once she noticed it, it was extremely hard to ignore. As she sat in the waiting room, it crept into her nostrils like a dying gnat seeking its last resting place, carrying with it the scent of oil, acid, and, for some reason, rancid milk.

The entire building was starkly white, both inside and out. The doctors and nurses were also dressed in white. All of the furniture was either tan or wheat or eggshell-colored, and everything felt sterile to the touch. The glaring overhead lights only made the rooms and long halls appear even whiter than they already were.

The only sounds in the vicinity were the hurried footsteps of medical personnel. The lights overhead hummed softly, creating a strange sort of white noise that would have been soothing if it weren't for the circumstances. Beki tapped her foot against the floor, fidgeting in her purse, clicked her nails against the metal legs of the chair she sat on, all in desperate attempts to create some sound, any sound, before the silence drove her completely mad.

Her husband had not said a word since their arrival. He sat across from her, with a small table piled with outdated magazines in between. It felt like a wall, separating them physically and emotionally. His hands were linked in front of his bowed head. He might have been praying, but she couldn't tell. All she knew at the moment was that he had chosen not to sit next to her.

She couldn't stop replaying the moment in her head, over and over again like a broken record. It wasn't so much a scene as a series of sensations: the sound of the brakes, the moment of impact, which she barely felt, the sight of blood, and the way his bike lay there afterward, its pedal still spinning slowly as it hung half-on and half-off the curb. She couldn't stop blaming herself, though at the moment her 'self' felt like another person. She wanted to point a finger at someone and scream, "You did this! This is not my fault, it's *yours*!"

The question she kept asking, however, was "How?"

She didn't know why she was asking such a question, since it seemed to make no sense. Accidents happen, everyone knew that, no matter how tragic, but her mind wouldn't let the question go.

How could

It bore into her head, deeper, deeper.

it happen?

It wasn't logical, not the fact that she was here, not her son in the emergency room hooked up to a dozen tubes and machines, not her husband sitting across from her with his head bowed. It wasn't supposed to happen.

Then why did it? How could it?

Had her husband not looked up at that moment, she may have kept going in her little logic loop for hours. But he raised his eyes and met hers. There was so much sadness in his eyes, which she was sure must be mirrored in her own. But to her endless relief, there was no accusation in his eyes.

"I love you," he said weakly.

It's not your fault.

That was what his stare said, but she hated to admit it, because he didn't seem convinced. Hell, she wasn't convinced herself.

A set of white-clad hips stepped in front of her, blocking her off from her husband. Beki looked up to see a dark-haired woman she initially mistook for a nurse. Upon closer inspection, however, she realized the woman was a doctor and immediately felt rather guilty about making the assumption so quickly. It wasn't that she assumed the newcomer was a nurse because she was female. No. She had made that assumption because she was a very beautiful female.

"Mrs. Tempest?"

"That's me."

Her hair was honey brown, flowing down her shoulders like Willy Wonka's chocolate waterfall. Her body was sculpted to perfection. In fact, Beki wouldn't be the least bit surprised if the woman was a veteran of plastic surgery. Her nose was perfectly shaped, her skin flawless, her eyes and brows a masterpiece, and her breasts worthy of a Greek Goddess. The only thing that looked real on her, in fact, was her lips. Her rosy, pouting, perfect lips. In that white doctor's coat, she looked nothing if not professional, but perhaps that was what made her appear to be a perfect Playboy centerfold. She looked as if she was ready to toss it aside, take off her glasses, and spread her legs for the camera.

"Are you here alone, ma'am?"

Beki shook her head, partly to answer the question and partly to clear her head. She gestured behind the woman. "That's my husband."

He looked up at her, at the doctor, then smiled. Beki wasn't sure who the smile was meant for.

"I'm Doctor Patton," said the woman, offering a hand as Beki stood up. She shook it. The doctor had very cold skin, albeit smooth and flawless. "Your son is in a stable condition. Would you like to see him?"

"Yes," she answered quickly, almost pleading. "Please."

Dr. Patton cracked a thin, brief smile. It was a strange expression, as if she wasn't used to smiling. Not that Beki blamed her, having to work day in and day out in this depressing place. She motioned for her to follow. Her husband did the same. No one said a word as they strolled through the waiting room and down a series of long halls, each one whiter than the next. She wrapped her hand around her husband's and squeezed, feeling strangely relieved when he squeezed back.

As they neared the white doors behind which lay their son, Beki found herself surprisingly calm. Dr. Patton raised a hand to open the door, but paused briefly as her hand came in contact with it, as if hesitating. It only lasted a split second, but Beki caught it, and it dissipated her calmness like a two-ton weight thrown into a tranquil lake. But before she could go into a panic, the door was open.

IMMORTALITY 101: The Intro Course

Eric lay on the – what else – white bed. He was very pale, so much so that he seemed to blend and get lost in the surroundings. His body was covered by a thin sheet, his head wrapped in bandages, and his face, once full of life and smiles, was now covered by a mask. Beki didn't understand any of the equipment currently maintaining her son's life, but she was grateful for and at the same time completely terrified by them. There were so many strange things hooked up to him that she could barely tell where one started and the other ended.

An IV drip was hooked up to his left arm. The fluids in the bag dripped slowly into his body. She could hear the soft sound of each drop falling, accompanied by the beeping of the heart monitor.

Drip. Drip.

Beep. Beep.

It was almost rhythmic, almost musical, like a little tune lulling the dying into death.

She shuddered. Her husband wrapped a comforting arm around her and kissed her forehead. Dr. Patton held the door open for them.

"You may stay until nine o'clock," she informed them. "Visiting hours end then. After that, I'm afraid I'll have to ask you to leave."

"Will he live?" It seemed such a morbid question, but it had slipped out of Beki's mouth before she could stop it.

Dr. Patton looked at her, a hard look of the kind elders gave to children when it was time to teach them a particularly unforgiving lesson about life. "He is stable right now," she said. "We will observe him for a while. If he wakes up, it should be in the next few days."

"If?"

"He has sustained considerable trauma to his cranium and brain. There is a slight chance that he will enter a permanent and profound state of unconsciousness."

"Which means what?"

"Coma." It was her husband who spoke. Beki glanced at him in surprise. There was a tragic smile on his face. "That's what it means, isn't it?"

Dr. Patton paused. Her head dipped a bit as she said, "yes, I'm afraid so."

Then she left. Or perhaps she stayed a little longer, her eyes showering them with sympathy, but Beki didn't notice. Instead, she went to the bed where her son might now lie for the rest of his life, pulled the nearest chair to its side, and sat down. Her husband did the same. And there they stayed, side by side, as their son's small chest rose and fell.

The room was a semi-private one. In the other bed, just as blaringly white, lay an old woman. She looked to be at least seventy-five years old, with salt-and-pepper hair and light brown skin that still glowed with remnants of youthful vitality. Her face, however, did not share that attribute. She was thin, and looked very worn. Her bones jutted out from under her skin, making jagged, unnatural angles. She was broken, whether by sickness or by medical treatments didn't matter – the end result was the same. The whole time they sat there, she slept on, not moving a muscle, barely breathing.

At some point her husband rose to go to the bathroom, and she stayed seated in the silence. Every now and then she would reach out to touch her son's hand, or brush the hair out of his face. They were merely excuses, however, just excuses to touch him and make sure he was still warm, still breathing. The sun was beginning to set outside, washing the room with a golden light brighter than her spirits.

All this time, however, she didn't cry. She had thought she would, had worried about it, not wanting to break down in public, not even in front of the old woman dead to the world. In situations like this she'd always thought it would be important to maintain control over oneself.

But, of course, she'd never been in such a situation, and if she had the energy to think more on it, she might even be proud of herself for keeping a level head.

Though was it a level head? She had no idea. Her mind was racing, clamoring. Sometimes she wallowed in memories: his first steps, his first words, and the first time he called her Mama. Other times she wondered, planned for the future, just in case he never did wake up. What would she do when she went home if that were to happen? The house would seem so empty. She had a hard time imagining tonight without him, or tomorrow, or next week.

And, for some reason she could not comprehend, in between those thoughts, a stranger's face kept coming to mind.

How? Why?

All of this, she felt, was somehow started by *him*.

IMMORTALITY 101: The Intro Course

The sound of a metal cart being pushed in the hall woke her from her trance. Beki looked up to see the sky had darkened completely, a dome of starless black. The woman in the other bed had not moved. She checked the clock on the wall. It was almost nine o'clock. Visiting hours were coming to an end and her husband still had not returned from the bathroom.

She rose from the chair. Her legs were a bit stiff from the long sit. Before leaving the room, she took one last look at her son, who did not acknowledge her departure, just as he did not notice her arrival. She considered praying, but somehow felt it wouldn't do any good. After a momentary debate, she settled on something simple.

God, if you're there, please watch over him. Her eyes fell on the old woman. *And her.*

As she wandered through the hospital's vast halls, Beki realized she had never wanted to be home so badly. Not just the house – her home – with her husband and son, and without the fear and doubt that has plagued her more and more lately. It was as if life had suddenly changed recently. Something had shifted out of balance. Maybe she and her husband would fall to a fatal accident on the way home, and their son, should he wake up, would be left an orphan at the tender age of eleven. Wouldn't that be a trick in luck?

Third floor, no sign of her husband. She descended to the second without much success. He could have wandered off to a restroom on the first floor, since those were larger and cleaned more regularly. Even hospitals kept up appearances for visitors. Rounding the elevators on the second floor, she passed a series of empty rooms on her way to the stairs.

Had she decided to take the elevators, she would not have seen what she was about to see. She could have gone on with the rest of her life without knowing what she was about to know, because it was something that was never going to happen again. But, as Luck would have it, that was not the way to go. As she approached the stairs, movement in one of the dark rooms caught her eye, and she stepped back to look inside through the small rectangular window on the door.

Two figures were inside. She could barely make out their shape in the darkness. Again, even if she arrived just a second later, she would have taken a short peek and moved on. But as she slowed her step, the figure on top lifted his face to the dim stream of light, and she saw him, her husband, the only human she trusted unconditionally in the world, with his limbs tangled in that of the beautiful Dr. Patton.

Then she went home.

She didn't particularly remember how she got there, but she must have driven because her car was parked outside, lined neatly with the driveway as if she'd done it with the utmost care. She didn't remember turning around, didn't remember getting into her car, and wasn't really sure how she made it home without running someone over. She would say that luck was on her side, but under the circumstances, it certainly didn't seem the right way to put it.

Throughout time and the history of man, many poets, novelists, and writers of all ages, shapes, and forms have written about doom. Doom was interesting. Doom was captivating. Doom was what happened when the world came crashing down, whether literally or figuratively, and those inside it had to keep on living. Some wrote of the fall of the Earth, others wrote about one person's world collapsing, leaving them desolate and alone, as if all else had been torn away and locked up. There were words to describe these things: darkness, sorrow, dreariness, pain, angst.

And yet, at this moment, as she locked the front door behind her, went to the nearest couch and sat down without reaching over to turn on the lamp, Beki realized that they were all full of shit. Every last one of them.

The true sound of a world collapsing was silence. At the moment she could hear nothing as she sat there in the dark that seemed to envelop her existence. At some point she wondered whether her husband would realize she was gone and thought about how he would get home. But of course that didn't matter. The later he came home, the better. Better yet, he shouldn't come home at all. In her younger years she had always thought that, if her betrothed should betray her, she would raise hell and make his life miserable, that he would regret ever getting near another woman. She had thought about how she would burn his things and toss them out on the front lawn when he returned. It would be satisfying. She had always thought it would be.

But now, in her mid-thirties and no longer the energetic, idealistic girl she once was, Beki Tempest found herself tired. Somehow, even with the memory of him and the doctor burned into her mind, she found it hard to muster up the strength to do anything, even hate him. She couldn't hate him. He was her husband. Ever after all that, even if it was on this day, he was her husband. She didn't want him to come home, but only because she didn't want to confront him about it. She wanted him to walk in the door, pretend it didn't happen, and the two of them could go to bed, lay under the same covers, and drift off to sleep thinking about their son.

She linked her hands together and twiddled her thumbs, then considered getting up and vacuuming the carpet. What else was there to do really? Cry? It would be the right time to do so, but she didn't feel like it. It didn't seem very productive. The room seemed to have blurred as she got to her feet shakily and walked around it, just so some part of her body moved as her mind worked.

Eventually she wound up in the kitchen, washing a pile of dishes left from dinner the previous night. In her distracted state she had turned on the water too hot. It ran over her hands, turning them lobster red and coating them with soap bubbles. She barely felt it. She washed each dish, cup, and bowl, then lay them neatly in the dishwasher, which she left open after the dishes were finished. She looked around for something else to wash. The cutting board, the milk saucer they put out for the stray tabby that occasionally wandered by. Finally she made her way to the knives, dumping them out of the holder unceremoniously into the sink and washing them one by one, blade and handle and all.

As she scrubbed the blades with an old sponge, she found herself staring at them, at the way the water glided off them. For several long minutes she simply stood there, watching the water slide off the blades and inevitably into the drain.

How?

She simply couldn't let the questions go. Some things always happened to 'other people', and she was, in her entire life, never part of the 'other people'. Things didn't happen to her, good or bad. She would never die in a hostage situation or win the lottery. Those things didn't seek her out and never would. Or so she'd thought until today.

Her son was dying and her husband was with another woman. It was like trying to figure out a particularly difficult math problem, searching for the reason behind it. Yes, this is how it's calculated, but why? Why this way and not that? Why now? Why today?

Of course at this point logic wasn't important. Humans weren't logical, or they would be machines. And the inability to grasp at logic was what sent her mind reeling as she picked up the nearest blade, a steak knife. It was still new. They were supposed to have a barbecue this weekend, and he was going to teach their son how to grill. Change of plans.

She thought about her son. Their son. Daytime television always made comas seem so common, almost casual, almost ridiculous. But right now, the idea of sleep, of her son lying there sleeping for the next God knows how long, seemed anything but funny. It was terrifying. The rest of the world faded from existence as images of her son and the white bed ballooned and suffocated everything else.

Ten o'clock was approaching. Usually she went to bed around this hour, but at the moment it was the last thing on her mind. Her husband still wasn't home. She supposed she didn't expect him to get home any time soon. How could he? She had the car. He also didn't know where she was.

As if on cue, her cell phone began to ring, a muffled little tune from the bottom of her purse. She didn't answer it. Eventually it stopped and she still stood at the sink with the steak knife in her hand.

What's it like?

She lifted the blade, then touched it against her other wrist. It was cold, almost comforting. She didn't press down right away.

Would anyone miss...

A knock came on the door, startling her out of her trance. Suddenly, she was very much aware that she was holding a knife to her own wrist. Shaking her head hard, she dropped it into the sink.

Another series of knocks, more urgent this time. Was her husband home? She dreaded facing him. But perhaps it wasn't. He had keys. He wouldn't knock. But then who could it be at this hour?

The visitor rang the doorbell. Twice.

Usually, common sense would have stepped in and told her that it was best not to open doors to strangers at night, especially for a woman alone at home. But right now it didn't matter. She needed something, anything, to take her mind off those knives. Quickly, she dried her hands on the nearest dishtowel, turned on the living room light as she passed the switch, and ran a hand through her hair.

Knocking again. She unlocked the front door and opened it.

It was like a thunderbolt striking through her body when she saw his face. All words escaped her as he grabbed her wrist, where a knife had been held just seconds ago.

"Come on," he said forcefully. "We're leaving."

Instead of struggling, or reaching back to close the door, she let him lead her, this stranger named Michigan Von Phant, who, for all she knew, was the catalyst to her misery. And yet, she said nothing. He pulled her down the driveway and past her car. One of her shoes fell off and instead of trying to retrieve it she kicked off the other one and walked barefoot on the asphalt.

Whether it was her dazed mind or her broken heart that clouded her judgment, or that she was seeing the world clearly for the first time, she was very aware that the night was chilly, and his hand was warm.

9
CALISA AND RO

Michigan Von Phant drove a red truck.

Were she aware of the full aspects of the situation she would have found it ironic. But at the moment, it was the farthest thing from her mind. He had parked it clumsily, half-on and half-off the curb two blocks down. A few hundred feet from her house, however, he let go of her wrist, since she was not attempting to resist or run away, and she simply followed him. The sidewalk still held a small remnant of the day's heat.

At first he seemed surprised that she was coming so willingly. He kept glancing back at her as they walked, as if to make sure it wasn't a trick. When they arrived at his car, he opened the passenger door for her and she got in willingly, even accepting his hand to help her step up. It didn't seem to matter where they were going, or what he was going to do to her.

In the moment he took to step round the front to the driver's side, she noticed that the truck seemed brand new. It was impossibly clean. There was not a scrap of paper on the floors, not a single cup in the cup holder, and not one item of personal memento on the dashboard. There was no dirt on the floor, no stains on the seats, and no air freshener hanging from the rearview mirror. In short, it looked as if no human hands had touched it until tonight. They rode in silence. He did not turn on the radio. She sat in the passenger seat, rubbing her arms to relieve the chill. Even now, she remembered to buckle her seatbelt. The night was dark and quiet as Michigan took a seldom-traveled route to the edge of town. She recognized the route. Her husband used it to take her to a hole-in-the-wall Thai restaurant that had surprisingly good noodle dishes. It had closed down just last year.

"What should I call you?"

He seemed surprised by the question, though it was only indicated by a slight arch of one eyebrow. He kept his hands on the wheel and eyes on the road. "Did you forget my name already?"

"I remember." Beki gazed out the side window, watching the trees pass by, silent and stiff in the darkness. "But your name doesn't really mean a lot at this point, does it?"

"Why not?"

"Because I don't know you."

She wasn't even sure why she was speaking. For the sake of making conversation with this stranger who might have just kidnapped her? She could be dead by the end of the night, although that didn't seem to hold much bearing in her thought process at the moment.

Unexpectedly, he smiled. She saw it when she turned momentarily to adjust her position in the seat. He had a friendly, if washed out, smile, as if he was very tired, and a little worried. "What do you want to call me?"

"A kidnapper?"

"If I am that, then I've never had a more willing victim." He made a turn onto a smaller road. There were no streetlights on either side of it. Michigan tapped the brake lightly and slowed down. "But no, I am not kidnapping you. You are free to go back at any time. In fact, I'd drive you back myself if you want me to. Although you should trust me when I say I am acting in your best interest."

"How would you know what's in my best interest?"

He turned to look at her for a moment, and she thought she saw amusement in his eyes, as if he expected her to already know the answer. But when she said nothing else, he returned his eyes to the road.

"How about the fact that you're here?" he asked. "Why are you here, with me, a stranger, driving off to God knows where?"

She started to answer, and then closed her mouth when she realized that none of the answers in her head were remotely coherent. So she sat back in her seat and tried to arrange the words in her mind. It was surprisingly easy. The hard part was admitting it to herself.

"Because I don't want to be home."

"And why is that?"

"Shouldn't you know? You act as if you know everything about me."

"Educated guesses only." He leaned over as if trying to make a move on her. But instead, he opened the glove compartment and removed a pack of cigarette and a silver lighter. "Smoke?"

"Smoking gives you lung cancer."

Michigan laughed as he removed one of the sticks, stuck it between his lips, and lit it, all with one hand. "Ever the good girl," he teased. "So tell me, are you not afraid that I will take you to a secluded cabin, have my way with you, and leave your corpse for the dogs?"

She had considered the possibility. It still seemed more attractive than staying home alone, waiting for the inevitable confrontation. "A little."

"And yet you came anyway. This means that, at the moment, you can think of nowhere else you'd rather be, or anything else you'd rather do. Either this is best or everything else is worse. It doesn't matter. Because you made this choice and I am part of it, I am acting in your best interest."

Beki was too tired to follow his logic, but it sounded good enough to her muddled senses. She eyed the cigarettes sitting in the cup holder. Michigan must have noticed, because he tossed the lighter at her without taking his eyes off the road. Moving quickly before she lost the nerve, Beki lit one of the sticks and put it to her lips. She inhales and coughed violently.

Michigan glanced at her. "How's it taste?"

"Like shit." But she took another careful drag. This one was slightly better.

"Didn't think you had it in you."

"To smoke?"

"To curse."

"Am I that vanilla?"

IMMORTALITY 101: The Intro Course

He didn't answer, but the smile stayed on his face and she found herself laughing as she took another careful drag.

"You're right," she said. "I am. So what are you, anyway?"

"Don't you mean who I am?"

"No, I mean what. I'm starting to think you're some kind of alien, or a ghost, or some visitor from the future trying to change the past. Or keep it from changing. Or maybe I'm dreaming this whole thing and pretty soon I'll wake up in bed and laugh at myself. I don't know. You tell me."

Michigan rolled down the driver's side window and tossed his cigarette outside. "The last two were pretty close," he replied. "But still wrong. I am from the present. I just happen to know a little more about *your* future – not *the* future – than you do. And this is pretty close to being a dream, I suppose, but no. To explain this whole thing would take too long. Besides, you don't need to know everything."

"What *do* I need to know?"

The truck was slowing down. After at least twenty miles of dense foliage and blank concrete, a small bushel of lights appeared ahead. Michigan turned to her. All laughter and amusement had disappeared from his eyes.

"Do you want to save your son?"

She started. "What?"

"Save your son. And yourself. You can save your life tonight. It's not to keep yourself from dying. But to save your *life*."

She looked away. For a moment she'd forgotten about her life. It was like a child's flight of fancy: for a brief moment, she was on a journey to the unknown, leaving the old life behind.

"It doesn't need saving."

"Don't lie." The truck pulled into a small parking lot filled with potholes. "I'm giving you a chance. It can be very simple, if you want it to be. There is someone who can help you. You can call it supernatural or what not, but this is your only chance."

For a long moment she sat there. If it was a dream, she wanted desperately to wake up. But when she did not, she realized she didn't want to go back. The last place she wanted to be at the moment was the house she called home. She looked at him. He had to be an alien.

But if she was about to be abducted, at least it'd be a tale to tell her son after he woke up, if indeed he could deliver what he was promising.

"Alright," she said, and was surprised at how firm her voice sounded. "Where are we going?"

"The Rabbit Hole."

The place they wound up going, however, was a dry cleaner's.

In fact, it wasn't even a good dry cleaner's. Once, running late and desperately pressed for time, Beki had left a skirt and two blouses here. It was run by an Italian man with a heavy accent, whose English was not merely broken but completely and utterly shattered. Her clothes stayed there for four days and came back in worse condition than they were left there.

The place was called Newt's, as was printed in blocky red letters right above the door. Someone, probably delinquent teenagers, had spray-painted an extra "e" above the space between the *e* and *w*. It must have been an inside joke because Beki certainly didn't get it. When she stepped out of the truck, she was suddenly aware that she wasn't wearing shoes. The concrete had turned cold in the night, sending a chill up her legs. She shivered and tried to walk on tiptoes.

"Here."

A pair of loafers knocked against her feet. Michigan had taken off his own shoes and kicked them to her. She regarded him in surprise as he stood there in socked feet, waiting for her to put them on.

"Well?"

She wanted to refuse, but something told her he wouldn't have it. A bit apprehensively, she slipped her bare feet into them. They were too big for her and looked rather ridiculous with her clothes, but at least now her feet were no longer cold. As she stood there looking at them, she suddenly realized that she was very grateful.

"Thank you," she told him.

He looked away and muttered something that sounded like, "You're welcome". If she didn't know better, she'd have thought he was embarrassed. But before she could get a better look, he was already headed toward the doors.

At first she fully expected it to be locked. After all, even a place with very little to steal didn't want to take the risk. It wasn't exactly the

IMMORTALITY 101: The Intro Course

best neighborhood and a shop with such meager means was sure to want to protect its few assets. But Michigan pushed down on the metal handle and the door opened easily. There was not a single light inside, but the small television in the corner was playing a rerun of *Friends* dubbed in Italian. When she was here last time, it was playing *Master and Commander*.

Using what little artificial light the television provided, she could see that the shop had obviously fallen on hard times. Paint peeled off the walls. Two chairs were stacked unceremoniously in the corner. There was a stack of newspaper and a cash register that didn't quite close on the white counter. The "lobby" was very small, probably less than a hundred square feet. A small door to its side led to the innards of the shop. It was closed tight save for a sliver of light making its way out from underneath.

Michigan reached up and turned off the television. Darkness shrouded them. Beki blinked hard as her eyes tried to adjust. Michigan was little more than a silhouette in the shadows.

"Listen to me closely," he said. "And this is vital."

"What is?"

"What we're about to do."

"Which is what?"

He turned a bit and glanced at the closed back door, as if paranoid that someone might emerge or overhear them. "We're going to get past the gatekeepers."

Maybe he's an elf, she thought to herself. Some elfin creature from a fantasy world on a quest. In that case, she was about to either be recruited as a warrior or was some unwitting princess he was saving.

"I don't even know where to start asking questions."

"Then don't. It's easier if you don't ask questions right now and just follow my directions. It will make it easier and less dangerous for the both of us."

She raised a brow. "Dangerous?"

"Only if you don't follow my directions."

The day was getting weirder and weirder. Part of Beki was intrigued, despite the fact that her common sense was protesting loudly, arguing that this was all a bad idea, something horrible would happen, and she should turn around, head home, and hide under the covers. The only things that kept her there were her piqued curiosity and the fact that this day couldn't possibly get any worse. As she stood there, four very definitive words came to mind.

To hell with it.

Out loud, she said, "alright." Then added as an afterthought: "but you have to explain everything eventually."

"I will." Somehow it didn't sound very convincing, but Beki found herself not quite caring. "All you need to know right now is that there is a person who has a chance at saving your son."

"Is he a doctor?"

"She. And no. It's more complicated than that. I'll explain more when we get to the Rabbit Hole. Now, no more questions." She started to open her mouth again and he shushed her by touching a hand to her lips. She drew back in surprise and he quickly pulled his hand away. "Sorry about that. Now listen up. The gatekeepers at this door are Calisa and Ro. If you're lucky, there's a temp, which would make things much easier. But with the way your luck's been running lately, they're probably on duty. Although they're not the hardest of the gatekeepers to get past, you will still have to be very careful."

"Careful how?"

"Stay back, keep quiet, and let me do the talking. But don't lurk, and don't hide. Look casual, maybe a little bored. And two major things: do not talk to Calisa, and do not make eye contact with Ro."

"Why?"

"You're asking questions again. It doesn't matter right now. If Ro speaks to you, you can answer, but don't look directly at her. Look past her at the wall or whatever you want. Just *don't meet her eyes*, got it? Now if Calisa speaks to you, do not answer. Let me answer."

In her mind, Beki saw a woman with a head full of green snakes. For some reason it struck her as very funny. "So is Ro Medusa or what?"

Michigan didn't laugh. She could almost sense him glaring at her in the dark. "If you mess this up," he said sternly, "you will never have a chance to save your son again."

All humor drained out of her as her son's pale, blank face drifted to mind. Beki nodded. Michigan began to raise a hand, as if to comfort her, but seemed to think better of it and scratched his arm instead.

IMMORTALITY 101: The Intro Course

"Are you ready?"

"Yes."

"Then it's now or never." Turning away from her, Michigan pushed open the back door.

"Wait, which one is…"

White light washed the room and Beki found her voice vanishing into the air. Michigan gave her one last look and stepped through. She followed. The door swung closed soundlessly behind her.

There were no clothes racks in the room. No coats wrapped in plastic, no skirts and blouses. There were no jugs of organic solvents, no machines, and not even a single rag tossed on the floor.

Instead, the room was large and bare, much larger than the lobby and certainly larger than Beki had suspected. It was a perfect cube, impeccably clean, and every inch of its surface – walls, floor, and ceiling – was covered in stainless steel. Not only that, Beki noticed out of the corner of her eye, the place was *seamless*. Every surface and corner was folded, instead of pieced together as had in a normal house. No one built this room. Rather, someone had glued a piece of steel onto the end of an enormous straw and blown a perfect cube-shaped steel bubble. The air was chilly and scentless. The whole place shone like an icy sun.

Suddenly, it wasn't so surprising that they had done such a bad job on her dry-cleaning.

In the center of the room was a table. Actually, it was more like a stainless steel cube. It sat squarely in the center of the room, and two silver chairs were placed on either side of it. It was quite possible that, on close inspection, they would also be revealed as stainless steel. Upon these chairs sat two women.

The word "sit", however, was hardly an appropriate term. At first, Beki thought her eyes were playing a trick on her, but with a second look, she had to bite her tongue to stop from gasping.

The women were both beautiful. More than beautiful. They were gorgeous. The one on the left wore her dusty-blonde hair in long layers at shoulder length. It was smooth and flawless like her sun-kissed skin, framing her well-proportioned face and cherry lips. She wore a lavender spaghetti-strap top, exposing just enough cleavage to warrant a second look. On her right arm, wrapped around her milky skin, was a bracelet of round amber stones strung on rawhide. Her companion on the right side of the cube was equally stunning. She was of Asian origin, with a mane dark as the night, hanging all the way to her waist. Her eyes were sharp and hot, and her skin white as snow. Though not as well-endowed as the other, she also sported tight, breathtaking curves, caressed by her red-and-blue striped tube top. Around her long neck she wore a large pendant that seemed to be a flat piece of white stone.

But those killer curves only took the two so far. Beneath those perky breasts and tiny waists, the women simply... ended.

Beki tried her best not to stare, but it was difficult. Where their hips ought to be, the two women had nothing. It was almost an atrocious sight, a horrible joke. They looked like magician's assistants after a particularly bad day of body-splitting tricks. Not only were they half, they were perfect halves. Their bodies ended as if they'd been cut by the careful blade of an artist.

The Asian woman turned to them. The other did not; Beki guessed that she was Calisa. Whereas Ro sized them up and down with her onyx eyes, Calisa 'sat' still and did not move. Where her eyes ought to be she wore a mask. Like everything else inanimate in the room, it was also steel, and without eyeholes. Without sight, her face was expressionless, like a strange, futuristic doll.

Ro fixated her eyes on Beki, who was suddenly very aware of her stare. It could have been her overactive imagination. After all, she was still somewhat convinced that Michigan was an alien bent on experimenting with her body. She could feel Ro's dark eyes roaming her body, and wherever they stopped, she felt a tingling heat, like someone burning a pinpoint on her skin with a magnifying glass. She waited to be asked a question, but it was Calisa who spoke first.

"Who is there, sister?" she asked. Her voice was extraordinarily soft, barely audible, and yet it was not a whisper, more like someone had turned a knob and lowered the volume. There was a hint of something unidentifiable in her voice. Exhaustion? Confusion? Despair?

Ro turned to her, but instead of speaking, she climbed onto the table in between them, dragging herself on her hands and arms with amazing dexterity. Beki saw her ropey muscles strain with the effort as she pulled her torso onto the cubic table, lying prone. With practiced efficiency, she crawled to Calisa's side and whispered into her ear, then trained her eyes on Beki and Michigan once more.

"Ah," Calisa said, her stony expression completely unchanged. "Welcome, rule-breakers."

As per Michigan's instructions, she kept her mouth shut and averted her eyes from Ro's hot gaze. It was difficult; the woman's eyes were like whirlpools, pulling her in with undeniable force.

"We're not rule-breakers."

At this, Calisa finally gave some form of emotion. She smiled. "I'd love to hear you justify that, V.P. Only rule-breakers need cross the gatekeepers. Have you forgotten that already?"

"Of course not, but we all know special exceptions are made for VIPs."

"You think of yourself as a VIP? How presumptuous!"

"I may not be." With one hand, he nudged Beki forward with one hand. "But do you recognize her?"

There was a pause. Ro leaned over once more and whispered into Calisa's ear.

"Why have you come?"

It took Beki a moment to realize the question was addressed at her. She almost answered reflexively. Michigan cut in. "She has important business. VIPs are allowed to break Rounds under special circumstances."

"And what circumstance would that be?"

Ro's eyes were boring into her skull. Beki fought not to squirm, and was more than thankful when Michigan stepped between them, blocking the heated gaze. He spoke something softly into Ro's ear, who in turn passed the message to Calisa.

"No."

Michigan blanched. "*What do you mean 'no'?*" he demanded heatedly, slamming his fist on the steel cube. Ro peeked over his shoulder at Beki, who quickly focused on a spot behind the woman's head. It was quite the hard thing to do with the entire room being colorless and bland. There was nearly nothing for the eye to hold on to.

"No," Calisa said again.

"Why? It's a legitimate reason."

"I want no part of this. I do not want to be the one who allowed a rule-breaker inside in order to defy…"

"It's not defiance! It's the settlement of a Bet. It's…"

Slender hands shot up and wrapped themselves around Michigan's throat, choking off his words in midair. He coughed, gagging and struggling as Ro's skinny fingers tightening around his esophagus. His face was turning an unsettling shade of red as Beki started forward. The woman seemed intent on killing him on the spot!

But even as he fought to breath, he waved her off.

"Sorry," he choked out, gagging on each syllable. "I'm sorry. I'll behave."

Ro released him. The entire time, her expression didn't change. Calisa, who must have been aware of this, didn't move or speak. Blood pounded in Beki's ears. Michigan, however, seemed less than fazed by the whole ordeal. Instead of backing away, he leaned down and spoke directly to Calisa. Beki couldn't make out what he was saying, but thirty seconds later he straightened and returned to her side, looking rather smug. Ro took the time to crawl back into her seat, where she fixed her hair using the reflection on the cube.

Calisa sat in silence. Then, slowly, she lifted one arm and ran it lightly through the tips of her hair. It was an unsettling gesture, and the first movement she had made aside from talking since Beki and Michigan entered.

"Alright," she said at last. Michigan threw up his hands like a child whose baseball team had just scored a series of homeruns.

"Yes!" He grabbed Beki's arm and pulled her past the two incomplete women. "Let's go."

As they walked past the two, Calisa spoke, a bit louder this time, and perfectly clearly. "Good luck," she said, "Miss V.I.P."

Beki turned just long enough to look at her, and to see the steel mask floating in front of her face. It drifted in midair, roughly an inch and a half from her face, held up by nothing. She was not blind. Her vision was blocked, just enough so that she could see the faintest light from its edge, like allowing a starving man one lick of a scrumptious meal.

IMMORTALITY 101: The Intro Course

10
BLACK AND WHITE

A great man's greatest luck is to die at the right time.

-Eric Hoffer, 1902-1983, Philosopher

Stat hadn't been sleeping.

Recently it seemed pointless to sleep. What would sleep bring him exactly? Dreams, nightmares, useless things that he was better off without. Sleeping was useless, entirely and utterly useless. Sure, he walked with a mild stagger. Sure, his vision blurred a bit. Sure, his mouth was dry as cotton and his tongue had the texture of sandpaper. What mattered was that he was awake.

He liked being awake. He loved being awake.

His presence was already treated like radioactive waste. Now, with his head hung low and dark circles under his eyes, he looked like... *what was that expression they picked up in the Round?*... death warmed over. Nah, he looked better than that. He looked like death after fifteen minutes of full blast in a microwave.

The plus side was, without sleep, he could work twice as much, and since his job generally involved wandering about town making people nervous, his sleep-deprived face actually helped. After a shower, he tossed on a slouchy brown jacket and black pants that made him look like a down-and-out mobster, then examined himself in the bathroom mirror. His eyes were bloodshot, and his hair, brown and shaved close to the scalp, was starting to grow a bit too long, giving him a messy peach fuzz. That was fine. No one was going to look anyway.

There were only so many places where large crowds of people gathered. He'd already hit most of them today. The Pink Pony he preferred not to visit, knowing it was Sasha's favorite hangout. He didn't think Geoffy would appreciate him dropping by twice in one day. There were a few other places he could frequent, but they all shared the same sentiment regarding him – the further away the better. Though he held no particular affection for the general population, being stared and pointed at could get old. He could drop by the Club and visit Lisa later, assuming she wasn't busy. Aside from Grimm Sullivan and Sasha, she was perhaps the only other person who did not greet his presence with apprehension.

In the end he settled on the Square, and that was where he wound up half an hour later.

Despite being the center of all known establishments, the Square was usually near-deserted. It was in the shape of an equilateral triangle, about half a mile on each side. On each of its tips was one of the three most coveted businesses. The Saffron Stallion, Club Meow, and the Pink Pony. Beyond them, tiers of buildings rose and fell in turn, dense as honeycombs. The triangular Square, by contrast, was empty and flat. The ground was layered neatly with bricks, painted a happy shade of yellow, spaced out evenly so that they resembled some prehistoric maze mosaic. At the center was a large round fountain of gray stone, many yards across, its edges bearing six nooks where water flowed out and wound itself between the yellow bricks, underneath the feet of the few pedestrians.

It was on the edge of the fountain that Stat sat, listening peacefully to the water trickling away underneath his feet. It was soothing, almost therapeutic. Here, no one disturbed him. No one walked in an arc to avoid being close to him, since there was plenty of room to maneuver here. They could spot him early and turn around without him noticing them doing so.

He took off his shoes and socks, spun around on the stone surface, and sank his feet into the water. It wasn't exactly clean, having taken on a slightly pink shade from all the doped-up drinks dumped into it by customers of the Pink Pony, but it was nice and cool. He wiggled his toes.

A statue stood on a tall pedestal in the center of the fountain. The pedestal was solid gold, but the statue was made of cement, here and there patched with clay. It was a statue of Lady Luck, the symbol of this place, the Goddess who controlled the dice and cards and Round. Stat wasn't the first to notice how ironic it was that, instead of visiting her regularly to pray for luck, the people have decided she ought to be isolated in this lonely Square.

The first thing they did was walk through the steel wall, Beki nearly stumbling in Michigan's shoes.

At first Beki was quite certain that some magical door would appear in the smooth surface as Michigan dragged her towards it quite determinedly. Some alien technology or whatnot, it didn't matter to her. In fact, she was a little disappointed when they simply passed through the seamless steel wall without so much as a fanfare.

Michigan stopped quite suddenly so that she ran into his back. Turning quickly, she saw the wall behind her shine transparent briefly. She could see the gatekeepers "sitting" in their chairs by the steel cube as if through a veil of mist. Then they were gone, replaced by a wall of smooth limestone. She looked at Michigan, who adjusted his collar and ran a hand through his hair.

"Were you expecting the mother ship?" he asked.

In truth, she was.

They were standing in a bustling city. It didn't occur to her until now that having the strange gatekeepers meant there was a *gate* of some sort to be guarded, one which they had just passed through quite unceremoniously.

Despite her initial surprise, the place where they had newly emerged seemed to bear nothing out of the ordinary. It appeared a bit run-down, a bit dark, and was painted with more than its share of neon lighting. Directly to their right was a wave of buildings, extending outward in a manner similar to a Chinese fan, each more gaudy than the next, flaunting its own array of neon letters and colorful graffiti, each lovely and vulgar in its own way. People entered and exited the buildings, most with their head down, looking quite drunk, high, or some combination of the two. They wore all forms of fashions, from business suits and evening gowns decorated with fake peacock feathers to leather biker jackets and green Mohawks. Every now and then there would be a scantily clad woman or two, parading their goods on the corners. The scent of alcohol, tobacco, latex, and an interesting mix of body odor filled the air.

It was just like Las Vegas, only a little cleaner.

To their left was a vast square. Michigan turned around and looked up. Beki did the same. A two-story building rose behind them, its outer walls were made of limestone and marble, here and there chipped and bruised with age. From where she stood, it looked small and stuffy. Around the corner, she spotted an Asian stone lion statue, probably half of a pair, an undisguised attempt to look "ethnic". The pointed roof almost resembled an English cathedral. A shiny brass horse, at least as tall as she was, its head raised and hooves kicking into the air, stood proudly atop. Someone had spray-painted "ASS" down its flank in pink. A red neon sign beneath the horse flashed "Saf ron Stalli n".

"Close enough," she heard Michigan say.

"To what?"

"To where we're going."

"Which is where?"

He ignored the question and peered to the right, scanning the buildings and crowds. No one seemed to be paying any attention to them, even though Beki found it hard to believe that no one saw them appear through the wall. She laid a finger on the wall, then her entire hand. It was solid.

"Well, we lucked out."

"I'll take your word for it." She drew her hand away, suddenly aware that the wall was probably very dirty. If they were indeed in Las Vegas, or somewhere similar, it made good sense not to touch anyone or anything. Michigan didn't seem to share her apprehension as he paced unwarily in his socks. Eyeing the back of his head, Beki found herself surprisingly calm. If watching popular movies had taught her anything, it was to always keep her guard up when in an extraordinary situation, although she had never imagined herself to be the type to wind up in some alternate realm that strangely resembled the back alley of a bar. As he craned his neck to see further, she stepped to his side and looked also. No two-headed aliens, no talking animals, no cronies of evil overlords.

"So," she said conversationally, "where are we?"

Fishing around in his pockets, Michigan removed yet another pack of cigarettes and a lighter. He offered the pack to her. Without hesitation, she took one. With this place, she felt almost out of place if she didn't smoke.

"Hell."

"What?"

"You asked where we are."

"And you're telling me we're in hell?" She waited for him to light his cigarette. "Can't you be more creative than that?"

"I'm keeping it simple so you'll understand." He took a long drag and held the flame out to her. "We could go into a long discussion about Heaven and Hell and whatnot, but that's not my cup of tea and I doubt you're in the mood for that sort of thing. So we'll save it for never."

Two women stumbled out of a nearby building, both quite large and unattractive, both wearing shorts cut so short Beki could count the dimples on their ample behinds. One had at least six piercings in each ear. She grabbed the other, who wore a spaghetti strap top three sizes too small, and licked her face. Her partner giggled.

Beki took a short drag. She herself had never had a problem with homosexuals beyond the whole "ick" factor, but to see two women make a spectacle of themselves in public was still surprising and made her more than a bit uncomfortable. "We're not in a Republican state any more, are we?"

Michigan looked at her, opened his mouth, then closed it again. "Right," he said distracted. She wasn't sure he heard her. "Something like that." He stuck the cigarette between his lips. "Ready?"

"For what?"

"I told you, we're going to the Rabbit Hole."

"I thought that was just an expression."

"Expression for what?"

IMMORTALITY 101: The Intro Course

The two women disappeared around a corner. They passed a group of men and women in 3-piece suits that screamed "lobbyists", none of whom batted an eye at their blatant display.

"You know, 'down the rabbit hole', Alice in Wonderland."

"Alice who?" Sticking the lighter back into his pocket, Michigan took one last glance around. "Ready to go?"

Beki turned around to take in the surroundings one last time for good measure, and found her eyes wandering through the vast empty square. Compared to the bustling streets, the square's emptiness was almost blinding.

The cigarette fell from her hand as she saw the silhouette sitting at the edge of the square, its feet bare and disappearing into the water, pants rolled up. She knew that head of brown hair anywhere – the boy she gave birth to eleven years ago.

Michigan was waiting. "What's wrong?" he asked her.

She quickly turned around. "Nothing," she said, and snuffed out the cigarette with Michigan's shoe.

When Stat entered Club Meow, an impeccably dressed young woman greeted him and somehow managed to show him inside, seat him, and take his drink order without lifting her gaze above his neckline even once. She brought him a hot towel to wipe his hands with and a menu printed on parchment paper. Lisa and her obsession with parchment paper. It was really quite ridiculous.

According to her nametag, the young server's name was Alex. She wore a tight black skirt that ended smack in the middle of her milky white thighs, just long enough to be conservative, and just short enough to pique the imagination. It was topped by a white blouse, black leather vest that pushed her breasts neatly to her throat, and a pair of knee-high boots with four-inch heels. The standard uniform for Club Meow. And as per club standard, her left boot was black, and the right white.

Though not as big as the Saffron Stallion, the club was quite well-endowed. The lounge was populated with leather couches and armchairs, arranged in small squares around glass tables with slender legs for the ease of entertaining small groups. Waiters and waitresses included, everything was black and white, spaced just right so that no two of the same color occupied spaces next to each other. The walls were covered in interchanging black and white panels, with black and white round paper lanterns hanging from the ceiling. In the center of the white-legged glass tables were black wooden carvings of tasteful nudes. On the far wall was a massive shelf, each level alternating black and white. Large tin jars, alternating black with white label and white with black label, lined its entirety, containing every flavor of tealeaves imaginable. Club Meow only served tealeaves or whole flowers. Ground tea powder and teabags were considered an insult.

"Jasmine," he told the girl, who nodded, smiled at his neck, and walked off. He settled back. A group of sage-like old men dressed in colorful Asian robes stood up and moved off to a table not quite so close to him, never pausing their conversation.

A young man approached him not long after. His toned muscles bulged attractively as he poured tea from a round white pot into a black cup sitting on a white plate for Stat, then asked how many lumps of sugar he took. Stat mused on the fact that this man, a gift to women by any standard with his flawless chocolate skin, carved body and onyx eyes, had probably not known the pleasures of the flesh in a very long time. He wore a tight mesh shirt and leather pants, molding his pecs and rear end into perfection respectively. Like the girl, he also wore a vest. The whole ensemble was white as new snow. His nametag read "Leslie".

"Two lumps," he said, then added, "if you please."

The man almost looked up, as if surprised at his politeness, then caught himself, kept his eyes down, and dropped two lumps of sugar – one black, one white – into his cup. As he walked away, Stat picked up his cup, blew lightly on the steaming tea, and leveled his gaze on the taut rear wrapped in obscenely white leather.

"Let's not get anything into that putrid little mind of yours now." He nearly dropped his tea. The woman behind him smiled in amusement as he set it down in haste and stood. She spread her arms warmly. "Status!" she cooed. "My dear, it has been much, *much* too long!"

Stat hugged her, tightly and sincerely. "I'm missed you," he said, "Lisa."

IMMORTALITY 101: The Intro Course

Michigan smiled to himself. It seems the gatekeepers had kept their word. No one in the streets batted an eye as they came through. No one looked at them with curiosity, and no one tried to sell them anything.

As his traveling companion stood there, gaping and clueless, he found himself wishing he could take her into the Saffron Stallion and buy her something extra strong. It would certainly make the next step easier. If she were drunk, she wouldn't notice him throwing a paper bag over her face.

The woman bearing the unfitting name of Rebecca Tempest didn't even know how much attention she would attract. Granted, her vanilla getup would help his effort to stay inconspicuous, but sooner or later someone would take a closer look at her face. It was a pretty face. She had always been pretty though right now she'd probably deny it. He couldn't comprehend what a Plain Jane she'd become, but, at the very least, the meek, timid personality she'd picked up in the Round would make it easier on his part. Maybe he could convince her to cover up her face?

The coast was clear, as far as he could see. Rebecca, or "Beki" as she called herself, was looking rather ill at ease. He didn't blame her. This place was a lot to take. It's like a person who had never seen an insect studying the underbelly of a tick through a microscope.

He took off his jacket and handed it to her. "Here."

She looked at it. "I'm O.K."

"Not that." He stepped behind her and draped it over her shoulders. "Put it on, then raise the collar and cover your face."

He expected her to ask questions, and was surprised when she didn't. He watched her pull the jacket on and lift the collar. It was too big on her slender body and hung in an almost ridiculous fashion. But most people in this place were ridiculous to begin with.

"Want another smoke?"

"I'm good."

"Then we're off." Despite the circumstances, he was excited. He turned and set off along the side of the Saffron Stallion. Rebecca was studying the place curiously.

"Interesting place," she said quietly.

"Cheap place," he corrected. "The walls are falling apart inside and the roof leaks. Not much of a problem though, since it never rains. And see that lion?" He pointed at the statue as they passed. It held a ball under its paw. "That ball comes loose real easy. Geoffy's just too lazy to stick it on right. One of these days it's gonna…"

"Michigan."

"Yeah?" It was the first time she had spoken his name. It sent a shiver down his back, but he hid it well. He motioned for her to hurry. "Keep up. We gotta get outta here."

"Those women. How are they alive?"

"Who?" The streets were just crowded enough to blend into. "Ro and Cali? That's a funny story actually. Well, not so much funny, but Cali was…" His words vanished into the air as something hard and cold met the back of his head. As the ground rushed up at him, he faintly thought, *I should have expected that.*

Club Meow, despite its provocative name, was a teahouse and nothing more, at least in the business sense. Though the owner's fetish for two-tone irritated the eye at first glance, visitors found themselves melting into the surroundings the more time they spent there, and it wasn't just the opiates in the tea either.

Lisa Gasolina was an entrepreneur.

Well, there were lots of words for what she did, and she wasn't particularly picky. Like anyone with any success in this place, her business was diverse, involving deals and contracts of all sort and nature. Under the dome, it was rather hard to hold anyone to a contract, and she was one of the few who could do it. Not only that, she could do it without much effort. In her chrome bedroom at the back of the club was an intricate little cabinet, about three feet tall and one foot wide. It stood on four inwardly curved legs, each bearing carvings of dancing dragons and phoenixes. Inside, arranged in olive green folders she personally labeled, were the above-mentioned contracts.

Compared to the serving girls, she was older, statelier, and did not share in their nervous regard of Stat. Her curly maroon hair was tied back into a loose ponytail. Instead of skirts, she wore a tailored black pantsuit that fitted her curves loosely. Though age has left its lines on her face, it was easy to see that she was once a knockout, a beauty by any standard, now aged – for the better – by experience. Her matronly eyes were a captivating gray.

As she pulled away from Stat, she looked him up and down, the way a mother would size up her son returning home. The armchair next to his was black. She glided around the table to a white one and sat down, taking care to smooth out the wrinkles in her pants as she crossed her legs.

"How's the tea?" she inquired.

"Excellent as usual."

She seemed genuinely pleased. "Fantastic." A delicate gesture and a dark-skinned girl in a white uniform came to her side. "Earl Grey, dear," she said, "if you please."

The girl bowed. "Yes, madam."

"I have told you, child, you needn't be so formal." Reaching over, she took the girl's hand. "How long have you being here?"

The girl hesitated. "Four hundred and sixty-five days, Miss Lisa."

"Such a good memory you have. Then you ought to know that you needn't tiptoe around me. Right, dear?" The girl nodded timidly. Lisa waved her off. "These young ones," she said to Stat, sighing melodramatically, "so awkward. I do wish they would relax around me. It's simply not good for the atmosphere."

"You are quite intimidating, Lisa."

She scoffed. "Oh, I am not. Now then, what are you doing here? Is there something I can help you with, or is this a social call? If it's the latter, I can spare ten minutes. I am quite busy."

"Too busy for an old friend?"

"Of course not. For an old friend I spare ten instead of five." A knowing smile appeared on her face. "You've gone to see her again, haven't you? Honestly, Stat, you're addicted. I ought to fix you up with a little distraction. How about it?"

Stat started to object, but found it rather hard.

Lisa clapped her hands together. "I knew it," she exclaimed excitedly. "So, what's your poison? Leslie or Alex? Or how about my little pudding pop Prescott?"

"Don't call her a pudding pop, Lisa, it's so…"

"Obscene?"

"Something like that."

Lisa bent ever so slightly, her warm fingertips connecting with his knee. "Are you jealous?"

Her touch shouldn't have had an effect on him, or at least he thought it shouldn't. And yet, the moment her touch landed, he felt an involuntary shiver down his spine. It wasn't pleasant. Nor was it unpleasant. It was simply her.

"Do you miss me?"

He shook his head. "No."

She smiled. "You're lying. Don't lie to me, Status. I can always tell when you're lying. That's the only time you look me in the eyes."

He had no retort for her. Retorting did no good when she was right. Her pale hand snaked around his neck, creeping as if looking for a pulse to strike. She guided him close until their mouths connected, tongues intertwining like a mating dance. The other patrons in the lounge paid them no attention, not because they weren't curious, but because they didn't dare.

"Like I said," she whispered when they had parted a few inches, "I'm very busy. Had you come at a different time, I may have had time to amuse you myself."

"You're always busy, Lisa. And I don't want to be amused by you. I can't afford it."

She flicked his chin playfully. "Smart boy. Too few people in this damned place know their price. How about five minutes with Prescott? You can turn off the lights and pretend she's that bitch Sasha."

Stat sat up and scanned the lounge. The way the black-and-white-clad wait staff dashed out of the way, his eyes might as well have fired laser beams. "I don't think your people like me, Lisa."

Raising one finger, Lisa wagged her hand as if reprimanding a child. "No, no, dear. That doesn't matter. You take your pick. They will like you if I tell them to."

"I'll take half an hour with Leslie then."

"Good choice." Lisa raised her delicate long arm and clapped her palms together twice. "Oh, Leslie dear?"

The young man in white tensed visibly at the mention of his name. In some sadistic way, Stat enjoyed it. This was Lisa's power – the power to draw people in instead of dragging them. Those who came to

105

her were like will-less rag dolls, being pulled by her invisible puppet strings. Leslie handed his tray to the nearest waitress, who looked at him sympathetically as she took it. He approached Lisa, who motioned for him to lean down, took his face gently in both hands, and kissed his forehead.

"Are you tired, dear?" she cooed. "You've been working so hard."

Leslie glanced at Stat quickly and started to shake his head, but Lisa's brow furrowed ever so slightly, and he nodded instead. Though the room was fairly chilly, he was sweating as he straightened.

"I love Leslie very much, Status," Lisa said teasingly. Stat smirked.

"You love them all very much."

"Good to see you remember. Do you promise to be gentle? I can't have you roughing up one of my precious boys."

"Yes, Lisa."

"Promise?"

Stat fought the urge to roll his eyes. Lisa was always overprotective. Had he been anyone else, she been anyone else, he might have thought she was putting him on. But she wasn't. He knew all too well how Lisa felt about her "boys" and "girls".

"I'll be nice."

"Very well." Reaching over, Lisa hooked one finger in Leslie's belt loop and pulled him close. She squeezed his hand and whispered, "If he's not nice to you, you run and tell Mama, OK, dear?"

Leslie looked beyond nervous. To be honest, it upset Stat ever so slightly. To live under Lisa's room meant the young men and women was used to all manners of things, and yet, they were all so ill at ease around him. Just him. He felt he didn't deserve it. There were worse things than spending half an hour with him.

Lisa left Stat alone to his fun. The boy always liked to play, that was what she liked about him. He liked to play though he would never admit it. Mind games, body games, he enjoyed them all, but it was a bitter sort of enjoyment and it pained her to see him trapped in those games. It was like a chess master forced to live on a chessboard. He could do nothing but be good at his games. That was why he loved that dreaded Sasha. Such a pity. He was such a good boy.

She paced the lounge, working the room, pandering to the patrons and serving a cup of tea every now and then. Her wait staff needed a break. It wasn't easy to keep the place running twenty-three hours a day, but they were excellent workers and she was proud of them. She allowed two of them to retire and took over refilling the tea jars in the storerooms personally. As she climbed the ladder to the top shelf of the massive white store room, a black tin tucked under her right arm, she never failed to notice how the sweet aroma of tealeaves always seemed to relax her.

"Miss Lisa?"

She looked down to see an olive-skinned girl in a white leather mini and black boots gazing up at her. Her name was Marky. Lisa knew the name of every person who served in Club Meow and the color of their uniforms. She made a mental note to acquire a white boot for the girl.

"Yes, dear?"

"There is a visitor here."

"We have many visitors, Marky. It is how we run business."

Marky fidgeted. "I thought you may want to greet her yourself, ma'am. She's one of your friends from the HRC."

Sasha. Lisa's grip on the tea canister tightened. The persistent little thing, never leaving poor Stat alone. She descended the ladder and handed the canister to Marky. It was a prime opportunity. She dearly wished to see the look on Sasha's face when she informed her that her beloved Stat was in the back room having his way with another.

Marky trotted after her as she re-entered the main lounge. She looked left and right for Sasha's trademark hair ribbons as a figure stepped into her way.

"Excuse me," said the woman, "are you the manager? I'm looking for my son. I think I saw him come in here." She pointed to Marky. "This young lady said you could help me."

Lisa looked at the woman for a very long time before smiling warmly. She took the woman's arm gently with one hand and reached into her pocket for a ring of keys with the other.

"Of course, dear," she said, "right this way. But please excuse me just one moment." Marky caught the keys she tossed into the air. "Lock the Jasmine Room, dear."

IMMORTALITY 101: The Intro Course

Marky paused. "But Leslie is in there with…" Lisa turned to her, her bright smile unchanging. "Yes, Miss Lisa."

A long dribble of water fell over Michigan's face. He opened his eyes to find, very gratefully, that it was coming out of a bottle. A pair of thick round glasses stared down at him and snorted.

"You alive?"

Michigan sat up, very aware of the throbbing bump on the back of his head. He reached up to touch it. No blood. He could be thankful for that much. The newcomer shoved his glasses and hooknose much too close to his face.

"You don't have her, do you?"

Rolling his eyes, Michigan pushed him away. "Sorry, Snip. I'll bring her by, don't you worry."

Snip, a lanky, perpetually hunched young man hardly out of his teens in ill-fitted flannel pants and a T-shirt that read *Jesus took three days to re-spawn*, jostled his glasses back up the bridge of his nose with a forceful twitch of his cheek muscle. "Don't be late now," he said, spitting as he spoke. "Don't forget how much you owe us. If you're late the Great Leader won't be pleased."

Michigan rose to his feet and dusted off his clothes. "Tell your Great Leader he can go f…"

"Thirty thousand, V.P." Snip picked his teeth, found something green, and wiped it on the seat of his pants.

Michigan sighed. "Fine, fine."

"And don't disrespect the Great Leader."

"I'll disrespect whoever the hell I want."

Snip snorted again. Michigan dearly wished he had a tissue to offer the kid. "You're so difficult," he whined nasally. "Sometimes I wish we could just, just…"

"Well, get in line."

"You'll bring her by soon?"

"Yes! For freak's sake, yes! Get off my back!"

Snip skulked off, muttering under his breath. Snip was harmless, but extremely annoying. In a way, it was a great power not to be abused. Michigan watched him go and contemplated his options.

He had just let down his guard and screwed up royally. It wasn't really his fault. It never was. This time it was Beki's fault for wandering off on her own, and after bashing him on the head no less. Did he deserve it? Of course not. But either way, if he didn't find her soon, things were going to turn into a right mess and Status Quo was going to have his head for it. Great. Wonderful.

He scanned the area. Where would she go? Into the Square? Toward the outskirts? Ask for directions somewhere? Pink Pony? Club Meow? Rabbit Hole? He ruled that last one out. If she didn't want to stick around him, then she obviously wasn't going to head to the same place he just suggested. If she was in the Square, he could seek her out quickly and maybe even without attracting much attention. But if she headed for the outskirts…

Michigan didn't want to think about it. This was getting too hard. He needed a plan. A formula of action. But before he could do that, he needed a drink.

So he turned around and entered the Saffron Stallion.

IMMORTALITY 101: The Intro Course

11
THE SISTERS

The woman named Lisa was the nicest person Beki had ever met. It almost seemed unreal to meet a person so warm and friendly these days, especially in a place like this – even though she hadn't quite figured out where "this" was. The two-tone décor of the teahouse was a bit overwhelming at first, but she soon began to find it rather comforting. The entire place closed around her like a warm shell. The young waiters and waitresses looked like they just stepped out of Calvin Klein and Dior commercials. Lisa was like a den mother amidst them all, waving them here and there, praising and reprimanding them with equally affectionate tones. In Michigan's oversized jacket and shoes, Beki felt grossly underdressed. She ruffled her messy hair in a weak attempt at looking halfway kempt.

Lisa asked the girl named Marky to bring a cup of tea for Beki on the house. Its wafting fragrance was wonderful and strangely homey. She tasted it. It was smooth and sweet like honey.

"Now, dear," Lisa said, settling down in the black armchair opposite her white one, "you are new in town, are you not?"

Was it so obvious? Beki nodded. "Yes, I am. I haven't been here very long."

"And you've already lost track of your son? Well, boys will be boys, am I right?"

IMMORTALITY 101: The Intro Course

From anyone else, it would have sounded like passing judgment on her parenting skills, but from this woman it simply sounded genuine. Beki felt herself relaxing, though her fingers still shook ever so slightly as she picked up the hot teacup.

She had left Michigan out cold in the alley, after knocking him on the head with the loose stone ball she pulled out from under the lion's paw. It was all too much like a bad movie, the way she hurried off with the collar of his jacket pulled over her face. Maybe it wasn't right to keep the jacket, but it was too late to worry about that now. A tall waiter of Asian descent approached Lisa. He wore a tailored vest that fit all too well. As they spoke, Beki glanced around the teahouse again.

If Hell had a teahouse, would it look like this? She always thought it would be brighter, with more reds and oranges, instead of the snow white and charcoal black. Or perhaps she was in Heaven, though she doubted Heaven would approve of the skin-tight leather outfits swathing the wait staff. Besides, everyone around here seemed to be living, breathing bodies of flesh.

"Tell me," Lisa said, "What does your son look like? Perhaps I have seen him."

"He's eleven." *And he's dying on a hospital bed.* "He has brown hair, light skin, and is tall for his age."

"Is that right?" Lisa's gray eyes washed over her. "He sounds like a lovely boy. And you said you saw him come in here?"

Actually, I think I'm out of my mind. "I thought I did. We were taking a walk, getting to know the new town, and he wandered off. I saw him wading in the fountain outside. When I went to get him, he waved and ran in here instead."

The lies had come easier than she expected. Beki felt an inward sigh of relief as Lisa nodded in belief. "He may have come in here then. But as you can see, I have many customers and cannot take notice of a few wandering in and out. He may have come through and snuck into the back rooms. Boys, always so curious. How about I fetch someone to check for you?" With a gesture of her slender fingers, she summoned the nearest waitress. "Alex, go check to see if anyone is in the back rooms, would you? A boy, specifically. Thanks, love."

Alex half-bowed gracefully and sauntered off. Lisa helped herself to a black sugar cube. Beki watched her with an odd sort of fascination.

"Can I ask you a crazy question?"

Lisa sipped her tea, her pinky extended. "Certainly, dear. Believe it or not, I have heard my share of crazy questions."

"Am I dead?"

Lisa laughed. She had a pleasant, matronly laugh, like a queen chuckling at a jester's tricks over a glass of expensive champagne. "Well, that certainly is an interesting question. The answer is 'no'. Why ever would you think that?"

Her hands were still shaking, but the warm cup was helping immensely. Beki took a drink and smiled. She felt a bit embarrassed, and more than a little foolish, but it was a relieved sort of foolishness. "I don't know," she said. "I suppose I was just... wondering."

"Everyone wonders." Lisa set down her cup, smoothed her pant legs twice, and stood. "I won't ask your reasons. Everyone has their own for asking the questions they do. But, for now, I think I can help you. Or rather, my daughter can. Oh, Prescott, dear?"

A hushed silence fell over the teahouse. A quick look around revealed that the patrons have not halted their conversation, but the wait staff seemed to have frozen in their place. The click of their boots against the wooden floor ceased; the clatter of glasses and cups stopped. As one, they turned to the rear of the lounge, where a small door, hidden in one of the black wooden panels, opened, and out stepped the prettiest girl Beki had ever seen. Standing at just over five feet, she sported a head of long shiny black locks that fell over her face and to her waist. Her eyes were a deep sapphire blue and her skin smooth as cream. Every line on her slender body flowed like water, from her narrow shoulders down to her slender legs. Like the wait staff, she was wearing a white shirt under a black leather vest and skirt. However, instead of boots, she wore a pair of white tennis shoes.

Lisa gestured for her daughter to come closer. The wait staff had returned to their work now, the momentary lapse past. But now, Beki noticed, they had parted to form a circle around the three of them, and walked with their heads down, as if shielding their gaze from something unpleasant. She couldn't imagine why.

Prescott walked with her head slightly bowed, too. She appeared very shy as she went to her mother and stood by her side, hands linked together, shoulders hunched as if wanting to shrivel up inside of herself.

IMMORTALITY 101: The Intro Course

Her actions were similar to that of a six-year-old afraid to let go of her mother's hand on the first day of school, though, judging by her figure, she was at least sixteen. Lisa placed a gentle arm around her daughter's shoulders and kissed the side of her head.

"Don't be so shy, darling, we have a guest."

Beki bent slightly and did her best to give a friendly smile to the girl. Having no sisters or daughters of her own, she'd developed a soft spot for gentle, shy girls like Prescott. The girl was fortunate to have a kind mother.

"Hi," she said softly. The girl looked as if she might flutter away like a spooked bird. "My name is Beki."

The girl's head suddenly snapped up, startling Beki. Her eyes were wide as she stared at Beki, then at her mother. She started to open her mouth, but Lisa shushed her with one finger.

"Now, child," she cooed, "don't be impolite. This nice lady is here looking for her son. Alex is checking the back room. Why don't you take her to the Earl Grey Suite and check there?"

The girl stared at her mother. To Beki, she almost looked panicked, frightened even. The poor child obviously suffered from social anxiety. Lisa gave her shoulder a squeeze. "You can do it, dear," she said, "it's nothing complicated. Go on."

Prescott nodded, then took a single step forward, reached out, and took Beki's hand. Her skin was cold and dry, and her grasp was limp as a cooked noodle, as if she had no strength in her whatsoever, and plastic straws instead of bones propped up her body. Beki felt sorry for the kid.

"Don't worry," said Lisa, "Prescott will help you. She's very good."

Beki was led away before she could ask *at what?*

Stat heard the lock click shut in the Jasmine Room. He pushed himself off Leslie and went to the door, turning the handle gently. It didn't budge. Behind him, he could hear the rustling of sheets.

"Tell me," he said, "does she usually lock the door for you?"

There was no answer. He turned around to see Leslie shaking his head, Lisa's crimson silk sheet drawn over his chest.

"Must be me then." He weighed the chances that Lisa wanted to give them some privacy and declared the possibility somewhere between "slim" and "nil". Leslie said nothing. Stat rounded the canopy bed, flicked the switch on the nearest lamp, and fished around for his clothing, well aware of Leslie's confused gaze as he slipped into his underwear. It was too bad. Leslie was a lovely person and a more than decent romp, but he had to do his job.

"Next time," he said to the young man. "And thanks for not closing your eyes."

Leslie favored him with a thin, uncomfortable smile. That was the best he could hope for, really. Shrugging into his jacket, he went to the door and pressed his right ear against it. The noises of the teahouse had drowned out whatever it was he hoped to hear. The temptation to turn around, snuff the lights, and continue having his way with Leslie was quite strong, but he had a sneaking suspicion that by the time someone opened the door, he would have already missed something imperative.

Good? Bad? Didn't matter.

The Jasmine Room was one of the four private rooms to Club Meow. The other three being Earl Grey, Rosehip, and Opium. The Jasmine Room was shrouded in various shades of red, from the cherry-colored canopy bed to the luxurious red carpet to the walls covered in fire-red silk. A painting hung on each of the four walls, two of which depicted delicately posed hands with long, gracious fingers, while the others depicted legs covered in black stocking and propped up by red heels. The reddish-mauve ceiling hung overhead like a bleeding sky.

The room held only a bed, two nightstands, and a tall lamp in each corner, with a red shroud draped over the one nearest to the headboard. There was also a single window with burnt orange curtains that felt like lambskin to the touch. When Stat pulled them apart, he saw that the window was also locked, or perhaps rusted shut. It was hard to tell. He tapped the glass, noting its thinness, and looked around for something hard and blunt.

The teahouse was larger than it looked from the lounge. As Prescott led her by the hand down a series of winding hallways, Beki found herself wondering if Club Meow was secretly a brothel. Judging by the vibrant colors and its obviously provocative name, she could easily imagine Lisa as a Madam of the night, directing her legion of beautiful wait staff to provide more profitable services than tea. But the thought quickly perished as she peeked into an open door and saw nothing but shelf after shelf of tea.

The girl named Prescott might be mute. She didn't utter a word as they walked together, and Beki noticed that the girl's hand was shaking and slipped occasionally, as if their hands were smeared with oil and she had trouble holding on. Her shy, mousy demeanor made Beki ache to reach out and comfort her.

The Earl Grey Room was a small lounge with several large leather couches, a coffee table, and an aquarium filled with exotic red fish, similar to goldfish in appearance but larger, with long tail fins that trailed behind them like tendrils of undying flame. Once inside, Prescott released Beki's hand.

To Beki's disappointment, the room was empty. Were she in the mood, she might stick around longer, just to admire the beautiful room. A bejeweled curtain covered the entire far wall, sparkling like a red waterfall.

"I don't think he's in here," she said to Prescott. "But thank you. Perhaps we should look somewhere else?"

"No."

It was the first time she spoke. Her voice was light and airy, as if talking in her sleep. As she watched, Prescott closed the door behind them, went to the large mahogany coffee table, and opened a wide drawer on the bottom. From it she removed a white handkerchief, which she spread carefully on the table's surface, followed by a small glass bottle the size of a prescription drug container, and finally a syringe. She looked at Beki, sat down on the nearest couch, and patted the space next to her.

"Do you want some?" she asked softly. "It's very lovely. And it makes everything easier."

It was as if she was speaking to the wall behind her. Her watery blue eyes soaked right through Beki's body. Receiving no immediate reply, she filled the syringe skillfully with the contents of the bottle. With the filled syringe resting on the handkerchief, she rolled up her left sleeve.

The crook of her arm was covered with red dots, marks left by needles from hundreds of injections. Prescott took the syringe in one hand, pressing her left arm against her body to keep her sleeve from rolling down. A tiny tip of tongue protruded from between her lips like a kid about to taste her first ice cream cone. "I only have one needle," she said, looking at nothing in particular, "so you can go after me."

"I hope that's insulin," Beki said lamely. Prescott tilted her gaze in her general direction, the needle less than an inch from her skin. Her face was one of bewilderment, as if Beki had just said something completely incomprehensible.

"No," she said very seriously, "it's smack."

Beki turned around and grasped the doorknob. It rattled on its hinge and did not open. Prescott let out a shrill giggle and pushed the needle into her white skin, emptying its contents into her vein. "It opens from the outside," she said, chortling, "it only opens from the outside, and only Mama and me can open it from the inside."

The girl was disturbed. Beki turned the knob forcefully with all her strength, but to avail. She snapped her attention back to Prescott. "Does your mother know you're doing this?"

Prescott pulled the syringe out of her arm. She had pushed it in too deep. The needle was covered in blood. She held it to her lips, carefully licked it clean with her tongue, and wrapped it up in the handkerchief. Her smile grew wider as the drug began to take effect. She fell against the back of the couch, one arm draped limply over her forehead and the other at her side, and laughed merrily.

Beki twisted the doorknob with both hands. It rattled loudly but was far from giving. She banged on the door.

"Hello? Is someone out there? Hey!"

"My Mama is beautiful, isn't she?" Prescott asked from the couch. "Even if you don't think so now, you will soon." Wobbling feebly, she pushed herself off the couch, stumbled over her own feet, and fell sprawling on the carpet. By the time Beki pulled her up, she had resumed her fit of uncontrollable giggles. She took Beki's face in her hands and held on tight, grinning so widely her cheeks threatened to split apart. "Do you want to see my sisters?"

Beki took Prescott's hands and pulled them apart. "I think we should go find your mother and get you some medical attention." *And me a get-away car.*

"No. No, no." Prescott withdrew from her grasp, nearly falling again as her rear bumped against the armrest of the couch. "If we go out now Mama will be mad. Don't worry. Come meet my sisters. They're wonderful. I love my sisters. They listen to my stories every day."

Quivering unsteadily on her feet, Prescott crossed the room, steadying herself on the aquarium on the way. She tapped the glass tank and whispered, "I love you, too, fishies!"

Beki considered banging on the door again, but something told her it would do no good. On their way to the Earl Grey Room, she hadn't seen a soul in the hallways. The girl before her no longer looked quiet and beautiful. She moved like a drunk, laughing and talking to no one in particular. Her left sleeve was still rolled up, her spotted arm exposed. She reached the jeweled curtain and nearly fell again. With some effort, she gripped the curtain and pulled it open by walking sideways like an inebriated crab.

"These are my sisters," she declared with pride.

Behind the curtain was a slightly raised white platform. Atop it were two mannequins. No, two halves of mannequins. The upper bodies had been removed, leaving surprisingly life-like legs behind. One was wearing a pair of embroidered jeans, and the other sported a short white skirt. Judging by the skin tone, they may have once been life-sized wax figures. Prescott fell to the floor heavily, landing on her bottom near the platform. Reaching out, she caressed one of the mannequins lovingly, rubbing her face against its waxen surface.

If it was some sort of exotic art piece, Beki wasn't surprised. The modern art museums of New York held a much more outlandish collection than the piece before her. But the way Prescott wound herself around the mannequins made her shudder.

And her son. Where was Eric? She suddenly feared that he was also here, locked in another room with another crazy girl.

"I love them," the girl said airily. "Aren't they lovely?"

Beki took a step back and bumped into the fish tank. She turned to make sure it was all right and found herself met with six pairs of curious round eyes. The school of fish stared at her through the glass, their mouths opening and closing, revealing needlepoint teeth. The only fish not paying attention to her was busying itself with a chunk of red substance at the bottom of the tank. With a sickening realization, Beki saw it was eating one of its own.

Swallowing thickly, she approached the platform and knelt before it. Prescott looked at but did not see her. She was much too preoccupied with her "sisters".

"Why don't you let me out?" Beki asked softly, knowing it probably wasn't going to work. "We can go out together and find your mother."

Prescott shook her head hard, her black mane swinging all over. "No," she said. "I have to do this first."

Carefully, she stroked the foot of the nearest mannequin. Following her hand, Beki saw the mannequin was nailed to the platform with a large nail through each foot. Where the nail penetrated, a sprawling red stain covered the "skin".

"My sisters," Prescott chanted. "My sisters. My sisters. My sisters. I will have a new sister soon, but I miss them. Oh, how I miss them."

Geoffy turned his bad eye to Michigan. "The usual, V.P.?"

To his surprise, his customer shook his head. "Just one. I haven't got a lot of time."

"Since when are ya too busy for a drink? If I didn't know better I'd think you were off yer rocker." He paused and strained his eye to peek over the counter. "*Are* ya off yer rocker? Where are yer shoes?"

"Fuck you, Geoffy."

"What'd I say about those words in here?" Geoffy shook his head, tossing the dirty dishtowel over his shoulder. "I kinda like you, V.P. Don't make me throw you out. You look like you got something on yer mind, but I don't really care. What'll it be?"

Michigan slumped onto a stool. Something was always up with him. Geoffy was too used to it. It wasn't his job to play psychologist or counselor. He just kept the drinks flowing. Considering time was a factor, he poured a shot of whiskey and slid it in front of Michigan, who downed it in a single gulp and wiped his mouth with his sleeve.

"Well, that didn't help."

"Ya want something else?"

"Could use a little Luck."

Geoffy rolled his eye, as much as he could manage. "I ain't lending you any more chips. You already got a tab a mile long and don't you owe B.C...."

IMMORTALITY 101: The Intro Course

"*Fuck B.C.!*"

Several patrons looked up at Michigan's sudden explosion. Embarrassed, Michigan hunched over, started to pull his collar over his face, and seemed to take a moment to remember he wasn't wearing a jacket.

"Get me another shot," he said, "please. I really screwed up this time."

"And getting drunk will help," Geoffy retorted, and poured him another shot.

Michigan raised the shot glass in a mock toast. "Here's hoping."

Geoffy leaned over the counter and tried his best to offer a sympathetic look. "What did you do?"

"What makes you think I did something?"

"How the heck do you screw up if you haven't done something?"

"Oh," Michigan said, "right. That."

"You find some way to get into more debt? Honestly, V.P., you owe everybody. Isn't it time you took a break from the games? You can at least work off your tab here."

"What the fuck am I gonna do, die on ya? I'll pay eventually."

"Well it's not that I don't trust you, V.P., but I got an inventory to keep, and..." Geoffy's mouth hung half open as he gazed toward the door. Michigan rolled his eyes. There was only one woman who could make Geoffy forget a lecture half way. Lazily, he spun around on his bar stool and glanced toward the door.

The unmistakable features of Rebecca Tempest peeked through. She looked this way and that, and for a flickering moment their eyes met. Michigan was vaguely aware of alcohol dribbling out of his mouth, over his chin, and down his neck.

"Shit."

"Yer telling me," Geoffy said, having regained his composure. "I wish he'd quit dropping by so much. Gosh darn bad for business."

"*Shit!*" Michigan sprung off the stool and made a beeline for toward her as Beki's face disappeared out the door. Geoffy looked after him, shook his head, and began to wipe the glass he left behind with the dirty dishtowel.

Beki was starting to panic. The girl in front of her – an under-aged child with her veins pumped full of heroin – was long gone. Her body was still there, but judging by her incessant giggles, her mind had abandoned ship. Beki knew very little of narcotics besides what little she came across on the TV screen. It was one of those "other things" – things that other people had, and normal, safe women like her never expected to come across in their stable, sheltered lives.

Prescott tried to stand again and failed. Beki stepped behind her, slid her hands under the girl's armpits, and lifted her off the ground, then half-dragged her to the couch. Prescott laughed all the while, and then suddenly turned to her in all seriousness.

"Do you love my sisters?"

Beki forced herself to nod. "Yes, your sisters are lovely. How about we go out and your mother can tell me more about them?"

Prescott shook her head so hard Beki feared it would fly off. "No. No, no, *no*. I told you, I have to do this first or Mama will be mad."

"What do you have to do?"

The girl spread her arms outward like a baby seeking a hug. She grinned at Beki. "I have to welcome my new sister."

Beki looked behind her, then to the side. "Your new sister?"

"Absolutely." Prescott waved her hands, motioning for Beki to come into her embrace. "It's the polite thing to do. Come here, won't you? My new sister. We'll have ever so much fun together."

Unable to think of an excuse, she went to her. Prescott wrapped her arms around Beki's shoulders and squeezed. Then she nuzzled her face into Beki's neck, brushing away strands of hair to reach the skin. Beki started to pull away when Prescott kissed her neck, but the girl held on. She struggled. Prescott kissed her again. And again. Then something hard and sharp pierced her skin, like the needle of a syringe, and the world started to swim.

IMMORTALITY 101: The Intro Course

12
UNKEMPT REDEMPTION

Prescott sat on the couch in the silent Earl Grey room, her new sister cradled in her arms. She was sleeping like a baby, and she will be a baby. As the new baby sister, it mattered not how she looked. Even if she was grown, even if she was more beautiful than Prescott in every way, she will be the baby because she came last. Rocking her slumbering body awkwardly, Prescott began to hum a soft tune to the almost rhythmic gurgles of the aquarium.

A sour, metallic taste filled her mouth. Laying her new sister down on her lap gently, she reached up, peeled back her own upper lip, and removed the metal instrument. It was thin, but less delicate than it looked, a hollow metal frame formed to curve around her gums and conceals two tiny syringes. When she moved her tongue a certain way, the needles protruded. When she moved it the opposite way, they retracted. Needless to say, it had taken much practice, and more than a few hours passed out on the floor, to learn the exact ways of maneuvering it just enough to release the concealed sedatives without drugging herself.

Her gums were bleeding again. The instrument was made for function, not comfort. She started to feel inside her mouth with her fingers, but then thought it would be impolite to stain her sister's clothes.

Yes, for her sister, she would bear it.

So she wrapped her arms around her sister's body and cleaned her gums with her tongue instead, swallowing the droplets of blood as if they were syrup.

What did she say her name was? Prescott couldn't quite remember, but it was something plain and unfitting. Maybe Mama will let her be the one to name her new sister. She started to think of lovely, exotic names. Maybe Rosa, or Avril, or Francine. Or maybe she could name her something cute, like Strawberry or Bleu.

She ought to go outside and inform her mother that the job was done, but she had time. This was her first time making a new sister, after all, and her mother wouldn't be too upset if she took a bit longer than was necessary. Somehow, if she brought her mother in here, she felt she would lose some part of her precious sister. Why did she feel like that? She had no idea. But for now, she wanted a moment alone with the new baby.

She rocked back and forth, back and forth. Her sister moaned in her sleep and she shushed her softly.

"Hush little baby don't say a word..."

The fish tank gurgled. The enormous goldfish seemed to be watching her.

"Mama's gonna buy you a mocking bird."

She hated those fish. They always watched her like they knew she had some shameful secret.

"If that mocking bird don't sing..."

Did they know her secret? She tried to ignore them as they watched her with their lidless eyes. They were questioning her, judging her, and it wasn't right. They couldn't judge her. They didn't even know her. They didn't know how lonely she'd been without her big sisters. They don't know anything.

"If that mocking bird don't sing..."

They kept looking. They knew she was feeling bad. They knew it.

"If that..."

She felt bad. She felt guilty. He would hate her. Her arm itched. She scratched at it absently until red welts began to appear.

"...mocking bird..."

She couldn't take it. She couldn't do it. She loved her new sister already but she didn't belong to her.

"...don't sing..."

She burst into tears. Her sister rolled from her lap and landed onto the floor with a soft thud. Prescott gasped and quickly knelt down to see if she was hurt. Seeing she was all right, she continued to cry, tears pouring from her eyes in long streams.

"I'm sorry," she muttered between sobs, pillowing her sister's head on her lap. "I'm sorry. I know you want to stay here and be a family with us, but I can't do that. I'm sorry I'm so selfish, but you're not mine, and you're not Mama's. He had you first."

Leaning down, she wiped her nose and eyes with her sleeve before placing a kiss on the sleeping face. Her sister was so pretty, like Snow White.

And she was just a dwarf. She had to go find the prince. Giving her sister one last squeeze, Prescott lay her on the floor. Now she had to think. No, she needed something to help her think. Sitting on the couch, she retrieved the wrapped bundle and rolled up her sleeve again. This time she only used a little. A lot made her happy. A little made her think clearly. By the time she put the needle away, she had made a decision.

She went to the aquarium and reached inside, all the way to the bottom of the tank, where she pried the plastic castle off the sand and wrapped her fingers around a small key. The fish swarmed around her and punctured her skin with their tiny teeth. She ignored them. They wanted her to feel bad; now they wanted her to think it through before she acted. She wished they would make up their minds.

The key slid into the lock gently. The door opened carefully. Prescott remembered to turn and shush her sister, just in case she breathed too loudly. But her sister was very good and said nothing, so she stuck her head out into the empty hall.

What if Mama got mad? She'd apologize. If she apologized to her wonderful, loving mother, surely she wouldn't get mad. Besides, without a new sister, she was still the youngest, and Mama wouldn't possibly punish her youngest, would she?

And so she tiptoed into the hall, listening for her mother's voice. When none came, she headed for the back door, moving as quietly as she could manage in her sneakers.

IMMORTALITY 101: The Intro Course

"Why didn't you use the door?"

Stat allowed himself a thin, simmering smile. Lisa brought him a cup of tea personally. Two sugars. When she set it in front of him he noticed that her pinky was extended as she held the saucer underneath the cup. She was nervous. When she was nervous, she became more dainty than usual.

"No reason," he replied, and drank the tea. It was most likely that she wouldn't poison him. "I felt like breaking something."

"That's most uncouth of you. You must have given poor Leslie such a fright."

"Leslie's a good kid, and I'm sure he's used to a bit of roughhousing every now and then."

They were dancing around the issue, a well-practiced tango they were both much too familiar with. After climbing out the window and leaving Leslie to explain the shattered glass – which he sincerely regretted – Stat had taken a brief roam around the Square, searching for something he wasn't sure existed. Whatever it was that caused Lisa to lock him in couldn't have gotten far – his first assumption was that she had kept him out of the way so someone or something could be taken out of the tea house without his notice, in which case he would have a better chance of catching them if he hurried. But a quick trip through the popular establishments proved fruitless. Nothing was out of the ordinary. The Ponies were dancing, the Rabbit Hole was crawling with the scent of deodorant and fried food, Gypsy was bent over that ridiculous glass ball she kept insisting was crystal, surrounded by a circle of curious on-lookers, and the usual frequenters of the Saffron Stallion were drinking their day away as usual.

Stat was admittedly unskilled when it came to the investigating part of his job, but since he was the only one doing it, he had to make do with what limited skills he possessed. And so, unable to summon any brilliant schemes or even a bright idea, he returned to Club Meow.

Marky brought a cup of dark tea for Lisa, who drank it with her pinky extended once again. State hated to interrogate Lisa. She was, after all, the closest thing he had to a friend besides Grimm, who hadn't spoken two words in all the time they'd known each other. He would hate for the only person he could hold a two-sided conversation with to resent him.

Still, work was work. Stat tapped one finger against his teacup thoughtfully.

"Whatever it is you're doing," he said, "I want to see. Chances are I won't even care what it is. If you're making a new son or daughter back there with that freak of a girl you re-named Prescott, I'll look past it."

Lisa smirked under her wavy bangs. Well, a half smirk. Lisa would never smirk fully. It wasn't lady-like. "Will you, now? I can't say I'm not grateful, but also a bit offended that you would think I have anything to hide. And don't insult my dear Prescott. She's done nothing to you."

"Nothing to hide? Usually people lock themselves away from me, but to turn a lock and key on me is a new one."

She stood, laid her cup down, and went to him. She sat on the armrest of his chair and splayed her fingers over his shoulders. Then she squeezed, kneading his muscles with her fingers. He would be lying if he said it didn't feel damned good.

"I don't have to hide anything from you, Status. Nor anyone else. You should know that best. I'm not ashamed of my children. I love them, I take care of them, and I would give all of my Luck for them. Once they're here, they have to worry no more."

"Then let me see your new child."

"She is resting. You can see her later, when I introduce her to everyone."

Stat smiled inwardly. It wasn't often that Lisa made such a slip. She didn't seem to notice, however, that she had just confessed to having a new child on the way. There was a dreamy look in her eyes as she went on rubbing his shoulders. It was happiness, a warm sort of joy that he usually saw on her face whenever a new 'baby' was on the way. But this time, it was mixed with something else. The only thing Stat had become semi-skilled at in his job was reading faces. Especially those of the High Rollers.

He reached up and seized her wrists tightly. She let out a small gasp and the nearby waiters and waitresses instantly stopped to look in their direction. Stat turned and met their eyes with what he hoped was a warning glare. A few turned their eyes down, but most held tight. For their mother, they would brave the worst, even making eye contact with him.

"I really don't want to hurt you, Lisa," he whispered to her, pulling her down closer over his shoulders. "But I have a job to do. Just like I know you usually don't bother hiding anything, you know my job isn't exactly a cakewalk. I want to ask you a question. Just answer, alright?"

She paused. Then, lifting her head, she nodded to the wait staff, ordering them silently to continue their work.

"Be honest."

"I'll try," she whispered into his ear. "But I want you to know, I really don't like you butting into my business. Gentlemen do not manhandle ladies like this."

"Don't you know already, Lisa? I'm the scum of the earth." He squeezed her wrists tightly. "Just tell me, do you have a Rounder back there?"

He could feel her smiling. She did not lie. She played with the truth and teased with words, but she did not lie. "Yes," she said to him, "and I've already begun to love her."

Michigan was drunk.

But, having spent most of his time drunk, he was well practiced in it. While most would have stumbled back and forth, unable to keep their head straight under the influence of the alcohol, Michigan only had a little headache. His eyes were a bit hazy and it took a little extra effort to walk fast in a straight line, but he could manage it well enough to follow Beki's form around the Square. It was as if he could suppress the effects of the drink temporarily, hold them off until later, when he would probably be having the grandmother of all hangovers.

She was wearing a slouchy brown jacket and black pants, and she was walking slightly hunched over, head down, quick and alert. He watched her stick her head cautiously into the Rabbit Hole, then pause almost hesitantly before looking into the Pink Pony. This was followed by a maddeningly long three minutes of pacing back and forth in front of Club Meow, which Michigan watched from the shadows behind the statue of Lady Luck, all the while very aware of the sweat pooling on his forehead and armpits. It was either nerves or the alcohol; he didn't take the time to figure out which.

He hadn't been inside Club Meow in a long time. The main reason was that he didn't like tea. The secondary reason he would never admit to – he was deathly afraid of Lisa Gasolina.

Theoretically, there was no reason for his fear. He wasn't sure what it was – her kind smile, her soothing words, or her freakish, glassy-eyed "children". Really, all of those things had the same effect on him. They made his scalp itchy.

Perhaps the alcohol was giving him a false sense of confidence, or maybe it made him extra intuitive, but he was ninety-nine percent certain Beki was inside the teahouse. If that was the case, he decided, he might as well turn around, head back to Geoffy, and drink himself into a stupor, because all was lost. His punishment was sure to be prolonged and painful, so he might as well drink until he became brain damaged enough to breeze through it.

He wheeled around and nearly bumped into a life-sized porcelain doll with enormous eyes. He let out a very unmanly yelp before realizing it was a human, staring at him with intense concentration, dark hair falling all over her face.

"*Nyaa*," he said, and raised a hand in a stiff greeting, "hi there. Prescott, right?"

The corner of her lips twitched in an effort to smile. Michigan took small steps backward and nearly stumbled into the fountain. Failing to put more distance between himself and the flour-pale girl, he cracked an immensely awkward smile.

She didn't seem to mind that he was looking at her as if her clothing was made of leeches. To keep himself from running away, and thus acting rude, Michigan bit the inside of his cheek to calm himself. Prescott gave him the creeps. She moved like a ghost and looked like one, too. Her voice was thin and always breathy and weary, like she trying hard just to suck air out of her own lungs. And her eyes were much too big, like two enormous glass marbles shoved into a blob of dough.

His eyes darted back and forth. Hers stuck to him.

"So," he started.

"If I take you to her, will you kiss me like you want to kiss her?"

Stat not so much stood as leapt out of the chair. Still holding Lisa's left wrist, he nearly dragged her over the chair. She seemed a bit surprised at his sudden burst of movement, but her lips were still curled into a smile, one that told him he may be too late.

"*You picked up another Rounder?*" he demanded heatedly. "Damn it, Lisa! Can't you fucking learn? You can't keep Rounders!"

She didn't try to pull out of his grasp. "On the contrary, I think they keep rather nice."

"Where is she?"

"With Prescott. In the Earl Grey Room."

A vein. He could feel a vein throbbing in his head. He released Lisa's hand and made a mad dash for the back of the teahouse, leaping over a table that happened to be in his way. The customers gathered around it looked up very briefly, then picked up the cups he had knocked off and continued their conversation.

The Earl Grey Room was the last room in the long hall, kept far from the lounge. For good reasons, of course – screams tend to drive away customers. Stat was dimly aware of Lisa following close behind.

"You won't be able to get in," she said cheerfully. "You know that."

He spun around long enough to glare at her. "You don't keep Rounders," he repeated as they arrived at the door. He was almost afraid of what he might see once he opened the door. Lisa was looking both calm and smug now.

"You don't listen," she said. "Rounders keep just as well, if not better. Besides" – she ran a loving hand over the door – "my new daughter must be resting by now. I can't let you in to disturb..."

He grasped the knob and twisted. Not having expected it to open, he nearly fell on his face when the door swung open. His feet quickly sought purchase on the thick carpet.

The room was empty at first glance. The only visible movements were from the tank of cannibalistic fish in the corner, feasting on one of their own. Stat wasn't sure if Lisa ever fed them or just added new ones when the number ran low. They swam in slow, uncaring circles as he stepped inside cautiously.

The woman on the floor wasn't moving save for the shallow rise and fall of her chest. Prescott, whom he had expected to be bent over the body with bloody medical instruments, was nowhere to be seen. Just for good measure, he checked behind the door before approaching the unconscious woman. Though rusty in practice, he listened to her heartbeat, looked at her pupils after moving her into the light, and was checking her pulse when she began to stir.

Lisa's face had darkened when he turned to her. She was still smiling, but now it was thin and forced. She moved her tightly pursed lips slightly as if to speak, but only wet her lips. A shadow had fallen over her usually luminous eyes.

"Who did you get her from?"

"No one. She walked in all by herself."

"Stop shitting me."

"If she were anyone else, I just might be." Lisa pointed at the woman with one finger. "But for this one, I think you have good reason to believe me, don't you think?"

The woman cracked her eyes slightly and winced at the light. When her gaze fell on him, they suddenly widened. The look of shock, he was certain, mirrored his own. He hadn't recognized her at first, but there was no mistake. As she scrambled to sit up, she reached out to touch him. He grabbed her hands and held them.

"Did she really walk in here by herself?" he asked without looking at Lisa. The woman was still looking at him with such hot intensity that he worried if he looked away she may burst like a hot air balloon.

"That she did."

"Eric," the woman murmured. "Oh my God, Eric..."

She started to touch him again, and again he brushed her off. His legs were falling asleep in his awkward kneeling position. He pushed himself off the floor with one hand on the couch and the other on the woman's arm. She was unsteady on her feet and he kept her up. *Be gentle*, he reminded himself. Rounders had to be handled with care to prevent permanent damage. At the moment, she was not the woman he knew. She was a harmless, confused Rounder, and must be treated like one.

She held onto his arm and kissed his cheek before he could dodge. No matter. Let her do what she wished. It would make things easier later. Or at least he hoped so – this was a bit out of his short range of expertise.

"Thank you," she slurred to Lisa. "Thank you so much for helping me find my son."

Lisa nodded politely. "You're welcome, dear."

Son.

Right. That's useful.

Stat took her hand. "Tell me, Mother," he said, "how did you get here?"

Though her eyes were still unfocused, he could see clearly see the affection in them as she gazed at him. She was *definitely* not the woman he knew. Fooling her felt too strange ... and too easy.

"Where have you been?" she asked. "You really had me worried."

"Here," he said, enunciating as if speaking to a child. "But I don't know how to go back. Do you remember how you got here? Mom?"

She blinked. "Someone took me through a shop," she said, her words disjointed. "Dry cleaning. There were... women."

"What were they missing?"

She seemed confused. "Missing?"

"Arms? Legs? Were there two women? Or three?"

She nodded. "Yes, two."

"Alright, we'll figure it out."

Stat wrapped an arm around her shoulder. Lisa was still watching. She was angry now, and Stat knew her anger was not unfounded. Prescott had made a fatal mistake; she had just cost her mother the daughter that she would never be able to have again. Wherever she had gone off to, Stat hoped she would keep running and never return. But being Lisa's daughter, she'd probably come back. With the exception of Stat himself, they always came back.

He gripped the Rounder around the waist and walked her, one step at a time, out of the Earl Grey Room. Lisa sighed softly and didn't try to stop them.

"I still think you're a wonderful boy, Status," she said, "even if you *are* a bloody pain in the ass sometimes."

"I love you, too, Lisa," he replied.

The Rounder made a half-attempt to wave goodbye as he led her out the back door. He would have to ask what name she went by later, or maybe it didn't even matter – he could keep calling her "Mom" until this was over, which he hoped would be soon. The name she used here didn't apply right now, and she wouldn't know it, even if he tried to address her by it. Rounders always had their own names. It was such a hassle.

The room was empty when they arrived. Prescott turned her enormous eyes to Michigan and said in a pathetic, pleading voice, "She was here. She was *here*, I swear."

He didn't know if he believed her, but the fact was, Beki was nowhere to be seen. The only living thing in the room was the tank of red fish that kept staring at him like he was a piece of pork chop. Would Prescott lie? He wasn't sure. She wasn't quite right in the mind, that was a fact, but it was obvious she knew what he had been looking for, *whom* he had been looking for, and that alarmed him greatly.

She was looking everywhere, even under the couch and behind the gaudy curtains.

"She was here," she muttered as she searched. "She was here. She was here. She was here!"

"She *was* here."

Michigan spun around. His inebriated brain protested by sending his mind reeling like a cyclone and bringing lots of interesting colors to his eyes. When his vision cleared, the form of Lisa Gasolina slowly came into focus.

Shit.

She was a sweet, matronly woman. Reminding himself that he had no logical reason to fear her, Michigan cleared his throat.

"Sorry," he said, trying not to fidget.

"Mister Von Phant," said Lisa. Her voice, which he had never heard up close and personal, was surprisingly soft and kind. "You brought her here, didn't you? I guess I'm not too surprised. You gave us quite a scare, you know. That was terribly bold of you."

"No," Michigan said, thinking quickly. "It was bad, and it was stupid. If you would forgive me and please just let me take her…"

Lisa shrugged. "I really want to help. Really. But she's not here anymore. It was too bad. I was taking care of her, making sure she was comfortable."

He eyed her suspiciously. "You were?"

"Of course. Why wouldn't I? The moment I saw what state she was in I knew what I had to do. She and I are … very much the same, after all." Prescott was shaking. Michigan could see out of the corner of his eye. Lisa must have seen the same, because she crossed the room in a couple of long strides and wrapped her arms around the girl. "Where did you run off to, love?" she asked, brushing hair out of Prescott's face.

"M-mama…" Prescott stammered shakily. "I… I'm not…"

Lisa cradled her daughter's head. "Shh," she cooed. "It's OK, baby. I'm not mad." She looked at Michigan. "I think you should go. My daughter has been out of my care for too long and, as you can see, she is upset and frightened. I need to tend to her. As for the one you're looking for, she wandered in here lost and confused, and I tried to keep her here. Unfortunately, my dear Status was here ahead of you."

His throat tied itself into a knot. He uttered a short "Thanks" and was out the door.

"Michigan." He stopped shortly. "You brought her here because her bet turned over, didn't you?"

Lisa knew. Of course she would. He nodded.

She gave him a sad curve of a smile. "It's heartwarming what you're trying to do for her, but do be careful, dear. Sasha is a wily one. I worry that you're playing right into her hands."

He turned and gave her a half-drunken, half-confident grin. "I know I'm playing into her hands," he said, "but I'm really not that worried."

She seemed genuinely impressed. "Well then, you are far braver than I am."

Lisa watched Michigan go, Prescott still shivering like a dying animal in her arms. He was afraid of her, but he won't be anymore. Weary, perhaps, but not afraid. She knew that, and she was glad for it. She did not want to be feared. Fear spawned anger, and anger spawned rebellion. To control others by fear was a foolish thing. Anyone could bully someone into fearing them. To wield power through kindness — now that was a skill.

She gave Prescott a squeeze, then kissed her daughter's forehead. Her silly, stupid daughter who let such a big fish slip away.

"Far braver," she said to the girl, "and far more foolish. Why must the guppies keep trying to jump as high as the big fish do?"

Prescott nodded uncertainly. She was shaking so much her tiny body was rattling, as if her skeleton would soon fall apart. Lisa pulled herself back, caressed the girl's arms, and kissed her on the cheek.

"Why don't you go close the door, sweetheart? Then come sit on the sofa with Mama. Then we can have a nice talk about this little mishap."

The woman barely struggled as Stat led her through the Square, past the statue of Lady Luck. She tried to pause to gaze up at it, but he kept her moving. The less time she spent in the public eye the better. Until he figured out which gate she came from, he had to keep her out of sight. At least with the combined effects of the drug and relief at finding her son, she seemed more than cooperative.

She was dressed in an almost ridiculous fashion. On her body she wore a dark, conservative suit, fitting her body, if not her persona. But clunking awkwardly on her feet were a pair of ill-fitted shoes, looking almost as out of place as her jacket, which was much too big and hung off her shoulders. There were advantages to it, though. Stat stopped, reached over, and flipped the collar up to hide at least half of her face.

"What happened?" she asked him as they kept walking. From the way her eyes were glazing over in irregular intervals, he guessed she might not even be aware that she was talking. "I saw you in the hospital, but you're here. Talk to me, honey, what happened to you? Was I dreaming?"

"Sure, Ma," he said. "I'm fine. Everything's OK. Are you sure you don't remember how you got here?"

"Someone brought me here," she said with a light chuckle. He had to keep her from falling. "He said he knew someone who could save you, but I guess you don't need saving. You could always find your way."

She touched his face again. It was unnerving. He fought not to push her away. "Yeah, I found my way. Now, Mom, if we're going to go home, you have to think hard, OK? Who let you in here?"

"There were two women," she slurred. "They were terribly nice, and so pretty."

"Yeah, I got that."

Two women. There were four gates guarded by women that worked in pairs. He didn't have time to try all four. "Do you remember their names?" She shook her head.

"But there were only half of them."

"Half?" Now they were getting somewhere. Stat let his eyes dart across the Square quickly. Thankfully, it was as empty as ever. Although, the fact that he was in the company of someone other than Lisa or Sasha was bound to attract attention sooner or later.

"It was like a circus." She smiled. "You would have loved it. It was an amazing trick, the women with no legs."

Bingo. He grabbed her arm again and headed toward the Saffron Stallion. After this was over, hopefully fast and efficient and without an audience, he was going to have a good talking-to with Calisa. And then, he decided, he would seal the gates shut with duct tape.

"I'm so glad," she kept saying as they walked. "When we get home we can go buy that game you like. What was it called again? Metal something..."

He shrugged and quickened his step. "I don't know."

She stopped so suddenly that her arm slipped from his grasp. Surprised, he wheeled around to see her standing stiffly a few feet away, her body bent forward like a broken puppet. She brushed a lock of hair out of her eyes and stared at him long and hard. No matter what state of mind she was in, she always had a hard stare.

"Who are you?"

He sighed and reached out for her again. Her body jolted at his touch as if his fingers were electrified. When he seized her arm forcefully, she lashed out and struck him across the face, hard enough to rattle his jaw. He dodged her second hit and stepped back, a relieved grin on his face.

"Good," he said to her. "This will make things much easier. If you start acting like yourself, then I can, too. I always hated role-playing, anyway."

"Where's my son?" she asked in a tone that told him she expected him to tell her he had chopped her boy up and made him into little breakfast sausages.

"I really don't know, and it really doesn't matter to me." He gestured at the Square around them. "Since the charade is over, I'll be frank. This is my town. You can run, but it won't really do any good. I'll catch you and take you back where you came from. Or you can spare us both the needless exercise and just come with me. I promise I'll get you home safe."

She didn't trust him. Of course not. Even people who knew him didn't trust him, and she didn't know him. Or at least thought she didn't. Distrust was more becoming on her pretty face than that innocent, motherly look she was giving him a minute ago.

"Who are you?" she demanded again, as if that would explain everything. It never did.

"Lady," he said truthfully, "I'm the law around here."

IMMORTALITY 101: The Intro Course

CALL

The race is not always to the swift nor the battle to the strong – but that's the way to bet it.

– Damon Runyon

IMMORTALITY 101: The Intro Course

13
THE TRICK SPIN

Sasha bent over the pool table and played with her dolls. There was one with long brown hair that she meticulously brushed and tied into a ponytail herself. There was one with cropped red hair that she styled with a pair of safety scissors. There was a smaller one with dirty blond pigtails and cute overalls. Then there was the anatomically incorrect male, with his plastic helmet hair and permanently flexed pectorals. He was Sasha's least favorite, mostly because he always looked so awkward in front of the females, as if he was always nervously smiling because deep down he knew he couldn't please them with the mysterious lump in his paint-on boxers and hoped that they would never find out.

She bent their legs at the hips and sat them all in a circle, even the male. Just because she didn't like the male didn't mean he wasn't important. He still had a purpose. The brunette sat across from the little blond in overalls. Sasha dealt them cards. Five each. The redhead and the man watched intently with their plastic eyes.

She turned the cards over, added up the numbers. The little blonde won with a higher total. She got to roll first. Sasha picked her up and set the die into her stiff arms. The doll balanced Sasha's treasure like it was an enormous beach ball.

"Watch closely," Sasha told the brunette. "This is how you play the game." The doll didn't reply. "The rules are just that simple. You put down your chips, and you draw. Higher total rolls first."

No answer. Silence meant concession. Sasha held the blonde doll in her left hand, made a circle with her right thumb and index finger, and flicked the die. Her treasure bounded out of the doll's arms and rolled across the pool table, knocking down and running over the impotent male doll as it went. Had he been alive, he would've died from the encounter, not that he had much to live for.

The die slowed, wobbled, and came to rest. The blonde doll walked over to the side of the pool table, balancing gingerly. She and Sasha both gazed down at the die, at the only side facing the ceiling. A grin crept to Sasha's lips. She covered her mouth with her free hand and giggled.

"Looks like I win," she said in a tiny, shrill voice, allowing the blonde doll a victory dance in front its companions. "Did you all see that? I win. I always win."

The dolls all agreed silently. Sasha decided to reward their participation with a good brushing of their hair. Jean-Luc barged in, however, before she was able to indulge them. She rolled her treasure into the nearest corner pocket with a flick of her wrist before acknowledging him.

"You have a customer," he told her. His eyes were following the die as it disappeared into the hole. She didn't like that.

"Since when do you play messenger boy?"

"Since I discovered you like my package."

She didn't want to laugh, but a short chortle escaped anyway. "That was terrible even for you, Jean-Luc."

He grinned. "I can live with it. Back to the subject at hand – maybe you didn't hear me – you have a *customer*."

She brushed the redheaded doll's hair, yanking it out in bunches with the rough metal brush. "Tell them to go away if they don't have the minimum."

"That's my point. They have the minimum."

Her hand froze. The doll might have breathed a sigh of relief as Sasha turned to Jean-Luc slowly. She studied his face to see if he was yanking her chain, but for once he seemed serious, which surprised her to no end. It had been a very, very long time since someone met the minimum.

"The new minimum is fifty-five. They have that?"

Jean-Luc choked on his own spit and quickly recovered. "Fifty-*five*? You're poisonous, Sasha."

"Do they have fifty-five or not?"

"Fifty-seven. If you don't hurry, it'll be sixty by the time you get out there. The guy's doing *something* right."

Sasha laid the doll down on its back and the brush tangled with its damaged hair beside it. "Tell me," she said patiently, "who is spinning?"

"Bethany, I believe."

Sasha looked down at herself. The sheath dress she wore, which she also slept in not long ago, was wrinkled. Her hair spilled down her shoulders in a mess, and the ribbons on her shoes weren't tied. It was amazing she hadn't tripped over them. She couldn't greet customers like this. "Since you like playing messenger boy, tell this to Bethany." She yanked a handful of doll hair out of the brush and ran it through her own mane. "For every slot that man goes up before I come out, so increases her own debt."

The Rounder squatted where she stood, her legs pressed together, face buried in her hands. She looked as if she was trying to make herself as small as possible, or trying to wake her brain up from a nightmare. She must be distraught. Rounders always became distraught when he announced himself. He really, really hated his job.

"Hey," he tapped her on the shoulder. "Are you alright? No need to be upset. You're not in trouble or anything."

"I'm nauseous," she said, her voice muffled through closed fingers.

"Oh," he said. There was nothing to sit or lean on in the Square save for the fountain, so he helped her up, guided her a few steps back, and let her sit down heavily on the fountain's edge. She ran both hands through her hair, rubbed her face, then puffed out her cheeks and let out a short puff of breath. "Better?" She nodded. "That stuff'll wear off in an hour or so."

"Do you know what kind of day I've had?"

IMMORTALITY 101: The Intro Course

He looked around. She was trying to have a conversation with him, not exactly what he anticipated. When he didn't answer, she tilted her head toward him and gave him a despondent gaze. "It was a terrible day, and I mean awful. My boss is dead, so I might be out of a job. Some crazy person tells me I killed him. I ran over my son with my car, and while I'm at the hospital, my husband decides to sleep with the doctor. It's a really, *really* bad day."

He started to mutter an answer but she cut him off. "But that wasn't bad enough, you know? Then I let the crazy person take me from my home and drive me to this dry cleaning place – I think it's a dry cleaning place, but I'm not thinking so clearly right now. He took me there and now I'm here. I'm pretty sure he killed me and left my body there, so I must be dead even though that woman in the tea house told me I'm not. But dead people sometimes don't know they're dead, right?"

It took two repeats of the question for him to realize she was actually asking him. "Nobody's dead."

"You're lying." She linked her fingers together, pulled them apart, and hooked them together again. "You pretended to be Eric, and now you're telling me you're a cop."

"I'm not a cop," he corrected. Even though he hated explaining himself to Rounders, he was willing to do whatever it took to get her out of here faster. "I said I'm the *law*. That's the truth. But you don't have to believe me, because I'm taking you home either way."

He reached for her arm again and she pulled out of his grasp. "Weren't you listening to the story? I had such a terrible day that I let a crazy person kidnap and kill me and I don't even feel that bad about it."

Stat took a very deep breath. "*You. Are. Not. DEAD!*" She looked at him and he reminded himself not to lose his temper with a Rounder. "You're not dead. You're not *dead!*"

She stared at him for a long time. "I'm not? So you're not a ghost then."

He briefly wondered which one of them needed a slap on the forehead more. But since she didn't know any better, he slapped himself. "No. I'm not."

"Then those women cut in half. They were real?"

"Yes, they're real. If I'm guessing correctly, Calisa and Ro let you through. I'm going to have a good talk with them, believe me. Now let's go. You're alive and well so I'll do my job and take you home."

She stood abruptly and stepped out of reach. The drugs must be wearing off. She pulled the oversized jacket tightly around her body. "I'm not going home," she declared. "The man who brought me here said there's someone who can help my son, and I'm not leaving until I find her."

Stat snatched her left wrist and, before she could protest, spun her around and locked his arm tightly around her throat. She let out a frightened gasp but did not struggle as much as he thought she would. When her nails began to sink into the skin of his arm, he tightened his grip to show her he meant business.

"I don't intent to hurt you," he told her in a coarse whisper. "But you're making my job hard. You don't even know how many rules you're breaking by being here and I don't have time to explain it to you. Hell, you don't even know what almost happened to you back there in that teahouse, do you?" she shook her head. "Trust me when I tell you it's bad, but it's not the worst that could happen to you if you stayed there. Now, I'm going to ask you a few questions, just because it's part of my job. You will answer them, and then I will take you home."

She said nothing to the contrary.

"First, what's your name?"

"Rebecca Tempest."

"Who brought you here?"

There was a pause. "Will he get in trouble if I tell you?"

"Damn right he will."

She turned, as much as the little space between them allowed her to, and he saw a smirk on her face. It was the smirk of her old self, but she, of course, didn't know that. "Good," she said. "His name is Michigan."

"V.P.," he muttered to himself.

"You know him?"

She didn't seem as tense as before. He loosened his grip and allowed her some breathing room. "He told you there's someone here who can help your son?"

145

"He said there's a woman who can help, but didn't tell me very much." She chuckled sadly. "The more I think about it, the more foolish I feel. He's never told me anything that made sense. The first time we met, he was wasted, and he kept talking about games and wheels. Something about a bet he thinks I made."

Several things dawned on Stat at once. His arms slipped a bit. The woman named Rebecca Tempest wiggled out of his embrace and spun around to face him.

"If you're going to get rough with me," she said, "at least take off my son's face."

"What did he say exactly?"

"Nothing that made sense."

"Humor me."

"I think," she told him, "he said 'your bet has rolled over'."

The circumstances have changed. 'Rebecca' didn't know that and was still looking as if she might bolt with a single false move from him. It didn't matter. He could catch her no problem. But more important than taking her home, more important than anything, he needed to think. Right in front of him was a possibility that V.P. was smarter than he looked, at least smart enough to set something very interesting in motion. Stat decided he had to find out. Curiosity over duty. It's not like anyone was going to give him a demerit for letting her stick around a little longer.

"Let's hold off on taking you home," he said. "Let's find some place private to talk. You like tea?"

"I'm not going back into that teahouse."

"No, no." He shook his head. "Home brew. Come on."

Sasha took a little extra time to get ready. By the time she arrived at the Wheel, Bethany, the pudgy, pathetic-looking woman manning it, was near tears. The customer must have done well. Sasha gave Bethany a disapproving nod and the woman stepped aside, her eyes puffy and red, straining to keep tears from spilling over her freckled cheeks. Sasha rubbed her temples and Jean-Luc ushered Bethany away, offering her a pristine white handkerchief from his pocket.

The Wheel was the only furnishing in the gigantic room underneath her private quarters. It was roughly five feet in diameter, balanced by its center on a single stand shaped like a tall, skinny bell so that when it spun, its entire bulk rotated on the stand, spinning, rotating, but never faltering. Its appearance was very much like a giant roulette wheel – with minor exceptions. Instead of red and black, the pockets were painted gold and white. As she bent over the wheel, Sasha saw that the wheel currently contained sixty-three numbered gold pockets and one white.

A fat man with a cloudy white beard and no hair from the eyebrows up was beaming. Sweat drenched his forehead and white T-shirt. He grinned broadly at her, revealing two rows of pearly white teeth. Sasha curtsied politely.

She had put on a loose white blouse and ruffled skirt trimmed with blue lace, in a shade matching the ribbons tied into her pigtails. Her knee socks were trimmed with tiny blue bows, and she had taken care to put on a blue sapphire hanging from a thin silver chain around her neck. She looked like a perfectly wrapped present.

"Pleased to meet you, sir," she said to the fat man, whose body odor tested her gag reflex. "It's an honor to meet with a customer by the Wheel. It has been a very long time."

The man snorted. "No kidding. Not after you rammed up that damn minimum." He slapped a hand against the Wheel. "But I'm here to bet, and I'm gonna win everything you got. You're looking at the next owner of the Wheel, Miss B.C. My name is…"

"Your name isn't important."

A murmur ran through the crowd. At least a hundred people had gathered by the Wheel at this point, and more were coming in. Everyone wanted to watch. Every time a fool like this one came by, he attracted a crowd, and the crowd always loved it.

"You're cocky," he told her. "But that's alright. I'm cocky, too. But I'm 'bout to be the one who's cocky last. See, everybody keeps tellin' me that you got a trick spin, that the ball always goes in white when you spin. But ain't no one's got up to sixty-three before, and that tiny little hole? There ain't no way."

The rules of the Wheel were very simple. It began with two large pockets – one white, one gold, each covering half of the Wheel. To start, one bet small, a Luck chip or two, five or ten if they were rich or adventurous. When the ball landed in white, the game was over and the chips lost. When it landed in gold, the game was won, the chips doubled, and the Wheel set up for another spin. The white pocket is contracted to cover one-third of the Wheel, and the golden pocket extended and divided into two, each covering one-third. Should the player hit a golden pocket again, the white pocket is shrunk down to one-fourth and the golden pockets divided into three. And so on.

The fat man wiped sweat out of his glazed eyes. Sasha knew that look well; it was the look of someone caught up in the game, pulled in. There was no way out at this point, because he was the one who wouldn't allow it.

The minimum bet for the first spin was one chip, the second spin two, the third spin three. One could play over and over, winning small fortunes and never losing. But no one ever wanted to win small – that was the beauty of the Wheel. As the white pocket grew small and smaller, the chances of winning grew larger, and no one ever placed a minimum bet after five rounds. No one. Studying the fat man closely, Sasha wondered how much he had riding on the line. He was betting chips he didn't have. He had to be. Everyone did. Usually, the more they bet, the more excited they became, and the more they sweat. The fat man was drenched.

Reaching out, she stroked the Wheel lovingly. "To have met the minimum is an achievement in itself," she said, "but not a very great one."

One would think that, with the odds stacking higher and higher in the gambler's favor, to win was nothing, but those more experienced with the Wheel knew better. There was another game being played. To spin the wheel, the gambler laid one hand on its side, while the person manning the wheel – the Spin Doctor, as Sasha called them – grasped the opposite side. Not anyone could become a Spin Doctor. An S. D. was trained. They were skilled, strong, and they could spin the ball into the white pocket with a simple flick of the wrist from any angle – assuming no resistance, which was provided by the gambler. Thus, in addition to ponying up the bet, a gambler had another task – tripping up the Spin Doctor.

Judging by the man's girth, Bethany had worn herself out, especially after so many rounds. She would pay later for allowing the man to get this far. He was the first in a very, very long time to pass the minimum rounds required to earn a spin from Sasha.

"How much do you bet?" she asked. "The minimum for the final spin is fifty thousand."

The man licked his lips. "I got that."

"And should you choose to wager for the Wheel, the price rises significantly."

The Wheel was passed down from winner to winner, though not all winners chose to wager for it. As long as anybody remembered, Sasha had owned the Wheel, and there had been no winners since.

"I want the Wheel," the fat man said. "How much?"

"Fifty million."

The crowd bristled in excitement. The gambler wrought his sausage-shaped fingers together and stared at her, as if trying to figure out whether she really had tricks up her sleeve. Then he glanced at the wheel. The miniscule white pocket stood out from the vast field of gold. To roll the ball inside was indeed difficult. Sasha wondered if the fat man was doing math in his head – probabilities and such.

"I'll take it."

A cheer erupted from the onlookers, the number of which had doubled in the last two minutes. The gambler took his place at the Wheel, hand grasping its side tight. As the rule went, they spun at the same time, in whichever direction they wished. A smart gambler would wait a split second after the Spin Doctor, get a feel of the opponent's direction and push the opposite way. A smarter gambler may spin in the same direction, speeding the Wheel far faster than the Spin Doctor's intentions.

A good Spin Doctor knew how to control the Wheel despite these strategies, and the Wheel itself hid other secrets that worked in the owner's favor.

Sasha slid her tiny hand under the Wheel and found a nook to hook her fingers into. She looked tiny next to it, as if she could barely budge it an inch. The fat man was trying very hard not to smile. He had a sure thing. He had to. Just by sheer strength, there was no way she could win. He could simply hold the Wheel down, allowing it to spin no more than a lazy quarter of the way. In his free hand he held the painted glass ball.

IMMORTALITY 101: The Intro Course

"Drop," Sasha purred. The glass ball flew into the Wheel.

She gave the Wheel a nudge to the left. Feeling the movement, the fat man pushed in the opposite direction with all his strength. She let go and the Wheel carried him forward before he could steady himself and he kissed the ground amidst a wave of excited gasps. His hand released the Wheel. It moved lazily, the glass ball drifting toward the nearest golden pocket. She bent forward, planted her hands against the ground, and lifted her legs off the ground. Then she flipped, her heel knocking hard against the Wheel and sending it spinning. It spun on its stand, so fast that the white pocket would no longer be spotted. When she came out of her flip, she turned her wrist ever so slightly.

The fat man let out a pained yowl as her heel came down hard on two of his fingers, breaking them with two crisp *snap*s.

Jean-Luc was sure to lecture her later for letting so many people see her underpants.

There was not a closed mouth in the room. Sasha smoothed her dress and fixed her hair as the glass ball clacked away, spinning inside the Wheel. The gambler cradled his hand, but his eyes were on the Wheel.

It spun for what seemed like eternity to the eager spectators. Then it slowed, teetered, and ground to a halt. The glass ball did not stop, however. It went another circle. Then another. Until finally, it bounded across several divided golden pockets, almost falling in, but not quite, and dropped inside the white pocket.

The gambler did not howl with rage or remorse. He did not cry or shout as the others dispersed, shaking their heads. He knelt on the ground, his eyes glassy and empty. A single sound like the dry croak of a dying frog escaped his throat. Sasha gestured for Bethany, who had dried her tears and now bore the calm, resilient look of a wax figure, to return to her post.

"How much did you win before?" she asked the gambler. "A million? Two? Ten? No matter. You can owe me the rest. Everybody does. It's sad, really, the way everyone keeps holding out on me, making the bet and not paying, picking on such a tiny little lady like me."

He shifted toward her stiffly, still deep in shock no doubt. Sasha didn't want to touch him. He smelled disgusting. She nudged him with the tip of her shoe to get his attention. "You're too clumsy to be a Spin Doctor," she told him, "not to mention ugly. That's too bad, because there's plenty of good Luck in it."

The room had cleared very quickly. No one stuck around to watch the tragic aftermath. They all told themselves that they didn't really expect him to win – Sasha was a High Roller, which meant she always won. The losers became little more than chattel property. It was all routine.

But they enjoyed it. It was fun to see someone lose. The bigger the fool, the better the show. Like all the drinking, fucking, and shooting up, watching someone lose was a marvelous high.

Prescott sat on the couch in the Earl Grey Room, her head pillowed against her mother's shoulder. Her mother held her legs in her lap like a doll's. Her mother smelled very good, like roses, milk, and tealeaves. And her voice was soothing, so comforting and warm. Her mother held her, rocking gently.

"Girls make mistakes," said her mother, and she nodded in agreement. "Girls fall in love with boys they shouldn't. They love boys who only want to do them wrong, boys who don't care about them. Isn't that right, honey?"

She nodded again, tears in her eyes. Her mother was always right.

"I know you love him, and yet you know he loves her. You wanted to please him, right? You thought you could make him pay a little attention to you if you gave his girl back to him. But did he say 'thank you'?"

Prescott shook her head.

"He didn't even shake your hand or give you a hug, right?"

She shook her head again. Lisa gave her a light squeeze.

"It's OK, sweetheart. You'll find someone else. You've made a mistake and you've learned from it. Just don't forget – your mother will always love you more than those boys ever could, so you should never go against your mother. Never speak in a way that could hurt your mother. Because you really hurt me today, Prescott."

Something wet and cold slid down her cheek. Prescott reached up and wiped away the cold tear, careful not to touch the thick black stitches that now held her lips together.

151

IMMORTALITY 101: The Intro Course

There was a prince, and he loved a princess. But she was not the princess. She was only the dwarf, the peasant, the frog who opened her big fat mouth and done wrong. And the Queen had punished her for it.

She deserved it. Ugly frogs shouldn't open their mouth and croak. It was a good lesson learned. Prescott felt very grateful to her mother for teaching her a proper lesson.

14
GO FISH

"So, what's your name?"

The boy who looked too much like her son stared at her as if surprised by the question. "You can keep calling me his name if you want. It doesn't bother me."

"It bothers *me*." Now that she knew he wasn't Eric, Beki thought she could spot subtle differences between the kid – who might not be a kid at all – and her son. Though he looked to be no more than twelve, he seemed taller than Eric, with a sort of oily darkness in his eyes. His mouth was a bit crooked so it sometimes looked as if he was sneering when he tried to smile. And there was something unsettling about his face. Even when he stood still, it appeared to be moving, as if his skin was made of liquid, shifting and changing ever so slightly.

"What do you want to be called?"

The boy/person/man scratched his head. "Stat is fine."

His voice sounded different, too. Just a few minutes ago it had sounded the perfect pitch for a boy on the verge of puberty – light and a bit high with the occasional crackle. But now it was deeper, with a slightly rockier timbre. The voice of a man.

It was all highly disturbing.

"You can stop pretending like you don't want to stare at me in horror."

"I'm not," she said quickly, turning her gaze away, "I…"

"You can also stop pretending you're not looking at me. Everyone does that." His crooked mouth split into an awkward grin. "I look like a freak, don't I? Like some distorted holographic projection of that person you want to look at."

Beki considered giving the polite answer, but she was too tired for manners, so she nodded. It seemed to be what he had expected. "What now?"

He gestured down the nearest street leading out of the town square. "That way. It'll be a bit of a walk, but, hey, you have nothing better to do, right?"

"Actually I…"

"Trust me, you don't. Now just follow me. And seriously, don't run. If I have to run you down and tackle you, I will." He didn't look capable of it in that slender body, but if he could already manipulate his looks, he probably had other hidden powers as well. "And then I'll have to physically drag you to a gate and shove you out back to where you came from, which would be a pity, because you've piqued my curiosity. There are some things I think you can tell me."

"Why should I?" Beki asked, more defiantly than she felt.

The swimmy form of her son shrugged. "I don't know. Maybe because, after you tell me what I want to know, I'll tell you some things, too. Or we can just cut to the chase and send you back right now. Your choice."

"I'll go with you," Beki replied, before she had a chance to stop herself.

"Great." He pointed to Michigan's jacket. "Flip up your collar."

"Why?"

"Wouldn't want anyone to see your face. Trust me, it's more trouble than it's worth."

She did as he said. "Are you ever going to tell me the reason?"

"If I feel like it, but not here." He looked her up and down. "Do I have to hold your hand or will you seriously not run off on me? Be honest. I really, *really* don't feel like running a chase today."

Truthfully, she had already considered it a dozen times in the last minute. But as soon as she pushed herself off the edge of the fountain, Beki's legs nearly gave out. Her muscles tingled as they tried to wake up from the nap in the teahouse, and, in Michigan's enormous shoes, she would probably trip all over herself before she got out of the square. Judging by the changeling boy's expression, he was serious about running her down.

"I won't run."

"Promise?"

"What you do want, a pinky swear?"

Stat rolled his eyes. "No," he answered sarcastically, "because you wouldn't keep to it. Now let's go."

Beki linked her hands together and stretched. As she craned her neck from this side to the other, she found herself gazing at the fountain. There was a statue in the middle. She hadn't had a chance to get a close look until now. It was a woman, standing on a golden pedestal, though her body appeared to be made of cement or clay. Her hands were outstretched, her long hair falling down her back. She had a solemn, pretty face and holes where her eyes should be.

Carefully, she took several steps around the fountain, turning to the statue's front. Stat was watching her, but something about his posture and expression told her that he was unsurprised at her curiosity. The statue reminded her of the Spirit of Justice statues guarding the steps leading up to courthouses. This woman also wore a toga that draped from her shoulders to her feet. But the gray cement fabric was wrinkled and hiked up in front, resting on what she originally thought was a hook that protruded from her nether region. A closer look revealed it to be something entirely different.

"It wasn't always like that."

Beki turned to Stat, who appeared to be entertained by her shock. She shouldn't stare so hard, she knew. She probably looked like an ignorant tourist; she couldn't figure out another way to describe herself right now. Gazing at the statue's erect member, at least ten inches long and carved in stunning detail, she wondered if it was some sort of political statement.

"The Roun – I mean out-of-towners — are always surprised by her."

The statue's right hand was held at shoulder level, its thumb and index finger held in a half-circle, as if something it had been holding had been removed. Or maybe it was some strange cultist hand gesture.

Its other hand was at waist level and cupped two bronze spheres – her eyes.

"I can tell you about her later." Beki looked over to Stat. He was anxious to go. She supposed she should follow suit. "Although it's not really important. She is... oh, what's that word you people use in there? *God*. Yeah, that's it."

The hermaphrodite nymph didn't seem particularly god-like, but, Beki decided, there were plenty of gods stranger and odder where she came from.

"She's a god?"

"She's *the* God."

"Why is she... like that?"

Stat shrugged. "I hear she didn't used to be. She used to be just a normal, boring gal. But at some point it was decided she didn't accurately depict what she stood for, so they replaced the old one with this one. I think it's great."

Great wasn't exactly how Beki would have put it. "So what does she stand for?"

Stat smiled. On Eric's face, his smile looked wrinkled and loose. He said in a singsong voice,

"Lady Luck is fickle and blind,
She is bold and crass.
Turn your back for a minute or so,
And she'll take you in the ass."

It had to defy some law of physics, aerodynamics, biology, or whatever it was that applied in this case, but Michigan had managed to dig himself into even deeper shit. He didn't know how he did it, but he did it and he did it spectacularly. It wasn't enough that he dragged a High Roller out of the Round. It wasn't enough that he lost her. It wasn't enough that Lisa now knew about it, which meant the other High Rollers would probably know soon enough. But now the woman who thought her name was Rebecca Tempest had fallen into Status Quo's hands.

He had stayed close to the Saffron Stallion, keeping an eye on the gate. So far neither Stat nor Beki had come by, but that could mean one of several things.

The good news was she *probably* wouldn't fall into any harm in Stat's hands. He would protect her because it was part of his job, and he would be damned good at it. The bad news was, once she was back where she belonged, Stat was going to come after Michigan and beat his head in on Lady Luck's Fountain for being so supremely stupid. And he would deserve it. Why not? He did bring this on himself, trying to play smooth and cool, and convincing himself that he was doing a great job of it.

He was going to be made into a gatekeeper. *That* was the scariest thought of all.

"You suck, man."

He wanted to slap himself across the face and insist that he didn't just hear that voice. But a bony finger jabbed into his shoulder and he forced himself to turn around with a wide grin.

"Hey, Snip. To what do I owe the displeasure?"

"I just thought you'd like to know you suck," Snip informed him, and then made a sound like there was a hairball the size of Michigan's fist jammed in his throat. "It was such a simple task and you made the newbie mistake – turning your back on her. She was a *pro*, dude. Don't ever turn your back on a pro."

"Duly noted. Anything else? If not, I have to go hunt down... wait a minute." Snip flinched at the sudden invasion of his personal space as Michigan took a large step forward and seized his skinny shoulders. "You! Help me find her!"

Snip snorted and shoved his glasses a quarter inch along his nose with his middle finger. "And how do you propose I do that?"

"Stat has her."

"Oh," Snip said. "So it's done then. Alright, here's what you can do to pay us back. The server farm..."

"Listen!" Michigan shook Snip hard, rattling his skinny frame like a bamboo cage. "He's going to take her back for sure. Just do that voodoo computer thing you guys do, find out if he's taken her out yet. There's a chance he'll take her through a different gate, so check all of them. And then..."

"And," Snip said nasally, "if he's taken her out already, you're done for anyway. And if he hasn't, what do you plan to do? Wrestle Stat for her? That'll be a show."

"No. That's where you guys will come in."

"I thought we were already in."

"So you come in again. Would you listen?!" He released the kid and tried his best to think up an idea without a drink. "Alright, look, we'll find them. If they haven't gone out, we can find them. Monitor all the gates, and we'll check a couple of Stat's hangouts, too. I already went to Club Meow and he wasn't there. Lisa told me…"

Snip wrinkled his nose. "Lisa Gasolina is a witch."

"I thought she was rather nice, actually. Anyway, she told me he's taken her and left, and, if they haven't gone out, he might want to keep her from being seen too much so maybe he'd take her to his place and wait until the peak gambling hours when most people are off the streets before taking her out again. Then there's that weird guy who does exit procedures that Stat hangs out with. Grimm. We'll look there last because I doubt he'll take her there. Old man Grimm wouldn't have it."

"And if we find them?"

"You guys tackle him; I'll grab her and run."

"V.P.?"

"Yeah?"

"You're a lot dumber when you're sober." Snip brushed a layer of invisible lint off the sleeves of his shirt. Michigan couldn't help but grin inwardly at the annoyed look on his face. Being something of a germaphobe, Snip hated being touched, which was the only reason Michigan ever touched him. "First, hacking into the Round Entry/Exit system is not a game. It's *hard*."

"It's pro," Michigan said with a wink. He could see the word tugging at something deep within Snip. "It's a job for a pro and I see one right in front of me."

Snip cleared his throat, a weak attempt to hide his slow succumb to the flattery. "And even if we get in, we find them, we track them down. We are *not* going to physically assault Status Quo."

"Why not?"

"Because we don't like to be beaten black and blue. The Great Leader would agree."

"The Great Leader was the one who wanted to see her. So he would agree with *me*." Michigan leaned close to Snip. "And you agree, too. You've waited a long time to get to her, and, if you help make this happen, you can be the *hero*."

There was a pause. "How would we tell them apart when we find them?"

"She's wearing my jacket. It's black, with high collar, and red trim."

Snip wavered, wavered again, and gave in. "I'll talk to the guys," he said, and pulled a small gadget decorated with flashing LED lights out of his pocket. Michigan hummed to himself in satisfaction as Snip began to talk into it.

"And tell them to find me some shoes," he added. Maybe it wouldn't be a total loss after all. If he was going to be "beaten black and blue", as Snip put it, at least he was going to have company.

The walk was mostly silent. Beki wanted to start some manner of conversation but found it hard to start anything without asking questions first, which Stat refused to answer, at least for the moment. She tried to make small talk about the weather, but when she looked up at the sky, she saw no stars, no moon, not even a cloud. The sky was a vast canvas of bland, unchanging darkness. She couldn't even feel a breeze against her skin.

There were plenty of wide, paved roads, but Stat led her through small, curvy paths. She didn't try to run and he didn't turn back to check if she was trying to make a break for it. He probably didn't think she would, and he was right. She had long lost track of where they had come from and didn't know where to go anyway. Part of her was frightened, but it wasn't enough to send her running.

If he intended to lead her into harm's way, he would've simply left her in that teahouse with the crazy girl and cannibal fish. The thought of the girl's empty, drug-infused eyes made her shudder and she pulled Michigan's jacket around her.

They emerged from the shadows in a suburb. It was so astoundingly normal that Beki thought there must be some mistake. Rows of small houses with cinderblock walls and tiled roofs lined the streets. Some of them were lit inside, others dark. The lawns were mowed and decorated with gnomes and flamingos. Here and there were green shrubs and meticulously laid flowerbeds.

Stat approached a small cubic house with a red door. "I'd take you to my place," he said, knocking, "but I don't have any cards."

"Cards?"

"You'll see."

Five seconds passed. Then another five. Then a minute.

"I don't think they're home."

"Oh, he's home. Grimm's just a bit slow. He's got a bad leg."

Beki fell silent and waited. Out of the corner of her eye, she saw a curtain lift. Someone from the neighboring house was looking at them. Though she still hadn't been told why, she immediately turned her face away, pulling her collar higher to hide it. A few seconds later the curtain fell back, and the curious onlooker left the window.

The front door of the small house creaked open and a hooded figure appeared, holding a stunningly black staff in one pasty hand. Beki couldn't see the person's face, but its posture looked vaguely male, so she assumed as such. He looked toward her, face hidden under the hood, then at Stat.

"It's OK," Stat said. "She's, uh…" He raised his right hand and made small concentric circles at his right temple with his index finger.

The hooded man dipped his head slightly, his unseen eyes fixed on Beki. He reminded her of ancient sorcerers in the storybooks she used to read to her son. She imagined he had a massive laboratory inside that little house, filled almost entirely by a huge black caldron that he will dip her into, along with two pounds of pickled newt eyes. A moment later, he turned and re-entered the house. Stat gestured for her to come closer.

"O.K., we're good. Come in."

"Did you just tell him I'm crazy?"

"What? No."

"Then what's with the…" she mimicked him, making a circle by her temple with one finger.

"That's the sign for a Rounder," he said, gesturing impatiently. "Would you hurry? We're attracting enough attention as it is. I'll explain inside. And be polite, by the way. Grimm doesn't usually like company." He looked her up and down and for a second seemed about to add something else, but turned around and entered the house instead.

The house was even smaller inside than it looked from the outside. Beki almost felt as though she'd stepped into a Hobbit house. Still, it was homey and warm, and the old, decrepit furniture was threadbare but inviting. The bent man named Grimm was standing by the kitchen, his hands folded atop his staff as he gazed at her, or rather she assumed that's what he was doing – his face was still hidden.

"You home is lovely," she said stupidly. Grimm said nothing. Stat shrugged off his jacket and tossed it on the faded couch.

"You have tea, Grimm?" Without turning from her, Grimm pointed one skeletal finger toward the far cupboard. "Relax. She's not going to do anything. She's a Rounder. Want me to make it?" No answer. No movement. "You still keep your pot in the old place, right? Can I use the red one?"

As Stat carried on with the one-sided conversation, Beki tried to sidestep out of Grimm's dark gaze. She slipped past the fireplace and nearly knocked over the life-sized doll sitting hunched over on a stool. Someone made a soft, guttural noise. It might have been Grimm, but she couldn't tell. The doll was wearing a dress layered with white lace and silks of plum red and Christmas green. It sat with its back to Beki, arms folded in its lap and legs splayed lifelessly. Its hair, each strand meticulously curled, spilled down its back.

Once, when she was seven, her grandmother had bought her a picture book of Shankar Pillai's International Museum of Dolls. In it, she had seen images of some of the most beautiful dolls in the world, with perfect porcelain faces and hair like rivers of honey. She remembered seeing a blond doll and thinking its hair must be combed with stars. But now they all paled in comparison to this doll. Before she could stop herself, she was reaching out to touch the beautiful, lifelike hair.

A loud thump made her jump. She spun around to see Grimm taking lurching, stumbling steps toward her, his cane all but crashing against the floor as he did. She quickly stepped back just as he got close enough to raise his cane to strike. Stat rushed out of the kitchen and wedged himself in between them.

"Whoa," he said, taking Grimm's cane in both hands and lowering it gently. "Whoa, whoa, whoa."

Over Stat's shoulder, Grimm glared at Beki from under his shroud. She shuddered.

"Don't do that, Grimm," Stat said calmly, smiling broadly. "She didn't mean any harm. You of all people know Rounders are harmless, right? Adda's fine. Why don't you sit with her here and I'll take the Rounder over there, all right?"

Grimm's bony hands tightened around his staff, but he turned away, lumbered to the couch, and sunk into it heavily. Stat breathed a sigh of relief and turned back to Beki. "Seriously," he said, "don't touch that." Grimm had turned his face away from them. Though Beki couldn't see his face, he looked tired.

"Sorry." She wasn't sure if he heard. "I am. I'm sorry."

Stat ushered her toward the kitchen, where they sat at an old breakfast table. As Stat poured tea from a red teapot for the both of them, Beki looked past him to see Grimm stand, walk slowly to the doll, and kneel next to it with some difficulty. He examined its face closely, cradling it in his dry hands.

"Don't stare."

She snapped her gaze back. "I wasn't..."

"Sure you were. Don't stare. He doesn't like it when people get too close to her." Craning his neck, he called into the living room, "Grimm, where are your cards?"

Grimm stopped his task to look at Stat and said nothing.

"Oh. Right. I got it."

"Does he talk at all?" Beki asked, keeping her voice low as Stat retrieved a stack of white cards tied together by a red rubber band from the nearest kitchen drawer.

"Don't know. I hear he used to."

"What happened?"

"Can you play Poker?"

Stat removed the rubber band and slapped the stack of cards on the table. It was a deck of playing cards, but unlike any Beki had ever seen before. Their backs were white and their designs somewhat inconsistent. Upon closer inspection, they proved to be hand-drawn. Mirroring numbers and suits were drawn on each upper left and lower right corners, but at the center of each was a different inked picture of a young woman.

"Poker, yes or no?"

"No."

She was blonde, and very fair. Her hair was always done in ribbons and she smiled in each one. Sometimes she wore lacy dresses, other times more provocative pieces, like lingerie and a transparent nightgown.

"Gin?"

"No."

Beki held up one of the cards by the edges, careful not to damage the immaculately detailed picture in the center. Stat reached over, plucked it out of her hand, and shuffled it along with the rest roughly.

"Relax. He's got, like, sixteen sets of these. I think he's making a new set as we speak."

"He made these?" It was hard to imagine Grimm's pale hands painting these beautiful pictures. As she turned to sneak a peek at the hunched man, Beki saw with a sudden but not surprising realization that all the cards were painted with pictures of the blonde doll in the corner.

"How about V.C.? Can you play V.C.?"

"No."

"OK, what *can* you play?" Stat dropped the deck on the table impatiently.

"Why are we playing cards?"

"I'm trying to make a point here. And I need to think. Playing cards helps me think. Just tell me what you know how to play. Anything but Go Fish. I hate Go Fish."

"You're out of luck then."

Sighing, Stat dealt the cards. "Fine. Go Fish it is." When Beki reached out to take the small pile of cards in front of her, he raised a finger. "Keep something in mind though – you have to play like your life is depending on it."

The records provided by Snip's "teammates" showed that no re-entry to the Round had been made in many months, at least not through Calisa and Ro's gate. Michigan allowed himself a very, very small sigh of relief. He tried to peek over the shoulder of one of the hackers, but earned an annoyed look through thick glasses, so he took to teetering about the crowded room and humming to himself instead. That, apparently, was also quite irritating, and he found himself banished to sitting in the side hall of the Snyperx headquarters, twiddling his thumbs and kicking the pair of old loafers Snip found for him against the floor.

Snip poked his head out of the main computing room.

"The guys want me to tell you to be quiet."

"I'm not making noise."

Snip pointed at the folding chair he sat in. "You're thumping your chair against the wall."

It's true. He was. He had hoped they wouldn't notice. The digital display across from him, accurate to the hundredth of a second, showed that over two hours had passed since he'd been here. The Snyperx headquarters was a boring, boring place unless you liked Space Invaders, which Michigan didn't.

"Are you finished yet?"

Snip snorted. "Delicate operations take time."

"I say we grab a couple of guys and go to Stat's while the programs are running."

"You're *such* a newbie." Snip rolled his eyes all the way back in his skinny skull. "You don't storm an enemy stronghold without proper information and preparation."

"What 'storm'? What 'stronghold'? He lives in a one-bedroom flat. I don't even think he has a deadbolt on his door."

"Because he doesn't *need* one."

Sighing, Michigan slumped back into the chair, slamming the back extra hard against the wall. "Fine. Have it your way. How much longer?"

"Another hour or so. You want a snack?"

"What've you got?"

"Cupcakes and coffee."

"I'll pass."

"Suit yourself. I…" Snip turned his head toward the interior of the computing room. "Hold on a sec."

Michigan wasn't particularly curious. He was too busy thinking up all the ways he could entertain himself sitting in a chair all day long, sans a few body parts. What would they take? Arms? Legs? One of each? Or maybe all four and just leave him a stump, though that was unlikely since he would need to retain something to prevent forced entry. But that didn't mean they wouldn't assign someone big and strong as his partner and let him be the talker.

"This is real interesting."

"What?" Michigan asked half-heartedly.

"You know Sasha B.C.?"

"What's the bitch done now?"

"She's announced a dice game. A hundred and twenty minimum for entry."

15
IMMORTALITY 101

"Got any threes?"

Beki checked her cards and took a sip of tea. It was sweetened with sugar with a texture like shredded plastic – gritty and insoluble. But the tea itself, despite its soggy, almost tar-like appearance, wasn't all bad. "Go fish."

Stat drew a card. "You know, someone wrote a book called *Immortality 101*."

"What's it about? Got any fives?"

"Go fish." Stat glanced over her shoulder and she thought she saw concern in his eyes, but she didn't turn around. The old man must still be fussing over his doll. It was a rather woeful sight. The doll must be his only companion. "The first chapter's only a single sentence long. Two words, actually, and they're the truest two words one can use to describe immortality."

"Which is?"

"It sucks."

"That's what it really says?"

"Yeah."

When she looked up from her teacup, something had changed. Stat's face had shifted. At first she thought it was her imagination, or that the tea was filled with hallucinogens. But as the game went on, his face became more and more translucent. Spots of wavering shadows began to appear here and there on his cheeks, like the surface of moving water. His body also seemed a bit longer and larger.

"So why are we playing cards again?"

Stat scratched his neck, sending a wave of tiny ripples over his face. "So *Immortality 101* was hugely popular. But then people began to hate it, because it was too real. And eventually the guy who wrote it became an outcast, so he hid himself until people began to forget. Now no one knows who wrote it."

"He managed to hide himself for that long?"

"It's not hard."

"What's with your face?"

"So Michigan Von Phant brought you here, is that right?"

"I think that's his name."

"Brown hair; perpetually drunk?"

"I don't know about perpetually, but he was drunk the first time I saw him."

"You saw him more than once?"

"Got any Jacks?" Stat handed her a card. "Thank you."

"Answer the question."

"What's it to you?" There was something about this situation that made her feel defiant. Beki deliberately sifted through her cards as Stat waited. He didn't seem angry, however. Actually, she couldn't tell if he was angry or not. His features were becoming increasingly convoluted. Her son's face was now little more than a watery mask hanging over another face underneath.

"It would help me decide whether to help you stay here or drag you back to that gate and throw you out. Got any sixes?"

"Go fish. I saw him a couple of times. Once at a party. He was drunk off his ass. Then again at my boss's funeral. He said some really weird things to me, then laughed when I threatened to mace him. Then the next time I saw him he brought me here."

"What did he say to get you here?"

"That I could save my son's life if I went with him."

Stat laughed. It was a man's laugh. His voice had changed. He laughed so hard he had to set down the cards in his hand and take a sip from his cup to catch his breath. "And you believed him?"

Beki scowled, though she supposed she shouldn't be surprised. "Was he lying?"

"No, but you're still a moron to just believe him like that. What's wrong with your son?"

"I hit him with my car." It shouldn't be funny, but as the words left her, Beki heard herself chortling. It felt truly, genuinely funny. "He was riding his bike," she said, making a swiping motion with her hand as she spoke, "and I just mowed him down. What's in this tea?"

"Valium. It's your turn."

"Got any Kings?" She let his words roll around in her head for a few seconds. "You drugged me?"

"Only a little. It helps you talk. Plus it'll help negate what Prescott gave you – too much of that stuff and your muscles will cramp up." He handed her a King. "So is your son dead yet?"

"No. He's in a hospital, where his father's fucking a doctor."

"Ouch. Your husband?"

"Yep."

"Happily married?"

"Many years."

"Must be killing you."

"No so much," she replied, not sure if it's her or the Valium talking. At the moment, she was feeling very relaxed, and the game, honestly, was a lot of fun. "I thought maybe if I came with Mich, I can at least do something useful before I go back."

"He lets you call him 'Mich'?"

"I don't know." She turned to look at Grimm combing the doll's hair with practiced delicacy. "You know, this just occurred to me. If things go well and I find that person who can help Eric, take her back, and she saves him, then I'd stay with that bastard husband of mine, because I don't want Eric to grow up in a broken family."

"He told you it was a person who can help, huh?"

She nodded. "Yes. But if I can't find her, then I'll head back and file for divorce, start a new life. No husband, no son. It's going to suck. Like immortality."

"Nothing sucks more than immortality."

"I wouldn't know."

Stat started to say something, then seemed to change his mind. "What if I told you," he said carefully, "that if you lost this card game right now, your son would die? That his life rides on this game?"

"I'd say you're a very, very mean person, and question whether you can really do that."

"And if I can?"

"Then you're just a jerk."

"Got any Queens?"

A few seconds passed in silence. Stat's face was entirely transparent now. Beki could make out the face underneath. It was a man in his late twenties or early thirties, with dry features and light brown hair shaved close to the scalp. "Seriously though," she said, drinking from her cup, "what is wrong with your face?"

Stat grinned. The water mask also grinned. "You can see me, can't you?"

"Almost. It's a bit creepy."

"Rounders can usually see me after a while."

"What's a Rounder? And, for that matter, what the hell are *you*?"

"Do you have Queens or not?"

"Go fish."

The rest of the game went in silence. When they ran out of cards, Stat smirked down at the two piles in front of them. "Looks like I win." He began to stand. "It's too bad. I was really considering giving you a hand. Oh, well. Come on, let's go. I'll take you back."

Beki didn't stand. The Valium was making her body feel rather cloudy. "Rematch."

Stat arched a brow. "What?"

"I want a rematch. If I win, you have to help me."

"Why would I do that? I already won."

Beki lifted the teapot. It was heavier than it looked. She filled her cup, then his, and gestured for him to sit. "Because," she said, "immortality sucks."

Stat clapped his hands together and settled into his chair again. "Now you're getting it. Deal."

Status Quo lived in a very small apartment on Rolo Street. The gray-walled establishment was five stories high, with twelve apartments on each floor. Stat lived on the fourth floor. To Michigan's knowledge, there was one empty apartment to each side of him, as well as above and below. Even the other apartments that shared a floor with him were hard to rent out. Kind of a lonely existence, though it meant no one would ever complain of loud music or bedsprings.

Would anyone ever bed Stat? Michigan could only imagine such a thing happening under duress, or perhaps someone trying to get themselves out of trouble. Though it wasn't like Stat to take bribes. He wasn't the most righteous man, but he took his job somewhat seriously. Of course, if he ever broke the rules, there wasn't exactly a place to report him.

Snip and his five pals were looking rather nervous. An overweight, pimply-faced young man who went by Pix looked like he might faint at any moment. His face even redder than usual, he tapped Michigan on the shoulder. "I don't know about this."

Michigan waved him away. "Relax, would you? There's six of you and one of him."

"Six? What about you?"

"I'm supposed to get *her*, remember? Don't worry, I'll take her straight to your base as soon as we're out of Stat's sight."

"I don't like that idea."

"Hey!" Michigan snapped, making the other jump. "You wanted to see her, right? This is the only chance you'll get. You're telling me you won't even take a little risk for your prize? I thought you guys were the elite."

The group pursed their mouths and looked at each other. For fighters, they were lacking. For defenders, they were lacking still. As a cushion to stick between himself and Stat, most of them were a bit scrawny. Michigan felt himself regretting getting the Snyperx involved in the first place, but he only had two hands. He supposed he could always hope for the element of surprise. "Ready?" he asked them, and rolled his eyes when they nodded uncertainly. "If you run away when he opens the door, I'll tell him who's been hacking into the Round cameras."

His "backup" muttered uneasily to themselves. "Let's just get this over with," said Snip.

"Good man." Putting on what he hoped was a brave face, Michigan knocked.

No answer. Snip's buddies breathed an audible sigh of relief. Michigan waited half a minute, then grasped the worn knob and turned. The door opened much more smoothly than he'd expected. For some reason he thought Stat's door would have rusty hinges.

Rumor had it Stat never locked his doors. Michigan gave the knob an extra turn for good measure and saw that the lock couldn't close entirely and was therefore useless. Six heads peeked in behind him. He swung the door back and smirked to himself at the yelps of surprise and pain. Stat's living quarters were cold and mostly bare. It seemed he did little more than sleep and shower in this place. A book sat in the only chair by the window in the living room, and a bed could be seen in the bedroom. Someone had made a half-assed attempt at straightening it.

"This is so not cool."

Michigan nodded. "Yeah. They're not here."

"No, I mean it's not *cool*."

The speaker was a thin female with stringy brown hair and no chest. She was one of less than a handful of females in Snyperx, and a very unattractive one at that. She reminded Michigan of a female version of Snip, only more shrill than nasal. When she disapproved of something, she would scrunch her face up, leaving lines on her face that resembled the legs of a large mosquito.

"I thought he'd have, I don't know, torture devices in here or something. Or secret weapons. Or body parts in jars. Like a secret lab."

Michigan, actually, had expected the same. It wasn't realistic, but he wasn't sure what else to expect. Word by the slots was that Stat never locked his door because he had nothing worth stealing. Looking around, that appeared to be true. The most valuable thing was probably the book. *Immortality 101*. Pretty rare nowadays. It would be worth quite a few chips if anyone still bothered to read it. As the group fanned out, sifting about curiously with a careful touch here and a ginger prod there, he let his eyes wander into the bedroom and found himself searching for any signs that Stat ever had company beyond that door. There was a rumor floating around that he had a fling with Sasha, but Michigan knew not to put merit in those kinds of stories.

"Let's get out of here," someone said, followed by a nervous cough. "This place is giving me the creeps."

"It's just an apartment," said the skinny girl.

"Yeah," echoed Snip, "just an apartment. Don't be so noob."

"I'm not noob!"

"Hey," Michigan said, "shut up." A few of them made sounds of indignation but none really protested. "Where are we hitting next?"

"The Saffron Stallion?"

"Been there. Where else?"

"I hear he goes to Club Meow sometimes."

"Been there, too."

"The Square?"

"I was just there."

Some obscure part of his mind kept hoping that the small flat held some sort of clue to their next search. But all reason pointed to the suburbs, and Michigan really hated the suburbs, especially Grimm Sullivan's house. Why did Stat have to have such weird friends? He supposed only weird old hermits would break bread with Stat.

There was something else to worry about, too. He couldn't recall the last time Sasha announced a dice game. Before this, there had been only one that he could remember. Once upon a time. The minimum had been high. Very high. At least four hundred. But now she'd lowered it. A hundred and twenty, not easily reachable, but neither did it pose a sizable obstacle. He had a guess as to what her intentions were, and admitted to himself sadly that he was indeed playing right into her hands.

"Got any Queens?" Stat added another spoonful of sugar to his tea, although Beki hadn't seen him drink from the cup in several hands now. He seemed to be adding sugar just out of habit. "You like fairy tales?"

"No."

"No to which question?"

"Both."

Stat drew a card. "There once was a magical land, only it wasn't really magical, and the people weren't really happy. They weren't sad either. They just kind of existed, milling about their useless lives as the days wore on. Most of them were content that way, and didn't seek to change things, because the only thing really magical about the place was that it resisted change. In this world of constant, unchanging mediocrity, there were three queens who struggled for power. No one really knows why, because it's a pretty shitty place, even if you ruled it."

"I said I don't like fairy tales."

"Do you want another valium?"

"Not particularly. Got any nines?"

"Go fish. The three queens each had their own specialty, which they used to lure unsuspecting—and sometimes suspecting—people into their lair to become their slaves. One used lies, she was called the Queen of Tongues. One used trickery, she was called the Queen of Spin. And the last one used kindness."

"Let me guess," Beki interrupted. "The one who uses kindness winds up winning the support of the people, turns the other two around, and turns the land of mediocrity into a magical, beautiful place where dreams come true?"

Stat stared at her for a long time, five cards in his right hand. "It's funny how the mind of a Rounder works," he said slowly. Beki couldn't decide if it was an insult. Then, without missing a beat, he went on. "She was called the Queen of Soul."

"I didn't know Aretha Franklin was from here."

"Who?"

"Never mind."

"The three Queens vied for power, each seeking control over the hapless people. On the surface, they are polite and cordial to each other, claiming it was all fun and games, but behind the curtains they loathed, and were insanely jealous of, each other. One day, each Queen thought, the other two would fall under her own power, becoming her servants." He glanced at her over his cards. "Got any tens?"

She looked down at the ten in her hand. "Go fish."

"I'm simplifying a lot," he said, "let me know if you can't keep up."

"Should I let you know when I start listening?"

"One day the Queen of Tongues got a bit cocky and entered a dangerous game, because that's how everything in the kingdom is decided – through games. By winning games, by which I mean cheating, the three Queens gain control over the losers. While the Queen of Tongues was distracted by her game, the other Queens—or maybe just one of them—did something interesting."

"What did they do?"

"I knew you were listening."

"Get on with it. Got any Jacks?"

"Go fish. I really don't know for sure. Whatever it is they did, the Queen of Tongues was put at a big disadvantage. It's a bit like playing with an incomplete deck, and her opponents are the only ones that know which cards are missing. The Queen of Tongues, with the help of a lowly toad, has returned to the table to claim her place, only the rules of the games had long been changed."

"That's a terrible story." She drew a card. "Are you the toad?"

Stat arched a brow. "No. Why would you say that? Got a five?"

"Go fish. Just wondering. Got any tens?"

"I think I gave you too much Valium."

"I'm a lightweight. So am I right?"

Stat shook his head. "Nope. Not entirely. But I'm not the toad. The toad is an insignificant creature, and I'm lower than the toad. In this kingdom, I'm nothing but a pebble. No scratch that; I'm the blind, retarded beggar that everyone tries to pretend doesn't exist because I tarnish what little beauty this kingdom has."

"Do you have a ten or not?"

"Here. More tea?"

"No, thanks. It's disgusting."

"Isn't it though?"

From behind, Beki could hear Grimm speaking softly to the blond doll. She looked back at the cards in her hand, at the doll's merrily smiling face looking back at her. With a scoff, she threw the cards down on the table. "Get another deck."

"Why?"

"Because this is seriously depressing me. It's bad enough that I have to sit here playing cards while my son's dying, and that crazy old guy talking to that"—she dropped her voice— "*thing* is really creeping me out. And you," she made a half-assed gesture at Stat, "you're no help. All you've done is slip me drugs and tell weird stories."

"I told *one* story."

"And now you start in on how nobody likes you and no one wants to look at you. News flash, buddy," –she pointed one sluggish finger at him and grabbed her teacup with the other hand, slipped dregs of the thick tea into her mouth, and gagged– "it's your face. It's weird. I don't know what's wrong with it but I'm sure there's a plastic surgeon in Beverley Hills that can help. They couldn't fix Michael Jackson, but you're an easier case than he is."

A thin smile spread across Stat's face. "It's not my face. It's how people see it."

Beki scoffed. "Cut the emo crap."

"The what?"

"Never mind." She crossed her arms. "Do you have another deck or not? I'm not playing with this."

Stat didn't move. "Are you willing to ride your son's life on your pickiness about playing cards?"

Grimm was talking again. Beki could hear him. He was speaking to the doll, whose face she still hadn't seen, but she guessed was either as pretty as the cards illustrated, or was actually blank, with no features or expression, and the crazy old man was just imagining the whole thing.

"Fine," she said, and picked up the cards again. "It's your turn."

It took a while for Michigan to find Grimm Sullivan's house. He hadn't been there before, but everyone knew where Grimm lived. Even if they weren't familiar with the old hermit himself, it was well-known as one of the few places Status Quo frequented, and thus a popular place to avoid. Michigan didn't like the red door.

"I don't like this place," the skinny, annoying girl announced. "I think we should give up this plan. It's stupid."

"Hey," Michigan said, "shut up."

He rarely ventured into the suburbs. The neat lines of houses and pretty lawns disturbed him. But this was the mess he got himself into, and right now the creepy little houses were the least of his worries. The curtains to Grimm's house were drawn tight, another sign that Stat must be there. If Beki was here, too, he thought, he had a chance. If not, then he could at least use the nerds as a shield.

"Is everyone ready?" he asked. Most of them nodded hesitantly. "No running. No sneaking off. Remember the plan. You guys remember how to identify her, right?"

"The jacket?" Someone asked.

"Yes, exactly." Assuming she still had the jacket on. Assuming she didn't take the jacket off and throw it in a ditch as soon as they parted ways. Assuming Stat didn't tell her to take it off and leave it somewhere. Fortunately, no one brought these things up and Michigan left them unspoken.

"Who wants to knock?"

"Got any Kings?"

"No," Beki said, looking at the King of Spades in her hand. Her head felt a little woozy, but it was pretty easy to convince herself she was just fine. "Go fish. Got any Queens?"

He handed a Queen. "Do you have any questions?"

"Like what?"

"Anything. There must be something you want to ask, after that convoluted story. Got any threes?"

She gave him a three. "I'm thinking. It's kind of hard when you've been drugged up twice."

"I thought you'd ask more about my face. The other Rounders usually do."

"I'm thinking," she said again. "Got any nines?"

"Go fish."

"I still haven't fully eliminated the possibility that I'm dreaming. Is that something else Rounders do? Dream?"

"Something like that."

"So what do other Rounders ask?"

"Usually how quickly they can get home."

"You don't invite all of them to play cards?"

"You're the first. Got any Jacks?"

She did. "Go fish. I'd ask why I'm the only one but I'm really not all that interested. If none of this is real, then there's no point in asking about it."

"You're not going to ask me if this is all real?"

"Why? You'd just tell me it is, no matter what, even if my common sense says it just can't be real. There can't be women who are still alive after they're cut in two. Got any Kings?"

"Reality shifted a while back. So what was real then might not be real now, and vice versa. What do you think of that?"

"What do you mean by shifted?"

"I mean shifted." With two fingers Stat nudged his teacup away from the edge of the table. "Just like this. It moved away from one place and wound up somewhere else. I'd say it shifted about three inches, but Grimm over there thinks it's less than that, an inch and a half at most. I've also heard six centimeters. If you read *Immortality 101*, it's got this formula that calculates the precise shift down to the last millimeter. Doesn't matter though. The point is: it shifted."

"Ah."

At first she thought she had made that sound as an acknowledgement to Stat's strange statement. It was, after all, a feminine voice. But then she realized it wasn't her, and she couldn't be so deluded as to imagine sounds. There was a shuffle behind her, and she turned to see Grimm standing.

The doll stood, too, with the help of Grimm's pale hands. She stood woodenly, stiffly, as if her legs hadn't moved in many ages. Of course they haven't. They're doll legs. Dolls don't walk. Grimm gripped his staff tightly with one hand, and with the other guided the doll up and away from the stool she sat on.

"Do you need some help, Grimm?" Stat called. Grimm glanced at Beki and didn't answer. Stat shook his head. "He's a stubborn old mule."

The doll turned around slowly. She was lovely. No more than twenty years old by appearance, with the emotionless face of a stone angel. She didn't take notice of their guests nor try to speak. Her makeup was light and perfect, and Beki guessed it must have taken Grimm hours and hours to paint on. As she watched, the living doll parted her ruby lips and made the sound again. "Ah."

"Grimm," Stat said. "I'm serious. Do you want some help?"

Again, no answer. Grimm led the doll around the stool, away from the fireplace toward the hall, one step at a time. Though she moved and breathed, Beki still found herself wondering if she truly was a doll.

Her chest barely rose and fell with each breath, and she rarely blinked. Suddenly, the pale, immobile face quivered slightly. That was all. A quiver, and the girl fell to the floor on her knees. Then, expressionless, she urinated all over her painstakingly stitched dress.

Stat's hand tightened firmly around Beki's wrist as she darted up to help. "No," he said simply, and gestured for her to sit back down.

Slowly, unhurried, Grimm bent. It was like watching an ancient tree being forced to curve its husk against strong wind. He wrapped one hand around the girl's arm and pulled her up again. She didn't protest, nor give any signs of shame and regret at the accident. Then, he walked her slowly to a small washroom at the end of the hall.

"He wouldn't have let you touch her," said Stat lightly. "Come on, let's keep playing."

But Beki couldn't tear her eyes from the closed door of the washroom. She picked up her cards and looked once again at the smiling face of the blond girl. "What's wrong with her?"

"Lots of things. Whose turn is it?"

"Yours."

"Got any eights?"

"No," she lied. "Now I feel bad."

"For what?"

"For thinking he's crazy."

Stat snickered. "Yes, Rounders tend to feel bad about everything. Don't worry about it. Most people think he's nuts anyway. And truth be told, he's not all there. But without Adda he'd probably be worse. It's too bad what happened to her, but what can you do?"

"It's just sad, is all. Having a child like that."

"Adda isn't his child." He drew a card. Beki could hear water running in the washroom. "She's his wife." If he noticed the surprise and mild disgust on her face, he gave no sign. "I could tell you their story, but right now it's really not important, and it would take too long. If you really want to know, just ask Michigan to tell it to you. Everyone knows it, or at least bits and pieces of it."

"I..." She rubbed her face. "Wait, Michigan? I thought I'm never supposed to see him again."

"I didn't say that."

"Then..." Beki shook her head. "I'm very confused."

"That's OK. You're allowed to be confused. And it's your turn."

"Fine. Got any Aces?" He handed her the last card. She tossed it on the table along with the last Ace in her hand. "I win."

"How do you know?"

"I counted. I have more pairs than you do."

The sound of running water had ceased, followed by soft splashing, Grimm cleaning off his child-like wife in the tub perhaps. Stat was looking at her, and she wondered if he knew she had cheated. Had he asked, she might have admitted it, but he didn't. Instead, he pulled the red teapot closer and lifted the lid. "We're out of tea," he said, with a sad smile. "I should wash the pot."

He stood, went to the kitchen with the pot and both cups, and busied himself at the sink. Beki watched him incredulously.

"Are you going to help me now?"

"Help?" he said without a glance at her. "Oh yeah, that's what I said, isn't it? Well, I can't really help you. There's nothing I can do. But since you won, I won't drag you back to the Round immediately. In fact, I'll let you wait here until Von Phant gets here, which should be..." He looked over the kitchen counter toward the living room window. "Any minute now."

"He's coming?"

"He's here." Stat dried his hands on a yellow dishtowel, just as Grimm emerged from the hall. "Everything alright, Grimm?"

A slow nod.

"Alright then. Thanks for everything. Sorry I brought her here, but, well, you know." Another slow nod, and a glance at Beki from beneath the dark hood. Stat reached over and cradled his friend's head with one hand, leaning in slightly. "This is a token of thanks, old friend. Only for you. Just pretend I'm her," he said softly, and kissed the old man on the lips.

In the time Beki took to figure out a proper reaction to this, Stat had pulled back and started toward the front door as Grimm disappeared back into the washroom. "That jacket you're wearing. It's his, right?"

She looked down, having completely forgotten about it. "Yeah, it is."

"Take it off and give it to me. You can have it back in a minute." Seeing her hesitation, he grinned broadly. Under the watery "mask", he looked like the distorted reflection of a clown in a house of mirrors. "You'll see. It'll be fun. I promise."

She did as he said, and waited while he slipped the jacket on. It fit him better than it did her. He gestured for her to come to the door, where he moved to stand behind her.

"Ready?" he asked, and opened the door without waiting for her to answer.

For a moment nothing happened. Then she was on the ground, six pairs of hands holding her down. She cried out but someone held her down with a knee in her back, knocking the wind out of her rather quickly.

"Hey!" was all she managed. Craning her neck to one side, she saw Stat, smiling soothingly as he approached Michigan.

"Von Phant," she heard him say, "you're such a doofus!" Then he bent Michigan's arms back in a most uncomfortable angle and kicked his feet out from under him.

IMMORTALITY 101: The Intro Course

16
THE SNYPERX

The moment Beki walked out the ugly red door, Michigan knew something was different. By the time he figured it out, his "backup" was all over her, pinning her down while Stat leisurely kicked him in the kidney. Having realized their mistake, the Snyperx were too stunned to get up and help – not that they could do anything, and Michigan sighed as Stat rubbed his face in the neatly trimmed grass.

"Nice plan," said Stat, his knee jammed painfully into Michigan's back. "Did you really think it would work?"

Michigan shrugged, or rather made a respectable effort to with his twisted spine. "It was worth a shot."

"Admirable," said Stat, nodding in amusement. "Stupid, but admirable."

"Thanks."

Snip had gotten off Beki and was apologizing furiously as the others bowed, blushed, and muttered all sorts of convoluted condolences to the very confused woman. The skinny girl was cradling her own face, giggling like a maniac and reaching out hesitantly to touch Beki's clothing, only to pull her hand back with a squeal at the last second. Were he not so preoccupied already, Michigan would have slapped her upside the head.

"Did I pop your arm out of the socket?" Stat asked. "Sorry. Here, let me put it back in."

IMMORTALITY 101: The Intro Course

A loud pop and a bolt of pain. Michigan winced. "Mother *fucking...!*"

"I believe Geoffy told you to get off the swearing habit."

"Fuck Geoffy." Figuring he had nothing to lose at this point, he added, just for good measure, "and fuck you, Stat."

Stat patted his aching shoulder. "Sorry, you're not my type."

Then the pressure on his back was gone. Michigan was rather paranoid that it was a trick at first, but then Stat took a few steps back and waited, hands in Michigan's jacket pockets. Slowly, hesitantly, he got to his feet. He gave Stat a disgusted look.

"I really hate your face."

"Everyone does."

"Alright." Michigan threw his hands in the air. "Take me. Whatever you're going to do to me, fine. Cut off some limbs, remove my brain, whatever. I lose. I give up. I was wrong. Happy?"

"No, not really." Stat tossed a glance toward Beki, who was trying hard to pry herself away from the adoring prods of her assailants. "But I am interested. Intrigued, actually. Oh, and just for the record, I'm not the one who does all the surgical stuff. I don't have the stomach for it."

Michigan narrowed his eyes. "Are you kidding?"

"About what?"

"No, seriously, are you kidding me?" Swerving his head this way and that, Michigan scratched his scalp. "You're talking. You're just talking. Aren't you going to beat the crap out of me for, you know, *bringing her here?*"

Stat raised a hand to stop him. "All in good time. But not now. You know, I'm almost glad you brought her here. She's much more pleasant this way."

"What did you do to her?"

"Must you make it sound so vulgar? Geez." Stat removed the jacket and tossed it into Michigan's arms. "We played cards. Had some tea. Had a nice talk. She's very fixated on saving her son or something."

"Of course she is. She's a Rounder." Michigan snorted. "Even I know that."

"Right. So I told her if she won a game against me I wouldn't throw her back into the Round."

"Did she win?"

"She won the only way she always wins – cheating and lying through her teeth. Even after being drugged twice. It was fun." Beki was looking toward them. Stat curled a finger, motioning for Michigan to come closer. "Come here. Let's talk seriously for a minute."

The fat man moped all the way back to the Crescent, his fingers roughly bandaged. His name, even if it wasn't important, was Peg. Peg was a loser. He had lost everything to Sasha. That made the second time he lost everything. The first time was a very long time ago. It had been so long that almost everyone but his creditor had forgotten. Now, when he was so close to getting some Luck to pay some of it back, he wound up being indebted to yet another High Roller. On his way he took care to pass by Lady Luck's fountain and spit at her feet. Lady Luck, indeed. Luck was no lady.

It was fortunate that he didn't wind up one of Sasha's spinners. He already had to work for his first creditor. It seemed that Sasha had forgotten he already belonged to another, or she would have demanded that he stayed and worked for her, just to annoy his current master. Not that it would really affect him any – he would merely switch from being ground under one pair of heels to another.

As usual, Titi was there to greet him the moment he stepped inside, her enormous silicon breasts nearly eclipsing her face. Today, in keeping with her costume fetish, she was wearing a nurse's outfit that could only be described as skanky. She even added fake blood stains to the front, or at least Peg was pretty sure they were fake. A hypodermic needle hung like a gunslinger's pistol from a tiny hand-made leather holster on her waist. The right sleeve flapped like the feathers of a dead bird, concealing the stump that used to be her arm. Peg wasn't sure how she did it, but it seemed the worse he felt, the cheerier she was. That, in its own strange way, was Titi's talent.

"Was it good day, Peggy-san?" she asked, leaning in close enough to tickle his nose with her black dreadlocks. She was perfectly capable of speaking correctly – he had heard her do it after a couple of Pink Ponies. She simply chose not to.

He grunted a thick "no."

"Oh, my," she tittered, "it seems our Peggy-san has lost some games again. Did that mean old red whore Gypsy take your Luck again? Did…" she looked down at his crippled hand. "Oh, gee. What happened to your fingers?"

He tried to push her out of the way, but she grasped his collar with her hand and hung on. "If you *must* know," he said, prying her fingers open. "I lost fifty million at the Wheel."

A spark of surprise in her eyes. "The Wheel? Miss B.C.'s Wheel?" she giggled raucously. As far as Peg knew, only Titi, with her tiny body and thick lips, could manage a raucous giggle. And, like anyone else, she loved watching people lose. "How interesting! Now you have two masters. Oh, the curse of it all. It will be millions of days before you pay it all off, Peggy-san! Did Miss B.C. break your fingers because you could not pay?"

"She broke them for fun. And you don't have to tell *me* how long it'll be before it's paid off." Peg wrung his hands together, careful not to loosen his bandages. "I'm gonna do it, Titi. I'm gonna pilfer some Luck from the boss lady's stash. Just a thousand or so, then I can go play again, win big, get out of this debt."

Titi wagged her finger at him. "No, no, no," she said. "No. You not steal from Miss Neese. She will chop off your hands like she chopped off my arm. Debt better than handless, got it?"

"She'll never know. She won't be back from the Round for a while. By the time she's back, she won't be worried about a measly thousand chips." It sounded much more convincing than it should be. Peg hoped he wasn't just trying to convince himself.

"Miss Neese is back, I hear," Titi said with a pout. "At least I think I hear. Someone saw her in Square with that guy."

"Who?"

"You know, that one nobody likes and always sits at the fountain by his self." She tapped her chin thoughtfully. "I don't know why no one like him. I think he's sexy. Man who can do those things with his face? Very sexy. And I hear he can fight, too." Pursing her lips, Titi purred like a cat. "I love man who can use his body."

"Shut up, Titi."

"You're mean to me, Peggy-san," she teased with a smile. "But when you have no hands and need someone to spoon oatmeal into your mouth, we see how mean you are then. You'll be begging for chance to be nice to me."

"Either way," Peg said firmly, pointing at Titi with his broken fingers, "you're wrong. It has to be someone else. Neese Highwaters would *never* allow herself to be seen with Status Quo. They hated each other. Hell, everyone hates Stat, and Neese hates everyone. And nothing's going to happen to me unless you rat me out. And you won't do that."

"Maybe I do, maybe I don't."

"You *don't*."

"What's in it for me?" She winked her mile-long lashes. "What's in it for Titi, hmm?"

"A fifty chip and walking away with your lip unsplit."

"Unsplit isn't a word."

"Shut up, Titi. Just shut up."

At the moment, Michigan was having a very difficult time convincing himself he was sober. He couldn't be sober. As he stared incredulously at Stat's thin smile, he traced his thoughts back to the last time he had a drink. Maybe he'd passed out at the bar and dreamed the whole thing. He continued staring and thinking, until Stat snapped two fingers an inch from his nose.

"You haven't said anything for about two minutes."

Michigan shook his head quickly. "Um," he said, "yes. Could you repeat that?"

"I said 'you haven't said anything for about two minutes'."

"Before that."

Stat grinned. "I'm letting you go. You can take her and do whatever you want. If you really are trying to do what I think you're trying to do, then go do it. I'll look the other way for a while. It's not like someone's going to fire me for not doing this job."

Michigan narrowed his eyes, but they just looked sleepy instead of threatening. "Why?"

"I'm bored."

"Everyone's bored."

Stat nodded toward Beki. "See that woman there? I hate her. I hate her just for being who she is. But right now, she isn't who she is, and she doesn't know I hate her, so it's really kind of funny. I want to be there to watch when it all works out." A shrug. "Or collapse and make a mess of things. Either way, it's something to see."

"What is it that you think I'm doing?"

"I'm not entirely sure. But if it all goes right, it'll knock Sasha down a peg. When news gets out that *you* made it happen, it will be the ultimate insult to her."

"I think she already knows I'm doing it."

"Yes, but she never expected you to succeed." Stat looked Michigan up and down. "I mean, who does?"

It was an insult, but Michigan decided it would be smarter to sidestep it. "So you're letting me off the hook because you have confidence that I'll succeed?"

"I didn't say that."

"Then what *are* you saying?"

"I'm saying that I'm actually bored enough to want to watch this pan out. Whether you screw up or succeed doesn't really matter to me. If you pull it off, I'll give you a nod of respect and take delight in the fact that Sasha's not as all-powerful as she thinks, after all. If you fail, well, then I'll have to do my job. I'll drag that pretty woman back to the Round – after knocking her on the head, of course – and let it take its course. And you can go back to your role as the village idiot." Stat spread his hands casually. "All in good fun."

A curtain lifted across the street, reminding Michigan that it was best not to be seen in the extended company of Stat. "So, you drugged her and she still cheated, huh?"

"That's why you might have a chance. I'd even go so far as to say your chances are a little better than slim to nil."

"Fair enough." Michigan slipped his jacket on and began to head toward Beki and her small crowd of giggling, wheezing admirers. "One more thing."

"What?"

"It's not really important, but I always wanted to ask. Is it true you fucked B.C.?"

Stat laughed and clapped Michigan on the shoulder, making him wince at the contact. "You shouldn't believe everything you hear," he said, "but, yes, that's true. Quite the narcissist, isn't she?"

From where she stood, Beki could see Michigan and Stat quite clearly. From the side, Stat's watery mask was almost invisible. She could make out his features, thin and a bit hard, and his close-shaved scalp. Except for the occasional glimmer over his face from the streetlights, he almost looked normal. When her assailants helped her to her feet, Stat had also let Michigan up, and the two were talking quietly, tossing a look her way every now and then.

"Oh my gosh," someone squealed. Actually squealed. She turned to see a girl with her face scrunched tight in delight. The way all her features seemed to squeeze to the center of her face when she smiled reminded Beki of an artichoke. "Oh my gosh," she said again. "It's really her!"

Someone's hand was still on her arm. The girl slapped it away. "Stop touching her!" she snapped.

"I'm sorry," said a skinny teen with thick glasses while his chubby companion pulled an inhaler out of his pocket and took a deep breath. The kid was spitting while he spoke, a sign of nervousness perhaps. "I'm sho shorry. I mean, sorry."

Beki looked the group over. There were six of them, one female among five males. None of them were over twenty-five and the only girl was really quite unfortunate-looking. Two of them were blushing furiously while the others were gazing at her adoringly. Chances were they mistook her for someone else.

"It's alright," she told the kid apologizing to her, squinting to see the name sewn on his shirt. Out of the six, four had what appeared to be their names sewn over the left side of their shirts. "Brian."

"It's Snip," the kid said. "Please, call me Snip. That's the name I go by. Or, well, you can call me whatever you want, because…"

"Then why does your shirt say Brian?"

"Uh, well…"

"Never mind, I don't care." Brushing off dirt and grass from her clothes and face, Beki was suddenly very aware that her limbs felt like cotton and her brain was drifting several feet above her head. Thinking back to the past few hours, she wondered briefly if old man Grimm ever got his wife cleaned off. The rest was a mess of painted cards and gritty tea. She began to suspect that whatever was in the tea was much

IMMORTALITY 101: The Intro Course

stronger than Valium. She turned to the girl. "You got something for me to tie my hair back?"

The girl pursed her lips in embarrassment and scratched her scalp as she fished in her pants pockets. She had stringy hair and more than a little bit of dandruff. "No, I'm sorry, I…"

"Anybody else?"

The other five immediately reached into their pockets and rummaged around. Finally, one of then, a short kid with dark skin and wide, fish-like eyes, handed her a rubber band, which she used to tie her hair back in a messy ponytail. Even this small task seemed to put the group in awe. Untangling the knots in her hair, she glared at them. "A little breathing room, please?"

They took a step back, almost simultaneously, and continued to gaze at her. When she scowled, they stepped back a little bit more but the gaze never broke. Michigan was still talking to Stat. She considered joining them, but realized she wasn't all that interested in their conversation. And by the looks of this group, they'd follow her even if she tried to walk away, like sad puppies looking for love. Whoever they thought she was, they were quite smitten with her.

The kid called Snip straightened his glasses. He appeared to be the leader. "May I say it's an h-honor to meet you, ma'am."

"It's Rebecca," she said curtly. Common curtsey said she should be a bit nicer to them. They were just kids, after all. But after being drugged twice and having her face shoved in the dirt, Beki decided Miss Manners could go stick herself. "Don't call me ma'am. It makes me feel old."

Six pairs of eyes looked at each other. Then the girl grinned. There wasn't a name on her shirt. "We really are sorry," she said. "We're just not used to such, such…"

"You," someone cut in awkwardly.

"Yeah, that."

"And having you here…"

"Is such an honor…"

"I really think…"

"Could you please…"

"The Great Leader…"

Beki rubbed her temples. "Stop talking," she said, not expecting them to obey. But they did, ceasing the chatter immediately. "Can someone please tell me what's going on?" Several mouths opened. "In five words or less. I have a headache."

There was a prolonged pause. Finally, the fat kid stuffed his inhaler into his back pocket. "It was Michigan's idea."

"For you to tackle me on sight?"

"We were supposed to tackle Stat," the fat kid muttered. The name on his shirt said "Jossi". It was one of those names parents only gave their least favorite children. "But we got confused."

"It's a relief," the girl chimed in. "We wouldn't've been able to hold Stat. He would've hurt us. And that woulda been, well, bad. Besides, this way we got to…" she turned away, giggling and blushing. It wasn't an attractive look on her.

When Beki looked up again, Stat was gone. Michigan was heading toward them, shaking his head, a mildly perplexed look on his face. He pried Snip and Jossi out of the way, and Beki found it very difficult to decide if she was happy, relieve, scared, or disgusted to see him.

"O.K.," he said, raising one finger. "First of all, I am *so* upset with you for hitting me on the head."

She nodded slowly. "Alright."

"Second, he didn't do anything weird to you, did he?"

"Who, Stat? No, he was perfectly nice."

"Alright, good." Michigan rubbed his hands together, a nervous-looking gesture. "Good," he said again and, without warning, gave her a hug. Before she could decide whether to push him away, he had stepped back again. The others were giving him disapproving looks.

"Hey," someone said, "you can't do that."

Michigan rubbed his nose. "Shove it," he said. "We're getting out of here."

"Are we taking her to the Great Leader?"

"Well…"

Snip pushed his thick lenses up his nose. "We had a deal, V.P."

"Fine," Michigan said quietly, looking at Beki with an unreadable expression. "Please come with me this time. Don't run off again. I promise I'll explain everything, or at least try to. Believe it or not, we've both just been spared a world of hurt."

IMMORTALITY 101: The Intro Course

Beki crossed her arms. "I'm not going anywhere until you introduce me to your" – "friends" just didn't seem like the right word – "minions."

Michigan blanched, at the same time Snip said, "his what?"

"Whatever you guys want to call yourselves doesn't matter to me. Just tell me something I can call you by when I want you to get out of the way." She stepped out of the circle and stood in front of Michigan. "And you, Michigan, if that's your real name, this time you're going to tell me where we're going, why we're going there, and why I should keep believing anything you say."

He looked down at her. There was a glimmer of something in his eye. If Beki didn't know better, she'd have thought it was some manifestation of fear or apprehension. Patiently, she waited for an answer. Michigan cleared his throat.

"These are the Snipers."

"Sny-per-x," the skinny girl corrected. Beki threw her a hard glare and she quickly clammed up.

"We're going to their headquarters because it's the only place that's safe for you right now. And you should believe me because I haven't told a single lie to you so far."

"How do I know that's not a lie?"

He narrowed his eyes. "OK, what exactly did Stat give you?"

"Tea and Valium, so he says."

"Well it's sure turned you…"

"Bitchy?"

He smiled. She wasn't sure why.

The Snyperx headquarters was actually just a house. The outside walls were chipped and the roof was covered with holes, from which satellite dishes and antennas of a variety of sizes stuck out, which would be a problem if it ever rained. Thankfully, for as long as anyone could remember, it never rained. A trellis against the far wall was wrapped with wires and antennas, and one of the front steps leading up to the porch had fallen through. No one fixed it. The members of Snyperx weren't exactly the handiest with a hammer and nails.

The front door, most of its paint gone, was covered with many hand-made signs. Most of them read something along the lines of *Do*

Not Enter, Trespassers Will Be Shot, and *TOP SECRET*. One toward the bottom, written with red crayons on a blank sheet of eight-by-eleven-inch paper, read *ladies welcome*. They hadn't had many attempted trespassers, but it probably wasn't because of the signs, because they didn't get many ladies either.

The front hall had hardwood floors, dusty and rough from lack of maintenance. The first room on the right had been converted from a sitting room to an arcade, filled with classic games such as Space Invaders and Mrs. Pac Man. Had she taken noticed of them, Beki would vaguely recall passing time playing those games in her college days.

The upstairs contained five bedrooms, two of which were lined with futons and blankets here and there, though it was rarely slept in. A third was filled with cardboard boxes, their lids splayed open to reveal all manners of electronic thingamajigs and doodads. The fourth held only a large television and a variety of home-brew videogame consoles. The fifth, the largest, was a server farm, a term Beki only recently learned from her son.

All of this Beki looked at without seeing as she was ushered into the house. Her head was swimming and she couldn't remember the last time she wanted to take a nap so badly. Images leapt in her head like fish out of water. She was aware of Michigan's hand on her arm and was a bit paranoid that he might try to hug her again. There were many voices, more faces floating in and out of her line of sight, all of them jabbering in excitement.

Eventually, they wound up in the largest room on the first floor. What used to be two rooms was now one, with a jagged frame down its center where a wall used to be. The furnishing was massive in quantity, but lacking variety. Everywhere the eye fell was another beanbag chair and glimmering screen after flickering screen. Tables were smothered under pile after pile of cords and disks. More cords, like entrails of dead snakes, hung from rows of nails on the walls, which was adorned with various brightly colored posters.

Someone brought her some water and instead of drinking it, Beki dipped her hand into the plastic cup and splashed some on her face. It was almost refreshing. Almost. People were talking and she wasn't answering. Michigan was still hanging onto her, asking not so politely for the others to give her some room. A blanket was draped over her body after she fell heavily onto one of the larger beanbags. She wanted to sleep.

Across from her, on the far wall, the only one not covered with wires and old posters, was a large framed portrait. The face was familiar, but she couldn't for the life of her think of a name to match. She heard herself ask a question, but the words didn't quite come out right. Someone took the half-empty cup from her hand and told her to sleep. Somewhere in between slumber and consciousness, the girl with stringy hair knelt by her and asked if she was feeling well. She heard herself mutter, "Yes, I'm fine. And I'm sorry. I don't really think you're ugly."

Sasha took special care to pick out her dress for the opening night. A dice game was something to commemorate, even if, in this barebones existence, there was really no reason to commemorate anything. Still, many people were coming. It had been a very, very long time since a dice game was held.

The High Rollers were losing their touch, she had been thinking. They had grown too comfortable in their place, ruling over the masses, living a dreary existence, and forgetting the games that had gotten them this far. Few of them still played regularly, while most didn't play at all. They relied on their cronies too much, which was a dangerous thing to do. A true Roller of their rank should never rely on anyone. That was the main reason Sasha still took to the tables herself. The unwashed masses needed to see there was still one High Roller who knew how to play with her own hands.

She picked a gold dress, one with many layers of gold-trimmed ruffles that shone like a burning field. Gold was the color of riches, of success and prosperity. She might even dye her hair to match its color. And shoes. She needed matching shoes, even though no one would be able to see them underneath the enormous dress. With the tender tickle of excitement in her throat, she fished her treasure out of the side pocket of the pool table and tucked it into a hidden fold in the dress.

Lisa Gasolina spent all her time in that blasted teahouse, whiling away her time with those puppets she called her sons and daughters. Sasha could not recall the last time she picked up a card or die. Rat

Spence had disappeared, seeming into a hermitage, seeking one manner of enlightenment or another. Mojiha Jordan was too busy chasing skirts, both in the Round and out of it. And Neese Highwaters, who had gotten too proud and adventurous for her own good, was too cocky to play the games that bought her the position she coveted so much.

Sasha wasn't like that. She was a Roller at heart. She took pride in playing, in rolling, in spinning, in getting her hands dirty in more ways than one.

As usual, Jean-Luc walked in just as she struggled to pull the dress over her head, her underpants in full view. He clicked his tongue and stepped forward to help.

"Could you have picked a bigger dress, Sasha dear?" he asked with a hint of disapproval. "Sometimes less is more, you know. This thing is... well, a marshmallow. A giant golden marshmallow. Why do you always do this to yourself?"

She looked at herself in the full-length mirror by the far wall, hands on her hips, turning slowly. It was beautiful. No matter what he said, it was beautiful. And soon, when her hair would be colored like threads of gold, spiraled like stairways to heaven, and hanging in ringlets framing her face, it would be perfect.

"I'm going to need shoes, Jean-Luc."

"You have a mountain of those."

"I need shoes that match this dress. The same color."

Jean-Luc signed dramatically. "I'll see what I can do."

She liked Jean-Luc. She couldn't deny it. But she did not respect him. Like many others, he was one of those who forgot his place. He had forgotten how to be a High Roller, gotten too comfortable living his cushy life, and wound up her companion, even friend, and High Rollers should never have friends. They could take on acquaintances, partners, and lovers, but not friends. To make friends was to forget a Roller's place.

She was glad, however, to have him near. He was a constant, and he was fun. If she couldn't have friends by principle, then having someone who was almost one was nice.

"Do you think angel wings would go well with this?"

"I hope you mean as an oxymoron."

"That's the plan." She piled her hair in a messy bob on top of her head. "I may wear this up."

He used to be one of the greatest. Now he's a fashion consultant. Sometimes Sasha wonders if he missed his old ways, or even remembered them. He might regret having fallen to this position, or maybe he's relieved, because the position of a High Roller was not for everyone. It was dangerous and exciting, the kind of excitement that sent tidal waves of heat through your veins, filling your heart until it was on the verge of bursting. Every day as a High Roller was that way.

"Don't ever change, Jean-Luc," she said to him.

Not that he ever would. None who fell have gotten back up again. The downfall of a High Roller was a one-way ticket, a dangerous path, and she was going to remind them what it was all about – the thrill of the roll, the cutting edge of the cards, betting life and blood.

If someone got screwed over in the process? Well, that was a bonus.

17
NEESE HIGHWATERS

When she first opened her eyes, Beki was convinced she was strapped to a hospital bed with leather bands, doctors injecting all sorts of medication into her arm while the light overhead flickered and buzzed like a dying fly. But then she turned, and realized it was just the blanket twisting itself around her torso, the thing jabbing into her arm was the corner of a desk, and the buzzing and flickering came from dozens of flat computer screens all around her. In fact, there was no light overhead, or anywhere. The computers provided the sole source of light. Many faces turned when she stirred and sat up, the lights from every monitor reflected in their pupils and eyeglasses.

A figure sat next to her on the floor. It took a moment for her senses to focus on him. She was pretty sure she remembered his name. All the flickering monitors were hurting her eyes. She closed them and lay back down against the pink beanbag.

"About time you woke up," she heard him say. Michigan. That was his name. "Want some water or a cupcake or something?"

She shook her head. "I want to go to the bathroom."

"It's right outside down the hall on the right." He started to help her up, but she waved him off.

"Thanks," she muttered sleepily. "I can find it myself."

After her business was done, Beki slumped over the sink and washed her face. Her skin felt dry and irritated to the touch. There was a mirror stained with toothpaste and lotion over the sink and she looked at herself in it. Her hair was a mess and her blouse wrinkled. There was a stain on her neck that she began to worry was a wound until it came off with a light rub of her hand. Her eyes looked a bit sunken and her face had a reddish tint to it, which could be a result of anxiety, having slept awkwardly on a hard floor, or the overhead light reflecting off the date-colored walls.

She leaned forward and pulled down the lower lid of her right eye to examine her pupil. Her eyes, contrary to how she felt, looked sane.

Michigan had a cup of coffee for her when she returned. He gestured for her to sit next to him on the beanbag she had slept on just moments ago. Had her legs felt strong enough to stand, she wouldn't have done it, but as it was, she fell heavily into it. The coffee was laden with cream and sugar.

"How do you feel?"

"Like I should be in a padded room." Looking down, she saw that he was wearing only socks on his feet, and one of his toes was poking through an expanding hole. "Have you been walking around barefoot all this time?"

He shrugged nonchalantly. "Just for a while. These guys lent me some shoes eventually."

She kicked his shoes off her feet. "I should give these back."

He didn't move to take them. "How's the coffee?"

"It's alright." Though theirs were the only voices in the room, they were not alone. In front of every computer screen was a young man or woman, some looking hardly out of their teens. Beki thought she could recognize the backs of the ones who tackled her in front of Grimm's house. At the moment, they weren't paying attention to her or Michigan, each busying themselves with their work. She lowered her voice. "These screens are giving me a headache."

"You don't have to whisper."

"I don't want them to think I'm being rude."

Michigan chuckled. "Back to vanilla," he muttered between chortles. "That was fast."

"What?"

"Never mind." Dipping his head, he mimicked her whispery voice. "I'd say we can go to another room, but they like having you here."

"Why?"

"Because they like you."

"They're not even looking at me." She scanned the rows of heads silhouetted against the flickering screens. "And you're talking about them like they're monkeys or something."

"Don't worry about it. We can talk here. So, what did he say to you?"

For a long moment she couldn't connect the threads in her head. "Who?"

"Status Quo."

"Is that his real name?"

"Who knows? We call him that. He calls himself that. If he ever had another name no one knows it. You have to tell me what he said and did to you. It's kind of important."

She shook her head and took another sip of coffee. "You've been saying that nonstop. 'This is important', 'that is important'. I only came with you because you said I could do something about my son, and so far it feels like I've gone full circle. I don't even know where I am, and for all I know my son might be dead by now."

"You sound awfully calm about it."

"I know, and it's scaring me."

"It shouldn't." Michigan smiled. The light of the computers illuminated his face eerily. "Because that's who you really are." He raised an arm as if to put it around her, then hesitated and patted her knee lightly instead. "Let's try this again. My name is Michigan Von Phant, and this is the Rabbit Hole."

When the news of Sasha's new game reached Club Meow, it hardly caused a stir. In fact, it barely bubbled. Lisa wound a strand of Prescott's hair over the girl's head and held it in place with a delicate pink diamond pin. Her daughter looked beautiful, even with those stitches over her mouth. Lisa thought they added character.

"Do you still love games, darling?"

Prescott nodded and tried to smile. The effort tugged at her lower lip, causing a small droplet of blood to swell where thread met skin. Lisa wiped it away with a handkerchief.

"Then you ought to play. You were once a good spinner, and I bet you still are. You can win. Can't you?"

She nodded again, though there was uncertainty in her eyes.

"You can do anything you put your little heart to." Prescott lifted one hand and mimicked an invisible needle injecting into her other wrist, a gesture Lisa knew all too well. "Yes, you can go get your treat, as soon as I finish with your hair. If you're going to be in the game, you have to look good. You are playing for me, after all."

A disobedient hair wound its way out of the flawless weave and fell over Prescott's face. Lisa twirled it around her finger and pulled it out with a hard tug, then bent to kiss her daughter's cheek. Prescott gave no sign that she felt either.

"Run along."

Prescott disappeared into the back hall. Lisa gestured to Marky to bring her a cup of tea, green with no cream or sugar. As she blew lightly into her cup, she wondered if she could still spin herself. It had been a long time. She had given up the cards and wheels. Her children were her life and purpose now. Still, she couldn't help but be a bit excited at the prospect of watching Prescott play in the upcoming dice game. The chances of her reaching the final table were quite high indeed, and Lisa even believed she had a chance to humiliate Sasha. Prescott was the best daughter she ever procured.

And should she lose, well, there was something else that needed to be done. Something she should begin making preparations for.

She motioned for Marky to come closer. Marky was very pretty, too, with a clear china face, flawless olive skin, and dark green eyes. Reaching up, Lisa stroked her face gently.

"Why don't you have a seat, my dear?" she said, "and I'll do your hair?"

"There's this movie that came out of the Round a while back." Michigan paused. "Your life, by the way, it's called a Round. I'll get to why later. But if you tell me you saw this movie, it would make things a lot easier. It's called Matrix or Matrices or something."

"*The Matrix.*" Beki warmed her hands on the coffee mug. "I saw it more times than I'd have liked, but that's what happens when you've got movie buffs for a husband and son."

"Good, then you can probably guess what I'm about to tell you."

"That it's true, and I've just being unplugged from some computer-generated hallucination and we're waiting for some machine empire to come crashing down on us?"

Michigan clicked his tongue. "Well, no. I was going to say I think it's a convoluted movie that takes itself too seriously. But you're one step ahead of me. I'm trying to put this in a way that you can understand." Someone in the corner snickered. "Hey, shut it! Anyway, that movie's not totally off the mark, but it's a tad overdone. The real thing isn't so dramatic or dark or cool. It's not even that dangerous. There's no savior or machines harvesting humans, and no handsome hero running around in black trench coats. In fact, the real thing's pretty damn lame. I mean, you can wear a trench coat if you want, but it still wouldn't make it cool. Do you believe in the afterlife?"

"Sure, why not?"

"Alright. Let's say this is the afterlife, O.K.? Do you believe in re-entry?"

"Re-entry to where?"

"Wait, sorry." Michigan snapped his fingers. "Lost my train of thought. What's the word I'm looking for... Hey, Snip!" he rapped his knuckles on a chair a few feet away. "What's the word I'm looking for?"

"Reincarnation," replied Snip without turning around. "Are you sure you want to do this, V.P.? I think we can probably explain it way better with a slideshow."

"Cram your slideshow." Snip only shook his head as Michigan went on, gesturing eagerly with his hands. "Alright, reincarnation, where one life ends and you go on to another life as someone else. Do you believe in that?"

She never thought about it. "Sure."

"Good, so let's say that this is the afterlife, and if your life ends, you wind up here, then you get reincarnated as someone else, and whoever or whatever you get reincarnated as depends on how you play a bunch of games. If you win a bet, you win some points towards a good life, if you lose, you get some points toward a bad life. And it can get so good that everyone you touch gets to have a good life, or so bad that everyone around you drops dead like flies. Does that make sense?"

(It's your fault)

"And the bets, they can get pretty big, so big that everyone's in on it, or watching it. You can bet on anything. You can bet on weather, politicians, even small favors – very addictive, by the way."

(it's)

"And a life, they call it a Round here. If you like someone, you can play a Round with them. If you still like them after that, you can play another Round. But hey, sometimes the Rounds don't turn out the way you want. I've seen plenty of couples break it off because they wound up with someone else in the Round. Isn't that funny?"

(your)

"So generally, everything you're doing is a game, and it's fun because you never know that you're playing it. Your entry and exit are all according to procedure, because messing with the procedure is, well, it's kinda dangerous." Michigan paused. "Well, I suppose I did a really dangerous thing taking you out of that gate like that. Oh, the gates. The gates are like… holes in the Round. No one knows why there are gates, but when they find a gate, they plug it up with a couple of gatekeepers. It's a sucky job, but someone's gotta do it."

(fault)

"My head hurts," she said, sipping the gradually cooling coffee. Several eyes turned toward them. "But keep talking, or I'll start convincing myself that I'm really insane. It wouldn't be hard to do."

"I promise you're not insane; at least not by the standards of this place." He scowled at the curious faces and the eyes turned away. "Your head probably hurts because of that stuff Stat gave you. I don't think it's Valium – don't think Stat can tell one sedative from another. But it's fortunate because … you know what? This is really confusing, even to me. I'm not thinking clearly. I think I need a drink." He smiled awkwardly when she offered him the coffee. "I mean… *drink* drink."

"He did tell me you're perpetually drunk."

"Did he, now?" Michigan cleared his throat. "The point is, and don't take this the wrong way, your son's life isn't worth saving. It'll end eventually; he'll wind up back here, just another person who's got nothing to do with you. He just happened to be unfortunate enough in this Round to be associated with you."

"Was it really my fault?"

"Let me put it this way – you lost. You lost big, so big that a ripple effect wiped out everyone within eight sticks of you. But none of that matters in the long run. They'll just come back here and start up another Round. Unless, of course, they were really liking that Round they were in, in which case they'll probably grumble for a while, but they won't really complain – not to you, anyway."

"Why not? I screwed them over right?"

Michigan nodded to his right, at the portrait on the wall. "Did Stat tell you that stupid story about the three Queens? He's really proud of it for some reason. He tried to tell it to me back there but I wasn't really paying attention."

She thought back, and vaguely recalled it in a fog. "I can't even remember what we talked about."

"He may have already told you this, and you probably didn't believe him, but" – Michigan gestured at the roomful of people – "this roomful of admirers should at least give you some clue. In this cesspool of drunken, toasted, pathetic gamblers, there is a group of elite who somehow manipulated their way to the top just so they can watch the masses writhe under them like worms. Because, honestly, there is nothing better to do. Love'em or hate'em, they've made a name for themselves. And like it or not, babe, you're a Queen. When I said there was someone here who could help you, I wasn't lying; she's right in front of you."

She stared at the portrait for a very long time. The hair was a bit different and the eyes were harder, but upon closer inspection, there was no doubt.

"That," she said to the painting of her own face, "is very creepy."

Stat went home. He headed back to his apartment, noted that some of his things had been riffled through, and decided to ignore it. Chances were Michigan took his stooges and barged in, looking for the woman who called herself Rebecca. If anyone else came in, looking for something to steal, then they would've already gone away severely disappointed.

He was very tired. He couldn't remember the last time he slept more than three hours in a row. It had been an eventful day to say the least. Not only did someone drag a Rounder out of the Round, but it was a High Roller to boost. And Michigan Von Phant. He always was a fool, brash and impulsive. The strange thing was, Stat was pretty sure Michigan knew exactly what his position was — a lowly toad drooling over a beautiful queen way out of his league. But he had to admire the toad for trying. And Neese, well, she was a cruel sort of beauty. Right now, with her mousy personality, that beauty wasn't quite shining. But he saw a glimpse of it, he was sure. That beauty he hated so much.

Stat really hated High Rollers. They were a bunch of self-serving, indulgent hedonists who had nothing better to do with their time than screw other people over for kicks. Of course, he supposed he was in no place to judge. He himself couldn't think of anything to do with all this endless time besides staring into space and strolling about town making people nervous.

Picking up his copy of *Immortality 101*, Stat flopped onto his unkempt bed. It was the only book worth reading in his opinion. The author was a keen thinker. It was a pity no one knew where he was now. He might have sealed himself in a wine cask for all Stat knew.

When the book failed to hold his interest, he tossed it aside and rolled onto his stomach. His body was tired, but his mind was restless, and he hated to admit who it was he was thinking about. It was always her, and it made no sense, because he despised her in every way. Her ways and her words and her actions, how she was always plotting and finding new ways to get to him, to get to everyone. If she smiled, it was always sneaky or derisive. If she laughed it was always a jeer. The prettier the dress she wore, the greater likelihood she was about to make someone else fall, lift its hem, and kiss her feet.

But he liked to think he finally had an advantage. This time it would be different.

Like Neese, Sasha was beautiful. All the High Rollers were beautiful, majestic, and stately. It wasn't wrong to call them Kings and Queens, because they certainly looked the part. Some of their beauty was natural, and some the result of surgery. No one remembered which was which any more. Unlike Neese, who was brutal and fierce, Sasha was wily, sneaky, and that was how she gained the upper hand. She must know Neese was here, and she must be so excited. Everything must be falling into place according to whatever plan she'd made.

Tossing in that many chips for someone after a Round had already started. No one had ever thought of it before. It was brilliant, and utterly despicable.

He could've dragged Neese back and let things take its course. She might have survived whatever was coming to her, or she might have come out battered and broke in spirit. Everyone knew. Everyone was waiting to hear about this Round, about what will happen to the High Roller who was brave enough to take on a Round. But that was only step one.

Step two was Michigan Von Phant. Sasha had to know he would try to bring Neese out before things got out of hand. After speaking to Rebecca, Stat was quite certain this was Sasha's doing also. She must have prompted Michigan to do it, daring him even.

Step three Stat wasn't so sure of. Whatever purpose Sasha had for making Neese an air-headed Rounder was beyond him, but by accident he had found the perfect way to throw a monkey wrench into her plans, whatever they might be. He had never seen a Rounder do what "Beki" did, but then he had never tried it before.

For now, there was nothing else to do but wait, and for the first time in a long time, he felt a little excited. Even if it wasn't often, every now and then something came along that made staying alive and awake worth it.

"Status is kind of, how can I put it... an enigma of some sort." Beki was gazing at the portrait with empty eyes, but Michigan decided he ought to keep talking anyway. No point in dragging it out. He still had a lot of things he had to convince her of. "Did he tell you what he does?"

"He said he was the law around here," Beki replied absently.

"Well, he's right. I know he likes to tell people that, assuming they talk to him. There's no other way to put it, really. That is what he is. It's not like he has a title or anything. His job, as far as I can tell, is to go around the gates and grab people who wandered out of the Round and take them back. 'Cause even with the gatekeepers they slip through every now and then. Especially teenagers. Man, they're hard to keep in. But we can't let Rounders in here, not for long anyway, since they die and all."

IMMORTALITY 101: The Intro Course

"Die?" She turned to him. "Am I going to die just by being here?"

"What? No!" Michigan waved both hands almost comically. "No, no. I mean, you die of old age and stuff. You can stay here forever, but eventually you die of old age if nothing else kills you."

"And you won't?"

(immortality sucks)

Beki shook her head. "You can't be serious. I thought he was just babbling… that guy, when he was talking about being immortal and how it's no good. You people aren't really immortal, are you?"

Michigan smiled thinly and knew she needed no further answer than that. It must be hard for Rounders to accept, having just come out of a world that revolved around the idea of a finite life. They were obsessed with it from what he heard. They were always trying to explain it, coming up with different theories and stories. As far as he knew, none of them involved a dirty casino town. Of course, the stuff they did come up with was pretty interesting. Fables, myths, religions, etc.

Come to think of it, the general populace here really did take this thing for granted. While Rounders struggled to explain death, the true immortals had lost interest in explaining immortality a long time ago. It just wasn't that interesting.

"You were talking about Stat."

"Right. Stat. He's the law. He has been, as long as anybody can remember. He's kind of a loner, maybe not by choice, and he's great in a fight, probably out of necessity since some of those Rounders get kind of offended and violent when they're being dragged out physically. But usually he doesn't have a problem with it because of his face."

"His face is strange."

"Isn't it? Not many people know what his real face looks like, but it changes. He always looks like someone who's important to the person looking, so usually he doesn't have trouble avoiding a fight if he doesn't want it. I imagine it makes the job a lot easier, if you can get used to not having anyone see your face. But once you know it's him, you can see past it, just a little, *then* it looks extra weird, because you feel like you can almost see underneath his face. That's why nobody ever looks at him straight on. It's unnerving."

"How sad," Beki said in a low voice, "he's not bad looking."

"Yeah, I... wait, what?" Beki raised the coffee cup to her lips. Michigan reached over and put a hand over its rim. "You saw his face?"

She pushed his hand away. "Yes. It's like you said. I looked through the first face and saw the second. It was weird. The first face was like..."

"A hologram?"

"Water."

Michigan chuckled. Beki was probably scowling at him in the dark, but he couldn't stop himself. "Well," he said, "you learn something new every day. Apparently Rounders *can* see through him."

"Are you going to get to a point eventually?"

That was something Michigan hadn't quite thought through. There were too many things to think about and too much to explain. They was all building on each other and without the help of Geoffy's rum and cola, he had trouble getting from one point to the next. Scratching his scalp uneasily, he searched for an adequate answer.

"How about you ask some questions?" he said at last.

Beki nodded. "Are you lying?"

"Nope. You can't make this shit up."

"Is that person in the picture really me?"

"It's you before you went into the Round."

"Do I have a different name here?"

"Neese Highwaters." He jerked a thumb to the far wall. "You run a place not far away, called the Crescent. It's pretty damn posh. You are a High Roller, after all. We'll go there later, provided you decide you're really not insane."

She held the cup up to no one in particular. "I need more coffee."

Several people practically fell out of their chairs scrambling to get to the cup first. The chubby kid with the inhaler proved victorious. "Cream and sugar?" he asked Beki, grinning broadly.

"Black, please. Thank you. Is my life up to this point real?"

"Of course," Michigan said in all seriousness. "It's a very real game."

"Your life up to this point has been near-perfect."

Beki drank her second cup of coffee and thought about how to process that. "How is it perfect? I don't live in a mansion, I married middle-class, and even though my husband and I both work full time, our son's college education will probably bankrupt us regardless."

"You were happy, weren't you? This is going to sound insanely cheesy, but being happy is what it's all about. You were born into a well-balanced family, right? Mom and Dad were smart and open-minded and educated you about the world. Your husband was nice and attentive and loyal... well, until recently, that wasn't his fault and I'll tell you why—it's just part of the bad luck your bet ran you into. Same goes for your son. And the other twenty or so people whose Round ended because they got caught in your ripple effect. And it's not even a ripple anymore. It's a damn tidal wave.

"Your life up to date has been good, because you won small favors. That's Gypsy's racket, and it's super addictive. Rounders don't appreciate small favors as much as they should, mostly because they don't remember how hard they had to work at winning them before they entered the Round. But that's part of enjoying it. Getting to enter a Round with lots of small favors on your side can make a huge difference.

"But now everything's all turned around, because your bet rolled over. You originally had a huge pile of small favors on your side, but you entered the Round before the game was up, and someone else tossed in a bunch of chips for you. The turnout wasn't so good, and you wound up with a bunch of bad chips on your plate, and they all started cashing in at once. Your husband was feeling his worst and most vulnerable when that doctor came to him. He'll probably be filled with regret and never come out of hating himself. You son will probably die or become a vegetable for ten years, and then die. It's a pretty crazy thing. No one's ever messed with a Round half way through. Probably because nobody's thought of it up until now. This whole thing's kind of complicated, but the rule is..."

"Hang on," Beki cut in as Michigan took a deep breath before continuing his speech. "What you're saying, basically, is that someone changed the course of my life half way through?"

Michigan shrugged. "I suppose you can say that."

"Why would they do that?"

"You're a High Roller, and people are jealous of High Rollers – scared of them, too, and generally hate them. Lots of people could want to screw you over just for the heck of it. And frankly, you're kind of a bitch." He gestured around them. "But there are also some who worship the High Rollers, like these guys here, who are pretty much your number one fans. And really, your worshippers outnumber the haters by just a little, and even the haters come around once in a while if you're putting on a good show."

Beki wished she could feel guilty about it, but she didn't. The only feeling she could summon up at the moment was annoyance at being associated with the person whose face was in the portrait.

"Do you know who did it?"

Michigan smiled. "Now we're getting somewhere. I've been waiting for you to ask that question. Her name is Sasha B.C., and she's also one of the elites, a High Roller."

"Should I apologize to her?"

The silence that fell over the room weighed a ton. All clicking, tapping, shifting, and hushed conversations ceased. Beki wandered if she'd said something wrong. In the corner, someone stifled a chuckle. Michigan slapped his forehead.

"No," he said. It was almost a whine. "No, no, *no!* Please don't say that again. It's really bad for my health."

"Why not? You said I was a bitch to her, so she did it as a payback. If I just go settle things, I can get back on with my life. It's the simplest solution."

Michigan turned, faced her, and drew himself up on his knees. He looked her in the eyes with such intensity that she tried to scoot back to get away, but bumped against a chair instead. "If it was that easy," he said, "you wouldn't be here. Cripes, you really are vanilla, aren't you? This isn't a nice place. People cheat, steal, and lie just for fun, because there's nothing better to do. Don't you have a place like this over in the Round? Where chips do the talking and the sleaziest people always get away with the most? Las Vegas, right? Well this place is like Las Vegas on crack. If you keep this good-girl act up you'll get yourself in some fucked up messes, or worse, get thrown back into the Round."

"What's so bad about that? It's my life, isn't it?"

Michigan paused. "You saw Adda Holmes, didn't you?"

"Ad…" the image of beautiful blond curls came to mind. "That old guy's wife?"

"Yes, Adda Holmes. Seems Stat neglected to tell you this particular story, and I don't have the patience for it. To put it simply, she's the classic example of a Round gone wrong, so wrong that it broke her completely. No one knows quite what happened. She was one of the most notorious High Rollers once upon a time, and gorgeous to boot. Then, like you, she played a Round, came out after exit procedures, and hasn't said a word since. Everything she had was taken away, split amongst people who lusted after her wealth. And Grimm, thank goodness for him. He was just a lowly servant who conducted exit procedures, but he loved her, and was the only one who took care of her after that, and he's probably going to do it forever.

"The story was she got caught up in someone's ripple, like all those people got caught up in yours, but that's not true. One of the other Rollers screwed her, just like you got screwed, and Grimm didn't have the guts to go in there and stop it before it got too far. Now he has to spend eternity taking care of that woman, whom he loves so much, but who can never love him back, or even talk to him. It's a sad existence, and *I'm not going to follow his example!*"

Beki flinched. His hands were gripping her shoulders too hard. With a start, Michigan pulled his hands back.

"Sorry," he muttered, avoiding her eyes. No one spoke of the elephant in the room.

"So," Beki said after a long, awkward while, "who did it to her? Was it Sasha also?"

Michigan shook his head. "No, Neese, it was you."

As Jean-Luc fussed with her hair, toning each strand with highlights and lowlights, Sasha considered the possibility of arriving at the opening of the games with Stat on her arm. Sure, Stat wasn't big on being the center of attention, but most of the attention would be on her anyway. And with him by her side, even more eyes would be fixed on her, wondering and guessing what exactly it was that brought them together.

She liked Stat, really liked him. It was more than infatuation or fascination. It was almost an obsession, which wasn't right – considering their respective stature he should be the one chasing after her. But she didn't mind a challenge. Once this was done, when he saw the glory she was about to bring back to the elites, he would see just how special she was, and he would come back to her.

She ached for him. It had been so long since they were last together. Sometimes she cursed her body. Would he come to her more if she was taller, curvier, and had hair in places untouched by light?

"Have you decided on the Doctors you will use for the qualifying rounds?"

Sasha nodded. "Leonard, Tish, and Mozart."

"Are they the best?"

She smiled. "No, not the best in skill, but they have the biggest debts to pay, so they will try harder than the others, and that's what will really make the game."

He stuck a pin in her hair. "I still say it's too much gold."

She scowled. "I didn't ask for your opinion. Be careful with what you're doing."

"Stat won't like so much gold. From what can I tell he'll like a simpler style."

Sasha pursed her lips. "Stat *will* like it."

"You mean he'll like you."

"He loves me," she insisted. "He just won't admit it."

The upstairs bathroom of the Rabbit Hole was a bit messy, but at least the water was hot. Beki scrubbed herself hard, and turned the heat up until the water was near scalding, as if with enough effort she could wash the woman named Neese off of her skin. She knew it wouldn't work, but it was worth a try.

When she finished, her clothes were gone. Just as she began to call for someone to ask where they were, a timid knock came on the door. A towel wrapped around her torso, she opened it a crack and saw one of Michigan's "minions", the girl who had tackled her at Grimm's door.

"Um, hi, Lady Highwaters," she said, and bowed.

"It's Beki."

"Lady Be…"

"Just Beki is fine."

IMMORTALITY 101: The Intro Course

The girl's face turned beet red. "I'm sorry!" she exclaimed, then quickly composed herself. "If you'll come with me, we have some clothes ready for you."

She followed the girl to the room filled with cots and blankets, where she waited while the girl sifted through a large closet. "What's your name?"

The girl fumbled and knocked over a pile of shoeboxes. "Tawny," she said meekly. "My name is Tawny."

"Alright. Tawny. You don't have to be so nervous around me. I'm not this Neese person you guys keep talking about."

Tawny smiled and said nothing. A few minutes later she turned, her arms laden with clothes, dresses, pants, and shoes. She dumped the pile onto the nearest cot. "Please try these on," she said, "and pick whichever one you like."

Beki eyed the pile. "Will they fit?"

Tawny tittered. "They will. I'll go outside and give you some privacy, O.K.?"

Before she could respond, Tawny was out the door, closing it behind her. Sighing, Beki threw the towel aside and began to try on the pile of clothes.

At first glance she had thought they were nothing special, but, upon closer inspection, Beki could feel her eyes growing wider. The pile of clothes were little short of amazing, everything from Egyptian cotton to breathy silk, in styles that rivaled that of the most prestigious brands. There were dresses of crushed velvet, jackets of flawless leather, and pants Cindy Crawford would die to fit into.

She opened the shoebox, and was not very surprised to find a pair of black platform heels that looked like they would be more at home on a red carpet.

The first dress she tried on was a perfect fit, very comfortable, and the sort of dress she would never wear. It was cut low in the back, scooped in front, and hugged her curves like a second skin. The second outfit, a pair of brown pants and dark red top, had the same effect, and once again, were perfect fits. The shoes were in her size, and unbelievably comfortable for heels.

After trying on nearly everything in the pile, she finally settled on a black velvet dress that wasn't quite as tight and revealing as the others.

It was strapless and gave off a soft sheen in the right light. She slipped the matching cropped jacket over her shoulders and crossed the hall to the bathroom.

Rarely in her life had she thought of herself as attractive. She was an average woman, who'd had a child and worked at an average job. The reflection in the mirror, however, begged to differ. Her hair had dried and framed her face on both sides in smooth strands. The dress flattered her figure almost excessively and the contrasting tones made her skin appear white and flawless. She tilted her head slightly to the side and the reflection craned its neck seductively, lips parted in a "come-hither" manner she never thought she'd see on her own face.

She looked just like the woman in the portrait.

Michigan was waiting in the hall when she came out. He looked her up and down and smirked.

"Damn," he said, "you always did clean up well."

She didn't know whether to thank him or tell him to shut it. "I'll have to thank whoever these clothes belong to."

"They're yours." Michigan gave her a crooked grin. "Or rather, they were until you threw them out and they 'magically' wound up here. Didn't I tell you? These guys are your biggest fans."

IMMORTALITY 101: The Intro Course

18
MISTER JEAN-LUC

During her second day of stay at the Rabbit Hole, Rebecca (Neese) Tempest (Highwaters) acquainted herself with the habit of smoking. She didn't especially enjoy the taste of cigarettes, but it was something to do while she paced about trying to sort out her thoughts. The gooey-eyed young men and women who called themselves the "snyperx" milled about, going from one computer screen to another, pausing every now and then to gaze at her adoringly. She had yet to meet this "Great Leader" they kept speaking of and she didn't think she'd care to. The food they provided her consisted of a variety of sweets and caffeinated drinks, which, as far as she could tell, kept them awake and wide-eyed all day and night.

The storage room had a large window rimmed by a wide windowsill. After moving the boxes stacked over it and wiping it off, she found it quite comfortable even if the view was abysmal. Michigan joined her just as she started on her second pack.

"So," he said with what appeared to be genuine concern, "how are you doing?"

She lit a new stick with the dented lighter Tawny had found for her. "I'm still thinking."

"About anything in particular?"

"Just what I should do right about now, with all this information, and this person that I'm supposed to be. You know, in the Round, as you call it, all the little girls want to grow up to be princesses. I didn't think I was already the evil queen." She took a long drag. "But I'm here. You brought me here because you didn't want me to wind up brain dead like that girl Adda, but you said if I stay here I'll just wind up spending the rest of my life here and eventually die. Isn't that right?"

"Yes, if all you do is stay here."

"So what should I do? I can't apologize to her and make everything better. I can't go back because things will just keep getting worse and ruin me."

"I do have a plan, you know. I didn't just bring you here without thinking it through."

She tossed him a slanted glance. "Is that so? From what Stat tells me, you're kind of a drunken idiot."

"I am," Michigan said honestly. "Most of the time. But I thought it through this time, and I had some help, of course. When I finally decided I was going to bring you out, I knew that if I just left you here you'd die eventually, being a Rounder and all. Besides, Stat would never allow you to remain here that long. So, the solution is, you have to fix your Round."

"Fix it?"

"Play another game, win enough good chips to balance out the bad ones, and then go back."

"Can I do that?"

"Anything's possible."

"What about my son?"

Michigan regarded her with amusement. "Why do you still care? He's just another guy playing a Round. If he dies he'll wind up here."

"Yes." She blew a haggard smoke ring into the air. "But... he's my son."

"Give me one of those." She tossed him the pack and the lighter. He lit one skillfully. "I'm really not used to this, you know. The way you are now is nothing like Neese, and if you want to have a chance at winning, fixing your Round, and, yeah, even doing something for your son if you want, you can't keep being so damn... nice."

"Why don't you just tell me what I have to do?"

Michigan took a deep breath. "Sasha knows you're here. I think, at least. I don't know for sure. She's the one who prompted me to bring you here, although I wasn't sure she was seriously expecting me to do it at the time. Not long ago I got word that she's setting up a dice game. It's one of the biggest, highest staked games here. She hasn't held it in a while, and the fact that she's holding it now can't be a coincidence. Well, maybe it is. I don't know. Originally I was going to take you to various games and hope you can win what you need from them, but with the amount of chips you need, the dice game is your best bet for now."

"But I'm not a gambler." Beki chuckled. "I haven't even been to Vegas."

"You don't have to be a good gambler." Michigan smirked darkly. "Do you think the High Rollers got to where they are by being skilled at gambling? Hell no. The High Rollers are skilled, yes, but the only thing they're skilled at is cheating."

(the Queen of Tongues)

"You want to me cheat?"

"You want to save your kid?"

"I suppose arguing for morals don't do much good right now."

"That word has virtually no meaning here, which you'd think would make this a fun place to live, but it doesn't."

Beki put the cigarette out against the windowpane. Ashes drifted down to the windowsill like black snow. "Fine. That's fine. I'll do it. It can't possibly get worse than this, and I can't stand all this thinking any more. If I'm not crazy, it's going to drive me there. Are you going to teach me the right way to cheat, or should I already know just because I'm this Neese person?"

"That would certainly make it easier, wouldn't it?" Michigan tossed the pack of cigarettes back to her. "Unfortunately, it doesn't work like that and, as far as cheating goes, the High Rollers are unrivaled pros, and nothing I could teach you would make a difference against Sasha. But, remember when I said I had some help in planning this?"

As if on cue, a light rapping came on the door, followed by a small, excited voice. "The Great Leader is here," someone said.

"I'll bring her right out," Michigan called, and grinned at Beki. "He's here."

"The Great Leader is your partner in crime?"

"It's not a crime. It's a game, and trust me, he'll be of much more help than me, plus he's something of an insider, so he'll definitely see this through."

"Why would he help me?"

"Because he's a huge fan, too. Come on, let's go meet him."

Unable to think of any reason not to, Beki followed Michigan downstairs. Most of the Snyperx had gathered in the hall, forming a half circle around a man who couldn't look more out of place.

Unlike his nerdy underlings, the Great Leader was tall, sleek, and well-dressed. His hair was dark as the night, smoothed back with gel against his scalp. His features were a sneaky sort of handsome, with a thin nose and high cheekbones. He wore a black suit with a crimson shirt underneath, and Beki silently swore that if she got close enough, she could see the pores on her face in the reflection on his shoes.

When she approached, he straightened, bowed, and brought her hand up for a gentle brush of his lips.

"Ms. Rebecca Tempest," he said. His accent sounded French, but blended in such a way that was difficult to decipher. It was oily and almost unbearably sweet. "Or should I say Lady Neese Highwaters? Welcome back. We have been acquainted in the past, but under the circumstances I will re-introduce myself. I am the owner of the Rabbit Hole and the leader of the Snyperx. My name is Jean-Luc Monaghan."

Peg paced the empty hall on the Crescent's top floor, his feet shuffling heavily against the lush crimson carpet. Every now and then he would crane his neck this way and that, quite a feat considering its thickness. He was nervous. Beyond nervous, absolutely terrified. But he had no choice, did he? At this rate he would never be a High Roller. He'd be someone's minion all his life.

Besides, if the rumors were true, then he had nothing to worry about. He closed his eyes, took a deep breath, and tried to work up his nerve just as a slender arm draped over his shoulder from behind.

"Hi!" came a shrill, cheerful voice. Peg nearly wet himself.

"Damn it, Titi!"

"Peggy-san is having bad thoughts," Titi cooed in a singsong voice, her enormous breasts pressed against his back and giving him a hell of a hard-on. "I'm going to *tell*."

"No you won't. You're not telling *anyone*. We had a deal, remember?"

"Nope. I'm going to tell. Then it'll be lots fun, because Miss Neese will cut your tongue off."

He grabbed her wrist in his meaty paw and yanked her off him like a scarf. "You listen to me, girly," he said, "Miss Neese ain't coming back. Didn't ya hear the story? She's done. She's done in by Sasha B.C. Everybody knows. When she comes out that Round, she's gonna be like that Adda girl, or worse. Then all of this"—he gestured at the luxuries around them—"will be gone. They're gonna carve it up and devour it and I'm gonna get my piece because I'm too damned fat to fight them for it later."

Titi pouted. With her fire-red lipstick and thick collagen lips, it looked like a tomato sprouting where her mouth ought to be. "You have no faith," she chided. "That won't happen. Miss Neese is best. She'll come back."

"Miss Neese is a bitch."

"She is, but that why I love her. If she come back, I'll tell on you. I'll tell her you try to steal from her and call her a bitch. Then you'll be in trouble." She bobbled her head up and down. "Yes, sir. Trouble, trouble, trouble."

"Yea, well, you tell her whatever you want." Peg shoved her aside. Titi stumbled and nearly fell, but the slanted smile never left her face. "When you're telling her, she'll be nothing more than a potato with great legs. She won't give a shit what you tell her. So yeah, when she gets back, go ahead."

"I will," Titi called after him. "You will look like roly-poly bug with arms cut off!"

It took Beki several long moments to look the newcomer over, and to adjust to the sharp contrast he presented opposite his underlings. But she managed a polite smile after drawing back her hand. "Nice to meet you."

IMMORTALITY 101: The Intro Course

He stared at her in surprise. It wasn't too different from the way Stat regarded her when she tried to make conversation with him. Gently, Jean-Luc cradled her face in his hands and sighed. "My goodness," he said, "what have they done to you, my dear Neese? Is this something you chose? And here I thought you were on your way back to us, looking almost as fierce as you once did. Had me fooled. But when I look closer, oh! Those empty eyes, that bland smile. It hurts me."

She had no good answer for him.

"But we have no time for sentiments." He snapped his fingers. "First, a makeover. To play the part, you must look the part. I assume Michigan here has filled you in on how I work?"

"I..."

"You've seen My Fair Lady, yes? One of the best products of the Round in my opinion. Brilliant. Wonderful. Couldn't live without it."

"Well...."

"This will be like that." Jean-Luc went on as he picked at her hair, moving strands, even single hairs, here and there. "You were always prim and posh, so perfect. There cannot be one thing out of place. Surely you understand. This is more than just a game. This is your second debut, the ultimate proof of your power, your style, your beauty, your...."

"Son," Beki cut him off. Slowly, carefully, she moved his hands away from her face. He seemed like the sort of person who loved to touch others but would be offended if touched by someone else. "We are doing this so I can save my son. Nothing else."

He blanched. "Son?" Perfectly tweezed eyebrows swerved to Michigan, who seemed to be trying very hard to vanish behind the stairwell. "You didn't tell me of a son." A gentle frown. It was almost as if he was trying to convey his annoyance without putting unnecessary wrinkles in his smooth skin. "I cannot work if you hide things from me, Michigan Von Phant. It's already a hazard to my person to be working with a lowly person like you, and if you wish to obtain my help in this, which usually does not come cheap, but since this is for..."

"He didn't know." Jean-Luc was obviously unhappy at being interrupted twice, but Beki felt her patience drain as he went on. The guy was a living cartoon. "He just thought he was helping. I want to save my son. He's a Rounder, too, as you call it. Can we get on with it?"

Jean-Luc's face split into a wide grin. "Well," he said cheerfully. "Well, well. You have spark, after all. That's wonderful. Just fabulous. I'll overlook this little matter then, just because I got to see a bit of your old spark. It's worth it, yes. Alright, as you wish, let's begin." He waved his hands in a nonchalant manner. "I do not care about this son of yours, but we are going to win anyway, because it will be fun. Something like this doesn't happen often enough."

"Something like what?"

"Excitement. Try to keep up, dear. I know your brain is all jumbled by that dreadful game, but it has literally been an eternity since we've had a good game. Let's get you pretty and ready. I would sing you a little tune like in those movies made by that man who made the cute little mouse with round ears, but I'm afraid I cannot carry a tune worth a pint."

For the first time in what felt like months, Beki thought about her son. *Really* thought about him. Eric, who had a crush on the girl next door. Eric, who loved to play video games and watch baseball. Eric, who had a warm, even smile like his father. Eric, who had a book report due next week. She wasn't even sure he'd cracked open the book yet. He was a bright, lazy boy who would probably cruise through life without a worry and barely getting by. That thought used to upset her, but now it seemed good enough as long as he had a life to cruise on.

She loved her son. She loved him because she was his mother.

(odd)

The thought was odd. She wasn't sure why. She revisited it on and off, trying to make sense of it. In the back of her mind she seemed to remember describing the accident to someone, in a voice she could barely recognize.

(I mowed him down with my car)

(it was funny)

(haha)

Jean-Luc was tugging at her hair painfully, pulling it this way and that, now up, now down. He made her wash her face, tested various makeup products, produced beautiful jewelry seemingly out of thin air and compared their looks against her skin. His underlings ran in and out of the room, following his every order, tossing an adoring gaze her way every now and then.

"You have to look the part," he kept saying, "*look* the part before you can play it. Oh, I worry about that personality of yours. So darned... what's the word you used, Michigan? Vanilla. Neese was not vanilla. She was so deliciously bitter. You are not half what Neese was, and yet somehow you must fill her shoes. It wounds me. It truly does."

She said nothing. It was just easier that way.

"And you think acting is hard?" he said, as if she had made some remark in that regard. "Playing is harder. Neese was a marvelous player. Wheels, cards, tiles, dice – she could do it all and make everybody else look bad at the same time. And she can cheat. Oh, how she could cheat. It was an art in her hands."

(One used lies; she was called the Queen of Tongues)

"And Sasha. She is a damnable opponent. Admirable, that Sasha B.C. She is just as good at cheating. A real High Roller. But you'll win. No doubt. No worries. Even if she is a tricky one."

(One used trickery; she was called the Queen of Spin)

"Do you have that much faith in me?" Jean-Luc lifted a piece of lint invisible to the naked eye off her dress. Somehow, she felt she already knew the answer to that question when he gave an exasperated sigh.

"You were not listening," he said. "You are a *cheater*. Neese could play, but she cheated much better. You probably cannot play at all. I'm willing to bet my favorite loafers that all you can play is Go Fish. But I have faith in myself, and in my little helpers. We are going to help you cheat. All you do is look pretty and pretend you know what you're doing. Don't let me down." Jean-Luc took a step back and took a hard, invading look at her. "Don't move," he said, and left the room.

The moment he disappeared, Beki let out a long breath and leaned against the nearest wall. Apparently, beauty was tiring.

"Don't do that now."

Somehow, after Jean-Luc's nonstop fussing, Michigan's voice felt like a breath of fresh air. She favored him with a smile.

"Looks like I did something right," he said, returning it as he joined her against the wall. "Seriously, don't do that. He'll yell at you for wrinkling up the dress. That man's got crazy good eyes."

She wrinkled her nose. "You smell like alcohol."

"I snuck down to the Stallion and had a drink." He opened his jacket to reveal a small canteen in the inner pocket. "Got some to go. You like Vodka? Want some?"

"I do," she said honestly. "I really, really do."

He handed it to her. The first swig made her eyes water and burned going down. The second made her head swim. She must have made some colorful facial expressions, because Michigan looked as if he was trying hard to contain his snickers.

"What am I doing?" she asked, capping the canteen.

"Well, let's see. You're pretending to be someone you're not so your son can have a fighting chance. It's a bit silly the way we see it, but hey, for a Rounder, it's a noble cause."

"No, I mean what am I doing? What game is this? Craps? Blackjack? Poker? I only know a little Blackjack. Everything else is beyond me. How am I supposed to cheat if I don't even know the rules?"

Michigan regarded her in surprise. "You're getting into this," he said incredulously. "You're actually getting into it."

She laughed dryly. "I am. God help me."

"God cannot help you if you wrinkle up that dress."

Quickly, not unlike a mouse holding a piece of cheese when the kitchen lights lit up, Michigan scurried into a far corner as Jean-Luc entered, a large white object draped over his arms. As he drew closer, Beki saw that it was a garment bag, the sort used for tuxedos and wedding dresses.

"Try this on," he said to her, dumping the bag into her arms. "Let's see if we can turn Cinderella into the evil queen of Neverland."

She thought about correcting him on the numerous referential errors in that statement, but Jean-Luc seemed so pleased with it that she decided not to kill his buzz. As he left again he took special care to give Michigan a disapproving glance as Beki tried her hardest not to drop the huge garment bag.

"He doesn't like me," Michigan informed her, pushing himself off the wall with his foot. "He thinks having me around lowers your re-sell value, so to speak. I'll be outside." He began to follow Jean-Luc out, but at the door, he paused and turned. "I have a question," he said. "Something I always wanted to ask a Rounder but never got a chance to."

"What is it?"

With one finger, he pointed at his right temple as if ready to shoot himself in the head. "Can you feel her in there?"

(her)

She tried. For a brief moment she closed her eyes and tried to picture herself as someone other than the normal, boring, Good Samaritan she was raised to be, but someone else.

(Neese Highwaters)

Someone who wore beautiful clothes, did half the populace wrong without batting an eye, and charmed the other half into servitude.

(the Queen)

She opened her eyes. "No," she told him with a tired smile. "Not at all. Not even a little."

It seemed to her that Michigan tried to hide the disappointment on his face, though she wished he wouldn't. "That's too bad," he said with a shrug that seemed very, very heavy as it fell. "I was... hoping."

Jean-Luc took a quick break on the only balcony on the second floor of the Rabbit Hole, smiling as he thought about his new Cinderella. That was what she was – a pauper princess to be molded, and a Rounder to boot. It was all too perfect. He thought about what other pretty things he could make her put on.

He removed a cigar from his inner jacket pocket, bit off the tip, and put it into his mouth. He only smoked cigars when he felt a very specific combination of emotions, which right now was a nice mix of guilt and excitement. He felt a little remorseful for going behind Sasha's back, even if he never did declare his loyalty to her, unlike those wispy Spin Doctors she kept around. He liked her. She was a little ball of spunk who shared his flair for fashion. In some ways, they were very close and very similar.

Jean-Luc was a man of style. His life was one of whimsy and color, flares and silks. For this, he dearly loved fairy tales. Those Rounders came up with the most interesting stories. In fact, he'd written a few himself back when he used to play in the Round, but almost none of them could last the test of time. There was one, though, one about a little wooden puppet who wanted desperately to experience the desires and passions of a real boy. It became grossly misinterpreted as time wore on, but at least it was something.

He forgot to light the cigar, but decided it didn't matter. There was something to be said for oral fixations.

Fun as she was, Sasha was a bit of a fool at times, though that was to be expected, stuck in a child's body as she was, with the mind, wisdom, and passions of a woman who had lived too long and done too much. Jean-Luc hadn't paid much attention to her little game before – the rivalry between High Rollers wasn't in his interest nowadays. But then she called for a game. That was different. He, like anyone else, still loved games, and he knew exactly what she wanted – to win. She wanted to win against Neese, who was as good as brain-dead at this point. To go as she was now, Neese would be ensured a devastating loss, and he couldn't allow that.

He didn't care very deeply for either of them when it came to the grab for victory, but he couldn't allow a perfectly good game to go to waste. If there was going to be a game, it was going to be exciting, grand, and majestic. He wanted it to have pizzazz, excitement, to regain the thrill it once held.

Looking up at the dull, blank ceiling of the dome, he briefly wondered what was outside, and then decided he didn't care, not when he had such a lovely doll at his disposal. He was going to carve a princess out of that pumpkin.

News never took long to spread. When people had nothing to do besides gamble, drink, shoot up, and fuck, and when all news traveled by gossip, everything spread like wildfire. Everyone listened, and everyone talked. Ears opened and tongues wagged. *What's the story? What's the story? Is it true or false? Does anyone care if it's true or false?*

IMMORTALITY 101: The Intro Course

One thing was for sure – Sasha's gallery was closed. The rumors of a dice game grew by the moment the longer it stayed closed. There was no need for paid advertisement. Everything spread by word of mouth.

Why now? Why a dice game? Who will be there? What will they wear?

Someone claimed they saw inside the gallery. The large Wheel had been removed, they said, and three small ones had been set up. Silks hung everywhere, all in dazzling gold and silver shades. If the game was indeed happening, then it was also true that there was a leaked roster of notable players. Everyone can play, but not everyone can afford the stakes for entry into later rounds unless they were very, very lucky and/or extraordinarily skilled. In a world ruled by games, these notable players were royalty.

Prescott Asher was among the names. She was one to be reckoned with, and if she was playing, Lisa Gasolina just might make an appearance.

Rat Spence. His name had appeared, but he was not reliable. He did not, after all, attend the last three games he supposedly signed up for. Many suspected some follower of his continuously enrolled him in games. In vain, of course.

Gypsy Hoss, the handler of Small Favors. For her, it was personal.

Bice Tic, one of the fallen, hoping once more to claw his way back up to the throne of a High Roller.

One of the Wonder Twins is coming. Just one. Rumor has it the other one's in the Round.

And, the one of most interest and which spawned the most gossip, Neese Highwaters.

How? Why? It couldn't be.

Some say she was in the middle of a Round, but some claim to have seen her in the recent past. Supposedly Sasha was about to break her, or had broken her. She wasn't to come back whole. But yet, could that really happen? It's Neese. She's a fortress, a winner. Even Sasha couldn't possibly break her. Rumors. Rumors. More rumors.

Voices overlapped, bodies milled about like agitated ants. Eager spectators began to camp outside Sasha's gallery, hoping for a prime view when the game began.

Had Sasha known all this, she would have been very pleased, but she was too busy with her own endeavors. With the games coming up in four days, she had shut herself in. Even Jean-Luc wasn't to disturb her at this crucial time. She sat in the corner by the window, rolling her treasure over in her hand, inspecting every corner and side.

It wasn't a dice game, because there was only one die that mattered, and so much rode on this single die. It would be the single trigger to the rebirth of the true High Rollers.

IMMORTALITY 101: The Intro Course

19
THE THING THAT HELPS

"I have a lot of questions."

"Shoot," Michigan said through the door as she changed. "You may not like all the answers but I'll give them a fair shot."

"First things first, then. What is this place exactly? Is it some sort of parallel universe?"

"I guess you can say it's another universe. But it's definitely not parallel to whatever you're used to. Think of it as a dotted line – the Round are the lines, this is the spaces, or alternatively, two lines winding around one another, intersecting at some points. I'm not good with the metaphysical stuff, and honestly, I haven't ever tried to explain it to a Rounder."

"Fair enough. Am I crazy?"

"If I said 'yes', would it matter?"

"No, not really, I guess. Why did those guys jump on me?"

"They thought you were Stat. I did, too for a moment. He got us pretty good with that one, wearing my jacket and all."

"How could you confuse us? We look nothing alike."

"Remember how I said he looks different depending on who's looking? We all saw your face on him."

"I'm flattered."

The long forest-green gown flowed from her left shoulder along her curves like paint poured over the skin. The hem flared out slightly like the tail of a mermaid. In the right light, it glistened – sure to catch curious eyes. In shadows, it seemed to darken itself, giving an air of coy mystery.

More and more, Beki marveled at how little she recognized herself in the mirror. It was an eerie feeling.

"How do I cheat?"

"Jean-Luc has a plan. I'm not privileged enough to be in on it."

"What does he get out of this?"

"He's bored. This will keep him entertained for a while."

"Seems that's the only reason anybody does anything around here. Where I come from, people would kill, lie, and steal to be immortal. Now I'm really starting to rethink the whole eternal life thing." She looked at herself in the full-length mirror against the wall. "Does she love you?"

A long silence fell over the room. She had just begun to suspect Michigan was gone when he answered a quick, hard, "no."

"I didn't think so." With her hand, she slowly brushed a thick lock of hair off her bared shoulder. Jean-Luc had done a great job indeed. Even the women who frequented red carpets would eat their hearts out for such a talented beautician. "She looks like a mean woman. When I look at myself in a mirror, I think, 'if I saw a woman like this on the street, I'd steer clear'. She looks too proud to love, and she makes a living by cheating people. Why do you love her, anyway?"

It was meant to be a rhetorical question, and she didn't expect a reply, but she heard Michigan give a wistful sigh before replying, "because she's amazing."

Beki turned away from the mirror. "I just want you to know," she said, "I'm not doing this for anyone else but me and my son."

A light chuckle from behind the door. "That's fine. Here, no one does anything for the sake of strangers. You may not realize it, but you fit right in."

She had expected that thought to give her a mild wave of nausea, but it didn't. She looked down at herself. "If I don't manage to do something before my son dies, would he wind up here while I'm still here?"

"Most likely."

"I bet my husband has already filed a missing person's report," she mused with a sad laugh. "I haven't even thought about it until just now, but I've been here for more than a day."

"Actually," Michigan replied, "you've been here for more than two days. You slept a pretty damned long time on that beanbag. But don't worry, the Round is much slower than here – they can get more bets in that way. I don't know the current exchange rate, but I'd say it's been no more than two hours over there."

She was well past being surprised at anything at this point.

Rebecca Tempest began dating her husband while finishing up her second year in college. He was a year ahead and not bad to look at. The initial attraction was physical. But then, most attractions were. Anyone who denied it was usually lying. Physical attraction led to something a little more, then a little more, and they were married a year after college.

It was one of those things one didn't appreciate unless comparing to something worse. For all those years they lived a dull, boring life, undisturbed by famine, war, drought, or terrorist attacks. When a plane flew into the World Trade Center, they went home early and watched clips on television. When anthrax, SARS, and the chicken flu supposedly posed threats to the survival of the human race, they never got a box full of suspicious powders on their porch. They never smashed their car against rogue tree stumps and their son never thought smoking was cool, at least not yet.

She worked as a number-cruncher; he was a certified computer nerd.

In their life, there were no revolution, no jihads, no vendettas, and very few burnt dinners. They caught the housing bubble at just the right time, played the stock market with moderate success, and didn't have to feed their son Ritalin. They went to work in the morning, came home at night, had dinner as a family, and occasionally argued over whose turn it was to do the dishes. It was one of those dull, plain existences. A statistic, if you would.

Rebecca Tempest was a statistic. She was one of billions of women, one of millions of accountants, and a reasonably good mother. Her hair was brown and her skin was light. She wore suits to work and jeans and sweatshirts at home. She'd never been to Las Vegas but had been to Atlantic City twice. On one of those trips she won two hundred dollars on a single pull of the slot machine. She would have gone through life not remembering which trip it was.

But now she remembered. For no particular reason, she remembered that it was during the first trip. She had just turned twenty-one, and it was the last trip she took with her great aunt before the old woman's health deteriorated. It was a slot machine with pictures of pirates, wenches, monkeys, and treasure chests. She had hit three wenches. Had she hit three treasure chests, she would have won over a thousand dollars.

There's no logical reason why she would remember a thing like that, so she went with everything she'd seen in movies and read in novels growing up. The explanation, she figured, was because, deep down, she really was this Neese person, who seemed to be obsessed with games and winning, so by nature she was able to remember every time she won, including any details she could possibly use in the future to ensure she won some more. It didn't matter that she knew next to nothing about Neese Highwaters, but a guess was better than nothing. It gave her mind something to do while her body underwent its transformation.

And, though she didn't know it, she was pretty close to the mark.

Jean-Luc wasn't touching her hair anymore. He stepped back, hands on his waist, and tilted his head this way and that. She didn't know or care what she looked like.

"OK, children," he said, clapping his hands, "time for makeup."

She stopped the makeup brush half an inch from her face. "Can we take a break first?"

Jean-Luc's displeasure was apparent.

"Just five minutes. I'm tired." She leaned forward in what she hoped was a seductive way, although whether Jean-Luc threw straight or curved balls was still somewhat of a question mark. "Please?"

He sighed in exasperation. Either she exasperated him often or it was just a habit of his. Every time he began to sigh, she thought it might be awfully fun to reached up and flick his nose as hard as she could, just to see if he could choke that sigh back down his throat.

"Fine," he said after a nice, dramatic pause. "Five minutes. And don't touch the do."

"Ten."

"You said five."

"I lied."

Michigan was fidgeting absently in the hall as usual. A crowd of Synperx members milled around when she exited. She acknowledged them politely and most of them swooned. Then she nodded to Michigan. "I hope you have smokes."

He patted his breast pocket. "Always."

"Is there a more private place around here?"

"There's a balcony up on top. It's a little rickety but no one's ever fixed it. Just don't lean too hard on the railing and you should be fine."

She lit her own smoke again. Was that three times in three days? Four? Five? She lost count. It all came too naturally. Seemed Neese was quite the chain smoker. She probably had a high tolerance for alcohol, too. Those things tend to go hand in hand.

"Does the sun ever come up in this place?" she asked, gazing up at the sky that seemed to be perpetually black.

"Once in a while. Not always. Think the generators are on the fritz again."

"Okay," she said. They smoked in silence for a while. "I need a small favor right now."

"Name it."

She gestured at the door behind them, in the general direction of the cot room. "Can you go grab me a pillow?"

"What for?" he asked, and went to get it without waiting for an answer. She was nearly finished with the cigarette by the time he returned. "Found you a clean one. These guys don't do a lot of laundry."

She took it from him. "Thanks. There's just one last thing I have to do before I can keep doing all of this. I think it'll make things a little easier after I do it."

"If you just pretend you're dead, all of this wouldn't seem so confusing."

"Let me try my way first," she said, pressed the pillow against her face, and screamed into it. The thick cotton and starchy fabric muffled her shrieks. It sounded ridiculous even to her own ears. She screamed until her throat was hoarse and dry, and then she screamed some more. Finally, she lowered the pillow, brushed a lock of hair out of her face, and handed the pillow back to a simultaneously mortified and amused Michigan. "Thanks."

"Did that help?"

"Immeasurably."

Jean-Luc walked around her like a panther circling its prey. Or an ape in heat. It was hard to tell which. His eyes went from ecstasy to disapproval to annoyance to jubilation to confusion to deep in thought. Finally, as if with a conscious decision of their own, they settled on a look of misty triumph. A large group of his minions were peeking inside, their heads piled on top of one another, struggling for a better look. He slowly turned around.

"A masterpiece," he announced. "It is a success."

There was cheering, and clapping. Beki looked down at herself.

"You can't be serious."

"I can and am," Jean-Luc said, turning with a sharpness that dared her, absolutely dared her, to question his superior taste some more. "You know nothing, you sad little woman. I have struggled and strived to build you into half of what the glorious Neese once was, so you just hush up and appreciate it."

"Yeah, well," Beki replied, "bite me."

In all honesty, she didn't so much disapprove of Jean-Luc's final design as she was confused by it. After the seemingly endless parade of silks, leathers, buckles, dangling jewelry, strapped heels, and diamond-encrusted knickknacks, she was certain she would walk out of this place dressed for the red carpet, draped in Egyptian cotton or Asian silk with the weight of million-dollar jewels cramping her neck, and the Snyperx crowding around cooing, "Who are you wearing? Who are you wearing? It's by Jean-Luc, isn't it? You look smashing!"

But something was off. She looked at herself again. It couldn't be right. Instead of Gucci and Prada, he had put her in a pair of faded jeans and an oversized green sweater cinched at the waist by a wide black leather belt.

"I don't understand," she said. "I thought you were going to put me into something... fancier."

"Fancy?" Jean-Luc scoffed. "You're right; you really don't understand. It is not about the fancifulness. It's about luxury and effortless corpulence, style without the burden of fashion. We still need the finishing touches." A snap of the finger and a box was brought to him. He handed it to her. "Put these on."

She lifted the lid. Inside was a pair of black open-toe heels. The top cover was surprisingly soft to the touch and she guessed that it was formed by layers of silk. A thin strap went around each ankle twice. The real eye-catchers, however, were the emeralds.

There was one on top of each shoe, the size of a small marble and perfectly round. An excruciatingly intricate pattern that reminded Beki of hedge mazes she'd seen in photos of old English castles had been carved onto their surfaces. Beki could not remember a time in her life when she had been around real emeralds. Most of her jewelry items were semi-cheap imitations, and she had never thought of herself as knowledgeable in the ways of jewels. But one look at these precious stones told her they were real, genuine. Unlike their owner, they were immeasurably pure.

"Lovely, no?" Jean-Luc said with a smirk. "I call them Oz Greens."

She lifted them out of the box. They were surprisingly heavy. The sole and heel were made of a black, flawless stone. Perhaps onyx or obsidian.

"Shoes fitting for Cinderella."

Beki looked up at him. "Cinderella wore glass shoes."

"Only because she was a poor girl who had no sense of style. Can you imagine trying to walk like a princess in those clunky glass things?" He actually shuddered at the thought. "Horrible."

She slipped them on, well aware of the many eyes following her fingers as she knotted the straps around her ankles. Jean-Luc seemed as if he might pounce on her at any moment and berate her for wearing them wrong. They were very cold. The chill snaked from the bottom of her feet up her calves, thighs, all the way up to the crook of her neck.

"Pauper girls wear Mary-Janes," Jean-Luc said. "Princesses wear glass slippers. Queens wear Oz Greens."

"That'll look great on a billboard."

"Don't be cheeky. Those are loans."

"Fine, I'll give them back to you after…" After what? She still wasn't sure.

"Not back to me, Missy. You give those back to Neese after you're done. As far as I'm concerned, you two are two separate people."

Beki took a deep breath. "As far as *I'm* concerned," she said, "your fly has been open for the last three hours."

While Jean-Luc fumbled with himself in an angry sort of embarrassment, Beki held her head high and allowed the coldness of the Oz Greens to seep into her. It was strange, foreign, and alien. She expected a pair of shoes that belonged to Neese, her other half, to feel oddly familiar, but it only felt like an invasion. The heat of her body attempted to reject the cold, the way the immune system rejected a parasite, but it wouldn't go away. Stubbornly, the cold stayed.

She thought about *The Matrix* for the first time since Michigan brought it up. When they first inserted that metal rod into Neo's neck, it must have felt like this. It felt like an honest, legitimate reason to dislike that movie, at least in her mind. She half-expected to start hearing Neese's voice in her head, her own voice with a twisted edge, telling her what to do, how to walk, how to talk, and not to scuff up those shoes.

Nothing. Silence. She looked down at the shoes. They were very pretty.

"Is this it?"

Jean-Luc looked up in a huff, obviously upset at having his flawless visage disturbed. "Yes," he said shortly. "This is it."

"Then why did you put me in all those other outfits?"

"Because," the man replied with an uncharacteristically mischievous grin, "I always wanted to dress up Neese Highwaters like a doll."

Michigan stared when he came in. From the windowsill where she sat, Beki pretended not to notice as she drank the cold cup of water brought by one of her admirers. It was too cold, almost freezing, and she hadn't asked for it. It seemed they knew what she wanted, or rather what Neese wanted. From what she's heard so far, the water must match her frigid personality. She let Michigan stare at her until she ran out of water.

"Do I look good?"

"Um," he said with an embarrassed chuckle, "I, uh... you look like..."

She didn't try to stop his awkward stammering. Michigan tore his eyes from her with visible effort. The air in the room suddenly grew thick. Sighing, she proceeded to tear the Styrofoam cup into small pieces and let them fall to the floor like so many sloppy snowflakes. Someone would clean it up later. Though she hated posing as a stranger, having people cater to and clean up after her was quite habit-forming.

"What do I do now?"

"Jean-Luc didn't tell you?"

"He was kind of upset after I pointed out that his fly was open."

"Yeah," Michigan said with an absent nod. "Jean-Luc's kind of a jackass. But he knows what he's doing. Now the fun part starts."

Her stomach threatened to sink from dread. To drive away the feeling, Beki pushed her feet against the floor, concentrating on the coolness of the Oz Greens. As an afterthought, she knocked the heels together. The dull "clack" that resulted wasn't quite like Dorothy's clinking heels. "There's a fun part?"

"Sure. Right now you just look like Neese. But if you're really going to pass yourself off as her, you have to *be* her. You've already been here too long since you came back. We have to take you out and parade you around a little, make people think that Neese is actually back. Then you have to go home."

"Home?"

"Your home. Neese's home, I mean. I haven't ever been inside except in the lower floors, where the casinos are, but I hear it's pretty swanky. You'll have to go by yourself." From his pocket he produced a pair of small dangling earrings in the shape of golden crescent moons. "Jean-Luc's masterpiece. This one's a microphone. That one's a camera. Put them on and Jean-Luc will tell you what to do from here. Just follow his instructions."

She took the earrings. They felt as cold in her ears as the shoes. "This is like a bad spy movie," she said. "Why can't you come with me?

And why do I need instructions to go home?" Michigan stared at her again. "What? What'd I say?"

"Nothing," Michigan said with a quick clear of the throat. "Nothing. Just that you wanted me to come with you and…"

Beki got to her feet and dropped what was left of the cup on the floor. Surprised by her sudden movement, Michigan took a step back as she invaded his personal space in a way that surprised even herself. "Look," she said, "I'm not her. Get it into your head. I don't care if we share the same body or what, but I am *not* her!"

"All right!" Backing up and nearly falling over a pile of clothes, Michigan nodded sheepishly. "All right. You're not her. I get it. It's a little hard to ignore when you look just like her."

Beki sighed. "I'm sorry."

"Don't apologize. Neese never apologizes. You should start getting into the habit as soon as possible."

"Why can't I just stay here until…" she paused, realizing she didn't know how to finish the sentence.

"It's too complicated. All you have to do right now is get into the part so your cover won't get blown. There are already people out there who are suspecting that you're faking, and if you don't go home that'll just fuel the gossip, which will undermine your game, which will make you lose, which means you'll never save your kid." He arched an eyebrow at her bewildered look. "Are you OK with that? Need a pillow to scream into before you leave?"

She gave it some serious consideration. "No. I'm fine."

"Good." Like a party trick he produced a small yellow pill. "Here. Take this."

She looked at it. It suspiciously resembled an M&M. "What for?"

"It'll help you… mellow out some." Seeing her hesitation, he pushed his palm closer to her. "Come on, please? It's the same stuff Stat gave you in the tea. It'll help you relax. I'm sure you're nervous right now."

She swallowed it dry, surprising him as much as herself. If she waited, she knew she would only stop herself. In this world, it seemed the easiest way to get things done was to think as little as possible. Michigan looked too dim to poison her, and even if it was poison… well, she still hadn't quite ruled out the whole "dead" thing yet. Michigan looked impressed.

20
TITI CHANG AND THE CRESCENT

As it turned out, 'swanky' wasn't the best word to describe the Crescent. A better word, Beki thought, as she ascended the towering structure's front steps, half a dozen teetering followers trailing just out of earshot, would be 'majestic', or 'grandiose', or 'awe-inspiring', or 'extravagant'. 'Swanky' was a word used to describe a bachelor pad with a hot tub and a five-thousand-dollar surround sound. The Crescent was a contemporary palace.

For starters, it was enormous. Standing on its steps, she felt like an ant being dwarfed by an elephant. The feeling only lasted a split second, however, as Jean-Luc's voice boomed into her head from the tiny microphone on her ear. The sound quality was shockingly good.

"Own it!" he was yelling as she stood there gaping. "Act like you own it, you stupid…"

She pinched the earring between two fingers and sneered in mild satisfaction as Jean-Luc's voice fainted into a soft muffling blur. She considered taking it out and dropping it somewhere, maybe even stepping on it, but the noises behind her told her that listening to Jean-Luc was her best bet right now.

She had picked them up on her short trek through the town. Michigan had described to her in detail the half-hour walk to the Crescent and with every block she passed the group had grown. They were trailing her with a pretentious subtleness, following her but pretending to be occupied with something else the moment she turned around. They followed and gawked and talked amongst themselves.

And taking photos – actually taking photos of her. Every time she lifted her finger a flash went off just beyond the corner of her eye. Once or twice they even jumped in front of her, camera poised and ready to strike.

"Come on, Neese!" a young man wearing a red beret and a skinny mustache shouted, grinning widely as the flashbulb blinded her more with each flash. "Give us a pose!"

"Is it true you went into the Round?" a middle-aged woman yelled, thick lips flailing as she spoke. "Is it true you took an illegal exit? Is it? Is it??"

She had, of course, been warned of them. Both Michigan and Jean-Luc had repeated the golden rule to her for dealing with the 'stalkers', and that was to *ignore them*. In truth it wasn't exactly what she had imagined. In her mind, she saw people pointing and whispering as she passed, perhaps craning their necks to see if she was truly the great Neese Highwaters. She had been fully prepared to walk with her head held high, pretending to be proud and mighty as she strolled past the on-lookers. But this was different. For the first time since hearing the woman's name, Beki realized what her role truly was.

Neese Highwaters was a celebrity.

She kept walking through the crowd. Michigan was right about one thing: they didn't approach her. Not one person entered a seven-foot radius of her.

"Don't worry, they won't come near you," Michigan had said. "Neese hits."

"What if someone does get close?" she had asked nervously.

"Then you will have to hit them. Balled fist, bridge of the nose. Don't worry about hurting them either. They'll love it."

As she hadn't hit anyone since the boy who pushed her into the dirt in kindergarten, Beki spent the entire time dreading having to hit someone. She couldn't imagine herself doing it, especially since she couldn't even spank her son for misbehaving. Luckily, no one broke the unspoken perimeter, and as she approached the Crescent, they began to trail farther and farther behind her.

Now, seeing her hesitation, they began to approach again, like hungry rodents suddenly realizing that the big bad coyote wasn't so tough after all.

"Flip them off," Jean-Luc said, "flip them off and go inside the front door. Do it quickly."

She did as she was told. It sent a dozen cameras flashing.

As far as she could tell, there were no vehicles in this place. There were roads, however, filled with potholes and marked with fading yellow lines. It looked as if someone was periodically re-painting the lines, though she couldn't imagine what for. Once or twice she saw bicycles lying in disheveled piles on one street corner or another, abandoned and left to rot. Everyone seemed to walk with an unhurried swagger, as if they were in no hurry to be anywhere.

The town seemed small. Even though it appeared to extend infinitely into what she now figured was a dome, it felt very small. People milled about like ants, their scalps showered in cheap neon. A clock with a broken face atop a small gray building read thirty minutes after one, but she wasn't sure whether it was a.m. or p.m. The ground was littered with colorful pieces of paper; most of which were printed with photos of nude women who belonged to some group called "Pink Pony". She assumed they were a band.

There was not a bright light to be seen anywhere. People felt their way around in the dim, dirty light like moles. Every now and then they lifted their faces to one neon sign or another as if in awe, rather like a fly staring at a bug zapper. She could smell alcohol, cigarettes, and sweat in the air, a mixture of scents she was gradually becoming used to. There was something else, too. Something she hadn't noticed before. It was the subtle fragrance of cheap luxury and pretentious wealth, like a temporary high that lasted forever, strangely repulsive and alluring at the same time.

The flashing cameras and shouts as she passed by made her wonder if this was truly how celebrities lived. If so, Beki felt she suddenly understood why the stars had made a second nature out of indulgences and vices.

Her trip did not take her past the triangular square; Jean-Luc had instructed her to avoid all locations where she was likely to run into Status Quo, apparently unaware that the two were already on first-name basis. Beki didn't feel like informing him, being in the process of nursing a serious distain for Jean-Luc.

IMMORTALITY 101: The Intro Course

The streets seemed to fan out in a strange, inefficient way. She crossed a street at one point that grew wider to one side and narrower to the other for no apparent reason. Street signs were unstructured and unhelpful – the same street could be named one thing for two blocks, another for three, then back to its original name for a few more blocks. In fact, the signs themselves looked as if they'd been painted over many times, perhaps at the whims of the passersby. As she approached Neese's house, she saw what were once stop signs painted entirely yellow with large, three-stroke smiley faces. There were a total of eight leading toward the house, then they stopped a few hundred yards away. She couldn't begin to guess what purpose, if any, they served.

The front of the mansion was open to the public. The double doors, as wide as ten of her and twice as tall, were constructed from dark wood and thick, clean glass. The building itself was laid out very much like a hotel or casino. The door swung open before she could put her weight on it and a young woman slammed into her with full force, nearly knocking the wind out of her.

"Miss Neese!" the newcomer shrieked happily, her enormous breasts squeezed so tightly against Beki she feared they might burst. "You're back, you're back!"

"That's Titi Chang," said Jean-Luc as if that explained everything. "Push her away and say…"

"What did I say about touching me?"

Titi grinned. Possessing no expertise in differentiating Asian cultures, Beki guessed she was Japanese, Chinese, or some sort of Filipino mix. Her hair was dark and straight, and her skin had the sort of natural tan that came from birth as opposed to the sun. She was short, perhaps just over five feet, and her breasts stuck out like skin stretched over two rice bowls. She was also missing one arm. The sleeve of her outfit concealed the stump that seemed to end just past the shoulder.

"You say not touch," she said. Her accent, like her cherry lips, was very thick. Her eyes, round and colorful, reminded Beki of the large marbles the boys in her elementary school used to play with. In the nurses' outfit she wore, she looked as if she had just rolled out of a porno. "I'm just glad you back, Miss Neese. There's mean people out there saying nasty things, but I don't believe, no sir." She shook her head hard from side to side. Beki noted with slight amusement that her hair did not seem to move. Straight and long, it hung over her shoulders and generous bust line like wire. For all she knew, it was a wig. "I told them, I knew Miss Neese would come back. I told Peggy-san..."

"Alright, shut up," Beki said without waiting for Jean-Luc's order. The girl's voice was irritating her, she suddenly noticed. It grated on her raw nerves like sandpaper. And her outfit was so tacky. So unfitting of this place that seemed to burst with class and luxury. Her mannerisms were cheap and she was obviously a brownnoser, which might be the only reason Neese kept her around.

The reason I keep her around.

Titi circled her, leaping about like a puppy that had finally found its mistress. Beki expected her to stick out her tongue and pant.

"I draw you bath," Titi clamored excitedly. "I draw bath like you like it, Miss Neese. On third floor. Then I help you wash, just like old days!"

Beki opened her mouth to protest just as Jean-Luc hissed loudly in her ear, *"let her!"* By the time she'd recovered from the buzzing in her ear, Titi was already half way down the hall, leaving her alone in the echoing silence.

Actually, it wasn't quite an echoing silence. Standing with her back to the front door, Beki suddenly realized how noisy her new surrounding was. There was the metallic clanking of coins, the drunken clamor of gamblers, and the sound of drinks being poured and spilled. Even the smells that saturated the air were loud. Thick, obnoxious cigars, body odor, vinyl that had held one too many sweaty behinds... and she thought she could even smell the oil on the corners of ancient cards being dealt out again and again. Titi's sudden appearance had distracted her, but now, as she stood there taking it all in, she felt one singular feeling welling up inside her chest – nausea. The penetrating sounds and scents were filling her chest as if they were being funneled directly through her senses. She wanted to gag.

To her right was the hall down which Titi had disappeared. Beki saw the girl's wiggling behind disappear around the corner. To her left was a shorter hall that led to a double-arched carved door. It was at least three inches thick, carved with intricate designs of nude Grecian nymphs. The top half of the doors was fitted with wavy cascaded glass. Stepping close, Beki could make out the shapes of those on the other side.

The casino floor was vast, and absolutely packed. She had never seen so many people gambling at once in Atlantic City. Usually there would be empty chairs here and there, even during the peak hours. But try as she could, she couldn't spot a single empty slot machine. The card tables were packed, too. The closest was filled with overweight patrons, most of whose genders she couldn't quite make out, their meaty shoulders pushing into each other's personal spaces. One was raising a hand, pointing at the dealer and trying to start an argument. The dealer, a young man dressed in an impeccable tuxedo, slid a hand through his sleek hair and spoke a few quiet words. The gambler instantly shrank back into her spot. Glancing around, Beki saw that all the male dealers and waiters were dressed in tuxedos fit for the red carpet, and the females were in clad in gray, shimmering silk dresses that hung off one shoulder and ended just above the knees. Beki thought she'd seen something similar in a high-end mall back home. The price tag dwarfed her bi-weekly paycheck by more than two-fold.

To say Neese Highwaters had extravagant tastes would be an understatement, she thought to herself.

At the moment, standing in the alcove just inside the door, she realized for the umpteenth time that she wasn't sure what she ought to do. The nausea was turning into a headache and the place as a whole felt stuffy and offending to the senses. She rubbed her temples in annoyance and reminded herself that this was all for Eric. Fortunately, at least, the alcove hid her from prying eyes.

"What are you doing?" Jean-Luc's voice seeped through the microphone. "Turn right, go down the hall, and take the stairs to third. Don't let anyone see you. It's bad enough that you had to go through the streets. Pretty soon everyone's going to know that you're there and it's going to be pandemonium. Do you hear me? *Pandemonium!*"

"Pandemonium," she repeated. "Right. What do I do when I get there?"

"Take a bath. Do whatever Titi wants to do, just don't talk to her too much. She may act like a loony but she's pretty sharp, and she will wag that tongue of hers to anyone who's got an ear. Just go upstairs for now. Take the *stairs*. There's only two rooms on the third floor and Neese's room is the one at the end of the hall."

"How do you know all this about her?" Beki asked, heading down the hall. Before she reached the stairwell, however, she spotted three shiny doors standing side by side. Elevators. She wasn't surprised to see that the arrows on the call buttons were formed with small diamonds.

"Well," Jean-Luc scoffed. "Not that it's any of your business, but the lovely Neese Highwaters and I were once lovers." Someone coughed in the background, sounding as if he were trying to muffle laughter. Jean-Luc yelled at him to shut it. "I know all there is to know about her. Her styles, her tastes, her house, even her favorite positions."

"You're not gay?"

"What?"

"Nothing. I'm getting in the elevator now."

As she'd expected, the third floor looked like the hall of a luxurious hotel. The hall was wide and led to a large gym at one end, filled with every piece of exercise equipment Beki had seen in her life and a few she had not. The colorless field of steel made the gym look like a torture chamber. She wondered if Neese forced her staff to exercise every day to maintain their beautiful figures. At the other end of the hall was a single large door. When she approached, she noticed a keypad attached to the wall immediately next to it.

"Jean-Luc? What's the code?"

Silence. She tapped the earring with one finger.

"Hey, Jean-Luc! I'm sorry I called you gay. What's the code into her room?"

Silence again. Beki looked around quickly to make sure she was alone, then slipped the earring out of her ear. She held it up to the light and studied it. Having as much expertise as an electrician as she did at categorizing Asian people, she could see no visible damage and reasoned that something in the elevator must have shorted it. Electromagnetic waves or something. Eric or Jonathan would know better. She slipped off the other one. The pinpoint camera lens looked dark and dead, although she wasn't sure what it looked like before. Suddenly, she realized she was completely alone.

IMMORTALITY 101: The Intro Course

As she stood there debating whether to risk triggering an alarm by punching in the wrong code or simply turn tail and run, the door swung open. It was all she could do to stop herself from gasping and jumping back.

Titi grinned at her and stepped back, gesturing for her to enter. "Come in, Miss Neese," she said, "come in. I took too long. I'm sorry." She slapped her own cheek playfully. "Bad Titi!"

Beki swallowed thickly and stepped into the room. It was a suite and, from where she stood, looked bigger than her entire house. In front of her was a large living room, with an enormous black leather couch and a matching sofa, arranged in front of a flat screen television bigger than anything she'd ever seen in a Best Buy. *What kind of programs do they air in the afterlife?* she wondered. To the right was a bedroom with a large canopy bed draped in layers of silk and cotton. The bedposts were decorated with ornate jewels, luxurious and just bordering on gaudy. If she were to let down the thick red drapery, the tent it formed could comfortably hold four or five. To the left were two doors, one closed and the other ajar, tendrils of steam snaking out from the gap.

"Come, Miss Neese," Titi called and gestured, "come!"

Beki's head was swimmy and, for the first time since she had left the Rabbit Hole, she remembered the pill Michigan told her to take. It had seemed like a harmless pill, but she never did find out what it did. Absently, she followed Titi to the bedroom, where she paused by the bed, half admiring the indecently expensive fabrics and half in thought. A cold hand slipped under her shirt from behind and she let out a gasp and spun around.

"What do you think you're doing?" she snapped at the girl.

"I help you undress," Titi replied with an affirmative nod. "I know you no like me touching you, but I do it careful, see? You must be tired after coming back from Round. Titi just want to help."

The girl then proceeded to give Beki a set of sad puppy-dog eyes that almost made her proud. Apart from her son, there weren't many people who could manipulate her with pathetic faces. The truth was, she *was* tired, and her mind felt more preoccupied than ever. From what she could figure, Titi must be Neese's personal assistant, so it was best not to arouse her suspicion.

"Fine," she said. "Whatever. Just make it quick."

And she was quick. For a girl with one arm, Titi was surprisingly agile. She pulled off Beki's sweater, unhooked her bra, slipped off her Oz Greens, and even undid her pants with her nimble fingers without once brushing Beki's skin. Before long Beki was clad in only her underpants in front of the girl and was surprised to find that she wasn't the least bit self-conscious. Titi smiled broadly. "I go get bath ready," she said.

As soon as she was out of the room, Beki scrambled for the earrings. "Hello?" she whispered into the microphone. "You're a fucking prick, Jean-Luc. Pick up! *Hello?*"

Still no answer. She growled under her breath. Actually growled. She couldn't remember when she had ever done that. It felt both foreign and familiar. A noise came from behind her and she quickly tucked the earrings away and turned around. Titi stood at the door without a single stitch of clothing on her tan body. The fluffy pink towel she had draped over her arm thankfully covered her front. The stump that used to be her other arm was smooth and flawless. It was rather hard to tell whether it had been cut off or never grew.

"You ready for bath, Miss Neese?"

Beki looked the girl up and down. Not since junior varsity baseball had she showered with another girl, and even then she'd kept her head down and her eyes to herself. It seemed impolite to look, not to mention awkward. Now, faced with this exotic nude young woman, Beki could feel every hair on her body standing on end. They were going to *bath* together.

"Sure," she heard herself say.

The bathroom was every bit as luxurious as everything else she'd seen in the Crescent. It was at least as large as her first apartment in college, perhaps bigger. Felt-lined jewelry boxes were set in careful arrangements atop translucent stone countertops. Not a single light bulb was visible as the entire room was lit by LED lights embedded within the walls and ceiling. A fireplace was sunk into the far wall, near the large raised marble tub. Titi had already made a fire as well as lit three scented candles near the steaming tub. A mixture of lavender and vanilla filled the air as Beki stepped inside and noticed that the floor emitted a gentle, comforting heat. As she watched, Titi retrieved a large glass jar from the cherry wood cabinet just inside the door and sprinkled a layer of fresh rose petals into the water.

"You first, Miss Neese," she said politely.

Beki hesitated, but the water was so inviting. The tendrils of steam seemed to pull her in. *Why not?* she thought. *If I'm going to be here for a while I might as well take advantage of it.*

She removed her underpants and slipped into the water. Its warmth washed over her in waves and she sighed. A moment later she felt Titi slip in behind her. Never in her life had she been so close to another woman, not in this sort of situation at least. She waited for unease to rise, and was surprised when it didn't. Titi lathered soap on her back and massaged her scalp with alarming expertise, her slender fingers entwined in Beki's wet locks.

Beki closed her eyes and enjoyed it. Her mind felt a million miles away, drifting half in and half out of her body. Every sensation was dulled to a murmur as her brain sloshed about in her head.

"That feel good, Miss Neese?" Titi asked, obviously seeking praise. Beki was dimly aware that the girl's naked body and silicon breasts were no more than two inches behind her. Every now and then Titi's knee or nipple would graze her skin. It wasn't quite arousing, but some part of her body definitely enjoyed it. It was a very, very guilty pleasure.

"Yes," she whispered. "Fabulous."

This sensation, she realized in her dazed mind, was familiar. She had been this way before, her mind both clear and muddled at the same time. She imagined seeing her own reflection clearly in a pool of muddy water. Titi was talking and her voice seeped through the steam like water through cotton.

"Titi was good while you were gone," she was saying. "But others were bad. Yes sir, they were very bad." She rubbed Beki's back and kneaded her shoulders one at a time.

"Oh yeah? Who was bad?"

"Who else?" Titi scoffed. "Peggy-san. The big, fat, greedy pig. Peggy-san was very bad. He went gambling to the blond girl. The one you hate."

"I hate lots of people." She didn't know how she knew it, but it was something Neese would say. "And they hate me."

"I no hate you. But it was Sasha, Miss Neese. Nasty little Sasha with the ugly curls. Peggy-san went to little Miss Sasha and played her game, then he didn't know how to stop and lost very, very bad. Miss Sasha broke his fingers." She said this last bit with a hint of delight, making Beki remember something Michigan had said not too long ago – everyone in this place seemed to enjoy screwing each other over, probably out of boredom.

"That rascal," Beki muttered under her breath as Titi worked those magic fingers on her neck. "What will we ever do about him?"

"And that not worst part," Titi said. "Peggy-san not happy that he already belong to you; he had to run up debt with the ugly little blond girl, too." Beki had an inkling that all the insults directed at Sasha were for the benefit of Neese. "Now he owe her and he can't pay her. So he did *bad*."

"I thought he was already doing bad."

"Now he worse." Titi leaned forward, her plump lips brushing against Beki's ear. "He *steal* from you, Miss Neese."

Beki felt her back tighten, a reflex perhaps. "He what?"

"He steal from your safe. He betray your trust. He took Luck chips, many thousands. Maybe ten, hundred of thousands. I know it only pocket change to you, Miss Neese, but is trust, no? He betray your trust. He not satisfied to grovel for you and now he take from you. Peggy-san is bad person. Bad person who must be punished."

"And what sort of punishment should we give him?"

Titi leaned forward, and it took Beki a moment to realize that she was showing Beki the stump that used to be her arm. Her red lips were bent into a wide, almost devious grin that was somehow attractive on her. "Like how you punish me, Miss Neese. I used to be bad, too. Now I am good girl, see? You punish him just like you punish me, and Peggy-san will be good boy, too."

Beki stared at the stump through the blanket of steam for a long time, allowing the realization to sink in. In another world and under another name, she had ordered this girl's arm be cut off as a punishment. For something minor, perhaps, since this girl in turn reasoned that a man stealing pocket change from her ought to be punished the same way. What had she done? Beki wondered. Did she touch Neese Highwaters one too many times? Spill a cup of coffee?

Maybe bedded a man Neese was interested in? The last one sounded implausible but she didn't rule it out. Staring at the stump that ought to have sent dread and disgust through her body, Beki inexplicably found herself chuckling.

"Okay," she said. Her facial muscles were pulling her lips into an unnatural smile. "Let's do it. Let's teach that fat bastard a lesson. What should we cut off? An arm? A leg? Maybe one of each?"

(I mowed him down with my car)

Titi's fingers worked their way into the muscles of her back, pushing pressure points skillfully. "I think both arms. He will look like roly-poly bug, you know?"

Beki shrugged. "Sure," she heard herself say in an eerily pleasant tone, "why not? Make it happen. Teach him not to cross me."

Michigan waited for Beki in the bedroom. He had expected her to scream and struggle when he put his hand over her mouth from behind. Instead, she let out a muffled cry and drove an elbow into his gut, and then stepped on his foot. He let out a cry of pain and released her. That was a stupid thing to do, he decided, while she was still being affected by Stat's drug.

Beki spun around and the top of her bathrobe peeked open for just a second. Had she not cinched it at the waist it would've gone flying open. Michigan was sorely disappointed that it hadn't. She looked at him with surprised eyes and quickly closed the bedroom door behind her. "How did you get in here?"

Michigan rubbed his stomach. "I have my ways. You didn't need to hit me so hard."

"What the hell do you mean you have your ways? We're three floors up."

He pointed behind him at the window. "There's a trellis outside. There used to be a garden out there once upon a time, and when all the flowers died nobody removed the trellis. It's strong enough to hold me."

She eyed him suspiciously. "And you just happen to know that?"

"What are you implying?"

"You know exactly what I'm implying." She brushed her wet hair out of the back of her robe. "What the fuck do you do? Stalk this woman? Do you climb up at night and watch her change or something?" She rubbed her face. "I don't want to think about this right now. I think I just ordered that psycho Chinese girl to cut off some guy's arms."

Michigan arched a brow. She was doing better than he'd expected. "Are you going to stop her?"

"Wouldn't that expose me?"

"Yes, it would."

She brushed past him and sat down heavily on the bed. "I feel weird," she said. "Ever since I got here I've been feeling weird. It's like I turned into someone else after I walked inside the door. Look at me." She gestured at the silk robe covering her body and Michigan leered unsubtly. "I just ordered someone's arms to be amputated and I don't even care. It's like when I told Stat that I ran down my son. Nothing. I don't feel a thing. Like I'm this cruel person."

"It's the pill." Though he wasn't sure if that would make her feel better, Michigan thought she deserved to know. "Stat discovered it when you were hanging at his house."

"It makes me cruel?"

"It lowers your inhibitions, and apparently, when your inhibitions are lowered, you act more like Neese. Stat thinks it's coincidence, but a very useful one."

"What do you think?"

"I think it's because, deep down, after you peel away all that vanilla stuff you got going on, you're still Neese Highwaters." He shrugged. "But that's probably just wishful thinking on my part, you know?"

Beki sighed. When she was like this, with Neese peeking out behind those hazel eyes, Michigan found her most attractive. Her gaze was fierce and she seemed to radiate the same sort of cold energy Neese always did. The plus side was, she didn't insult him and order him to get out of her sight. The charm of it, perhaps, was that she didn't realize how much she resembled Neese's true self. Those little curse words, that standoffish frown, even the way she brushed off the plight of the man she'd just ordered to be punished. It gave him goose bumps.

"So," she said, turning her icy gaze to him. "Do you stalk her or what?"

He considered lying to save face, but decided it was pointless since she had probably already decided on the answer. "Yes," he said. "Something like that."

"Do you love her? Really love her, or 'I love her so much I want to keep her toes in a jar next to my bed' kind of love her?"

"I don't want her toes in a jar next to my bed, no. Maybe her lips and tits." Seeing her unease, he smiled. "No, I'm just kidding. I actually came to check on you, since the mike and camera went out. Did you break it or something?"

"They stopped working after I came out of the elevator. I thought Jean-Luc was pissed at me or something."

"Oh, he is," Michigan said with a nod. "He is. You shorted out pretty expensive equipment getting on that elevator. You should've seen him throwing a hissy fit after you got on. I mean, he did tell you to take the stairs. He said all the elevators that lead to this floor have some special wave emitter installed. I don't really understand it but I think it messes up cameras and voice recorders. Neese likes her privacy."

"Maybe because crazy little men often climb up to her window in the middle of the night and watch her undress. Ever think of that?"

Michigan clicked his tongue. "Man, you're bitter with that pill in you. So what have you been doing since the mike went out?"

She told him about the bath and rolled her eyes when his own grew wide. Michigan cleared his throat uncomfortably.

"So, tell me more about the…"

"Shut up."

"Will do."

"So what now?"

"Now you stay here for a bit, make believe that you're Neese. I think as long as Titi knows you're here, that's enough. She'll spread the word since she's got a big mouth. Having that guy punished was a stroke of genius, by the way. Now no one will doubt that Neese is back."

Beki looked irritated and tired, despite having had what must have been a heavenly bath. Michigan unsuccessfully tried to keep his mind from conjuring up a variety of steamy images involving Beki, Titi, and a lot of soap bubbles. "You'll be fine," he reassured her.

"I hate her."

"Who?"

"Neese. The bitch ruined my life."

"You know that you *are*..."

"Shut up."

Shrugging, Michigan picked up the earrings, turned, and headed for the window. "Well, you seem to be doing fine. Stay put and I'll see if I can get Jean-Luc to fix these. I'll probably have to listen to him get huffy about how you don't treasure his things."

"No," she said. "Stay. Let's have sex."

Michigan spun around and nearly lost his footing, bumping his elbow painfully against the bedpost. He expected to see Beki laughing at him for falling for her joke, but she was looking at him with dead-serious eyes. He looked behind her to see if those words came from someone else, then behind himself to see if she was talking to a third person. "Um," he said incoherently, "what?"

"Maybe it's the pills," she said. "They're making me impulsive or something. But come on." She patted the bed next to her. He'd be lying if he said anything in his life had ever looked more inviting. "Let's have sex."

"Um," he said again. "Why?"

She tilted her head. "You don't want to? I thought you were in love with Neese."

"But, you're not..."

"I know, I know," she interrupted with a wave of her hand. "I'm not her. That's OK. You can pretend I'm her. What do you want me to do? Hit you? Cuss you out? Does she have whips and handcuffs hidden somewhere? Whatever you want. You better hurry, because once this pill wears off I'll start regretting it."

Michigan thought this over, knowing well that Neese Highwaters would never proposition him again. Tuning his gaze to Beki, he found himself marveling at her beauty for the umpteenth time since Jean-Luc cleaned her up at the Rabbit Hole. Just being near her made his heart and body ache. But, once again, he reminded himself that, just by being a Rounder, she was not Neese.

"Just so you know," he said, "Neese would *never* go for this. Not with me, I mean."

She nodded, her lips breaking into a devilish smile. "I know. That's why she's going to hate herself when she comes back."

Michigan blinked. "You want to use me to take revenge on yourself?"

"Why not? Wouldn't she do the same?" She gestured for him to come closer. The silk robe slid away. "Besides, I thought I ought to even things up. My husband got one, I get one. So I'm offering. Do you want it or not?"

"Yes," Michigan breathed. "Oh, yes."

The sex wasn't the kind of squishy, passionate, headboard-thumping thing often seen in movies, but it wasn't bad either. Beki mused at the fact that Michigan was a very gentle, polite lover, either that or he was nervous and awkward and afraid to touch anything on Neese's body without permission. Being with him was warm and pleasant. He wasn't a bad-looking fellow and his body was firm and hot, though she could feel the sign of emerging love handles, probably from all those drinks he poured down his throat.

After it was over, they laid side by side. She wondered if he wanted to cuddle. He seemed like the cuddling type, but then again, he was probably still recovering from the fact that he had just boned the woman whom he'd always assumed was out of his reach. The thought of Neese Highwaters getting an aneurysm realizing what she'd done after she came back brought a sneer to Beki's lips.

Michigan propped himself up on his elbows, the silk sheet hanging off his torso. He looked embarrassed. She had noticed in the midst of it that he seemed disappointed by his own performance. In his mind, he must have imagined the earth-shattering pounding he'd give Neese if he ever had the chance. "Look," he said, looking like a little boy caught stealing candy, "I, uh…"

"Don't you start apologizing," she said, cutting him off. "It was good. Don't be such a wuss around me. I mean, her. Me. Whatever."

He smiled. "Okay," he said, and laid back. "Jean-Luc's gonna be fucking pissed."

"You shouldn't curse so much."

"Pills wore off?"

"Guess so. I can actually feel my brain shifting gears. It's not gonna give me brain damage or anything, is it?"

"Don't know."

"Wonderful." Beki gazed at the bathrobe lying in a crumble on the floor. "I really miss my son. I can't stop thinking about him."

"Not during…"

"No, not during." She sighed. "So what do I do now?"

"I guess try to get some Luck chips out of Neese's safe. You'll need them to enter the game. Sasha's games are pretty pricey. Jean-Luc says the code for the safe is the same as the door to Neese's private suite."

"Which is…"

"You don't know?"

She turned to him. "Titi let me in."

Michigan chuckled. "Well, crap," he said. "That makes things a hell of a lot harder."

"If we get the code, can't I just use the chips to overturn the bet?"

Michigan shook his head. "No. Neese is very careful about her money, and her chips are dispersed all over the place. Everyone knows that High Rollers don't keep more than a million or two in their main safe for show, which isn't nearly enough."

"Should I ask Titi for the code?"

"Hell no, that'd just blow your cover. And here I was hoping you'd somehow dredged the code out of your subconscious. Now we have a problem on our hands."

"Is it something we can solve with a little lying and cheating?"

He gave her a surprised look. "What?"

"Isn't that what Neese does?"

"Well," Michigan said, "you sound more like her every day. No, we may not have to lie and cheat for this one. But hey, it's nice of you to think of it."

Titi Chang watched from inside the wall of the bedroom as Michigan Von Phant boned the Rounder posing as Neese Highwaters. The crawlspace was small and tight, and her silicone implants were pressed so tightly against the wall that she feared they might burst. But the peephole offered a very good view. She took a picture with her cell phone. It might be good for blackmail later, even though she couldn't imagine doing such a thing to her beloved mistress. Then again, time would tell. Maybe one day she would feel the need to be bad again.

Titi smiled to herself. She knew the moment the woman stepped through the door that all the rumors were true. The all-mighty Neese had been reduced to a clueless Rounder. Although it upset her to see her mistress in this state, Titi was impressed at how the woman handled her prodding about Peg. She even ordered him be punished. Her words and the soapy feel of her skin sent a shiver down Titi's back. Wetting her thick lips, she leaned forward again to watch the two in the bedroom.

She considered blowing the top off the whole thing, but not seriously. Not really. She loved Miss Neese too much. Then she considered revealing to the Rounder that she knew her secret, but really couldn't imagine what that would accomplish. She didn't want to be the Rounder's friend. She was just a dirty pebble compared to Miss Neese. So, after some debate, she decided to stick with watching. Miss Neese did hate Sasha, so maybe the Rounder would do the work for her and knock the girl down a peg. Titi was very excited. She hadn't had this much fun since she snuck into that same bedroom and pleasured herself on Miss Neese's bed. Someone had squealed on her, however, just like she squealed like a piglet on Peg. Miss Neese had subsequently ordered that naughty hand she used be cut off, but it was worth it. Oh, it was worth it.

When they finished, she heard them talking about the code. Of course the Rounder didn't know the code. If she asked, Titi decided, she would give it up without a fight. But if she didn't ask, well, it was just that much more fun.

Titi began to slide out of the crawlspace ungracefully. For now, she had to go make sure fat, sweaty Peggy-san got his punishment.

21
FORTUNE

Gypsy Hoss sat in her tent and gazed absently at the crystal ball. It was actually made of glass but who was going to snitch as long as she insisted it was crystal? The tent was decorated in a distinct Arabian style, with draping fabrics and thick hanging rugs in a variety of explosive autumn colors – not that anyone still remembered what autumn was like. Gypsy sighed. She was bored. Her customers were a dull bunch with no imagination. All they want to hear were two things – will they win the next game and what's the latest gossip was on their favorite High Roller. She was considering closing shop early when a movement caught her eye.

Two people were lingering just outside. One was a man who looked vaguely familiar. Gypsy couldn't think of his name but identified him as one of Geoffy's regulars. He was with someone, a person slightly shorter and wearing a dark hood and cloak like some witch or sorceress out of a picture book. They were talking in a hushed tone, perhaps arguing about something. A moment later the man entered the tent, holding the drapery aside as the other ducked inside also. Judging by posture and movement, it was a woman. She came forward to the table that held Gypsy's glass ball, knelt on the lace-trimmed pillow opposite from Gypsy, and lifted her hood. Gypsy started just a little.

"We have come to request your help," the woman said formally. The man just scoffed as he sat down cross-legged next to his companion, raising a palm to Gypsy in greeting.

"Don't be so stiff. Gypsy's cool," he said to the woman. "Hey Gypsy. How's tricks? Geoffy been good to you lately?"

Gypsy looked from the woman to the man, then back. "It's true then."

"What is?"

She pointed at the woman, who was sitting properly with her slender hands in her lap despite the nervous look in her eyes. "This. Don't play stupid with me, boy. What the hell were you thinking?"

The man grinned sheepishly. "Yeah, Stat asked the same thing."

"So Status Quo already knows," Gypsy mused. This she hadn't expected, but damned if she was going to let her surprise show. "And he didn't beat your head in?"

"I'm sure he will later. I mean, he said he would."

"Alright," Gypsy said. "Fine." She reached over the table and grabbed the face of the pretty woman, who started a bit but didn't resist. "What's your name, sweetie?"

"Rebecca," she said. "Rebecca Tempest. You can call me Beki."

"Rebecca," Gypsy repeated. "What a nice, girly name. What can I do for you, Rebecca?"

"You could let go of my face." Gypsy released her grip and the woman currently named Rebecca flexed her jaw and turned to the man. "You said she'd know what's going on."

"Oh, she does," the man said. "She's psychic. She knows everything. Right, Gypsy?"

Gypsy rolled her eyes. "I hear you dragged her out of the Round, is that right?"

"Pretty much."

"And Status Quo caught you, but didn't drag her back, yes?"

"Yep."

Gypsy reached into a pouch strapped to her waist and pulled out a pair of bone-colored dice. She rolled them between her stick-like fingers. "Everyone knows Neese Highwaters went in to a Round," she said. "But not everyone knew that she came out a Rounder. There are rumors. Some saying she broke, some saying she stuck together and came back fine, and some saying she came through a gate illegally and is just posing. Which gate did you use, boy?"

"Cali and Ro."

Gypsy hissed through her teeth. She was a little impressed. "That Ro's maimed Rounders for less, you know." She turned to Rebecca, whose innocent eyes were wide with curiosity. "Say, pretty girl, did you know that Neese Highwaters is the one who came up with the idea to blindfold Calisa like that?"

Rebecca look horrified. "Really?" she stammered. "That's so…"

"Cruel? Yes, that's the sort of people the High Rollers are. Are you prepared to be cruel?"

"I ordered a man's arms be cut off today." Rebecca bit her lip. "I'm still regretting it, so I guess I'm not cruel enough."

"No, you're not," Gypsy said pointedly. "I think I can guess what you two are hoping to accomplish. You want to enter Sasha's game, best her at it, and then rub it in her face that she lost to a Rounder. Is that right?"

"Actually I just want to save my son."

"Your what?" Gypsy shook her head. "Never mind. I don't want to know. Rounders always have all these… reasons. Reasons to do this, reasons to do that. I don't care what you're getting out of it. Either way, it seems you've already got the wheels in motion. You got Status Quo to overlook your intrusion and" – she glanced at Rebecca's feet – "you're wearing Neese's shoes. Did Jean-Luc give you those?"

"How do you know?"

"She's psychic," the man chimed in.

Gypsy rubbed her temples with her thumb and forefinger. As the resident "psychic", she had long ago discovered that she was the only person around who didn't believe in such things. Through an efficient combination of secondhand information and practiced deduction, she had secured a steady income as a "mystical advisor". It was both frustrating and amusing to extort those who hadn't yet figured out that her "psychic abilities" were nothing but logic and secondhand gossip. Fortunately and unfortunately, that involved most of the population within a hundred square miles.

"What can I do for you?" she asked again.

"We need a loan, a big one," the man said. Gypsy suddenly realized that she hasn't asked for his name. No big loss though. "I know you want to see this game play out, too, if you already know what's going on, but we can't get into Neese's safe."

"How much do you need?"

"Enough for the entrance fee at least. Ten thousand."

"I'll give you twenty," Gypsy said, and the man nearly fell backwards.

"Wow," he said. "That was easier than I expected."

"But," Gypsy added, curling her thin lips. "It won't come cheaply." She turned to Rebecca. "You must win. If you do not win, well... you're a Rounder. You know what a 'life debt' is, don't you?"

Before Rebecca could answer, the man threw up his hands. "Whoa," he exclaimed. "Hey, whoa! You can't hold her to a life debt. Do you know who she is? Even if you try..."

"Not her." Gypsy pointed her long red nail at the man's startled eyes. "You."

Silence fell over the tent. Gypsy kept her bony hand up, pointing at the man and waiting for him to crumple. His eyes darted to Rebecca, who was gazing at him with her dark beautiful eyes. Gypsy marveled at the sight. Many men and more than a few women loved Neese Highwaters. They admired her from a distance and worshiped the ground she walked on. But this one, this fool, had taken it to a whole new level.

She waited as the man swallowed thickly. Gypsy could tell from his eyes that he was considering whether a life debt, measured in the sum of roughly forty-four thousand hours, was worth giving innocent little Rebecca this chance. Once she returned to her former self, she would promptly kick him to the curb, cursing herself for having come within ten feet of him in the first place. Gypsy and he both knew that Neese would never speak up for him, nor bargain him out of this debt. Neese wasn't one to appreciate foolish sacrifices.

"Okay," he said. Gypsy raised a red brow.

"Okay?"

"Okay."

Stat hoped that he wasn't turning his recent trips to the Saffron Stallion into a habit. He usually didn't hang out in places where crowds tended to gather, but staying at home just made him more grouchy and irritable. Problem was, being alone meant there was no one to be irritated at but yourself. So, after much hesitation and pacing in and out of the door, he finally relented and came to the bar.

He sat in a booth in the back this time, a place where he could comfortably see the rest of the place and melt into the shadows at the same time. Geoffy had hooked up a karaoke machine and a skinny woman was warbling drunkenly about yellow submarines. Stat wasn't sure what a submarine was. It was one of those things people saw in the Round. He tried to order water from Geoffy again, earning himself a curt look and a cold shoulder. A few moments later, however, Geoffy brought him a gin and tonic that he didn't order, set it in front of him, and walked off without a glance back. Stat wondered if it was Geoffy's attempt to get him drunk and not start any trouble.

I'm not the one that starts troubles, he thought to himself, but didn't have the energy to say it.

The bar was filled with its usual assortment of patrons, having drunk so much that their bodily odors carried the scent of alcohol. The whole place was a sweat-and-smoke cocktail. Stat wrinkled his nose and sipped his drink. It tasted awful.

A big man lumbered up to the bar, slapping a meaty hand on the counter to get Geoffy's attention. "Yo!" he yelled, his thick voice wafting above the general clamor, "Barkeep! Drink over there and make it strong!"

Geoffy filled a shot glass and slid it over to the customer, who tried to catch it with his left hand, but it slipped out of his grasp and shattered on the floor. Stat saw that two of his fingers were in splints. Grumbling in frustration, the man slapped the counter again. Geoffy looked up. "You're paying for that," he said.

The patron glowered. "Give me a break, will ya?" he said. "You see this?" He held up his splinted fingers. "You see this misshapen claw? I got it from that little bitch Sasha. Wasn't enough that she took all my chips, little whore broke my fingers, too. Just for fun!"

Stat took another sip and set his glass down on the table.

261

"Now I owe two of them," the big, awkward man continued. "*Two!* Those High Rollers. I hate'em. I hate'em all. Sitting there on their throne all high and mighty. What makes *them* so great?"

Geoffy said nothing. Stat had figured out a long time ago that by ignoring depressed drunkards when they're at their worst, they became annoyed and drank more, which meant more profits for Geoffy. He sold alcohol, not sympathy. A few moments later he'd lined up two more drinks on the counter.

The bearded man downed one and let out a dry wheeze. "Whoa, that's good stuff," he said, pointing his broken fingers at Geoffy. "You know what? I can't believe I'm saying this, but being a footstool to Neese is actually better than being under Sasha's heel. You believe that? All Neese ever did was call me names. Never broke nothing or cut nothing off. Sasha? Damn. And it's my spin hand too."

A pair of attractive young women passed by Stat's table, veering a wide arc to avoid brushing against him. He waited until they passed his table to check out their silhouettes.

"Keep yer voice down, will ya, Peg?" Geoffy said huffily. "Yer disturbing my customers."

"Hah!" said the man named Peg. Geoffy frowned and cleaned his spittle off the counter with the dirty dishrag. "It's not like any of them don't know what I'm talking about. Little Sasha, high and mighty." He tried to imitate a little girl prancing around. The end result was something of a walrus trying to keep from being tilted over by a strong gust. "She's the worst one of them all. Little girls should be nice, and she's just a grade-A bitch in a small package."

Stat finished off his drink and stood. A middle-aged bald man who happened to be standing nearby scrambled to get out of his way. He gave the guy a smile and was rewarded with a nervous glare.

"She's like an evil little dwarf," Peg said, sitting down on one of the red vinyl stools, his girth spilling over its edge. He gestured as he spoke. "I wish I could put her in a little jar and squish her little head."

Geoffy rolled his good eye. Stat approached the bar and put his empty glass on the counter. He tucked his hands into the pockets of his slouchy brown jacket and lingered as Peg continued his rant.

"I'll break *her* fingers," Peg said, finishing his second drink, a strong shot by the smell of it. "I'll break her little fingers and see how she likes it. She's nothing but a stupid little kid trying to act all grown-up. She's the worst of them, the *absolute*..."

Stat scooted next to Peg, leaning his back against the counter. Then, sighing, he dealt a swift kick to Peg's stool. It flew out from under the large man's body and Peg flailed momentarily, trying to catch himself in the air before his nose met the edge of the bar with a loud crunch.

"Fuck!" Peg cradled his nose as blood poured out of the nostrils. The rest of him tumbled to the floor with a force that shook the tables in the vicinity like an earthquake. The stool spun twice and stopped against a booth half way across the room. The booth's occupants looked their way briefly and turned back to their drinks. "You boke my nose!" he wailed nasally. "You 'ucker, you *boke* my nose!" Still on his knees, Peg grabbed Stat's leg with one hand and snarled. "You're gonna pay for this, you... you...!"

Stat waited for the man to lift his head. Their eyes met and Peg's hand loosened.

"S-Stat," he stammered, suddenly pale. Stat scratched his head and waited. Peg backed away, scooting on his fat bottom across the floor. "I'm sorry, I didn't mean to..."

Geoffy, who had left his post behind the bar, hoisted Peg to his feet. "Scram, ya ninny," he said, giving Peg a shove toward the door. Peg stumbled away, still holding his nose. Geoffy turned to Stat, opened his mouth to shout, then thought better of it and shook his head instead.

"Dang it, Stat," he said. "This is why nobody likes ya."

Stat shrugged narrowly, his hands still in his jacket pockets. "Nobody likes me anyway," he said.

"Do you think we'll win?"

The red-haired woman named Gypsy Hoss looked at Beki with warm eyes. The woman's fierce appearance and brazen outfit had originally startled Beki, but now she was beginning to feel that she was rather matronly, like a sharp-tongue older woman teasing her grandchildren. She also had a very interesting name that Beki found she liked very much.

"Why are you asking me?"

IMMORTALITY 101: The Intro Course

"Aren't you a fortune teller? Can you tell us if we're going to win?"

Gypsy looked at her like she was crazy. "Oh, why not," she said after a moment. "Usually I put on a dog-and-pony show for the paying customers, but here's a freebie." She flicked the crystal ball with her long nail. It made a soft clink. "Abracadabra. Hocus-pocus. Bibbity-bobbity-boo. Lady Luck says you got as much chance of winning as a cow does of retaining ownership of its vital organs in a slaughterhouse." She reached over and patted Beki on the shoulder with a wide grin. "But, hey, you'll look mighty nice losing, especially in those shoes."

22
LADY LUCK

Beki stood before the statue of Lady Luck in the center of the Square, which was almost deserted, just like the last time she was here. The statue looked the same, and she had thought seeing it again wouldn't disturb her, but the gray figure of the hermaphrodite woman still made her a bit uneasy. The Square was quiet, as if the noises of the casinos and the colors of the neon were shielded away by a protective bubble around the gurgling fountain. She looked down and saw the water winding between the bricks just beneath her feet.

She reached up and pulled her hood back. She had found the cloak in Neese's closet. It was a bit too "Lord of the Rings" for her taste, but it was comfortable and convenient.

"What are you doing?" Michigan hissed, looking around nervously.

"It's okay. No one's around." She gazed up at the statue. "Besides, she's a god, right? It seems disrespectful to keep the hood up."

"Whatever." Michigan peered around the fountain, seeking prying eyes. "Just do whatever it is you wanted to do and let's get out of here."

Beki reached into the inner lining of the cloak. It was weighed down with the chips Gypsy had given them. They were nothing like the poker chips Beki had expected to see. They were made of a variety of metals, with shapes reminiscent of snowflakes. Single-count chips had five corners, a perfect pentagon made of aluminum, light and flexible.

Five-count chips had seven corners and were made of copper. Ten-count chips were made of silver, with eight corners and sides that curved inward. Fifty-count chips had twelve pointy corners that pricked Beki's fingers every time she reached for them. They were gold-plated and much heavier than they looked. Beki felt around until she found a fifty-count chip. Also among the chips was a small bag. Inside was a single pill, the last one Stat had given to Michigan. That, luck, and whatever it was Jean-Luc was cooking up were all she had to go against Sasha, as well as all the other skilled gamblers who were sure to be drawn to the game.

"What are you doing with that?"

Beki held the chip out over the water. "Making an offering."

"Are you nuts?"

"We have a saying in the Round," Beki said. "*Lady Luck smiles upon you.*"

"Well, we have a different saying here."

"I know. Stat told me." She dropped the chip into the water. It sank to the bottom without so much as a bubble. "It still feels like the right thing to do." Pressing her palms together in front of her chest, she closed her eyes. She wasn't a particularly pious person. In fact, she couldn't remember the last time she went to church. It wasn't out of any prejudice against religion, but simply because she never felt the need to. Now, standing before this crude statue, she suddenly felt like she could understand what the churchgoers were talking about.

Please grant me luck where I need it most.

It felt good to have someone, even an abstract figure, to rely on.

"Amen," she said, unable to come up with anything better. Michigan, who had been shuffling about anxiously, came forward.

"Can we go now? I don't like this place. That statue creeps me out." He peered into the fountain. "You gonna fish that out? Someone else will, if you don't."

"You don't know how a wishing well works?"

"Sure I do." He looked longingly at the fifty-count chip. "*I'd* fish it out," he muttered.

"Don't worry about it." Beki pulled the hood over her face and took his arm. "Thanks for what you did back there," she said, and kissed him lightly on the cheek. "I hope Neese will be at least half as grateful as I am when she comes back."

SHOW

You first duty is to the Game; then come Mother, God, and Country

— *Motto at the National Press Club, Washington D.C.*

IMMORTALITY 101: The Intro Course

23
THE HEAD TABLE

Tish eyed her uniform mournfully as the boys dressed themselves. She considered averting her gaze but they didn't have a thing that she hadn't seen before. Leonard and Mozart had lost their modesty around her a long time ago, and she supposed she was the same way. Such was the life of a slave, she thought with a wispy sigh. How sad, to be in closer quarters for so long that they had forgotten what it was like to be humble.

She was just about to go on contemplating the pointless void that was eternity when something hit the side of her head. She looked up and glared at Mozart, who was cinching up his pants. Leonard was still in his briefs.

"Get dressed, will ya?"

Tish looked down on the floor and saw the hat that Mozart had thrown. She always hated the hat. It was shaped like a white half-dome, with a square base and four flaps peeling from its sides like the petals of a flower. From the top of the dome rose a tiny white sprout. If not for the red cross on one of the sides, the hat would look identical from all four sides. Tish knew the red cross was supposed to mean something, maybe only as a joke, but she didn't know and didn't care to ask.

"Hurry it up," Leonard said, snapping his fingers an inch from her face. She winced unhappily. "Get dressed or we're do it for you."

IMMORTALITY 101: The Intro Course

"So rude," she said, picking up the hat and setting it in her lap. "I will dress myself when I am good and ready. My body is not to be so easily touched by your dirty hands."

The boys rolled their eyes. Mozart grabbed his jacket and slapped Leonard on the shoulder with the sleeve, and a wrestling match promptly broke out. Tish sighed again, holding the hat against her chest as the boys rolled about on the floor, taking turns pinning each other down and laughing. They were such a barbaric bunch and Tish often found that her own immeasurable suffering was nothing but a joke in their eyes. How could they joke and play as such when their own lives were as dark as hers? Their life was nothing but servitude. They had debts, too, that they could not pay. The future was bleak and eternal and they only responded with futile laughter.

Tish cursed her own poetic soul, but without her poetic soul she would be just another ruffian. Slowly, as if the weight of life bore down on her shoulders, she stood, uttering another long and wistful sigh as she did so, and began to dress. Leonard and Mozart paused mid-grapple.

"Hey, check it out!" Mozart said, pinning Leonard down with his knees, "Tish is gonna take her top off!"

"Shake it, baby!" Leonard said, his hand tangled in Mozart's blond hair.

"I bet her panties match her bra," Mozart said, administering a wet-willie.

"I bet she stuffs," Leonard said, delivering a mean purple-nurple. The grappling ensued and Tish felt sorrow well up in her heart like an oily pool. She folded her hands against her chest and mourned her lost youth. She was young, barely into her teens. Mozart and Leonard were a bit older, but eternity had made age irrelevant. She wished she could have a window to look out of, perhaps into a cemetery, although there hadn't been any cemeteries as long as anyone could remember. Perhaps after the game she would compose a few sonnets that compared her withered youth to a wilting flower.

"She's doing it again," Mozart said.

"Yep, that's her sonnet-composing face alright," Leonard said.

"Now she's gonna mope."

"And cry."

"And lament how the world treats her wrong."

"I hate it when she does that."

"Me, too."

Another hat hit the back of Tish's head. She spun around, angry tears in her eyes. The boys looked away innocently, whistling as they untangled their limbs and put on their uniforms. "Better get dressed, Tishy," Mozart said, combing his bleach-blond hair into spikes. "You know Sasha gets mighty pissy if you're late."

"Or you can just go out there with your ta-tas hanging out," Leonard said. "It'll be okay. No one'll be able to see them, anyway."

Tish gazed down at her flat chest and quickly slipped into her uniform. The cropped jacket was a little big and the skirt too loose from the waist up. She was too skinny. She started to sigh at the thought that her body would never mature into the curves she so richly desired when the three monitors hanging from the dressing room's ceiling turned on.

"Check it out," one of the boys said. "All the big wigs are here."

"That's Prescott."

"There's Mojiha. He looks more orange than ever."

"Is that Rat Spence?"

"Nope. That'd be his rep. Looks like he's playing by proxy."

"Gypsy."

"Where?"

"Right *there*. How can you miss her?"

"Random people, random people, random people... hey, there's Neese!" Yet another hat flew at Tish's head. It seemed the boys were unable to get her attention through any other means. "Hey, Tish, there's your idol!"

Tish nearly stumbled. With one boot on and the other foot bare, she limped to the nearest monitor and gazed up, her eyes glazed with adoration. She watched the camera focus on the endlessly graceful Neese Highwaters, long hair spilling down her shoulders and milky thigh peeking out from underneath shimmering silk. And her Oz Greens. Tish had spent many nights in between woeful laments imagining herself being carried by those Oz Greens.

Neese raised her champagne flute and mimed a toast to the camera. For a split second it was as if their eyes had met. Tish nearly melted. She could hear Mozart and Leonard's jeering from behind but she didn't care. Hands clasped before her flat chest, she sighed, this time in awe and not a little bit of jealousy.

Someday, she promised herself, *when the heavens finally open up and smile upon the wretch that is me, when the floods of pain and sorrow finally wash away with the tide, I will be just like you.*

Neese Highwaters sat at the head table, sipping bubbly from a crystal champagne flute. The head table was reserved for High Rollers. If the drooling masses were to contest, Neese looked as good as she ever did. Eyes sparked as she crossed her legs. Tongues rolled when she brushed a strand of hair off her shoulder. When she lifted the glass to her pink lips thousands let out a sigh of pleasure as she sipped. She turned to the crowd and raised her glass, then tipped it and let a thin trickle of liquid fall to the floor. A dozen people dove to catch the droplets on their tongues as if it were the nectar of the Gods. She gave them an approving glance like a mistress feedings her dogs. Neese Highwaters was queen, an unrivaled Goddess, the empress of the high life. She glided over the wave of the common people on her mesmerizing Oz Greens.

The one problem, of course, was that the person sitting in her seat was a common, plain woman name Rebecca Tempest. She went by the nickname Beki, which she spelled B-e-k-i because it looked cool in middle school and sort of stuck since then. She crunched numbers for a living, couldn't tell Chardonnay from Merlot, and had never bought a pair of shoes that cost more than ninety dollars.

Sitting on the raised platform at the head table with the rest of the High Rollers, Beki struggled to keep her hands from pouring more and more alcohol down her throat just to calm her nerves. She breathed deeply, drank slowly, and tried to look the part, all the while aware that her hands were shaking uncontrollably. Up until this moment, everything had seemed like a dream and part of her was still expecting to wake up. Unfortunately she was now here, sitting amongst the elite that were supposed to be her peers and thinking about how ill-prepared she was. There was even a little engraved plaque on the table that read *N. Highwaters*. It all seemed like a bad joke. After she had settled into her seat in the most graceful manner she could manage, a waiter arrived with a tray of drinks and rattled off their names at lightning speed. Thankfully, he held out the tray for her to pick from, instead of asking her to select one. If he had, she probably would have answered, "The first one," blowing her cover from the get-go.

After that, she had accidentally tipped her glass and spilled some champagne trying to look classy by raising a toast to the crowd, and the sight of them fighting to get a drop reminded her of a concert she had attended in college. It was a popular band made of cute boys that had since faded into the same oblivion as all the other popular bands made of cute boys. One of them had thrown his baseball cap into the crowd and Beki watched as thousands of female attendees dove for it at the same time. There were bloody noses and broken wrists; a dozen fights broke out that soon led to the concert being halted while security hauled a handful of girls, missing chunks of hair and teeth, out of the stadium. One of them was cradling the coveted baseball cap as if it were a baby and shouting praises to God, Joseph, and the Virgin Mary.

I could do that, Beki thought to herself. *They would go crazy like that over me. Any of us.*

Michigan was in the crowd somewhere. She couldn't single him out in the sea of people. For now, she pretended to drink from her glass and studied the other occupants of the table over its edge. There were four others at the table, only one of whom she recognized – the pretty, pale girl with blue eyes and dark hair from the teahouse. She would have forgotten her name but for the list Jean-Luc and Michigan had provided her the night before and instructed her to memorize. *Names and faces*, Jean-Luc kept saying, *names and faces. Neese must know all the names and faces of the High Rollers and proxies*. Beki ran down the list in her head. Prescott. Daughter of Lisa Gasolina. She was not an official High Roller. She had been playing in her mother's place in many prestigious games.

Upon her initial arrival, Beki's first instinct had been to place herself as far away from Prescott as possible, but Jean-Luc had specifically asked her to refrain her from doing so. *Sit next to her*, he had said, *sit next to her and tease her. Call her names. Call her mother names. Badger her any way you can about why her mother isn't coming.*

Beki didn't like to insult anyone's mother. It was impolite to say the least. But never in her life had she felt so many pairs of eyes on her, expecting her to act the part. The other High Rollers were looking at her also. Biting her lip to calm her nerves, she turned to Prescott.

"So," she said, trying her best to remember a movie she had seen about snooty high school girls who got what's coming to them. "Is your mother too good to join us again?"

Prescott seemed to shrink in her seat and Beki instantly felt bad. The girl looked even paler than she remembered, and there was a circle of oddly shaped scars framing her small mouth, perhaps a rash.

"Lay off the girl, Neese," said the man sitting across from her. Mojiha Jordan, if she remembered correctly. He was tall, muscular, with a head of wild, untamable dirty blond hair, and a tan the color of a sunburned tangerine. He winked at Beki. "You're so mean, you know? But that's what I love about ya, that little ball of heat in yer loins. I got some heat in my loins, too. How about we rub it together and see if we can't make a fire?"

Beki rolled her eyes and recited one of the lines Jean-Luc had fed her. "If it burns when you pee, Mojiha, it's not heat you're packing."

Mojiha grinned, blinding Beki with the reflection off his three gold front teeth. A crowd of girls nearby made a sound as if they had just simultaneously wet themselves. Beki averted her gaze lest her nervous eyes gave anything away. The other two occupants of the table had not spoken since her arrival. Sitting across from Prescott was an old man with salt-and-pepper hair and a face that had long lost its battle with gravity. He wore his long beard like a sage in an imported Asian movie. On his thin, sagging body was a white wife-beater with a yellow stain on its front – mustard, drool, or perhaps something worse. Underneath it, he wore a pair of banana-yellow windbreakers and worn sneakers. All in all, he couldn't have looked more out of place. He had arrived last and since then had sat in his chair and mumbled to the tablecloth. If she didn't know better, Beki would have expected security to walk onto the platform and escort the confused old man back into the crowd where he belonged.

Bice Tic didn't meet her gaze when she turned to him. He continued to converse with the table as if it was the most interesting dinner companion in the world. True to his name, he appeared to suffer from a mild form of Turrets Syndrome. The tic in his neck, however, didn't slow his conversation the least bit.

The last member was a man in his late thirties, medium height and well-groomed, dressed in a powder blue shirt and khaki slacks, the sort of clothing men put on when their wives told them to "dress nice" for dinner with the parents. His hair was black and cropped in the manner that Beki was quite familiar with – the fifteen-fifty "number-cruncher special". Like Bice, he also hadn't made any attempt to start a conversation with anyone. Instead, he sat with his head propped up on one hand, gazing into the crowd and looking absolutely bored and miserable. Out of all members of the High Rollers present, Beki would've liked to have conversed with him most, as he seemed every bit as uncomfortable as she felt. Unfortunately, Jean-Luc had warned her against doing so by slapping her wrist when she pointed at his picture.

"No!" he had barked. "You do not talk to him. He's a commoner."

She rubbed her wrist and thought horrible things about him. "Why? Isn't he a High Roller, too?"

"He is most definitely not." Jean-Luc's voice dripped with distain. "He is a proxy, just like Prescott is. His name is Boxcat, and he is playing as a proxy for Rat Spence, who is the real High Roller. The only reason you would have to speak to him is to insult him. You must treat him worse than Prescott."

"Rat and Boxcat? Cute." That had earned her another slap on the wrist.

According to the plaque in front of him, his name was Boxcat Pincher. Rat Spence's name had been added underneath his in a smaller font, the same way Lisa's was added under Prescott's. Mojiha was winking and licking his lips at the girl now, and Beki's maternal instincts urged her to pull the poor girl into her arms and tell Mojiha to sod off. She thought of Eric and a wave of despair washed over her. *What am I doing?*

"What are you doing?"

She looked up. Boxcat was looking at her. There was an odd spark in his eyes and Beki suddenly realized she had dropped her mask. Quickly, she fixed her features into the icy nonchalant look that Jean-Luc had trained her to do. "Were you talking to me?" she asked, trying hard to picture Boxcat as a roach.

Boxcat blinked in a way that made Beki feel like the girl who showed up at prom in a potato sack dress. "Um, yeah," he said.

"What does it look like I'm doing?" She sipped from her glass, only to realize it was empty.

"That," Boxcat said. "You've been sucking on that empty glass for five minutes."

Mojiha snickered. Beki was certain her face was flushed. Prescott was also eyeing her timidly. She hesitated for a split second, then raised her hand and chucked the glass at Boxcat's head. He tilted his head to the side to avoid it and it sailed past him, over the railing behind his chair, and into the crowd below. There was a mad dash by at least a hundred people to claim the glass as it fell. Boxcat turned to eye the milling crowd below, shook his head, and went back to looking bored. Beki stifled her sigh of relief.

"When in doubt, throw your glass."

"What would that accomplish?"

"Lets people know you don't want them butting into your business."

"Seems awfully rude."

"When you're Neese Highwaters, you don't have to waste time being nice."

It seemed to work, at least. Mojiha turned his head away and whistled as if nothing had happened, and Prescott drew her legs onto the chair, wrapped her arms around her knees, and kept her head down. With her pale complexion, white satin dress, and red cloak, she looked like Red Riding Hood after one too many overdoses. Beki wondered how many times she had shot up to get up the nerve to attend the game. The crook of her right arm was filled with tiny red dots, some still oozing pinpoint-sized droplets of blood.

A waiter brought another tray of drinks and Beki picked one, not knowing what she would do with herself otherwise. She almost wished she could bend over and talk to the tablecloth like Bice, then she wouldn't have to bother with the other High Rollers, who all seemed to hold some form of contempt for her as well as each other. The only person who appeared to be having a good time was the orange-smeared Mojiha, who had left the table to wave to a crowd of shrieking girls gathered around the platform. One of them threw a pair of lacy panties onto the platform. It landed next to Boxcat, who eyed it in disgust and kicked it back off.

On one side of the platform was an ornate stage. Three of the biggest roulette wheels that Beki had ever seen had been set up in front of heavy gold curtains. They were different from the roulettes she was used to. Instead of being attached to tables, they stood on their own, and their pockets were white and gold instead of red and black. Jean-Luc had briefed her on the rules of the game, but nothing prepared her for the sight of the wheels. It didn't take much to see that their presence commanded the room. They stood on thick wooden stands, like a trio of one-legged dwarves guarding their treasure. Each wheel looked as if it had been carved out of a single piece of wood, completely and utterly seamless.

To the other side of the platform were three rows of round tables. Each table seated four people. As far as Beki could tell, every seat was occupied. These were the 'common' participants – in other words, those who were a tier below the High Rollers. Instead of plaques, they were given numbers. Among them, Beki recognized the red-haired Gypsy Hoss, who was sipping a glass of water and speaking to no one. She seemed to have her own little fan club – a small crowd was gathered around her table and several people were taking pictures. The rest of the competitors seemed to regard her with envy, as none of them had a single follower.

None except one, she suddenly noticed. There was another member of the commoner's table who seemed to be attracting a fair bit of attention, a thin young woman with short black hair. She wore a blue dress and had a flat body like a pre-pubescent boy. Though she didn't have quite the fan club Gypsy had, there was more than a handful of people taking photos of her and trying to make conversation as they passed her, and many more pointing and whispering. She gave them no attention, however. With an uncomfortable twinge, Beki realized the girl's attention was fixated on her, and her black eyes were cold as ice. She quickly tore her eyes away and pretended not to notice the girl's dark gaze.

Beyond the contestants was a crowd, the likes of which Beki had only seen once, at a baseball game her cousin dragged her to when she was little. A team whose name she could no longer recall had been playing, and it was something of a big deal because the sea of people made her feel dizzy. Their colors, their movements, the endless wave of bodies ... right now, she knew that if she were to step off the platform, her eager fans would cling onto her and tear her from limb to limb.

Like zombies, she thought to herself, and allowed herself a soft chuckle. Boxcat turned to her and raised a brow. She decided that if she put a little effort into it, she could really dislike him.

Sasha's gambling parlor was something of a theater crossed with a club. The floor where the crowd gathered flashed a spectrum of colors in sync to booming techno music. People danced and ground against each other as they hailed the High Rollers. Something about it was almost tribal. Beki watched, mesmerized, until silence suddenly fell over the crowd.

The music paused. The colors faded. The lights darkened. The only sound remaining was Bice mumbling to the tablecloth. A single spotlight cast a circle of light over the head table, and two more turned to the stage as the golden curtains slid open, revealing a sparkling staircase. A figure, no more than five feet tall and draped in gold as bright and warm as the sun, descended – a bubble of satin, silk, lace, and frill.

"There she is," she heard Boxcat whisper.

"Always making an appearance," Mojiha said. "Could she wear any *more* gold?"

"Sa-sha, Sa-sha!" someone in the crowd chanted, and soon, like a ripple, the rest joined in, even some of the competitors. They pumped their fists in the air, shouting with drunken glee. The waiters had saturated the entire room with alcohol twice over. "*Sa-sha! Sa-sha!*"

Boxcat and Mojiha raised their glasses in a half polite, half mocking toast. Prescott pulled her legs away from her chest and did the same. Bice tilted his head toward the stage, coughed, and turned back to the tablecloth.

Beki sat in her place, too stunned to raise her glass. Suddenly, she realized, through all the training, all the lectures, all the makeovers and preparations, not a single person had thought to tell her what Sasha looked like.

Sasha did not see the crowd, nor pay attention to the cheers. Her sapphire eyes landed on the head table and met the eyes of the person she had been waiting for. She had come and, moreover, she did not squirm under Sasha's gaze. This was a game for the two of them. Sasha smiled. All the others, though they did not know it, were nothing but spectators.

Michigan Von Phant chewed on his nails. He never thought that he would be too nervous to drink, but there he was, swimming in a sea of alcohol, free of charge, yet unable to bring himself to swallow any of it. He looked up at the stage as Sasha appeared and admired how well Beki was holding together. He was a wreck himself, trying to reconcile the fact that he'd just signed a potential life debt to Gypsy – fifty years wiping down her crystal ball was not going to be fun – and a barrage of new and unfamiliar thoughts that had invaded his unusually sober mind very recently.

The way she had kissed him on the cheek and said, "Thank you." It was very nice. Very unlike Neese. He'd always loved Neese for her fire, style, and even the way she strutted over everyone else on her Oz Greens. He loved that she was powerful. But Beki … Beki needed him. She actually needed him to help her. It felt nice to be needed. Never in his life had he imagined Neese Highwaters would need him.

Well, fuck, he thought to himself as he worked on his third nail, his thumb and forefingers already a scraggly mess, *I think I'm starting to like her.*

IMMORTALITY 101: The Intro Course

24
PRESCOTT'S BRAND

The cheering and chanting went on for several minutes before a man emerged from the side stage. He was tall, with a hooknose and sleek hair, and wore a black silk tuxedo and shoes so shiny Beki could see the entire audience reflected in their surface. He took a step into the light, raised his hands, and the crowd quieted instantly. Then he turned to the head table and gave a shallow, almost mocking bow. When he lifted his head, Beki nearly bit her tongue.

"Jean-Luc," she heard someone say, and suddenly realized it was her own voice.

"No duh," Mojiha said with a scoff. "Jean-Luc, once one of us, now nothing but an errand boy for Sasha."

"He…" Beki bit down on her tongue again to stop herself. *He didn't tell me that part.*

"Welcome, esteemed High Rollers," Jean-Luc purred. His eyes betrayed no recognition of Beki. "We are honored to have you here at the Dice game. For the pleasure of the crowd, why don't you stand and be recognized by the unworthy commoners?"

The crowd cheered again. Jean-Luc spun on his heels and raised a hand to Sasha, who curtsied cutely. Beki couldn't help but swoon a bit at the bouncing curls framing her cheery smile. She was like a doll. A perfect little doll meant to be admired inside a glass case.

IMMORTALITY 101: The Intro Course

"*You saw that movie* Chuckie, *right?*" *Michigan had asked her when she first asked about Sasha. She hadn't caught his meaning at the time.*

It was hard to believe that a girl so young and sweet could have caused the miserable turn in her life. Beki was much more inclined to believe Neese's list of crimes than Sasha's. Neese was an evil woman. But Sasha... Sasha was the same age as her son!

"...Highwaters!"

Beki nearly jumped out of her seat, a conditioned response from her school roll-call days. As it was, she merely made a jerking motion and caught herself with one hand on the edge of the seat. Jean-Luc had turned to her, extending one hand in her direction. The crowd had begun a chant of *Neese, Neese, Neese!*

One of her most important lessons had been to never acknowledge such things. When prompted to make an introduction of some sort, she was told, simply ignore it. The most she ought to do was make a slight nod to the crowd as if annoyed. This lesson, however, had been imparted to her by Jean-Luc, whom she realized less than a minute ago she knew next to nothing about. How was she to know that anything the man told her was true? That what he had taught her was not some elaborate lie to trip her up? Maybe all this time she had been acting out of Neese's character and never knew. Maybe Sasha had already won.

All eyes were on her. She turned and gave the crowd a half-hearted wave and thought she saw a familiar head of brown hair. Michigan. Could she trust Michigan? He had said that Jean-Luc was an "insider", though Beki wondered if Michigan knew how much of an insider he really was.

Or maybe it was all a setup. Her mind raced and she could hear the blood pounding in her ears, louder than the raucous crowd. There was nowhere to go but forward.

"Ladies, for all your love, the delicious Mojiha Jordan!"

The crowd switched its chant to Mojiha's name without missing a beat and Beki allowed herself to relax for the moment. Mojiha sprinted out of his seat, ran to the edge of the platform, and tore open the front of his shirt, exposing his chiseled orange chest and abs to his screeching female admirers. Beki was pretty sure there were a good number of males drooling as well, although she couldn't imagine what they saw in the man besides an orange creamsicle.

"Playing for the sage Rat Spence, Boxcat Pincher!"

The crowd began to chant Rat's name. Boxcat looked over the railing and sighed, not bothering to lift his head to give a nod, then went back to looking miserable again.

Jean-Luc took a pause. Beki saw that he was looking at the mumbling old man with unbridled distain. Bice didn't notice it, or anything else for that matter. Jean-Luc cleared his throat with a look of indignation as if he'd been forced to present a cockroach at the queen's banquet. "Bice Tic," he said shortly.

The crowd erupted into a tidal wave of booing. Many people raised their hands with their thumbs pointed down, jeering and hurling insults at old Bice. Mojiha was doing the same, she saw; even Boxcat, who up until now had been completely apathetic, raised one hand with his thump pointed at the table. She quickly did the same. Bice's wrinkly head twitched on top of his skinny neck. He kept talking to the tablecloth, completely oblivious to his unpopularity.

"And last but not least, Miss Prescott Asher, playing for Lisa Gasolina. Give her a hand, folks!"

Shakily, Prescott got to her feet and walked to the center of the platform, facing the crowd that had begun to chant her mother's name. She gave them a thin smile, straining as if two-ton weights were hanging from the corners of her lips. Her skinny ankles were weighed down with a pair of red heels decorated with ruby studs. Carefully, she turned her back to the cheering crowd, reached over her shoulders, and lifted her cloak upward. Beki let out an involuntary gasp that was thankfully drowned out by the noise.

The enormous heart-shaped scar gaped at the crowd. Prescott's white dress was backless, dipping in a curve almost to her waist. The scar covered almost her entire back, the top mounds touching the line just above her armpits, and the fabric of the dress hid the tip. It was a sickly dark, pulsating red, here and there framed by dead black skin.

At the sight of the scar, the crowd exploded into frenzy. Cameras and cell phones flashed, snapping hundreds of pictures within a few seconds. They began to chant Lisa's name even louder as Prescott stripped off her cloak and tossed it over her shoulder into the crowd. She raised her white arms to the ceiling and allowed the crowd to drink in her mutilated form to their satisfaction.

"Would you look at that," Boxcar said, as if he had just spotted an interesting pebble on the side of the road. "Lisa branded another one. A heart, too. Cute."

Mojiha shook his head. "Damned shame if you ask me. Such a pretty girl. Seems a waste of all that pretty skin."

Beki understood the meaning of branding. She had seen it done to cattle once, when her grandfather took her to a ranch at age eleven. Growing up, she had always thought it was a cruel thing, cowboys burning their marks into those poor cows. But it was never like this. As Prescott skulked back to her seat, her back bare, Beki shivered. She couldn't take her eyes off the girl's damaged skin. It wasn't *just* a brand, though. She still remembered the neat, clean brand on the cow's skin after the branding iron was removed. Prescott's brand was rough and messy, here and there exposing raw, damaged flesh underneath.

As if someone painted her back with gasoline and set it on fire.

Jean-Luc was saying something else, but Beki couldn't tear her gaze away. Noticing her unease, Prescott turned to her and smiled eerily. "My mama gave me this," she whispered thinly. "It was a prize. If you had become my new sister, you would have got one, too. But only if you were good."

Beki swallowed and looked away, pretending she didn't heard Prescott's words. Sasha was descending to the bottom of the stairs and for a split second her round face turned to the head table and her eyes locked onto Beki's. Then she smiled and looked away, waving to the crowd like a queen before her subjects. Beki simply sat still and waited, continuing the endless cycle of asking what exactly she had gotten herself into the moment she met Michigan Von Phant.

Tish watched the screens from backstage along with Leonard and Mozart as Prescott presented her brand to an eager audience. Her eyes were on Neese, however, who seemed a bit disgusted at the sight. Of course she would be. Neese and Lisa never got along. She would be upset to see Lisa's mark displayed so proudly. Tish felt for her, but she also envied Prescott. Prescott was so pretty, so pale, so solemn. Her white dress and red cloak were fitting for a long, reflective stroll in a snow-covered cemetery. Tish looked down at her own gaudy getup – gold-trimmed cropped jacket, white mini dress, studded belt, and that ridiculous hat – and couldn't help but feel like a dime store doll admiring a porcelain masterpiece.

"Ew," Leonard said.

"Gross," Mozart said.

"Lisa always does weird stuff like that."

"Prescott looks like a ghost."

"What did she do – roll in flour?"

"How else do you get so white?"

Tish sighed. Instead of a pale, troubled princess who whiled away hard days waxing poetic, she was a common bumpkin trapped in a school of ignoramuses. She closed her eyes and tried to imagine herself as one of Lisa's beautiful daughters, or as one of Neese's handmaidens. She would love to have been at Neese's beck and call, wearing silver dresses and running tables instead of spinning. She hated spinning.

"Who do you think's gonna win?" Mozart asked.

Leonard tilted his head in thought. "Hard to say. Maybe Neese or Mojiha."

"Bice and Boxcat are the long shots, I think."

"Prescott's pretty good."

"You know it's not about how good you are."

"True that."

"The commoners still don't stand a chance, though."

"True that, too."

Tish spun around to face the boys. "Would you stop your gibbering?" she snapped. "You're ruining something special and beautiful with your incessant chatter."

Mozart grinned. "Aw, come on," he said. "We're just trying to make things a little livelier around here."

"Not everyone can be like you," Leonard said.

"Glass-eyed."

"Obsessive."

"Quiet."

"Angsty."

"Emo."

"What's emo?"

"I donno. I heard it the other day from some guy who just came out of the Round."

"Is it a fish?"

"Maybe a bear."

"Emo bear."

"Cool."

Tish wanted to tear her hair out by the roots, but to be presented to the High Rollers with bald spots would be unthinkable. So she adjusted her uniform and turn away instead. If Mozart and Leonard were going to play the part of jesters, then she could still headline the show as the star. They were the Spin Doctors, after all, and for a good portion of the night, all eyes would be on them. She had to impress someone today. Neese, Prescott, Mojiha, anyone. She simply had to. If all went well, by this time tomorrow she could be living in the Crescent, or serving tea in Club Meow. One of the other High Rollers might purchase her debt. It had happened to others before and it could happen to her.

As if on cue, Jean-Luc's head poked through the door. "I sure hope you're dressed nice and proper," he said as if he expected to find them naked and rolling in mud. "You're going to be presented to the guests of honor and you better not embarrass Miss Sasha."

"No problem," Mozart said, giving a thumbs-up.

"No sweat," Leonard echoed, putting on his gloves.

Tish nodded. "Of course."

Jean-Luc looked them up and down as if they had no idea what they were talking about, but motioned for them to follow him anyway. Tish walked between Mozart and Leonard, because that was how ladies were escorted – by gentlemen on either side. Although Mozart and Leonard were no gentlemen, she couldn't exactly do much better.

And then, without warning, she was there. Neese Highwaters. The Queen. The Goddess. And she was breaking away from the group gathered in the lounge to approach Tish. Tish felt light-headed but kept her feet on the ground.

"Whoa, here she comes," Leonard whispered out of the corner of his mouth.

"Don't choke, Tish," Mozart teased.

She resisted the urge to elbow them both in the nuts and stood straight and proud as Neese drew near. Their eyes met and she couldn't speak. Neese smiled and leaned down, her lips barely an inch from

Tish's ear. She could smell Neese's perfume, fragrant and indecently expensive.

"Sweetie," Neese whispered and Tish shivered with excitement, "you've got some toilet paper stuck to your shoe."

Beki was nursing her third drink when she spotted Jean-Luc entering the lounge. She had gotten over her initial fear of getting drunk and letting something loose after realizing that she just might have been set up for failure by a goofy Frenchman and his band of geeks. Fortunately, the High Rollers had as much to say to each other in private as they did in public. The only one attempting to make conversation was Mojiha, who alternated between throwing lines at Beki and trying to cozy up to Prescott. Boxcat appeared to have fallen asleep on the sofa and Bice was carrying on a most invigorating conversation with a hat rack.

Based on Jean-Luc's briefing, the High Rollers were to receive royal treatment in a private lounge while the rest of the contestants competed for spots in the final round. The High Rollers were automatically qualified, and five more spots were reserved for the other contestants. The lounge was small and cozy, with a banquet table full of delicacies and a champagne tower, as well as an open bar. There were six sixty-inch television screens affixed to the wall in two rows of three. The top three each showed one of the three wheels on stage, while the rest showed the grand hall from different angles. Beki thought she spotted Michigan briefly on one of the screens.

When Jean-Luc walked in and closed the door behind him, she set her drink down and motioned for him to come to her. He did, but with a most displeased look on his face.

"How can I help you, Miss Neese?" he said loudly as he crossed the room, and dropped to a low hiss as soon as he got close enough. "What are you doing? You can't be seen talking to me like this."

Beki looked over his shoulder. Prescott was sitting with her knees drawn as Mojiha tried to lay his arm around her in a fake yawn. Boxcat was snoring, completely undisturbed by Bice's conversation two feet away. "Who's looking?"

"You never know." Jean-Luc looked over his shoulder nervously. "You're doing fine. Just remember what I told you and you'll do fine."

287

"Why didn't you tell me you worked for Sasha?"

"Because it doesn't matter," Jean-Luc replied pointedly. "You made it here, didn't you?"

"How do I know you're really helping me?"

Jean-Luc snickered. "I'm not helping you," he said. "I'm not helping her either. I already told you, I'm doing this because I'm bored. My job was just to make sure the game happens and a good show gets put on. Everyone's watching, you know."

Beki reached out and grabbed his wrist as he tried to walk away. "What about my son? You said you'd take care of everything so I can win for my son. He's dying in a hospital while I'm here pretending to be some high society bitch."

Jean-Luc shrugged. "I don't care about your son. If you want to save him you better win." He eyed her hand in annoyance. "And if you could, please do not manhandle me. It is very unsanitary."

"You said you'd rig it so I would win."

"I said I'd rig it to give you a chance. It wouldn't be a good show if I already knew you'd win."

"You bastard."

Jean-Luc grinned and wrenched his hand free. "Why, thank you," he said.

Beki bit her lip and restrained herself from giving him a thrashing. Knowing what she'd learned about Neese so far, no one would bat an eye if she pounded on Jean-Luc's head with a punchbowl right now. "Whatever," she said, and pointed to Bice. "What's wrong with him?"

"He's fallen."

"What's that mean?"

"Did something to screw himself out of his fortune and fell in bad with the other High Rollers. Do throw a couple of insults at him when you get a chance."

"Are all the fallen ones like that?"

"Just him and Adda. Actually, we're still not quite sure if he's faking. But if you'll excuse me, I must go alert the Spin Doctors to get ready." He raised a finger in front of her face. "Remember my lessons now, little girl."

Beki considered throwing something at him, but after a moment decided to have another drink instead. She was beginning to understand why Michigan was perpetually drunk – something about this place and these people made alcohol slide right down. She looked over at Prescott and considered offering her a drink. She looked like she needed it.

A moment later Jean-Luc reappeared, this time accompanied by three others. They were younger than Beki had expected, especially the girl, who had straight dark blond hair that ended at her narrow shoulders, and small budding breasts; she looked fourteen years old at the most. Her companions were older, two boys perhaps in their late teens. One had a head of bushy brown hair that reminded her of Eric and the other's bleach blond do was spiked with gel. They all wore the same uniform – gold-trimmed white jackets above white pants (skirt for the girl), studded belts around their waists, and an oddly-shaped hat with the Red Cross symbol on its front. Beki supposed it was a pun. Spin Doctors. Clever.

"May I present to you the Spin Doctors for today's game," Jean-Luc announced. No one but Beki turned to look. He pointed to the brown-haired boy. "Leonard Haze." The blond boy. "Mozart Dupont." Then the girl. "And Tishia Wellington."

Mojiha turned away from Prescott and waved half-heartedly. "Yo," he said, and went back to wooing Prescott, who didn't raise her head once. Boxcat snorted in his sleep. Bice's head jerked upward. He rubbed his eyes and stared at the Spin Doctors, as if suddenly realizing that there were people in the room other than himself and the hat rack. He gave them a single nod and went back to his conversation.

The girl named Tishia looked nervous, almost as bad as Prescott. Her knees seemed to be shaking as she stood there between the boys, who were looking around nonchalantly. Beki felt for her. She looked like a sweet girl thrust into a situation she didn't like, and she was staring at Beki with an awkward smile, as if she might burst into laughter or tears at any second. There was also a small strip of toilet paper stuck to the bottom of her right heel. Beki looked around quickly, noting that the others weren't paying attention, and quickly made her way to the girl.

"Hey sweetie," she whispered to Tishia, "you've got some toilet paper stuck to your shoe."

289

Tishia let out a sound like a bird trying to swallow a frog too big for its narrow throat. She looked down at her shoes and her face instantly turned a shade of unhealthy red. Without a word, she spun around, nearly fell, and bolted out of the room. The boys exchanged a look and a nod.

"Hey!" Jean-Luc called after her. "You can't leave now, young lady! Come back here!"

"She's just being dramatic," said the boy named Mozart.

"That she is," said Leonard.

Guilt overwhelmed Beki. She hated to think that she had just embarrassed the poor girl. It must have been important to her, spinning in front of the High Rollers tonight, and Beki had just humiliated her in front of the most important audience. The side of her that was a mother above all else wanted to go after the girl and comfort her, but she quickly reminded herself that showing sympathy would only undo what she had done so far, even if she wasn't quite sure what that was. Would screwing up make a good show? Maybe Jean-Luc would secretly love it if she were to screw up in public. So, instead of going after the girl, she turned on her heels, returned to the bar, and let Jean-Luc go after her instead.

"Look at that, Neese. You made her cry."

At first she thought Prescott had spoken. The voice was soft and young, but Beki had never heard Prescott speak above a breathy, eerie whisper. She turned, paused, and turned back to the bar, where she poured herself a shot of hard liquor and downed it in one gulp before turning back again.

"How was the Round?" Sasha asked, smiling like a perfect Stepford child.

Beki had taken two years of drama in high school. At fourteen, she had the delusions of grandeur that so often infected young minds not yet familiar with the ways of the world. She thought about going to Hollywood some day and becoming an actress, maybe even making it big. Her biggest dream had been to become a white Halle Berry, though an independent film star wouldn't have been the worst thing in the world. By age seventeen that dream had mostly died after she

290

discovered that she wasn't such a good actress. Talent was a birthright, impossible to acquire through practice.

The point was she was terrible at acting. She had no idea how to play off the actions of her partner, couldn't think on her feet, and every time she exchanged more than three lines of dialog with someone the fourth could come out with a strange stammer as she struggled to remember the fifth. She was never even cast as the lead in the small plays they put on for the middle-school kids. In her senior musical she danced in the back and didn't say a single line.

Now, with her son's life on the line, Beki suddenly realized she had to recall all the lessons she failed to learn in drama class nearly twenty years before. She took exactly one second to think about the difference between upstage and downstage, then tried to remember the definition for method acting, then attempted to remember if she was ever good at improvisation, and finally decided on one thing – play it by ear. She smiled back at Sasha.

She was a very beautiful child, golden curls above alabaster skin. Her lashes were long and her lips were painted as if by an artist's brush. Next to sad, gloomy Prescott, Sasha looked like a ray of sunshine. She was far above any preteen beauty queens Beki had seen in magazines or on television. Even in the enormous golden dress she walked as if on a cloud and, when she acknowledged Beki, she had curtsied, a little half-bow too adorable for words. Everything on Sasha was the image of a perfect little girl with the exception of one thing – that fleck of frustration in her eyes. Beki had seen that same look before, when her son was eight years old and too short to ride the roller coast at Six Flags. He had whined and pouted and sulked the rest of the day with that look of frustration in his eyes, as if growing up took much too long. Now, looking at Sasha, Beki thought she saw the same thing – a combination of envy and annoyance. It must be awfully frustrating, she realized, to have a body that never grew.

"Uneventful," she said, trying her best to act bored. Jean-Luc was standing behind Sasha. He gave a very slight nod of approval.

Sasha tilted her head to one side ever so slightly. "Is that so?" she asked. "I had heard otherwise."

"Around here gossip flows like shit in the sewers. I would think you of all people would know better than to pay attention to idle chatter."

Sasha's neatly trimmed brow raised for a split second then dropped back down again. She walked past Beki to the bar and pulled herself up to its level on a stepping stool. Beki had been wondering what the stool was for ever since she had arrived in the lounge. She waited while Sasha made herself a drink – a shot of gin with a little paper umbrella in it. Beki held back the lecture about underage drinking that immediately sprang to the tip of her tongue.

"Come with me," Sasha said. It wasn't a request so much as a command. "I have something to show you."

Beki glanced at Jean-Luc, who looked as surprised as she did. "I don't think you have anything that would interest me."

Boxcat let out another snort in his sleep, almost as if he was laughing at her. Prescott looked up. She had turned her back to Mojiha and was sitting barefoot on the sofa with her knees drawn up to her chin. Her blue eyes bore into Beki. Mojiha was rubbing her shoulders and every now and then would gently touch the scar on her back as if it was the most erotic thing in the world. Beki shuddered.

Sasha pouted mockingly. "Aw, come on," she said sweetly, "... Rebecca."

25
REBECCA

Sasha watched the Rounder squirm. It was a delicious feeling. So unfortunate that the humor was lost on the rest of the idiots in the room. She drank her gin slowly and waited for the Rounder to come out of shock, perhaps make a slip. She would wait as long as she had to.

"Why not," said the woman pretending to be Neese Highwaters. "I have nothing better to do at this sad little party. Entertain me."

Sasha frowned, but only a little, as frowning was not very ladylike. Once was a fluke. Twice was luck. But the way the Rounder had parried her goading comments was surely not by chance. She studied her closely. She was wearing Neese's face and clothes, right down to those tacky Oz Green shoes. Her hair was parted slightly to the right, as Neese usually preferred it, and she was wearing two rings with black stones on the second and fourth fingers of her right hand and a red ruby ring on her left middle finger, as was Neese's habit. Her lips were painted a reddish brown and she over-enunciated her words slightly.

To retain one's character after passing through to the Round ought to be impossible, and yet there she was. The sound of the name she used in the Round had rattled her a bit, but she had quickly regained composure.

Surely Michigan Von Phant couldn't have trained her this well... or could he? Sasha had always prided herself on being an excellent judge of character and Michigan had always been a fool of fools in her book, a spineless sniveling coward. But then, he did risk having his ribs broken by Stat to pull Neese out of the Round.

The thought of Stat saddened her. He wasn't there. She had ordered the cameras to sweep the crowd at least half a dozen times, capturing every corner and shadow that he might hide in, to no avail. Not only did he refuse to squire her, he hadn't even thought to come to this monumental event.

"Well?" the Rounder asked in the manner of the contemptuous Neese.

Stat stared at the clock above Grimm's fireplace. It was an ugly little clock, he realized. Very fitting for this ugly little house with its ugly little furniture and ugly little red door. But somehow all the ugliness had its own charm. He waited for Grimm to make tea in the kitchen. It was another twenty minutes before the tea was placed in front of him. He added sugar to his cup as Grimm made himself comfortable across the table. The old man leaned with both hands on his cane and faced Stat.

"What?"

Grimm said nothing.

"Don't look at me like that."

Grimm took his own cup and blew on the surface, sending tealeaves dancing over the ripples. Then he looked at Stat again.

"Let's play cards."

Grimm shook his head.

"If you're just going to give me a hard time about this I'm going to leave." He pretended to stand. "I'm serious. I'll leave."

Grimm thumped his cane once on the floor heavily, then made a sound that was almost a laugh. Sighing, Stat sat back down and sulked over his tea, adding a second lump of sugar.

"Yeah, I know. I have nowhere else to go. But that's only because everyone's at that stupid game so there's nothing for me to do." He caught Grimm tilting his head out of the corner of his eye. "Don't look at me like that! I said I'm not going. This isn't any of my business."

Grimm turned to the clock.

"It's too late, anyway. It'll be almost over by the time I get there."

Grimm shook his head.

"Yes, that *is* what this is about. It's not about her. Why do you even care anyway?" Stat added another lump of sugar to his cup. "I thought you hated the High Rollers. Why are you pushing me to her?"

Slowly, Grimm raised one bony hand and placed it over his heart.

"No, I don't need to be going to her. It's not healthy."

Grimm shrugged.

"Yes, it matters."

Grimm looked down. Stat followed his gaze and saw that his cup was overflowing with sugar cubes. With an exasperated sigh he pushed it aside and folded his arms defiantly. "I'm not going."

Grimm said nothing.

"I'm not."

Grimm shrugged again.

"You can't make me, you know? I'm an adult."

Grimm reached under his hood and scratched his nose.

Stat threw up his hands. "Alright!" he exclaimed. "Fine! I'll go! Damn it, quit it with the third degree!"

Grimm nodded in satisfaction and poured himself some more tea.

Beki followed Sasha up a flight of winding stairs to what looked like a small library. It was very stuffy, and the shelves lining the walls were more than a little dusty. There were a few books here and there, but most of the shelves were lined with dolls that reminded her of the knock-off plastic Barbies one could get for a dollar or less. In the center of the room, taking up almost all of the space, was a large pool table. There were four more dolls sitting along its edge, their plastic legs bent in ninety-degree angels at the hips.

Sasha hiked her skirt up and hopped onto the table, her legs dangling over its side. "How long have you been here?"

Beki looked at the dolls. There were two women, one of whom had red hair that had been cruelly mangled, one man, and one little girl. Something about them gave her the creeps, though she couldn't quite figure out why. Maybe it was the way they were sitting, with one arm raised and their heads turned toward the door – toward her – as if they had been expecting her. She tore her gaze away and focused on Sasha.

"Five or six days. It's hard to tell since the sun only came up twice."

"The generators are on the frits." Sasha swung her legs back and forth. "Have you been with Michigan all this time?"

"I don't think that's any of your business."

Sasha giggled shrilly. "You can drop the act," she said. "We both know who you are, Rebecca."

Beki rolled this fact around in her head, weighed the pros and cons of admitting to her own "vanillaness", thought about different directions she could go with the whole "don't know what you're talking about" act, and decided that Sasha wasn't so cute once she started talking. In fact, she was kind of obnoxious, like one of those evil mafia queens on television, just in a smaller package.

"Beki is fine."

Sasha's pouty, painted lips split into a wide, triumphant grin. "I'm Sasha."

"I know." Then, taking a long shot, "I'm sorry."

Sasha blinked. "Sorry?" she echoed, mimicking Beki's tone. "Neese would never say that. What are you sorry for?"

Although Jean-Luc and Michigan were well out of earshot, Beki imagined the two of them weeping in disappointment and despair as she went on. "I was told that I did something to you—well, the me in this world, Neese – did something to you, so you retaliated by screwing up my life. It's all very complicated to me."

Sasha giggled again. "So you decided to say you're sorry?"

The way the little girl – a child no older than her son and wearing ribbons around her pigtails – was looking at her gave Beki an uncomfortable shiver down her back. It was as if their roles were reversed. Beki felt like a child in the principal's office, being coaxed into confessing to a prank she didn't play. She cleared her throat and tried to remember that she was the adult here, not the other way around.

Damn it, Neese. Help me out here.

"It's actually not complicated at all," Sasha said before Beki opened her mouth. "I don't know how Michigan got you to dress that way but he didn't teach you the technicalities very well. See, a Round game is always changing. It's based on the black chips that make good things happen and the blue chips that make bad things happen. You're supposed to roll for a pile of each before you start, but you got cocky and didn't allow for that last roll to finish before you started the game."

It was a simplified version of what Jean-Luc had already told her. It didn't make much sense then and it wasn't making much sense now. Beki kept her mouth shut and nodded. The dry air in the musty room was making her lips crack.

"I just put in a couple of extra chips for you." Sasha crossed her legs and shrugged. She was wearing white knee socks underneath the dress, with a pair of gold kitten heels. "Who knew it would turn out so... bad?"

"You did," Beki said. "Isn't that what High Rollers do? They lie and cheat to get what they want?"

"Spoken like a Rounder." Sasha scoffed. "This is why I hate people who play the Round. Some of them come out all preachy. Morals this, principles that. Nothing but hypocrites. Within a couple of days they're back of their old *sinful* selves." She stretched the word "sinful" with dripping sarcasm. "What we use is skill."

"You call lying and cheating skills?"

"I don't see you doing any better. You're the one pretending to be Neese. And by the way, you're sucking at it."

It was like arguing with a twelve-year-old. Scratch that, she *was* arguing with a twelve-year-old. Beki wanted to slap herself for getting goaded into it. She also wanted to yell at Sasha to pull down her dress and send herself to bed without dinner. Instead, she collected her thoughts and focused on what was important.

"I apologize for everything," she said. "Whatever you want. I'm sure you like hearing that coming out of Neese's mouth. Just fix everything. I want my son to live. Undo whatever it was you did and let him live."

"No."

Beki started. "No?"

"No," Sasha said with a shake of her head. Her curly pigtails swung like whips. "I don't want to."

"Why not?"

"I don't like you," Sasha said simply. "I got you here so we can play. I want to beat you."

297

"If I let you beat me, will you fix everything?"

"No." Sasha picked up one of the dolls, the one with long brown hair, and began to comb its hair with her fingers. "Then it wouldn't be fun. If you play to lose then you won't try. You said your son's life is depending on it, right? I want to you play like that. Like both his and your lives are depending on it."

Beki watched Sasha's manicured nails disappear and reappear from the doll's haywire hair. It looked helpless as Sasha's nails scraped against its scalp. Beki thought she could relate. "Why? What did I do to you?"

"Nothing," Sasha replied, hopping off the table. The doll dangled in her hand, much the same way a hanging body would after rigor mortis set in. "You didn't do anything to me. Nothing out of the ordinary, anyway. This is what we *do* to each other as High Rollers. We do it for fun. I wanted to put on a good show this time, and nothing would make a better show than someone playing for their life. Nobody plays for their life around here, and any other Rounder wouldn't be high profile enough to attract attention. So you were perfect."

"You set Michigan up. You knew he would bring me here."

"Yep." Sasha strolled over to Beki and placed the doll in her hands. "Now don't disappoint me. Try to win. We could have a great show tonight. You can't get into Neese's safe, right? So you must have conned someone else into giving you the chips. Kudos. If you win you'll have enough chips to overturn the last bet."

Beki looked at the doll and nearly dropped it. There were two bright yellow thumbtacks stuck into its eyes. The doll was smiling, however. Always smiling. "I thought you wanted to beat me."

"And I will." Sasha stepped past Beki and paused at the door. "I just called you here to gauge how much competition you are. Now I know that you stand no chance against me at all. Who knew Neese would turn into… you? You have nothing compared to her. You can't do a fraction of the things she does. And when she gets back here, I'm going to thoroughly enjoy rubbing *you* in her face."

Beki pulled the tacks out of the doll's eyes. It seemed cruel to leave them in. They left perfect little holes in the doll's pupils. "Am I going to turn into Adda?"

Sasha's eyes betrayed surprise. "So Michigan told you about Adda, huh?"

"I saw her. If I lose, will I turn into her?"

The hard slam of the door made Beki jump. The thumbtacks fell to the floor. She looked up and saw that Sasha's cool, teasing demeanor had melted into anger. Lips pursed, hands on her hips, Sasha stomped her way in front of Beki, blue eyes burning as she stared up at her. "When did you see Adda?" she demanded.

"I met a guy named Status Quo." Suddenly nervous, Beki set the doll carefully back onto the pool table. "He took me to…"

"Grimm's house," Sasha whispered softly. "Quo took you to Grimm's house."

"We had tea."

Something had changed. But before Beki could quite figure it out, Sasha reached past her, grabbed the brown-haired doll, wrenched its head from its torso, and threw both across the room. The mutilated doll struck the corner of a shelf and the head bounced back onto the pool table, where it spun twice before coming to rest. With a shriek of rage Sasha spun around and stormed out of the room, slamming the door behind her so hard it rattled on its hinges.

Beki looked at the doll head. It looked back at her and smiled brightly, not missing its eyes and limbs one bit. Its hair was the exact same shade as Beki's. She hoped dearly that it wasn't an omen.

In a hidden fold on the breast of her dress she had hidden the pill. If she wanted to pass herself off as Neese for the rest of the night, it was her best bet. She felt for it through the dress, and felt a surge of relief to find that it was still there.

Sasha hadn't meant to throw a tantrum. She was half way down the stairs before she remembered that temper tantrums were very unladylike and quickly paused and patted her cheeks, hoping they were still a proper, natural color despite the simmering rage in her gut. She looked behind her and saw that the Rounder had not followed and breathed a sigh of relief. She didn't want to see the infuriating woman. Not now. Not until the final game, when she would crush her in front of millions of watchful eyes.

She couldn't figure it out. Couldn't understand why Stat would pay attention to that woman. Rebecca. Such a disgustingly sweet name. He had never offered to take Sasha to Grimm's place, which was his second sanctuary. And tea... he never took Sasha out to have tea, or make tea for her, or even ask if she would like to have tea with him. Anywhere. Anytime. He never did. So why her?

Sasha wanted to cry, but she couldn't do it in the stairwell and with so many people waiting just downstairs. Besides, she would ruin her makeup, and ladies should never be seen with running mascara.

Neese was a sneaky one.

She hadn't expected this. Without every advantage, brainwashed by the Round, mixed up with a moron like Michigan Von Phant, she still managed to strike Sasha where it hurt most. The humiliation she caused would not go unpunished.

Sasha swallowed her tears and continued down the stairs with renewed resolve. She had more reasons than ever to win now. She would defeat Neese, remind the commoners of the true High Rollers, and win Stat's heart, all in one summary strike. When he saw her as the winner, he would come back to her. He would realize once and for all that the only one he wanted was her.

26
THE ODDS

The hall was filled with the scent of excitement.

Thousands of spectators held their breaths at once as Gypsy's wheel began to slow. It ticked past a gold space, then another gold space, then another, inching ever closer to the single white space. Then, it stopped. The little ball teetered on the divider, and then fell into the gold space adjacent the white. The breath of relief was simultaneous, creating a sound as if an enormous balloon had sprung a leak, followed by cheers. Gypsy Hoss had qualified for the final round. Those who had bet on her shouted with joy.

The television screens surrounding the hall changed from a close-up of the last round of spins to a display of the finalists. To qualify, one must reach at least one hundred and twenty thousand points within twelve spins. Out of the qualifiers, the five who score the highest after fifteen spins would earn coveted spots alongside the High Rollers. The competition was fierce this time, more so than anyone could remember. The scent of Luck pumped through the veins of the crowd like liquid adrenalin. As the contestants heaped on their own chips, vying for a spot at the top, the others rushed to the betting tables set up along the perimeter of the hall, throwing their own meager fortunes into the pot.

The screens went black for a split second, then returned with the updated scores.

Contestant	Score	Qualified
Neese Highwaters	N/A	Y
Mojiha Jordan	N/A	Y
Lisa Gasolina	N/A	Y
Rat Spence	N/A	Y
Bice Tic	N/A	Y
Gypsy Hoss	789,120	Y
Kam Hurley	762,200	Y
Tracer pane	723,129	Y
Moria Banners	699,946	Y
Lexicon Powell	690,724	Y

Never before had the scores been so high. Never before had they gone over and above the limit in a way that made the audience salivate with anticipation. Something was fueling it endlessly, ruthlessly. It was almost supernatural, almost unreal. People talked amongst themselves between downing alcohol and placing increasingly larger bets.

Was Neese Highwaters really a Rounder? Did you see the way she waved to us?

Is Bice Tic really sane enough to compete? What about the rumors that he'd already gone over the edge like Adda?

Will Gypsy Hoss really become a High Roller? I thought she hated them.

Why is the Wonder Twin competing alone? Where's her sister?

Did Sasha rig the game to soak the other High Rollers? She hates to lose.

Tracer is aiming to win.

Betting on Lexicon could pay off big.

Is Rat watching Boxcat play?

Is Neese a Rounder?

The display faded from the screens and was replaced by a new chart.

	Contestant	Payoff
1	Mojiha Jordan	3-1
2	Lisa Gasolina	3-1
3	Gypsy Hoss	4-1
4	Rat Spence	5-1
5	Bice Tic	6-1
6	Kam Hurley	15-1
7	Tracer Pæne	17-1
8	Moria Banners	20-1
9	Lexicon Powell	25-1
10	Neese Highwaters	50-1

Silence fell over the crowd. There was a pause, followed by a mad scramble to place the last round of bets. Voices erupted from all around. People climbed over each other, shouting across the room and trying to debate the significance of the high payoff for Neese's victory while at the same time getting a piece of the possible profit before the betting tables closed. The rumors were true, they all agreed through exchanged glances and nods. Neese had never been given a payoff higher than 2-1. Something was different. Something had to be wrong. Was it a dig at Neese? Was it a joke? Was it a trick to get their chips? Was it an error?

But the display never changed. There was Neese's name at the bottom of the list. Fifty to one. Everyone knew it had to be wrong. Everyone knew it couldn't happen. A professional like Neese would never be given that kind of odds. It was fishy as high hell. No way Neese could lose to the commoners.

And yet, as tickets worth millions and millions of chips exchanged hands, none of them read *Neese Highwaters*.

Michigan Von Phant had to duck out of the way when the crowd around him started toward the betting tables like mad. He was elbowed in the ribs, slapped on the head, and nearly trampled by a trio of large women in bright pink sundresses. Granted, some of it might have been due to his slowed reflexes. The endless flow of alcohol – doubtlessly supplied by Geoffy at exuberant prices – had finally won over his nerves. He shuffled into a corner, out of the way of the stampede, and looked up at the display monitors. Far as he could figure, Sasha was confident. The huge payoff was obviously an insult to Neese, but Beki probably couldn't care less. Michigan smiled at the thought. Still, it made him worry that Beki had already made a mistake to stoke Sasha's confidence like that.

He was dirt poor. Most of his Luck had already gone to paying off the Snyperx for their trouble, bribing the security at the Crescent to let him in, and, of course, the many drinks to calm himself through this whole thing. As it turned out, drinks were free only during the first hour, serving to loosen up the wallets of the gamblers. Since then, prices had grown with every half-hour. The strategy was brilliant. After all, when faced with losing one's entire fortune, what was another fifty-chip for a consolation drink?

If Beki lost this, he was going to owe Gypsy a life debt, which currently went on the market for half a million chips. Everything he owned had gone into this. In the hands of a Rounder. It made him think maybe everyone else was right. Maybe he really was stupid.

He fished into his pockets and came up with a single fifty-count chip, the one he had fished out of Lady Luck's fountain when Beki was busy preparing for the competition. At the time it had seemed like a waste but now having it felt wrong. He was never one to believe that luck actually existed, or that the funky statue had any sort of power over how this night was going to turn out, but he suddenly felt guilty, as if his taking the chip had somehow doomed Beki to failure. Had he already inadvertently pissed Lady Luck off?

He looked at the display again, sighed, and headed to the nearest betting table, where he exchanged the fifty-count chip for a ticket with Neese's name on it. The lone number "50" looked so small printed on the ticket. Peeking over at the nearest person, he saw their ticket was for a seventy-eight thousand bet on Gypsy.

"Vote of confidence for you, babe," he said to no one in particular.

Tish gripped the wheel and pushed it to one side, her finger almost missing the trigger under its rim as it flew past. She extended her middle finger and felt the gentle impact against it as the switch flipped from the off position to on. Then, sighing wistfully, she stood aside and waited for the magnetic field to guide the ball into the white pocket. She waited for the contestant to finish his uncouth howl of desperation before signaling him to move along. The routine could get tedious, especially in a game this large.

They were a greedy bunch. Tish mourned her fate as she set up for the next game. The memory of the embarrassment she had endured in front of Neese was unbearable. And Neese was her usual cruel self, pointing at her shoe with such mock sincerity. Tish bit back bitter tears and tried to focus on the job. Like most everyone else, she had debts to pay. Sasha had promised that if the winnings tonight were kept under control, she would drop up to ten percent of the Spin Doctors' personal debts. Tish vowed to stop gambling after the debt is paid off. Never again, she promised herself. Never again unless it's for Neese.

The job itself was also quite humiliating, she often felt. Leonard and Mozart didn't seem to mind, but those idiots never minded anything. Tish knew she was skilled. More skilled than Leonard and Mozart put together, because she was the only one who took the training seriously, wearing her fingers to the bone learning how to manipulate the wheel, practicing day after night after day. Back then she had been so devoted, so blinded by her admiration of Sasha that nothing was too hard when it came to impressing her. She became good. Very good. Unfortunately, her skills weren't necessary when it came to the crucial moments. The magnetic fields, invented by that irritating man who always hung around Sasha, made skill irrelevant. When a score rose too high, she simply had to flip a switch and the ball would fall into the white pocket as if guided by a magic hand. Tish didn't understand the mechanics behind it, but it angered her no end. It was a safety net that reduced a game of chance to nothing but a sleight of hand. And so, Sasha was never impressed with her skills.

But Neese would be, she promised herself. Neese would be impressed by her. Next time it would be different.

The woman in front her began to sob as her ball fell into the white pocket on the first round. Tish gestured for her to move along when the crowd suddenly went quiet. She looked around to find the cause and saw that every pair of eyes in the room was glued to the display monitors.

"Check it out," she heard Mozart say.

"Fifty to one." Leonard whistled.

"I want to get in on that."

"Me, too."

"Damn this job."

"Damn it three times."

Tish took a few moments to process the numbers as chaos broke out on the floor. The few remaining contestants, realizing that their chances of entering the final round were abysmal, withdrew from the competition and made a beeline for the betting tables to put their chips on Prescott and Mojiha. Too busy sorting through her feelings, Tish didn't notice Leonard and Mozart flanking her from either side.

"Your hero's gonna lose."

"Sasha's never paid fifty to one."

"She must be confident."

"The game's gonna be rigged."

"Wonder why."

"Why indeed."

"She hates Neese."

"Gotta be it."

"Gonna be fun."

"Sure will."

Tish reached out and clapped one hand against each boy's mouth. "Shut up," she snapped. "Shut up, shut up, shut up!"

She began to pace up and down the stage. Mozart and Leonard watched her with the same interest kittens gave a mechanical mouse. Tish ignored their idiotic gapes and tried to think. Sasha had to be rigging the game. A loss like this could cause Neese to become one of the fallen. That couldn't happen. Neese was going to be her way out of this place. She loved Neese. Respected her. Worshiped her.

"She's thinking," Leonard said.

"Uh-oh," Mozart said.

"She might hurt herself."

"I think she already has."

She had to even the odds. Tish racked her brain. What could she do to even the odds? What could she do as one measly, miserable girl? Her head and heart felt equally heavy as she continued plodding up and down the stage. This was it. If Sasha had rigged the game then she had no chance to be by Neese's side because Neese's humiliation would drive her to become one of the fallen. Tish wanted to cry at the thought of beautiful Neese standing in front of a lamppost and trying to carry on a conversation with it.

Then it dawned on her. It was all so simple. Tish stopped in her steps and spun around to face the two boys, who continued to look at her incredulously.

"I've got it," she said.

"By George, she's got it," Mozart said.

"By George," Leonard said.

"We throw the game," Tish announced. "It's all in our hands. All we have to do is *not* hit that little knob."

"Sasha will be mad," Mozart said.

"She'll do terrible things to us," Leonard said.

"More debt."

"More work."

"Ugly outfits."

"And she might beat us with a stick."

"You're cowards," Tish said heatedly. "Cowards of the lowest grade!"

"Why don't you throw the game?" Leonard asked, scratching his scalp. The hats often became itchy after long periods of wear. "Just make sure you spin for Neese."

"Yeah," Mozart said. "Then you can tell her about it after she wins. She'll love you so much that she'll take you under her wing."

Tish's heart skipped a beat. She was far too excited to notice the sarcasm in their voices.

When Beki returned to the lounge most of the High Rollers were gone. The only one left was Prescott, who was kneeling on the sofa with her back to Beki. The hideous heart-shaped brand jostled up and down and with an uncomfortable quiver Beki realized the girl was masturbating.

Before she could formulate a plan to slip out quietly, Prescott turned around. Tears were streaming down her pale face and Beki saw that she had picked the scab off of a few of the oddly shaped scars around her mouth. They were bleeding thinly.

"Why?" she asked a spot on the wall right behind Beki. "Why does it have to be you? I love him, too."

IMMORTALITY 101: The Intro Course

"The dice game is painfully simple." Jean-Luc combed his hair in front of the full-length mirror while Beki shrugged into yet another satin dress. He turned, motioned for her to turn in a full circle, then shook his head and pointed at a different outfit. "There is one die. You take turns rolling. Only once. Whoever gets the higher score wins."

"That's..." Beki tried to search for a respectable word and failed. "Stupid."

To her surprise Jean-Luc grinned at her through the mirror. "Isn't it? I always thought so. But that's the best Sasha could come up with. What can you do? She's forever young and lacking in creativity. But in a way that makes the game more interesting, don't you think? Everything rides on that one roll. No second chances. No strategy. Nothing. It's more nerve-racking than you think. The game is charming in its simplicity. There's also something else."

"What?"

"The die used for the game is a special die. As far as I know, there's only one like it."

"Must be valuable." She pulled another dress out of the pile. It felt a lot like she was rummaging through someone else's stuff. Beki kept expecting its rightful owner to barge through the door and demand to know what she was doing.

"Not really. It's just an ugly orange thing. Sasha's got some unnatural attachment to it. Unfortunately this means she's become rather adept at rolling it. She claims it's magic but that's probably all in her head. Still, she's very good at it nonetheless. She can hit a hundred and twenty almost every single time."

"A hundred and twenty?"

"The die has a hundred and twenty sides."

"My son's got a friend who plays something called Dungeons and Dragons. I bet he'd love something like that."

Jean-Luc stared at her, then sighed. "Less talking, more changing."

27
THE WHITE POCKETS

Jean-Luc peered under the wheel set up in the gallery upstairs. Moving the pool table was troublesome, but thankfully he had Leonard and Mozart to do most of the work so he didn't have to get dust on his suit. This part, however, couldn't be avoided. He squatted under the wheel and fiddled with the intricate mechanism underneath it, careful not to dirty his cuffs.

Sasha had instructed that "Neese" be allowed to win until she reached the final round. All others were to be eliminated as soon as possible. The small magnetic wave generator was his personal invention. Its design involved long hours of calculations, delicately balanced geometry, and many days with a tiny screwdriver. It ought to guide Neese to the final round with no problem.

Jean-Luc scoffed at the thought. That woman was not Neese. It was only for Neese's sake that he was setting this up. He double-checked the switch, flipping it smoothly and soundlessly back and forth. All it took was a gentle touch to turn it on and off. While spinning, the Spin Doctor need only extend one finger, usually the middle finger since it's the longest, a few millimeters a certain way to hit it. Even Tish, with her head in cloud nine, couldn't mess this one up.

The second round was quite a bit different from the qualifying round. Jean-Luc felt a twitch of excitement as he finished tuning the machine. Instead of becoming easier and encouraging larger bets, the second round was designed to eliminate contestants. The gold pocket became smaller and smaller and white pockets are added after each spin. It was a true test of the contestant's skills and he couldn't remember the last time such a game was held.

It amazed him, really, that no one had caught on to his wave generator for this long. Perhaps people were so consumed by greed that they refused to notice anything that might possibly take that glimmer of hope away. To admit that the game was rigged would be admitting that no one among them will ever win enough chips to enter the elite ranks of the High Rollers, when in reality that was actually the case – most of the games had been rigged to prevent new meat from trying to muscle out the incumbents. The High Rollers were perfectly comfortable on their thrones and had no plans to move.

Adjustments finished, Jean-Luc stood, fished a ball out of his pocket, and dropped it into the wheel, flipping the switch to the on position with his other hand. The ball slid downward with the pull of gravity, then suddenly made an impossible ninety-degree curve and landed in the gold pocket.

Jean-Luc applauded himself inwardly. It was perfect. Everything was going right. It was really rather ironic that Beki didn't know that her winning would be playing right into Sasha' hand. That wasn't Jean-Luc's problem though. He had fixed things just so that he could please them both. Now as long as those Spin Doctors remembered to hit the switch everything would go perfectly.

There was one last thing to do, but Jean-Luc was still debating on it. In technical terms, he'd already had the fun he was seeking. He dressed up Neese, made the new wheel, and now would watch it all play out. However, he still hadn't decided whose win would make a better show.

Aside from Gypsy Hoss, the other contestants who had made it through the qualifying round all had two things in common – they were very young; not a single one looked over twenty-five, and they were very ill-at-ease in front of the High Rollers, especially Beki.

After her awkward encounter with Prescott, Beki had quickly backed out of the room to collect herself, only to be greeted by a grinning Mojiha, who had no concept of personal space and smelled like six different perfumes. Beki didn't want to think what – or who – he'd gone off to do while she was upstairs.

"Where have you been, Neese?" he asked her, smiling broadly. "You missed the posting of the odds. Didja piss off Sasha or what? Looks like she's got it in for you."

Boxcat and Bice followed soon after. Bice kept his head down and was mumbling "six-to-one, six-to-one, six-to-one" to himself. They strolled past Beki and entered the lounge, followed by Gypsy, who didn't give Beki a single look. A few steps behind was a group of four kids. They looked about the right age to be high school or college students. They stuck close to each other, eyeing the High Rollers timidly, and were painfully obviously out of their element. Spotting Beki, they bent their path in a wide arc around her, scraping the doorframe as they entered the lounge, as if being within five feet of her would set their hair on fire. Despite her innate instinct to pity them, Beki found herself amused.

All this pretending to be Neese is finally going to my head, she thought to herself as she made eye contact with a chubby, brown-haired girl. The girl whimpered and scooted to the back of the group. The second round hadn't even started and Beki could already tell that these children were no match for the High Rollers.

And Gypsy.

Watching the red-haired woman fix herself a drink and settle comfortably on the sofa next to Prescott, Beki wondered why she wasn't one of the High Rollers. It was obvious she had no love for them, but the High Rollers themselves weren't exactly fond of each other. So what was the reason? That was a question for another day, she decided. When she became Neese again, she would surely know the answer.

That was another thought that disturbed her as she stood in a room full of what was supposed to be her peers. She was eventually, inevitably, going to revert to being Neese Highwaters, a woman she came to like less each day. She had power, money, influence, looks, a great wardrobe, and a personality like a porcupine with a firecracker up the wrong end. As soon as the life she knew was over she would change back, and probably laugh at all the effort she was putting in now to save her son, who wasn't even really her son outside of the game they called the Round. Beki disliked Neese terribly. It was a whole new kind of self-loathing unknown by most renowned psychiatrists.

Prescott was sitting on the sofa with her hands folded in her lap when she re-entered the room. Gypsy was sitting next to her. Mojiha, drink in hand, approached the two wearing his perpetual grin.

"Say, Gypsy," he started.

"You have to make an appointment like everyone else." Gypsy said without raising a brow. "And back off. You smell like rotten fruit."

"Six-to-one. Six-to-one," Bice said from the corner, making the group of youngsters very nervous.

"Don't worry about him," Beki heard Boxcat say. "You should be worrying about yourselves."

"You're not even a High Roller," one of them muttered like a kid in class, afraid the teacher would hear. It was a boy with a ponytail. In his baggy jeans and white T-shirt, he was very, very underdressed.

"Wouldn't wanna be one," Boxcat replied, eyeing Beki as if her very existence made his point.

Beki tried to come up with some clever retort but failed to do so. It didn't seem to matter, however, as the kids were huddled against each other, looking in her direction nervously, as if expecting her to wrestle Boxcat to the ground and tear him apart with her manicured nails. Maybe it was something Neese would do, but Beki couldn't imagine herself doing that. So she did the next best thing for appearances sake – grabbed a glass off the bar and chucked it at Boxcat's head, deliberately missing by a few inches. It shattered against the wall. No one even looked up.

For a good minute or so no one talked to each other. The air in the room was thick and uncomfortable. The High Rollers milled about, doing whatever they pleased, which mostly involved drinking and staring into space. The kids continued occupying themselves fidgeting and looking around like a couple of spooked rats in a roomful of cats. The only sound besides the clinking ice cubes was Bice saying, "six-to-one, six-to-one, six-to-one."

Sasha entered.

She was so quiet that she seemed to materialize next to Beki, who almost jumped out of her way in surprise. She had changed her hair ribbons from gold to red. Just inside the doorway, she paused to give Beki a poisonous glare. Beki pretended not to see.

"So these are the finalists," she said in the general direction of the trembling kids. A boy with a brown bushy Afro and an unusually large nose made a sound like he was choking. "What a sorry bunch. I can't imagine how you could have possible done well enough to enter this game." She turned to Gypsy and smiled insincerely. "Gypsy. Good to see you."

Gypsy returned the smile, raising her glass. "Can't say the same."

"Uncouth as usual, I see."

"I always thought the guest ought to reflect the hostess."

Beki decided that the fact Gypsy was so willing to help her suddenly made a lot of sense. It was really rather funny, almost a schoolyard *I'm-rubber-you're-glue*. She kept quiet as Gypsy and Sasha took a moment to glare at each other through their smiles.

"Alright then," Sasha said, addressing the entire room. The four kids in the corner took a deep, nervous breath simultaneously. "Let's begin the second round. I assure you this will be a game to remember."

There was a time in Beki's life when she made peace with the fact that she would never do anything awe-inspiring, extremely admirable, or leave her name in the history books. She was probably never going to save anyone's life, start a foundation that saves half the population of a third-world country, have a prime time talk show on television, or make a Nobel-Prize winning discovery. This was still true less than a week ago, when she was sitting in her car on a rainy night debating whether or not to go to a boring party hosted by someone she didn't like. At that moment, it seemed like a very important and energy-consuming decision.

Now, about to step into an otherworldly competition wearing someone else's skin and name in order to save her son's life, Beki suddenly found herself thinking about Gilligan Milani – her chubby, clueless friend who thought everyone and everything in life either loved her or was plotting against her. Gilligan, who had no mind for anything but parties and men. Gilligan, whose view of the world ranged exactly from her house to the bar down the street ("they have three-dollar martinis on Wednesdays," she always said). Beki had always been annoyed with Gilligan and treated her with only polite tolerance for the sake of their years of schooling together. Gilligan was selfish and narrow-minded, didn't know anything about anything but preached about it anyway and didn't know what to do with herself if she didn't have a man's arm to hang onto.

She wasn't sure what made her think of Gilligan, except that she suddenly felt guilty about thinking all those things about the woman. Despite all her faults, Gilligan never deserted her friends. Though her view of reality was skewed, she never intentionally lied, at least not to Beki. Surrounded in a world ruled by greed and games played by cheating, with people who either empty-mindedly fawned on her or eyed her as if she was poison incarnate, Beki decided there were worse things in the world than having a friend like Gilligan Milani.

I'll buy her a nice sweater once I get back, she thought to herself, *a sexy one with a low-cut scoop neck so she can go pick up guys in it.*

Stat got as far as half way before the welcoming committee caught up to him. He was taking a shortcut across the Square when he heard the pattering of footsteps behind him. Someone was running to catch up. He stopped and turned around to face the five panting Snyperx members.

"Give us a minute," Snip said, huffing tiredly, his hands on his knees. Stat recognized a few members of the group as the same group who came to Grimm's house with Michigan. There was the girl with the stringy hair, the fat kid with the inhaler, and two others, slightly older, that he didn't know. He waited for Snip to catch his breath.

"Is that him?" the girl whispered to Snip. "It's not her?"

"No, it's not," Snip whispered. "Look at the clothes – not the face."

"Can I help you guys with something?"

"Wait," Snip said, straightening himself. "Wait... OK. Status Quo, I am Snip, and we, the Snyperx special squad, are here to stop you."

"Stop me?" Stat scanned the group. The fat kid looked like he was about to pass out. The girl was looking at Stat's face as if trying to decide whether she was fascinated or disgusted. He considered just turning around and picking up his pace, but it seemed kind of rude. "From what?"

"From ruining Neese's competition." Snip pointed an accusing finger at Stat, although the dramatic effect was somewhat deadened by his flannel shirt and the tape holding his glasses together. "We know that's where you're going. We're going to stop you."

"You are?"

"Yes." Snip sounded quite determined. The others gave a hard nod. They certainly looked resolute in their decision. Stat was moderately impressed and a little surprised.

"What is it that you think I'm going to do?" he inquired.

"You're going to take her back before she can compete. Michigan said she has to compete. It's vitally important."

"He sent you guys to stop me in case I interfere?"

"No. He inspired us." Snip gestured to the others, who surrounded Stat with a wide circle and struck awkward, ridiculous, quasi-karate-like poses. "He was willing to do something brave for her, so we're going to also. We're going to stop you from messing his plan up."

"Right," Stat said. He considered his options. He really wanted to get to the game before it was over. "What if I told you that I just wanted to go watch?"

"We can't take that chance." Snip raised his skinny wrists and curled his hands into fists in a manner that told Stat he had never formed a fist before in his life.

"I'm not lying. I just want to go see."

"We don't know that."

"So you want to stop me by force?"

One of the Snyperx, a balding older man with a potbelly, balanced precariously on one foot, with his hands raised in hooks above his head. The fat kid was still panting from the run. Stat felt very, very sorry for them.

"Yes."

"You don't have to do this, you know. Just step aside and let me pass. I don't have time for this."

"We can't do that."

Stat tapped his feet on the gold-colored bricks impatiently. "So you want to try to stop me, even if it means getting the snot beaten out of you?"

"Even if it means getting the snot beaten out of us."

"OK," Stat said, rolling his eyes. "But remember, I'm only doing this because I respect what you guys are trying to do." *And because it wouldn't be nice to just outrun you after you tried so hard,* he thought, then cracked his knuckles and proceeded to beat the snot out of them.

The ten contestants stood in the gallery upstairs, the same one where Beki and Sasha had spoken not fifteen minutes before. Beki had to admire how quickly they worked, removing the pool table and bringing in the wheel. She leaned against a bookshelf and tried to look nonchalant as the others milled about. It was obvious that most of them had never been inside this room before. Most everyone, with the exception of Bice and Prescott, were looking around curiously, seeming surprised that the second round was to take place in such a small, uninteresting room.

"I need to show mama."

Beki hadn't noticed Prescott come up to her. The girl was standing much too close to her, and it was difficult to tell whether the girl was making conversation or talking to herself.

"I need to show mama I'm good," she said quietly. "I need to be good."

You need professional help, Beki thought, and quickly came to the conclusion that a psychiatrist could probably make very good money in this place. Although who would want to spend eternity playing psychiatrist to these lunatics was beyond her.

The Spin Doctors filed in following Jean-luc, the same way they had done before. They stood in a line behind the wheel. Beki was glad to see that the girl named Tish seemed to have recovered. The wheel before them was slightly different from the ones downstairs. It was much larger, almost taller than Sasha, who looked very small next to it. It also looked older. Though it had no visible marks of age, something about it gave the impression that it had been refinished many times. The inside layer was almost the same as the other wheels – half white and half gold to start. But instead of the wheel being divided down the middle, the white and gold squares alternated. There were six of each, twelve total, lining the side of the wheel.

"Welcome," Sasha said, and curtsied. She was adorable, even if she *was* a cold-hearted harpy. "This is the second round, as you might have already guessed." She pointed to the ceiling, where six cameras had been mounted along the seam where the ceiling met the wall, their lenses pointed down like curious animals with a single glass eye. "Everyone will be watching," she said, looking at Beki. "But don't be nervous."

Someone let out a soft, nervous gurgle. Probably one of the kids. Beki swallowed thickly. The pill was still hidden in her dress.

"We will also be doing things a little differently," she continued.

"You trying to trick us, Sasha?" Mojiha clamored. He was visibly drunk. One of his arms was swung over the shoulder of the chubby brown-haired young woman, one of the finalists from the first round. She looked both horrified and incredibly thrilled. "Tricking people's not nice, ain't that right, sweetie?"

The young woman looked up, nodded, and quickly looked down again.

"There's no trick," Sasha said. "Just a small change of plans. Of course, there will still be one winner at the end who will play me for the grand prize. But instead of the Spin Doctors," she took a pause, blue eyes glistening at the anxious expressions around the room, "you will play each other. And for this special occasion, I'm going to allow *dueling*."

IMMORTALITY 101: The Intro Course

28
SNITCH

"You will be divided into two groups."

Beki looked across the room at Jean-Luc, and was rather displeased to see that he looked as surprised as she felt. She had hoped that this was somehow part of his brilliant plan. He tilted his gaze toward her, shook his head, and quickly turned away again. To say the least, this did not bode well. She searched her brain for anything that might be helpful from the last few days and came up empty-handed. *What would Neese do?*

"Each pair will consist of one member from each group." Sasha gestured at the wheel.

Carefully, Beki slipped into the back of the group, reached into the folds of the dress at her breast, and removed the little pill. It was her best chance, she figured.

"One group will play against the other. I will now announce the names of group one, the rest of you will be group two." Sasha removed a sheet of paper seemingly from nowhere. "Kam Hurley."

The girl with short black hair stepped forward. She tossed an unreadable look at Beki.

"Tracer Pane."

The underdressed boy with a ponytail joined her. Compared to the others, he looked a bit more relaxed. Back in her college days Beki had been around marijuana only once, when a friend had scored a small bag

319

and they had experimented by baking them into brownies. She hadn't seen said friend in over ten years, but she would always remember the glassy look on her face after eating the brownies. It was like watching a frog try to focus on a single piece of dirt in the air. Of course, she herself wasn't faring too much better. The expression on Tracer's face made her think that the boy had a little extra "help" to calm his nerves.

"Gypsy Hoss."

Gypsy did not step forward. She merely nodded and stayed in her place, apparently occupied with her long nails.

"Lexicon Powell."

The young man sporting a fro looked around nervously, hiccupped, and stayed in his place.

"And Moria Banners."

"Wait!" The brown-haired young woman who had been standing with Mojiha's arm around her suddenly stepped forward, flinging Mojiha's arm off as she went. Mojiha muttered something disappointedly. "You can't do that. You're putting us against the High Rollers!"

Sasha lowered the sheet of paper. Her eyes carried the indignity of a teacher being interrupted in class. The girl named Moria shrunk back, as if just realizing that she had spoken up out of turn. "Is that a problem?"

"Well, no, but..." she looked morosely at Beki. "We can't... win against *them*. It's not fair."

Sasha sighed dramatically. "To call you stupid would be a compliment," she said flatly. "In a game that will end in one winner, what difference does it make who you play against?"

Moria's lower lip quivered. Beki continued her marveling at the amount of power the High Rollers were able to exert over the "commoners". It was both disgusting and intoxicating at the same time. She took the chance to bring the pill to her lips.

"Hey," Mojiha said, and nudged her elbow.

The pill slipped from her fingers and rolled into the forest of feet in front of her. She lost sight of it behind someone's heel. With a lurch in her chest Beki realized her only secret weapon had turned into a piece of debris on the floor. Her last hope had just vanished under someone's feet.

"We don't need nothing from Sasha," Mojiha was saying. "Hows about you and I throw this little match and go…"

Anger welled up in Beki's chest. "Bug off," she replied, and punched him on the bridge of the nose. Mojiha let out a yowl of pain. A few eyes turned to look, then turned back as if nothing happened.

Jean-Luc was confused. He stood to the side as Sasha announced her new rules and tried to figure out if it was a stab at him. This was what always fascinated and annoyed him about Sasha. She liked to change the rules. She was like a kid who hid behind trashcans and jumped out at people yelling "boo". Surprise was always her favorite element, and sometimes he wondered why she bothered throwing games at all if she was just going to alter the rules and manipulate herself into the winner's seat.

He scanned the room. Not that he particularly cared if the Rounder won or not, but this little twist had officially rendered his brilliant mechanical apparatus pointless. He had spent many hours with grease on his sleeves tuning the machine, and now it seemed to be nothing but a moot point.

Jean-Luc considered grumbling, complaining aloud, or storming out. But all of those would reveal that something had been done under the tables to rig the game, and thus ruin the whole tournament. Sasha would get upset and all those people placing bets downstairs would demand their chips back, which would mean a lot of fun killed for him. At least, he thought to himself, now he knew why Sasha had been so confident as to write up Neese's odds as fifty-to-one. Neese Highwaters would make mincemeat of these untalented rubes. Beki Tempest didn't stand a chance.

The first round was starting. The competitors, deeming by names drawn from a pile of scrap paper, were Boxcat Pincher and Lexicon Powell. Two commoners, one playing in the place of a High Roller. When Lexicon crossed Jean-Luc's path to reach the wheel, Jean-Luc caught a whiff of dust from the young man and had to pull a silk handkerchief from his pocket to stifle his sneeze. Commoners were highly disgusting. Out of the corner of his eye he could see Beki fidgeting, something Neese would never do. She was a pathetic rendition of the goddess that was Neese. He shook his head in disappointment. All the jewels in the world couldn't pass a pauper off as a princess. Still, it was amusing to see her hit Mojiha in the face. For a moment she was almost worthy of Neese's name.

Almost.

Sasha had stepped aside to watch. Jean-Luc couldn't tell what she was thinking as she stood there with that thin, devious smile on her face.

Lexicon and Boxcat placed themselves on two sides of the wheel. Lexicon was a ropey kid with big lips and a narrow nose. His eyes were enormous, sunken into his doughy, freckle-covered face. They seemed to dart from one direction to another as if perpetually under the influence of caffeine. He was wearing a collared shirt and black pants that made his legs look pencil-thin. Jean-Luc felt sorry for the kid. Even in eternity, he looked like he'd never get laid.

Boxcat put his hand on the wheel and yawned, which earned a round of frowns and gasps from the others since it was quite an impolite gesture. Jean-Luc, however, didn't expect anything more from a commoner. He looked over at Beki, who was still fidgeting. He wanted to walk over and slap her wrist.

"Let us begin," Sasha said.

Lexicon gripped the side of the wheel so tightly his bulbous knuckles turned white. He had very large hands for his size and Jean-Luc mused at what was said about men with large hands. He was very nervous and was trembling visibly, but his eyes betrayed a determination that that almost made Jean-Luc proud. Every now and then a commoner came around that made these games worthwhile.

Sasha raised a hand into the air. Between her fingers she held a solid silver sphere. Lexicon tensed visibly. Boxcat rubbed his eyes and looked supremely bored. She looked at them both, paused, and tossed the ball into the wheel.

The moment the ball struck the wheel's surface, Lexicon pushed the wheel forward, sending it into a smooth, flawless spin. The commoners held their breaths as it went. Boxcat, who did not even attempt to nudge the wheel, removed his hand from the wheel and picked at his nails as it spun. Jean-Luc took the chance to scoot next to Sasha.

"What are you doing to me?" he whispered. "What would putting them against each other do?"

Sasha batted her eyes, still watching the match. "Whatever do you mean? I think this makes the competition a lot more interesting, don't you?"

"Why did you ask me to rig the Wheel if you didn't want to use it?" He gestured to draw her attention to his hand. "Do you know what it did to my hands? There are calluses on my fingers."

"Well," Sasha said innocently. "Then you shouldn't have double-crossed me, should you?"

Jean-Luc started. He looked to the match, at the spinning wheel, then back at Sasha. "How…"

"I have my ways," Sasha said, twirling her hand in her golden curls. "I don't like it when people go behind my back. You've been a bad boy, Jean-Luc."

He looked at her for a very long time, then allowed his lips to split into a grin. "You know, Sasha," he said, "every now and then I'm reminded of why exactly I tolerate you."

"You mean why you like me."

"That, too."

The wheel had slowed and the ball was rolling lazily, bumping against the brackets as it went. Lexicon's hands were formed into tight fists as he watched. The ball hit a white pocket, a gold, then a white, and finally fell into a gold pocket. Boxcat, who up until this point hadn't even glanced at the wheel, looked up at the ball, then at Lexicon's devastated face.

"Aw, hell," he said with unabashed disappointment. "Did I win?"

There was a word for people like the Snyperx in the Round. Actually there were two. One was *nerd*, the other *geek*. The distinction between the two was that nerds usually elicited sympathy while geeks generally existed to annoy. Both, unbeknownst to Rounders, stemmed from the Snyperx, much in the way that ape and man stemmed from the same hairy ancestor. They were a twitchy, nervous, anti-social bunch, most of which would be virginal save for the fact that immortality meant most everyone got laid eventually. They also had an affinity for small collectables – immortality also meant that, eventually, you *do* get to collect them all.

Nerds and geeks were also generally associated with an image of inflexible, weak bodies, usually overweight or eerily thin. Many hours in front of a computer or book made them tender and soft. They tend to be bad at anything that involved physical movement and couldn't catch a ball or form a fist to save their lives. In many situations they would try to reason their way out of trouble, only to fail and receive additional pummeling for trying to be a smart-ass. This made them easy targets for bullies or anyone who wanted to pound on something to let out a little frustration. In other words, they were built to be victims.

Stat didn't see the Snyperx that way. He knew they were pretty smart—smarter than he could ever be – and usually kind of nice. But as he handed their asses to them in an orderly fashion, he mused that they were, in fact, kind of annoying.

"Damn it!" Snip exclaimed in exasperation. He had a bloody nose that Stat felt very guilty for. He hadn't intended to hit Snip that hard. Who knew nerds had such brittle noses? "Regroup! We have to regroup!"

Stat had no idea what regrouping would do for them.

The fat kid pulled out his inhaler and took a deep breath. Stat had been careful not to land any real punches on him. He looked like he would crumble like a gingerbread house. "Yes," he huffed. "Re-regroup. We have to…"

Stat shook his head and checked his watch. He could, he supposed, kick these guys around all day long, but he was a nice guy and there were better things to do. He turned to Snip, who he assumed was the leader. "Would you like me to dislocate your knee?" he asked.

Snip narrowed his eyes in an attempt to look angry. Instead, he looked sleepy. "Your threats don't scare us."

"I'm serious. I have to cut this short. I could just dislocate your knee right now" – he mimed the motion with his hands – "and you won't be able to run after me. You can wait here, and when I come back I'll pop it back in for you. I promise I will. I probably won't forget. Then you can at least say you tried. I really don't want to keep hitting you guys." He shook his right hand limply. The knuckles were slightly bruised. "You're really bony."

The Snyperx looked at each other uncertainly. Stat hoped that they'd come to the conclusion that this was a losing fight quickly so he could leave. The girl, whom he had dubbed Female Snip in his mind, had been staying away from the center of the action. He was glad for that. Hitting a woman just didn't feel right. She peeked at him and stepped forward.

"Just let him go," she said quietly to the others. Her friends looked appalled at the suggestion.

"Let him go?" Snip snapped. "Do you know what he might do if we let him go? Don't you care about Neese at all?"

"Why should I?" she muttered. "She doesn't care about us. Sasha's going to win anyway."

Stat arched a brow as the others gaped in horror, backing away from her as if she had suddenly sprouted a radioactive second head. She shrugged and looked at the ground. After a moment's consideration, Stat approached her, which only caused her friends to scamper even further. He took her chin and forced her to look at his face.

"Tell me," he said quietly, "whose face do you see?"

Female Snip averted her eyes.

"Do you know for sure that Sasha's going to win?"

Still no answer. Stat really disliked interrogating people without a good cup of tea.

"Did she promise you something?"

"She said she'd make me a Spin Doctor," Female Snip replied. "I want to be a Spin Doctor. I'm tired of hanging around these smelly guys." Unlike most people who stood within close vicinity to him, she didn't seem scared. Maybe it was Sasha's influence rubbing off on her. In fact, her nervous glances were directed at her friends, who were just out of earshot. "Aw, damn it," she said, shaking her head out of his grasp. "You're gonna tell them, aren't you? Are you gonna tell them that I'm a spy? That I don't really love Neese?"

Stat patted her shoulder. He already knew that Sasha would never make her a Spin Doctor. She wasn't pretty enough. But there was no point in crushing her hopes. He was, after all, a nice guy. "Nah," he said, "I don't care enough," and walked off before the Snyperx could think to chase him. Behind him, he heard the girl apologizing furiously to her friends for being out of line. They'd forgive her. He knew they would. Nerds and geeks were equally susceptible to feminine charm.

Beki stood alone in the hall, leaning against the wall, staring at the ceiling, and eating her fingernails one at a time, feeling grateful that there was at least one advantage to being Neese – no one questioned what she did. A few curious eyes looked back when she opened the door to slip out of the gallery, but no one stopped her or tried to ask where she was doing. The manicured nails that Jean-Luc had painstakingly painted for her turned to shreds between her teeth.

A hand grabbed her wrist right before she could finish off the third nail. She could tell by the sleeve of the immaculate suit that it was Jean-Luc. Pulling against him, she brought the nail to her lips anyway.

"What do you think you're doing?" he hissed, jerking her hand out of her mouth. "Do you know how bad it would look for Neese to have broken nails during a tournament?"

"Bite me," Beki replied, and continued to chew on the nail.

Jean-Luc smirked. "What's this? The little pauper girl grew a spine? It's a little too late for that. There's no turning back at this point."

"What do you care?" A piece of the nail tore off between her teeth. She spat it on the floor, next to Jean-Luc's perfectly shined loafers.

"I care that Neese doesn't look like a fool in front of the whole world *and* her peers."

"Yeah, well, I'm not Neese," Beki said. "I'm not a High Roller, I don't like gambling, and I hate how people act in this place." She raised one foot off the floor. "And these shoes are hideous."

Jean-Luc gasped in indignation. For a second Beki thought he might slap her.

"I hate Neese, too," she continued. "I have a son waiting in a hospital for me to win some game so she could look good. Does she care? No. And I can't even slap her for it. I hate how she cuts people's arms off and I hate how she treats Michigan."

"Michigan's a fool and a commoner and Neese treats him as much."

"I slept with him. On her bed. She can deal with that however she wants to when she gets back here." Beki bit off another nail.

"You *what?!*" Jean-Luc shouted, then quickly cleared his throat and dropped his voice. "You did what? How could you… you…"

"He helped me out and I rewarded him. You can yell at me about it later."

"Deal." Jean-Luc shook his head, looking extremely defeated.

"Too bad it's all for naught now. I'm going to lose. Your little rig's not going to work and my son's going to die. I might as well leave now and spend his last days with him." She spat the nail onto the floor. "God, I hate this place. It stinks and all you people are evil. Where I come from twelve-year-olds don't gamble."

"They don't?"

"Not so blatantly, anyway." She studied her ruined nails. "So who's winning?"

"Boxcat. He's not even trying. It's really an insult to even have him in the game. Are you coming back in or not?"

"Why should I? Without your little rig thing I can only lose. Neese will look bad, my son will die, my husband will run off with that doctor with the Playboy tits, and I'll live the rest of my life dreading the day I 'die'"—she raised her fingers in a pair of air quotes – "and become someone I utterly despise."

"You're an exasperating little woman, you know that?"

"I do, actually." Beki turned to Jean-Luc. "Are you really here to convince me to go back in there?"

"Yes," Jean-Luc said. "I am. For the first time in… who knows how long, a game of chance is actually depending on chance. No rigs, no cheats, all surprises. I haven't seen a show like this in ages; I'm not about to let one annoying woman cheat me out of it."

"Did Sasha change the rules because you told her you were helping me?"

"No. I told her nothing. Someone must be spying."

"You think it's Michigan?"

"No. He's a fool, but a traitor? No. It's not him."

Beki nodded. "Yeah, I don't think so either." Straightening, she smoothed her dress. "All surprises from here on out, huh?"

"Until the last round, anyway. Assuming you make it there. To lose now would be a pretty big blow to Neese's reputation." Jean-Luc grinned widely. "I have to admit, I'm excited. Not knowing is pretty fun."

"Do you believe in luck, Jean-Luc? I mean *really* believe in it?"

"Not really. No one here does."

"I guess that's what makes a Rounder different, isn't it?" With that, she strolled past Jean-Luc and back into the gallery.

Boxcat had won without trying. He sighed and shook his head when he was declared the winner and muttered something about Rat deserving to be hung from the roof by his toes for making him participate in the game. It was disrespectful. It was rude. Sasha didn't particularly care. She motioned for the Spin Doctors to come forward and take charge. Tish retrieved the ball and prepared the Wheel for the next match while Leonard and Mozart peeled Lexicon Powell off the floor.

"Come on, on your feet," Leonard said, grabbing Lexicon's left elbow.

"One, two, three," Mozart counted as he grabbed the right one and together with Leonard pulled the young man to his feet, patting his back. "Nothing to worry about."

"Just a game."

"Lessons to be learned."

"Lives to be lived."

"Well, just one life really."

"Don't blubber like that. Cheer up."

They escorted Lexicon to the door, opened it for him, and booted him out quite literally. "Off you go."

"Don't forget to write."

Sasha retreated to a corner and fussed with her hair. She was restless and agitated, which annoyed her because this was supposed to be her day. She was supposed to be beautiful and happy. The game was going swimmingly. The last-minute change she made to the match had sent the crowd downstairs into an all new frenzy. She could hear the cheers through the floorboards and faintly feel the vibrations of the dance music under her feet.

Leonard and Mozart were still jabbering to each other. She turned and gave them a hard glare. They annoyed her. With mountains of debt on their shoulders they still went on and on, carelessly living their pathetic lives as if spinning was just a gig they played when they were bored. Though she had no love for the mousy Tish, at least she knew her place. She wore a sad look of despair in her eyes most of the time, as if doom was right around the corner. Even now she was moving with a heaviness that made Sasha glad deep down. What was the point of stepping on the vermin if they didn't even struggle?

"We seem a little down today."

Sasha tried hard to keep her lips from parting into a snarl when she turned to face Gypsy. "Shouldn't you be worrying about the game?"

"I don't care about the game."

"Then leave," she snapped, and started to walk away.

"My, my," Gypsy purred. "Something *must* be bothering you." She paused, just long enough for Sasha to think she was finished, then said, "Could it be that pretty little Rounder out there is getting under your skin?" Another pause. "Did you know that Stat caught her and let her go?"

Sasha stopped in her tracks. She quickly looked around the room. The commoners were engrossed in the match between Tracer and Mojiha, and the High Rollers – if the remaining ones in the room could even be called that – were preoccupied with dozing, talking to the bookshelves, or staring into space. She spun around and walked right into Gypsy's personal space.

"What do you know?" she asked, heat roaring in her eyes and chest.

"Just what I've heard," Gypsy said nonchalantly. "I am merely a repository for gossip. You know that."

"*What*," Sasha repeated, "do you know?"

"He picked her up, fresh out of the Round, but for some reason didn't force her to return. Now I don't know what could've happened." She blinked innocently. "But Stat is no slouch when it comes to his job. She must have done *something* to convince him to let her stay instead of drag her back by the collar. Don't you think?"

Sasha bit her lower lip.

"Of course I don't even know if this is true. For all I know they never ran into each other."

"They did," Sasha said in a small, trembling voice. "She said they did."

"She could be lying."

"She said he took her to Grimm's house."

Gypsy gasped mockingly. "Oh, my," she said, fanning herself. "That boy sure goes to Grimm's a lot doesn't he? It's like a second home to him, I hear. Now these are just rumors but I hear he even spends the night there sometimes, that Grimm has a spare *bed* for him to crash on. Oh, I wouldn't know. Listen to me prattling on."

Sasha longed to reach up and scratch Gypsy's eyes out, then pull her fire-red hair out of her pale scalp by the handful. She wanted to stomp the floor and scream and most of all, she wanted to do terrible, unimaginable things to the woman just outside the gallery door. Her cheeks were burning and she quickly patted them in an attempt to return them to normal color. In this she had succeeded. She was, after all, talented in putting on masks, like every worthy High Roller. Then she drew a short breath and let it out, her fingers kneaded into the folds of her dress to keep them from lashing out. She refused to give Gypsy the satisfaction. Ladies do not lose control. Ladies do not betray their emotions.

She turned away again and walked out of the gallery for some fresh air, and nearly bumped into the infuriating Rounder.

"Oh," the woman said. "Sorry."

Sasha cringed at the sound of such an unsightly word coming out of Neese's mouth. The Rounder tried to squeeze past her to return to the gallery. She reached out and seized her wrist.

"What did you do with him?" she demanded, hearing the words leave her lips and unable to stop herself.

The Rounder named Rebecca looked down at her. "Who?"

"Status Quo. Don't play dumb. What did you do with him?"

"Stat?" The endearing shortening of his name was a stab in Sasha's heart. Rebecca turned and peeked down the hall. "Why? Is he here?"

Beki watched Sasha storm down the stairs, shrugged, and returned to the gallery. As far as she could tell, Sasha didn't like her hanging around Stat. That was fine with her, since Stat made her feel awkward and uncomfortable inside with his weird, watery face. Still, she pitied him a bit. He was a pleasant enough guy, and it was really unfair when nice guys had that one weird quirk that made them woman repellants.

Gypsy gave her a nod when she walked inside. She started to return it, and then remembered Neese probably wouldn't and turned her attention to the competition instead. The Spin Doctors were running the show now. With Sasha out of the room, Beki felt significantly more relaxed. If it weren't for the gnawing dread in her stomach she would almost be having fun. Mojiha had easily beaten his opponent, who stood in a daze until two of the Spin Doctors pushed him out of the room. His glassy, doom-filled stare reminded Beki of something Stat had said.

You have to play like your life was depending on it.

That was how everyone played, she realized, at least the ones who made it this far. They played as if it was the most important thing in their lives, even if their life was eternal. One would figure that if someone was immortal, there was bound to be some other, more important thing along the way. Maybe, she reasoned, it made the games more fun. Why not stake your life on it if there's always more of it coming, anyway?

Mojiha was making a big show of his win, posing and showing off his muscles and golden smile. The brown-haired young woman looked on with lingering infatuation in her eyes while the others clapped obligatorily. Beki tried to remember her name and couldn't. She was insignificant in this situation, just like all the other commoners who qualified. Beki hated to think this way, because it was surely what Neese would think, but as far as she was concerned, nothing mattered right now except getting to the final round with Sasha.

Bless me, Lady Luck, she thought, and felt kind of stupid for thinking it. Still, it was the best she could come up with for the moment. Luck was the only thing left on her side.

IMMORTALITY 101: The Intro Course

29
DUELISTS

Tish eyed Neese sadly while she prepared the wheel. All was lost. All her hopes had been dashed to pieces. She would never be one of Neese's servants, wearing beautiful silver dresses and dealing cards. She was going to be spinning forever. Here she was, so excited to throw the game for Neese, and the chance was so cruelly robbed from her. She tried to compose a sonnet or poem about it but was in too much despair to even manage that.

"Moria Banners," she called. Moria was a round, curvy girl with large features. Large eyes on top of a large nose on top of large lips. Before stepping forward, she looked over at Mojiha, who blew her a kiss.

"Good luck, pretty baby," he said. She swooned. Tish rolled her eyes and looked down on the sheet of paper Sasha had handed her.

"Neese Highwaters." Her heart skipped a beat.

Neese, who had been standing in the back of the room alone, emerged like a rose blooming in a field of weeds. The moment she did, Moria's face fell and the other commoners breathed in relief. Neese stepped in front of the wheel in her elegant Oz Greens and smiled a bit at Tish, who nearly fell over. She clutched the piece of paper and stepped aside.

"P-please," Tish stammered. "Please take your positions."

Neese did so, laying a slender hand on the wheel. Three of her nails were damaged, Tish noticed, and knew that Neese would never step outside with any part of her perfect image flawed. It must be the new style, she reasoned. Once this was over, she would rush back to her room and tear the tips off of three nails on her right hand.

Moria stood in her spot. Tish eyed her in distain. "Hurry up," she said. "Don't keep Miss Highwaters waiting."

"It's alright," Neese said, her crystal eyes zoned in on the competition. Tish pitied Moria, who was shaking and having trouble making eye contact with Neese. "Let her take her time."

Moria let a half-choked sob. She looked small and pathetic in front of Neese, who continued to burn her with a steady gaze.

"*Well?*" Tish snapped.

Moria turned around, pushed her way through the other contestants, and ran out of the gallery, her face flushed a pale pink. Mojiha looked around, grinned, and ran after her. For a moment no one spoke.

"You've done it again, Neese," Gypsy said after a long moment, and clapped twice. No one followed.

Tish smiled. This was what it was all about. This was the power of the High Rollers. This was why she spent days and nights worshipping this amazing woman, who was able to end a competition before it even began. She moved to Neese's right and raised her left hand.

"Winner, Neese Highwaters," she announced proudly. Neese just smiled.

The bar downstairs was ample and abundant in variety. It would have to be to keep thousands upon thousands of people plastered just the right amount to keep throwing money into the competition. The borrowing and lending had already begun. Those who bet on Lexicon, Tracer, and Moria have divided into two groups – one sauntered off to the bar with their heads hung low and the intent to drink themselves into a stupor, and one milled about the floor, begging for a few chips here and there, promising high-interest repayments so they could put in another round of bets. Most of the second group put their chips on Mojiha.

The combination of alcohol and thumping music was giving Michigan a strangely pleasurable headache. All the flashing colors, bodies, and continuous noise was making it quite easy not to worry about both the immediate and not-so-immediate future. He loitered around the outer perimeters of the room, then wandered onto the dance floor and attempted to dance, only to be knocked down by something large, round, and familiar.

"That you, V. P.?"

Michigan blinked. "Geoffy? What are you doing here?"

"Checking in on business. Ya wanna get off the floor there?"

Michigan considered this. "No, I'm quite comfortable here, thanks." And he was. The ceiling wasn't quite as colorful as the rest of the room and therefore didn't hurt his eyes nearly as much.

"Yer gonna get trampled."

"Yeah, that's the downside."

Geoffy offered a meaty hand. Michigan took it after a moment's hesitation and allowed Geoffy to hoist him to his feet. He weebled, then wobbled, but didn't fall down. Geoffy gave him his usual patented disapproving look. "How many drinks did ya have, V.P.?" Michigan held up three fingers. Geoffy arched a suspicious brow. "Three?"

"Three this round."

"How many rounds?"

Michigan held up two fingers, realized it was wrong and held up another two, then realized that was wrong, too. "Don't know," he said, trying hard to focus on at least one of the two Geoffys in front of him. "What are you doing here?"

"You already asked that."

"OK. What else are you doing here?"

Geoffy turned his good eye upward to the nearest monitor. The image was a semi-close up of Prescott. "Watching my baby play," he said dreamily.

"Prescott? That's sick, man. She's so creepy. She's like one of those sad clowns you see in the weird paintings in the Round."

"Not her!" Geoffy snapped, pointing to the edge of the screen. "Right *there!*"

Michigan squinted through his inebriation just enough to make out Gypsy's skeletal form leaning against a bookshelf behind Prescott.

335

He gaped at Geoffy and shook his head, which made him dizzy enough to consider falling down again.

"You're still after her? You know she doesn't like you any more than all those other…"

Geoffy huffed in indignation. "Right, an' I assume you and Neese have *such* a great future together. Did she let ya lick the dirt off her shoe this time?"

"Uh," Michigan said, and that was all he could think of.

"Rumor has it she ain't even herself," Geoffy continued as the screens switched to a shot of Neese. A damned good shot, too, if Michigan had any say. He wished Beki was here to see it. "Have ya heard the rumor that she snuck outta the Round? Some folks 'round here are saying she's faking, pretending to be Neese when she… well, who knows what she was in the Round. Don't matter." He nudged Michigan in the ribs. "I bet if ya met her now ya wouldn't even like her. I mean, what if she's… *nice* or somethin'?"

"Uh," Michigan said again, staring at Beki's figure molded in the silver satin dress. "Yeah."

A roaring cheer suddenly erupted from the far side of the room. Geoffy craned his neck to see above the crowd. "Hey!" he exclaimed.

Michigan continued to stare until Geoffy grabbed his head and wrenched it to one side.

"Look over there!"

"I rather look over here."

"Yeah, well, look over there for now. That's Boxcat over there! He just came down the stairs!"

Michigan looked in the direction of Geoffy's chubby finger reluctantly. It was Boxcat indeed, pushing his way through the crowd, an annoyed look on his face as the commoners struggled, climbing over each other to shake his hand or pat him on the back. Several pairs of panties flew at his head, one landing on his shoulder. Boxcat frowned, brushed it off onto the floor, and kept walking.

Geoffy shook his head. "I dunno why he keeps showin' up if he don't even enjoy it. Look at him; he looks like he wants to go home and take a nap. Why does he keep coming?"

"Maybe he's bored."

"Maybe you should go soak your head."

"Hey," Michigan tried to wag a finger and found it tremendously hard to do. The motion made him nauseous. "That's not nice."

"No, I mean really, go soak yer head in the sink. Ya look like a mess warmed over twice."

"Oh," Michigan said.

Boxcat didn't like to gamble. It was weird – extremely weird – for someone who resided in this glorified ghetto not to enjoy gambling. After all, there was nothing to do but gamble. He was good at it, too. Someone had once taught him how to gamble without cheating and actually win a good deal of the time. But even when he won, he didn't like to gamble. He longed to return to his restaurant, where he could mix drinks, serve food, and take bets instead of make them. He would have to see Geoffy at some point to make sure he could get a small shipment of alcohol for the after-dinner hours tomorrow. The days after a major game were always followed by an influx of people eager to drink their woes away, and those were the only days when Geoffy would willingly share the liquor business with others.

He squeezed his way through the crowd to the nearest bathroom. There was a nicer washroom in the lounge upstairs but he didn't feel like doing his business in the same place the High Rollers did theirs. They wouldn't want him to, anyway. He was common.

Undoing his belt, he cursed Rat under his breath. If they weren't friends, he always swore, he would never come within a mile of a slot, wheel, or table. Damn Rat, running off and sealing himself in a wine cask and spouting philosophies about eternity and immortality and all that. Boxcat was pretty sure that's what Rat went off to do. He couldn't come up with anything better, not when he had to keep entering Rat's competitions for him all day.

Actually, this one would only be the fourth in the past ten years or so, but he still felt justified to gripe about it.

The door opened and a man stumbled inside. He was barely holding himself upright. He looked one way, then the other, and his eyes finally landed on Boxcat, who really didn't like to be stared at when he did his business.

"Hey," the man said. "You're... uh... that guy."

"Yes," Boxcat said. He could smell the alcohol on the man's breath halfway across the room. "I am."

"Don't mind me," the man said, and went to the sink, where he ran the water for ten seconds, turned it off, grabbed some paper towels, stuffed it into the drain, and ran the water again. When it was nearly full, he turned off the water and dunked his head into the sink. "Just soaking my head," he said.

Boxcat cinched up his pants, rolling his eyes. Despite the theory that, in a society of non-reproducing immortals, there ought to be no change in population size, he could swear that there were more and more weirdos on the loose every day. His theory – as well as Rat's – was that the population of immortals was growing weirder and weirder with each passing day.

The guy who came in still had the top half of his head dunked in water by the time Boxcat made his way to the other sink to wash his hands. He briefly considered which would be more unbearable – heading back upstairs to wait for his turn at the Wheel among the insufferable High Rollers, or watching this guy wash his head a little longer.

"You want to wash your head?" the man asked. He had pulled his head, dripping wet, from the sink. Water streamed down his shoulders, soaking his clothes. "It's pretty refreshing. Bit of a mess, though."

Boxcat dried his hands and eyed him. "Are you drunk?"

"Very much so."

"Maybe you should go home and sleep it off."

"Nah," the man said with a wave of his hand. "Gotta stay. Gotta watch B— I mean, Neese, play."

Boxcat shrugged. "Suit yourself," he said, and headed for the door.

"Hey," the man said. "You *won*, right?"

"Yes. I did."

"So you're gonna be competing in the next round, right?" The man made an expression like he was thinking very, very hard. "You think you'll go against Neese eventually?"

"Maybe."

The man thought for another moment. "Hey," he said, pointing to a spot on the wall behind Boxcat. "Look at that."

Boxcat turned, saw nothing, and heard the man mutter something that sounded like "sorry" before a hard object hard struck the back of his head.

Beki couldn't believe she made two girls cry in the same day. She stood in the back of the gallery again, feeling very, very guilty and hoping that Moria was alright. She couldn't even figure out what she had done to scare the girl so badly. After all, she had been nice, asking Tish to lay off and let the girl collect herself before the match. She herself had been too nervous to think of anything else and was hoping that Moria would take her time so she could calm her own pounding heart.

But she had won. Somehow, through some bizarre hidden charisma that undoubtedly belonged to Neese, she had won without having to spin. She wondered what Jean-Luc made of this, but he was nowhere to be found. Gypsy was giving her an approving nod, which she didn't return.

Tish, the only female Spin Doctor, was giving her a look that was almost like worship. Beki hoped she would find herself another idol.

"Bice Tic."

Bice talked to the bookshelf, asking if it had had a nice day.

"Bice."

Beki considered giving the old man a prod, but he seemed to be having a really good time and she hated to disturb him.

"*Bice!*"

Slowly, hesitantly, Bice looked toward the Wheel, then started, as if just remembering where he was. Rubbing his brow absently, he walked unhurriedly past the others and took his position by the Wheel. His back was bent and his legs arched to either side awkwardly. "Six-to-one," he muttered, "six-to-one."

"Pipe down," Tish said, looking at the list again. "Kam Hurley."

Kam stepped forward. She looked a little ill at ease, though not quite as much as Moria. She was flat and lean. Close up, Beki saw that the blue cocktail dress wrought around her body was ill-fitting and her nonexistent chest could barely hold it up. She gave a single nod to Bice, who looked at her and said, "fifteen-to-one."

IMMORTALITY 101: The Intro Course

The two contestants took their place. Beki looked from one to the other and decided to root for Bice. The old man looked like he'd weathered hell and came back to tell about it. But in a world where there was no heaven, hell, or anything in between, he had probably just weathered too many martinis in front of slot machines.

Kam gripped the Wheel with her right hand.

The glazed look on Bice's face suddenly vanished as he took the Wheel. It was as if his face had blinked out of existence and was replaced by a new one. His beady eyes narrowed with concentration and his fingers tightened around the Wheel's edge until his knuckles turned white. Beads of sweat were rolling down his forehead as Tish approached the Wheel, the silver ball in her hand.

"Ready?" she asked.

"Ready," said Kam.

"Ready," said Bice. It was the most coherent word Beki had heard him form.

The ball went into the air, then onto the wheel. Bice spun, sending the Wheel into a hard, twirling spin that seemed impossible for his bony hands. It spun with such speed that the brackets and ball became nothing but a blur. The Wheel rotated on its axis, and each time it faced Beki she saw the silver ball making its own orbit around its core.

Kam spun on her heels gracefully like a ballerina, her arms extended on either side, and caught the wheel with the heel of her left hand as it spun toward her. The entire Wheel seemed to jostle and pause before it reeled in the opposite direction. Two turns later Bice caught it with an agile flick of the wrist and it spun in its original direction without so much as a hiccup. Kam retaliated by holding her arm flat against the Wheel's side, slowing its pace before pushing it in the other direction.

While the others looked on with bored expressions, Beki fought to keep from looking too impressed at the exchange. Every trace of senility had vanished from Bice's face and movements as he kept up with Kam, spin for spin. Kam alternated hands on each spin, her feet moving her body ever so slightly after each turn, perhaps to put herself at the most advantageous angle. The wheel changed direction seamlessly. No more than two seconds passed between spins.

Four hands manipulated the Wheel in a blur.

"Every now and then someone really talented comes along," Jean-Luc said, sticking things that looked very much like metal chopsticks into her hair. "And they play a different way, called dueling. Theoretically, the two people spinning are allowed to touch the wheel as many times as they wish. But usually the first spin is so calculated that further spins are pointless. If you're really talented, however, you can calculate the cumulative effect on the spins that follow. What's really amazing to see is if you have two people like that. They start fighting on the Wheel, spin it this way, then the other, then the other, and so on."

Beki cringed as the chopsticks scraped her scalp. "Doesn't that mean they can just keep the game going forever?"

"Well, sure. There's a rumor that a game went on for days. Until one of the contestants collapsed from exhaustion." He smeared more gel in her hair.

"What do I do if I come up against a person like that?"

"Try to hit the switch like I told you."

"No fallback plan?"

"Nope. If the switch doesn't work then you're screwed. But, don't worry, they don't show up often. Some of them get lynched as soon as they're discovered because people hate it when they hold up the game. Plus I don't think any of Sasha's Spin Doctors can duel for very long. She considers dueling to be a commoner's game so she rarely allows it. Still, there's some commoners who made a name for themselves dueling, like the Wonder Twins for example, they..."

"They what?"

"Not important," Jean-Luc said shortly. He stepped back and looked at the hairdo he just spent three and a half hours on. Beki couldn't see it, but it felt like a ten-pound helmet. "Nope, we'll have to re-do that."

The Wheel stopped and Beki realized she had been holding her breath and let it out in a soft huff. She expected Boxcat to give her one of those annoyed looks he was so good at but he was nowhere in sight. *Good*, she thought, *irritating guy, anyway.*

The ball made two more circles around the core before losing to gravity. It rolled downward along the Wheel's tilted inner surface, bounced off one bracket, two, three, and settled into a white pocket.

"Winner, Kam Hurley," Tish declared.

For a moment nobody spoke. Then a soft, rhythmic sound wafted to Beki's ears. It sounded like a voice. She peeked through the dwindling group and saw Bice still standing at the Wheel. He was gripping the side with both hands and muttering something.

"Six-to-one," he said with wide, disbelieving eyes, which had once again taken on that glassy gaze Beki had become used to. "Six-to-one."

Kam walked past him without a word and found a spot against the wall, where she stood with her hands behind her back. Aside from Gypsy, she was the last remaining commoner, and the first to win a match against a High Roller. She was breathing hard, but doing well to control it.

Bice was still standing at the Wheel. Tish nudged him. "Hey, old-timer," she said. "Move along." Bice didn't move. "Leo, Mo! Get him out of here!"

The boys came forward, each took one of Bice's arms, and tried to drag him away. When he held on, they bent and pried his fingers off. The old man didn't resist. In fact, he was fairly cooperative as they pulled him toward the door.

"Six-to-one, six-to-one," he muttered as they pushed him into the hall and closed the door behind him.

"All done," said Mozart.

"He's gonna keep talking out there," said Leonard.

"But we won't hear."

"We sure won't."

"Wonder if he's any good at math."

"He knows his ratios at least."

"Hey," Tish said. "Shut up. Last pair, please come forward. Gypsy Hoss and Prescott Asher, who is playing for Lisa Gasolina by proxy."

Prescott, timid and quiet, walked to the wheel; the brand on her back stared back hideously at the others. Her head hung low and her eyes downcast, a complete opposite of Gypsy's brazen hair and confident stroll. They took their places at the wheel just as Beki came to a realization.

The building had gone quiet.

Up until now she had become used to the thrumming of music from below, the faint buzz of conversations, and occasional shout of joy or despair that found its way up the stairs. But, as soon as Prescott stepped forward, it all stopped. The air had gone dead and all sound vanished without a hint of warning. Beki started to turn to look around the room, but the sound of her own hair brushing against her shoulder seemed to disturb the silence.

Prescott took her place at the Wheel. Fortunately for Beki, the brand was shielded from her view. The girl's slender arms didn't look as if they could lift a pebble, much less spin the heavy Wheel. Tish walked forward, her heels clacking thunderously against the floor. She raised the ball over the Wheel.

"Contestants ready?"

"Ready," Gypsy said with a flip of her red hair.

Prescott nodded shallowly.

Tish tossed the ball into the air. Neither Prescott nor Gypsy touched the Wheel. The ball made a thin arc and fell into the Wheel with a gentle *chink*.

Then Prescott grew a thousand arms.

"There's this girl named Prescott," Jean-Luc said. Beki chewed on the stale cupcake the skinny girl had brought her. It tasted awful, but having food from her own world brought a small sense of comfort, even if it *was textured like sandpaper. "She's not a High Roller, but she plays for her mother."*

"The lady who owns the teahouse, right?"

"You met Lisa?"

"Uh," Beki said. *"No. Michigan told me about her. So what about Prescott?"*

"Right, Prescott," Jean-Luc said, sipping what appeared to be water from a bone china cup. He was holding the cup with his pinky extended. "You can't beat Prescott."

"I can't?"

"Neese can. You can't. Whether it's one-spin or dueling, you can't beat her."

"So what do I do?"

"Hope that someone else beats her. Hope really hard."

IMMORTALITY 101: The Intro Course

Michigan looked down at Boxcat, who was lying splayed on the bathroom floor and looking rather serene. He scratched his head and looked at the metal soap dispenser in his hand, trying to figure out if he should have done what he just finished doing.

If Boxcat had really wanted to go to the competition, he reasoned, he would've left in a hurry. In fact, he would've used the private washroom – there surely was one for the High Rollers. If he was concentrating on the game, he wouldn't have been easily fooled. If the soap dispenser hadn't been loose already, it wouldn't have come off the wall so easily. If Michigan hadn't been drunk, he might've hesitated and not hit Boxcat that hard.

Therefore, he reasoned, trying to put the soap dispenser back over the sink and failing miserably, everything was fate. Well, not everything. Just the last five to ten minutes. Fate as assured by Lady Luck. Lady Luck was rewarding him for putting that chip in as a token of faith in Beki, who was probably the only person to ever pray to her.

So, having fulfilled his role in destiny, Michigan happily dragged Boxcat into a stall, wedged them both inside, locked it, and crawled out from under the door – a tight fit. Then he washed his hands, smoothed his hair, and went out to rejoin the party.

30
ERIC

Jean-Luc found Sasha storming about in the stairwell, making quite a mess of her dress. He sighed and waited for her to slow her pace before approaching. Just to be safe, he had brought a carton of her favorite smokes and a few pieces of milk chocolate. Usually, one or the other would distract her long enough for him to think of something to calm her down. When she got tired and sat down on a step heavily, he came up from behind and offered the carton.

"Smoke?" he asked graciously. "You look like you need one."

Sasha shook her head. It wasn't that she didn't want one, Jean-Luc could tell; she was in one of those moods where she refused everything for no apparent reason. He sighed. It wasn't all her fault, he supposed. It was part of being twelve years old for all eternity. It kind of sucked.

"Look at you," he said, gesturing at her torn hem. "You're out here making a mess of yourself while there's a great game going on. Want to come back in?"

She shook her head again, blond curls bouncing off her shoulders.

"Are you sure?"

She nodded so hard he thought her little head might snap off.

"Why not?"

Sasha raised a hand and pointed at the gallery door behind him. "I can't be in the same room as *her*," she said. "I'll go crazy. I can't look at her."

Jean-Luc scoffed. "You don't honestly think she did something with Stat, do you?"

"I don't know."

"You know he hates Neese." He offered her a piece of chocolate wrapped in gold foil. She took it, tore off the foil the same way one might tear the skin off a small animal, and put it in her mouth. Then, chewing angrily, she started pacing again, circling up and down the steps. "Stop, please. You're making me dizzy."

"I shouldn't have done this."

Jean-Luc arched a brow. "Are you kidding me?"

"I shouldn't have set this up. I don't want it anymore."

"In case you haven't noticed," Jean-Luc said slowly. "It's not like throwing away a toy. Besides, what's the problem? This is the biggest game ever. Have you seen how many people are making bets down there? Have you seen how many people showed up just to *watch?* Gossip's worth its weight in gold!"

She paused in her pacing long enough to glare at him.

"OK, so I helped her out. Big deal. If I hadn't, she would've just wandered around and eventually gotten herself into some trouble. Then the story would be all about her and nobody would pay attention to you. Is that what you want?"

Sasha said nothing.

"And I know you like Stat. I don't get it, but, hey, whatever floats your boat. You want him, go get him. You wouldn't want him to see you out here sulking when he shows up, would you?"

A gleam returned to Sasha's eyes. "He's coming?"

Jean-Luc gave her a mischievous smirk.

Sasha started to smile, then her face changed to a mask of horror. "My hem!" she exclaimed, looking down. "My hair...! I have to..."

She was up the stairs before the rest of the sentence could make it out. Jean-Luc watched her go, lit a cigarette, and breathed a sigh of relief, glad that the show would still go on. He had no idea if Status Quo was coming, but he found that it didn't matter since he didn't care.

Prescott's hands were little short of magic.

Beki could hear her own heart beating as Prescott moved with inhuman speed; her white arms seemed to split into a thousand, each manipulating the Wheel with a different formula. Nothing on the girl's body moved except her arms and hands, which were slowly becoming such an unrecognizable blur that she looked as if she had no arms at all. Her legs stood straight, heels pressed together making a perfect forty-five degree angle of her feet. Her shoulders were squared back and her eyes, usually dazed and unfocused, zeroed in on the Wheel as if the rest of the world simply didn't exist. The only thing that moved on her body apart from her arms was her hair. Every now and then, a loose black lock would quiver from the wind generated by the Wheel's movement. When they fell before her eyes, she didn't attempt to move them.

At first Beki found tracking the Wheel's movements difficult and presumed that its direction was being switched at random. It spun in one direction lightning fast, and then switched at Prescott's persuasion without a moment's pause. The change was seamless, almost undetectable, and completely silent. The only sound in the entire room was the sound of the Wheel gently grinding against its stand. The ball, Beki noticed after a while, was spinning at such a speed that it was levitating a hair off the surface of the Wheel.

Gypsy had not yet touched the Wheel, and instead was watching it with grim concentration while Prescott spun. Every now and then she would lift her hand as if to attempt something, then drop it again. Beki guessed – correctly though she did not know it – that Prescott switched the direction of the Wheel every time it looked as if Gypsy might make a move, changing the velocity and angle, making it impossible for Gypsy to cut in.

One minute passed. Then two. Then five.

Not a single sound disturbed the soft rustling sound of the Wheel. Beki imagined thousands of people watching Prescott's amazing feat on the screens downstairs, slack-jawed and wide-eyed. Then she marveled at how correct Jean-Luc was, which was quite an annoying thought. If Prescott were to win this match, she might as well write off any chance to save her son right then.

Ten minutes passed. Beki forced herself to stop wringing her hands and was suddenly aware that the only other contestant left watching was the flat-chested Kam, who was also looking a bit uneasy at Prescott's skill. None of the other remaining contestants were in sight.

Tish also seemed to notice this. She took a quick look around and turned to the pair of boys standing by the wall looking bored. "Hey," she said. "Where's Boxcat? And Mojiha? They're supposed to be getting ready for the next round."

"Mojiha's not coming," said Leonard.

Tish blanched. "What do you mean he's not coming?"

"He's banging that girl," said Mozart. "Moria or something."

"In the washroom."

"We asked him if he wanted to come back."

"He said 'no' and 'go away'."

"We think that's what he said."

"Awfully hard to tell."

"His mouth was kind of full."

Beki heard this clearly and decided Moria could do better.

"What about Boxcat?"

"No idea," said Mozart with a shrug.

"Maybe he's waiting his turn," said Leonard.

A hard, solid thud made Beki jump and she swiveled her eyes back toward the Wheel. Prescott had stopped moving, her arms frozen in mid-spin like a video on pause. Something was missing and it took Beki a moment to realize that it was the gentle scraping of the Wheel against its base. Gypsy was holding the Wheel now, and it had stopped dead in its tracks.

She looked up. The ball was in the air. It soared in a straight line upward, came within a hair's length from the ceiling, and came back down again. It struck the surface of the Wheel, bounced once, twice, thrice, and fell neatly into a white square after the fourth.

Cheers exploded from beneath. Beki steadied herself against a shelf, fearing the floor might be upended by the rancorous cheering. Tish walked over to the Wheel and raised one hand.

"Winner, Gypsy Hoss."

With a smug smirk Gypsy backed away from the Wheel.

Prescott, slowly dropping her arms to her side, did the same. She looked at Leonard and Mozart, who looked at each other, apparently hesitant to manhandle her like they did the others. She gave them a slow nod and walked out of the room unhurried.

When she passed Beki, she slowed her steps, pausing just long enough to say, barely above a whisper, "Mama's going to punish me, baby sister."

"There's this other technique I know of," Jean-Luc said, then shook his head. "Why am I telling you all this? You don't need it. It's not like you'll ever play against any of them. You're just hitting the switch."

"I want to know," Beki said, having figured out that as long as she kept Jean-Luc talking about spinning techniques, he wouldn't make insulting comparisons of her hair, facial expression, clothes, demeanors, or existence in general to that of Neese. "It's very... interesting. You're very knowledgeable."

"Well, of course," Jean-Luc said proudly, puffing out his chest like a peacock in heat. "I used to be one of them, you know."

"You used to be a High Roller?"

"That's right."

"Why did you stop?"

"Got bored with it. Now what was I saying?"

"The other technique."

"Right. I don't know if it's got a name, but I call it the stopper." He mimed with his hands as he spoke. "It's both tricky and cheap. Basically, an insult to the sport of spinning. Instead of spinning, you slam your hand down on the Wheel at just the right moment. Once the Wheel is stopped, no one can make any more spins, so if you stop it just right, the ball will go into your pocket and your opponent can't do anything about it. Of course, two people can't both use this technique because otherwise they'd just trip each other up and the result becomes random. It's a very hard, risky technique and I only know one person who's truly good at it."

"Oh yeah?"

"Yes. She's the inventor of it, too. I think she did it just to spite Sasha."

Tish eyed the room wearily. Something was not right. What was supposed to be a match with five had somehow dwindled to three. Two players, a High Roller and a proxy, had either withdrawn or vanished.

It wasn't that she minded Neese being the only High Roller left, or that she had any particular attachment to Boxcat and Mojiha, but losing participants in such an important game could come off as a sign of incompetence on her part. Sasha had left her in charge and she had somehow managed to lose two people.

She scanned the list and marked off the losers by making a mark next to their names with her fingernail. With three contestants left, she supposed, the only way to compete was to pair up two and have the last play the winner. Naturally, she figured, Neese should have the honor of dueling a winner.

An idea occurred to her, and it felt like a particularly good one.

She looked up at the remaining contestants. "We will have a short intermission," she said. "Please rest in the lounge while we prepare for the next round."

At first she thought they might protest, but none of the three women said a thing as they left the room, keeping a respectable distance from each other. Tish closed the door behind them and went to the Wheel.

Did she dare? It would be an opportunity she might never have again. When Sasha announced the duel she had been devastated, but now the chance had come around again. She could play against Neese. Kneeling, she peeked under the Wheel and found the subtle bump in a thin crevice that was the switch to activate the magnetic fields. All she had to do was not hit the switch, and Neese would spin the ball into a gold pocket. She was certain this would be a small feat.

But did she dare put herself in the competition without Sasha's permission?

She would, she decided. When Neese saw how gutsy, how smart, and sneaky, she was, she would surely whisk her away from underneath Sasha's claw.

She gave herself a mental pat on the back for being ever so smart, then made a note in the back of her mind to compose a poem about this triumphant moment as soon as the tournament was over.

The lounge felt very, very small to Beki. She thought about making herself a drink, but more alcohol probably wasn't the way to go. Gypsy sat on the sofa, chewing on pieces of ice and smiling in a way that made Beki think she was formulating some secret evil plan. The last remaining contestant, Kam, sat on a stool at the bar, drinking a glass of water and tossing glances at Beki out of the corner of her eye. No one was speaking. In fact, the three of them were going to lengths not to acknowledge each other's existence.

What made the uncomfortable silence even worse was the thin door that led to the washroom. Beki had used it not long ago. It was pristine and decorated in soft white and lavenders, with a couch for resting. At the moment, however, a panting, rhythmic thumping was coming from inside, a sound that said a certain sink or counter surface was being grossly misused. There was a clatter, like something being knocked over, followed by the sound of skin sliding against a smooth surface, perhaps the mirror. Beki cringed and pretended not to hear.

Gypsy stood and said, "You shouldn't chew on your nails like that, sweetie."

Beki pulled her hand out of her mouth in a hurry, which led to a chuckle from Gypsy. A movement to her right caught her attention. She turned to see Kam gaping at her, surprise filling her dark eyes.

"You ought to be more careful," Gypsy said. "Acting like Neese is a full-time job. Don't let down your guard."

With that, she left the room, leaving Beki alone with Kam, who continued to stare at her from down the bar. Frowning in annoyance, Beki chewed on her nails again. She had already destroyed four in the course of the day. Might as well finish off the rest.

When she completed the set on her left hand, Kam was still staring at her. With a start she realized Gypsy had just spilled her secret as a parting gift. Slowly, she unclamped her teeth from her mangled fingernail and faced Kam, trying to look as composed as possible.

"What?" she asked.

Kam quickly looked away, but a second later peered over again.

"Seriously, can I help you with something?"

Kam turned toward the washroom. The heated pair inside didn't seem to be paying attention to much of anything. "You're a Rounder," she said in a low voice.

"Right," Beki said, trying to decide if she was worried or annoyed. "And?"

"That depends," Kam said carefully. "Does the name Eric Joseph Tempest mean anything to you?"

While Beki took time to process her words, another series of thumps came from the washroom. This was followed by the sound of running water. A moment later Mojiha's face appeared at the doorway. Though he was shielded by the door from the waist down, Beki still got a better look at his naked orange body than she would have liked. He looked at Kam, then at Beki, then stuck a finger out and wagged it loosely.

"Hey," he said. "You guys keep it down out here, huh?"

Rebecca "Beki" Tempest never really believed in much of anything.

She wasn't religious. She didn't really think either way on reincarnation. She thought witchcraft, voodoo, and shamanism were just fancy words teenagers used to act cool during their "punk Goth" phase. She went through about six months of it herself at age fourteen. Vampires, werewolves, and Frankenstein's monster belonged in storybooks. Zombies belonged in movies. Magic was something magicians did to pull rabbits out of their hats. God and the Devil were as plausible as unicorns and fairies in her book. The bible was just another story. Everything had its place.

Luck was one of those things. She was never quite sure she believed in luck, fate, destiny, fortune, and all that good stuff. It wasn't that she disbelieved it either. Those were merely things she never really thought about. When the time came, she always figured, something would happen to change her mind.

Apparently, that time had come. Now, she believed. For the past week or so, she had begun to really, truly believe in something. There was something supernatural going on, something inhuman and beyond the explanations of science.

And whatever it was, it was fucking with her.

31
KAMELEON

The first thing Beki did was look toward the door where Gypsy had disappeared. It must surely be some sort of joke the woman had set up. But the door remained closed and the sound of Mojiha and Moria's rhythmic breathing continued from the washroom. She looked over at Kam, who sat on her hands with her legs crossed, looking both curious and nervous.

"So?"

"So what?"

"So do you know that name?"

"Yes," Beki said. "Yes, I do. That's my son's name. How do you know his name?"

Kam let out a relieved breath. "I was worried," she said, running a hand through her short hair.

"What do you have to worry about?"

"You sound *just* like a Rounder. Do you know what kind of insult it is to call Neese Highwaters a Rounder? Everyone's sneaking around whispering it, but no one dares to say it to your face. No one who knows better anyway." Kam hopped off the stool. She walked over to the washroom and pulled the door shut. The sounds from inside didn't cease but were at least muffled. She looked down at her feet for a moment, as if trying to compose herself, then cleared her throat. "You should leave."

"What?"

Kam sighed. "I'm telling you this because you're a Rounder and you don't know any better. You should leave. There's no place for you here. Go back home and try to fix what's left of your life."

Beki shook her head. "Do you think you're the first one to say that to me? Ever since I got here people have been telling me I'm ignorant, useless, ugly, and pretty much worthless compared to this Neese person that I'm supposed to be in another life."

"Well," Kam said slowly, "they're right."

"I'm not leaving."

"Why not? Even if you win, you don't even know what to do with the chips."

"I can find out." Beki planted her feet stubbornly. "I'm not leaving until I find a way to save my son. If you're going to threaten me—"

"I'm not threatening you," Kam said, interrupting. "I don't really have any reason to. I'm just telling you this because I don't want you to waste your effort on something hopeless. Trust me when I say, I don't like you. I would never do Neese any favors. I'm doing this out of sentiment for the last Round we played together."

"The last Round?"

"I entered my last Round as a male," Kam said. "There was a lot of jealousy because I was assigned a role as the child of Neese Highwaters by chance. It has been a long time since a High Roller played a Round. It was a big deal." She paused, just long enough for Beki to tear her own mind, which had being increasingly unstable in the past week, to pieces. "Yes, I underwent exit procedures two days ago, 'mother'."

Her knees felt weak. Beki felt her way to a stool and sat down heavily. She stared at the young woman in front of her, and tried to spot some resemblance to her son, but found none.

"Are you lying?" she asked shakily.

Kam rolled her eyes. Having learned that the person in front of her was a Rounder and not a High Roller, she seemed much more composed than a few short minutes ago. "I was born in the spring," she said like a kid reciting a boring essay. "I wet the bed until I was two. I had a red truck given to me by your aunt, whom I didn't really like because she kept kissing me with too much lipstick on. I became obsessed with an old Nintendo machine I found in grandpa's attic.

There were two moles on my back just below the shoulder blades, a clear scar on my right hand from a hot cookie sheet, and I can roll my tongue but not wiggle my ears."

Beki said nothing. She felt dizzy.

"Eric…"

"No," Kam said sharply, "not Eric. Kam. My name is Kam. Eric was just a persona I used in the last Round. It's like… I don't know, when you chat with someone over a network. You can use any name and identity you want."

"My son is dead," Beki said numbly.

"He never existed." Seeing the pain in Beki's eyes, Kam threw up her hands. "OK, fine. He's dead. He died in his sleep shortly after the car accident. I was kind of disappointed, but that's what happens when you get caught in someone else's ripple. I didn't know you were here until I exited. Didn't think you'd be stupid enough to actually come here as a Rounder."

"He's dead," Beki said again.

Kam scooted up to Beki and peered into her listless eyes. "You have *got* to stop that," she said. "You're going to ruin Neese's reputation. He *never existed.*"

The sound of skin against skin shocked Beki. She looked down at her tingling hand and realized she had slapped the girl before she could stop herself. The surprised look on Kam's face immediately elicited guilt, but other emotions rose up and drowned it out.

"He did to me," she said. It came out more bitterly than she had intended.

Kam touched her bruised cheek, which was taking on a shade of ugly red, and shook her head. "Whatever," she said.

Michigan drummed his fingers on the bar, humming to himself and feeling pretty damned good. He felt proud that he had done something to help. Lady Luck was smiling on him, he thought. Everything was going along swimmingly.

The next round should start soon, and he had a feeling Beki was doing very well.

As Luck would have it, the air in the hall was beginning to get to him. Long hours among sweat and alcohol made his eyes water. Beki wouldn't mind, he figured, if he stepped out for some fresh air. He would return later and observe the game with a clearer head.

The streets were eerily quiet outside. As usual, there were no wind or stars, and today, no pedestrians. Nothing moved, and if one had watched one too many movies from the Round, the scene was reminiscent of many stories that involved boogiemen jumping out to mangle pretty young girls. Michigan, not being a pretty young girl and generally disliking that sort of movie, found the peace comforting. After the mass of writhing bodies, it was nice to see the still streets. In fact, its stillness was what made it so easy to spot the figure walking away in a hurry not half a block away.

He broke into a run and chased her, which wasn't hard, considering she was barefoot, just like she had been when he first dragged her out of her home by her hand.

"Wait!" he called. "Hey, wait up! Where are you going?"

She stopped, but did not turn around. He saw the Oz Greens clutched clumsily in her hand as she hugged herself, her shoulders shaking in a way that worried him on many levels. Slowing his steps a few yards away, he waited.

"He's dead," she said.

For a moment he had no idea what she was talking about. "Who?" he asked stupidly.

"Eric. He's gone." A pause. "Why didn't you tell me?"

"What?" Michigan racked his brain, trying to remember if he knew something she didn't. "What do you mean he's dead? How do you know?"

She turned around slowly, her head dipped so low her chin was almost on her chest. The mascara Jean-Luc had so meticulously applied was running down her cheek in two dark lines. She looked like a woeful clown. He reached out to her, but she pulled back, wiping her cheeks and smearing the makeup all over her face in distorted blotches. Michigan decided not to point it out.

"Hey," he said. "What's wrong?"

Beki swallowed thickly. "I talked to this girl," she said, her voice shaky and broken. "She said she played Eric in the last round, and that she had 'exited' or something, which meant he had died. This is all for nothing."

"Wait," Michigan said. "Wait, wait, wait. That can't be right." He took her shoulders gently. "I know everything there is to know about Neese, OK? I know who played what in her Round, who was close to her, who she hated, what she did, why she did them, etc. The person who played your son was a pro spinner. She won some sort of bet by accident and got that part. Her name is Kameron."

"Kameron Hurley?" Beki gave him an accusing glance. "*Kam* Hurley?"

"Yes, and she's..." he paused. "Wait a minute..."

"So she was telling the truth." Beki slipped from his grasp. He followed suit as she sat down on the curb, the Oz Greens dangling from her fingertips. "That's it, then. All of this was for nothing. I could have spent my son's last moments with him, but instead I was here, playing this stupid little game."

"Where were you going to go?"

She shrugged. "Find Stat, I guess. Ask him to take me back. Kam told me to go home and fix the rest of my life the best I can, and that's what I'm going to do. Screw Neese. Screw Sasha. Screw this whole place."

"What if the rest of the Round breaks Neese like it did Adda?"

"That's her problem. Not mine. From what I can tell, she would deserve it." She handed the shoes to him. "Could you return these to Jean-Luc for me? Thank him for his help, then tell him I said he's a spineless prick. Oh, and that he wears too much hair gel. I'll stop by the Crescent and see if I can get the safe code from Titi. You can take whatever you want to buy yourself out of Gypsy's contract. Hell, take more. I don't need it. And Sasha... I don't care about Sasha. Write something nasty about her on a bathroom wall for me or something."

He took the shoes and briefly considered if he should construct a shrine of some sort for them, then decided that would be too creepy. He would sell them to one of Neese's other slobbering fans instead. There were a lot of them and chances were he could get a pretty decent price. Beki wiped her face again and he quickly put them aside.

"So... that's it?"

She nodded, turning watery brown eyes to him. "I guess so. Thanks for what you tried to do. Sorry it turned out to be a waste." She stood and dusted off her dress. "I should get this dress back to Jean-Luc... I don't even know where my own clothes are."

"Stay," he said.

Beki blinked. "What?"

Michigan replayed the last three seconds and made sure he had said what he intended to. "Stay," he said again. "I mean... yeah, stay. Stay here. Don't go anywhere."

She shook her head. "I don't want to compete anymore."

Michigan's mouth said, "stay with me," while his brain said, *shut up, stupid*.

"And do what?"

"I don't know. Stay with me. I think I like you."

She laughed a short, sad laugh. "You 'think' you like me?" Reaching out, she patted his shoulder weakly. "I know it's hard for you to get over, but I'm not Neese. That's why I have to go. I can't keep staying here and pretending to be someone else."

He grabbed her hand. "Come on," he pleaded. "I know you're not Neese. I do like you. Just stay here. You don't have to go back. You can stay here until you're old, then go back to the Round and do your exit procedures. You'll come back as Neese either way."

The disbelief in her eyes was a bit hurtful, but he kept quiet and waited for her to work the idea through her head.

"You want me to spend the rest of my life here?"

"Yep. I mean, that's the general gist of it."

"With you? Just hanging around, gambling and drinking all the time?"

"There're other things to do." He gestured toward the street. "We can live in the suburbs. A lot of people live there, pretending like they're in the Round, living what they think is a normal life. We can do that, too. We can get a house with a nice lawn, have dinner together, and go to bed together at night. It'll be fun. You won't have to go back and deal with your husband or your job or anything."

Beki looked at him closely. "You do realize what you're asking me, don't you?"

"I'm asking you to stay here and not worry about all that other stuff."

"You're asking me to marry you. Or pretend to marry you, whatever it is you guys do here."

"Oh," Michigan said. "Right. Yeah. That's the word."

"And you want this even though I'm not Neese? Even if I'm not glamorous and powerful and beautiful like her?"

"You *are* beautiful like her. Not many people get to choose their appearance when they go into the Round, but of course Neese gets whatever she wants. She didn't want any other face but her own. But that's not the point." He picked up the shoes and shoved them into her hands. "Put on your shoes. We can leave right now. You can stay with me until we find a better place. Come on, it's easy. Stat will probably forget about you after a while. You can just escape from everything. I mean, it's just a Round."

"Just a Round?"

"Yeah. It's nothing, right?"

Beki looked down at the shoes in her hands long and hard. She didn't speak for so long that Michigan began to wonder if she had passed out on her feet. But then she looked up, and her eyes were dry and bright. "I can't run," she said softly.

Michigan wondered if something was wrong with his short-term memory. "Wait, what? I said…"

"I can't run," she said again, half to herself. "I can't just escape like that. That wouldn't really solve anything." She dropped the shoes on the ground and slipped her feet into them. "I have to finish this."

He raised a hand to stop her. "No, you…"

She wrapped her arms around him, surprising him with her strength. "Thanks," she said. "I know that everyone here thinks the Round is just a game, but you just made me realize – it's my everything." Then, with a determined step, she walked past him and back toward the tournament. "I'll have to fix my makeup," he heard her say.

Michigan watched her go, then scratched his head and sighed. "Well, fuck," he muttered to himself in disappointment.

Gypsy was lounging comfortably when Neese – or at least a woman who looked a lot like Neese with a face painted like a sad clown – walked in. She was surprised, genuinely surprised. Kam looked up, too. The woman who wore Neese's face walked past both of them to the washroom, where she gave the door a hard shove. It struck the wall thunderously. Two intertwined figures looked up from the couch, startled.

"Whoa, Neese," Mojiha said as Moria busied herself blushing and covering her breasts as she straddled his hips. "Don't be a spoilsport, huh?"

"Get out."

Mojiha started. "What? You can't be serious. We were just..." He paused. "Dude, what happened to you? You look like a damn raccoon."

"I need to fix my makeup. Get the fuck out." Gypsy arched a brow as the Rounder pretending to be Neese strolled into the washroom, picked up the pile of clothes on the floor, and flung them into Moria's face. The girl let out a frightened cry and climbed over the back of the couch off Mojiha. "And you, I don't know you but if you're fucking him I'll assume you straddle anything that walks. Get yourself another hobby before you sprain something."

Moria struggled to dress herself as Mojiha rolled onto his feet. He cricked his neck, one side then the other. Unlike Moria, he didn't seem quite as bothered by his own exposed privates. "Neese," he said, "come on. I backed out of the competition just so..."

'Neese' reached up, grabbed his ear, and twisted. Mojiha yelped and tried to swat her hand away, but she held tight and dragged him toward the door by his ear. It was all very comical, and Gypsy stifled her chuckles out of embarrassment for Mojiha.

"I said get out," 'Neese' said. "Or did you not understand me?" She glared at Moria, who was still topless. "And you. What are you, deaf? Out!"

With a whimper Moria ran out of the washroom, her top clutched in her arms. She ran out of the lounge, past Gypsy and Kam, who tried not to gape. 'Neese' shoved Mojiha out and slammed the door behind him.

"Hey!" he yelled, hammering on the door. "At least give me back my pants!"

Gypsy and Kam waited politely while he did this for a handful of minutes before realizing they were there. Sheepishly, he turned to them. "Ladies," he said.

Gypsy raised her glass slightly. "Cheers."

"Right," he said. "Cheers. Damn Neese. This is just like her." Cursing under his breath, he walked out of the lounge in the buff, presumably to find some clothing, but more likely to find Moria and finish their tryst.

Kam glared at Gypsy. "You said she wouldn't come back," she said in a low voice. "You said if I told her that her son was dead she would back out."

Gypsy shrugged and took her sip of her vodka. "I merely made an assumption," she said, sucking on the lemon slice. "I never promised anything. What does it matter, anyway?"

"What matters is I was going to win," Kam snapped. "My sister's Round is being cut short. She never wanted to be in the same Round as that woman. This was her chance to get out. Now she's back. What the hell am I supposed to do now?"

"Beat her," Gypsy said evenly. "Honestly, Kameleon. Did you really think you'd lose to her? She's a Rounder. She lucked out before, because that sissy Moria chickened out." She pointed toward the washroom. "Tell you what, I'll even throw the next match so you can go up against her. How's that? Sound satisfying? You can beat her yourself. It would be ever so enjoyable, don't you think? Get Kameron out of there yourself."

Kam narrowed her eyes. "Why would you do that?"

Gypsy smiled. "Why not? I'm just bored enough to let it happen. A duel with some personal motive behind it is always more fun to watch."

There was some commotion when Neese Highwaters reappeared on screen. At first there was the usual wave of cheers of excitement, then it turned into a murmur of confusion. Some questions were raised as to why Neese wasn't wearing any makeup, and why she had tied her beautiful hair back. She looked better this way, some thought. More dignified and unique. Others thought this was strange and a little suspicious, as Neese had always paid such attention to her appearance. However, they did not speak up, since questioning Neese was never a smart thing to do.

There was another portion of the audience that was too drunk to form an opinion, so they cheered that Neese looked better than ever, and they cheered that she looked weird and suspicious. Then they poured themselves another drink.

Michigan started out in the first group and was slowly moved on to the third. He vowed not to wash his head this time, even if he got trampled. If he got trampled, he was just going to stay down until someone peeled him off the floor. So, with this in mind, he stayed by the bar and grumbled to himself that at this rate he was never going to find a good girlfriend.

Sasha dabbed her face with powder and looked up at the television screen mounted on the wall of her private washroom. The Rounder was up to something. She had taken away everything that made her Neese and was playing with her ugly face exposed, without a lick of makeup or disguise. How droll, she thought to herself. A lady should never be seen without makeup. Even if it was just a touch of eye shadow and blush.

But more important things were at hand. Carefully, she laid a thin layer of gloss over her own lips. Stat was coming. Whatever the Rounder was trying to pull, she would only expose herself and ruin Neese's perfectionist reputation. Besides, Stat could never fall for a woman who looked like that. Of this she was certain. He would think she was plain and dumb, which was precisely what she was.

He would know he'd been a fool, she mused, her heart pounding, *and come back to me*.

Lisa wound a strand of Marky's hair over her fingers and pinned it up with a pretty diamond butterfly pin. She was such a pretty girl, Marky was, so quiet and tame and obedient. She reached over the dresser and retrieved a jar of vanilla skin cream, which she applied to the girl's face and neck. Marky didn't move or say a word, the mark of a good daughter.

The large television in the main lounge was playing a live broadcast of the dice game. The few of her regular customers who opted out of the noise and hustle-bustle were watching intently, ordering very expensive cups of tea in the process, mostly to congratulate themselves for not having gone and made a fool of themselves by making the wrong bet.

Prescott had lost. Lisa sighed inwardly as she applied meticulous layers of gel to Marky's hair, curling and styling it with care. She was disappointed in Prescott, losing to a commoner, but as a mother she knew it didn't warrant punishment. Prescott merely needed to learn, and when she returned, it was lessons she would receive. Lisa had long vowed to be a good mother, and sometimes being a mother meant tough love.

She put the last pin in Marky's hair, then stood her up and looked at her from every angle. She would need a new leather skirt, and perhaps some heels to match. Lisa made a note to get her some sneakers so her feet wouldn't blister from wearing those boots all the time.

"You look lovely, my dear."

Marky nodded, her eyes glassy and unfocused. "Thank you, mama."

"Are you my good girl?"

Another nod. "Yes, mama."

Lisa bent and kissed the girl on the forehead. Marky received it without a sound. She stood, perfect and steady, like a wooden doll.

IMMORTALITY 101: The Intro Course

32
MIRACLE

Tish couldn't believe her eyes. The woman standing by the door with her arms folded couldn't be Neese Highwaters. She simply couldn't be. After all the years Tish had spent idolizing Neese, she had built up an impressive mental portfolio of Neese's outfits, makeup styles that transformed between day and evening, shoes for every occasion, jewelry that ranged from a simple silver ring to a diamond necklace that could buy Tish's life six times over. But this was new. It was different and shocking in a way she had never prepared for.

Without makeup, Neese looked almost plain. Almost. Her skin was still luminescent and light, and her eyes dark and deep. But it simply wasn't the same. Tish stared at her, trying to figure out the something that was off. With her hair tied in a neat ponytail and her face fresh and clean, Neese looked...

Common.

Tish quickly erased that word from her mind. It wasn't right. But it kept coming back and it was painful. The royal Neese Highwaters had become a commoner, and not just any commoner. She looked like she wouldn't stand out in a sea of wheat. The plainness was blinding to Tish after knowing the painted radiance that was Neese. She couldn't bear to watch and turned her attention to the paper in her hand instead.

IMMORTALITY 101: The Intro Course

"The third round will now begin," she announced, and looked around quickly, noting that Sasha was still not around. Sasha hadn't been around for the better part of an hour and she couldn't imagine where she had gone. But, she supposed, it didn't matter. "Since there are only three contestants remaining, I will stand in as a temporary contestant." She glanced at Neese and tried to swallow the bitter disappointment in her chest. "Neese Highwaters. Please step forward."

Neese came forward and there was a rupture of cheers from below. But it wasn't the same cheer her presence used to elicit. Tish could tell that many people were confused and cheering out of habit.

"You will be playing against me."

Neese shrugged nonchalantly. "Fine," she said simply.

Tish went to the Wheel and took it. Neese did the same. Her posture was different, too, Tish noticed. Instead of standing by the Wheel with her usual impeccable posture, Neese was half-leaning against it, her fingers gripping its side clumsily. It was as if everything that made her old self had drained out of her, leaving only the husk of a commoner in its place.

All of Tish's dreams of playing against the great Neese fell over her head. She could barely contain the sorrow welling up in her heart as she stood across from this person, whom she increasingly felt was nothing but an imposter. But who else could she be? It was Neese's face, and Neese's dress, and her Oz Greens. She choked back a sob and gripped the Wheel tightly.

"You disappoint me," she said in a low voice, barely above a whisper.

"Bite me," Neese replied, and spun.

By all accounts, Tish was not a great spinner. She could not duel and most of her skills lay in being able to make one decent starter spin. Usually, this was enough, as the majority of the people who came to the Wheel did not duel. Plus Sasha forbade dueling in her halls except for special occasions like this one. The one thing Tish could do, really, was feel for the switch. She could tell by the way it brushed against her hand whether it was in the on or off position.

Beki could not spin. She had never been near a wheel of this sort until today and, due to the unexpected result of the previous round, hadn't made a spin in her entire life. But she, too, knew how to feel for the switch, as it was the only thing Jean-Luc made sure to drill into her brain during her 'training'. She knew precisely what the switch ought to feel like when it was off, and how it ought to stay after it was turned on. She knew, theoretically, how to turn it on and make sure it stayed on, in case it flicked back to its original position during the spin.

Tish, disappointed that her image of Neese Highwaters had been shattered by her 'new look', had decided to flip the switch and win, thus driving Neese out of the competition, seeing how she no longer deserved to win. She was unaware, of course, that the Wheel had been rigged to ensure the ball would land in a gold pocket. She was also unaware that Jean-Luc had neglected to tell her this because he wanted the Spin Doctors to remain an X factor in the game, thus making it more interesting.

Beki, after blowing off Michigan inadvertently and working through some personal dilemmas, found that throwing her weight around as Neese was actually pretty satisfying, especially when one was feeling bitter. She had begun by kicking Mojiha out of the washroom in the buff, which was more fun than she had anticipated. Then, looking at herself in the mirror, she realized she had no makeup on hand to fix her face with. In a moment of defiance, she washed her face in a manner – though unbeknownst to her – not too unlike the way Michigan had dunked his head earlier. Then, standing there in front of the full-length mirror, with water dripping down her hair and soaking her dress, she realizing she disliked most everyone ever since she got to this place and was going to start acting accordingly, which involved defeating those who annoyed her in the game that apparently meant so much to them. What came after that, she hadn't quite decided. Win or lose, she made a vow not to turn into Adda, no matter what the rest of her life threw at her, so Neese could come back and surely exact some horrendous revenge on the people who did this to her.

"Alright, Neese," she had said to her reflection. It was a bit of a crazy thing to do, but she had decided to embrace the insanity if it wanted her so badly. "It's just you and me now." A pause, then, "you know, I really hate you."

Tish was waiting for something miraculous. Were she in the Round, she would be one of those girls who spend their entire lives waiting for a prince to come save her from a boring, dreary life. She would want this so much that she would eventually wind up alone, past her prime, and probably die from an alcohol-related death, dreaming of her nonexistent prince. She was waiting for something to show her that Neese was still the amazing idol of her dreams.

Beki had decided that she disliked Tish, much the same way she disliked nearly everyone else she'd met since coming through that weird wall. There were a few exceptions, but by and large she could probably live without them in the long run. What she didn't know was that by chance, or perhaps by Luck, this made her more like Neese than Stat's pill ever did.

The switch zipped by Beki's fingertip and she began to sweat. That was the third time. As she kept her hand on the bottom of the wheel, she was very aware that, with all her preparations, the one thing she did not do was actually touch a wheel. There wasn't one available for her to practice on, and all Jean-Luc did was fuss with her looks and bring her a mock-up of the mechanism for her to touch. She knew how it felt, but she didn't know how to catch it.

Tish had spun hard, and Beki merely went with the flow and groped for the switch. It dashed by again, and again she failed to catch it. Her heart began to pound and the confidence she had a moment before was quickly evaporating. Her hands were becoming clammy and moist as she watched the Wheel whiz by in front of her, gold and white blurring before her eyes. She reached for the switch again and came within a hair's breadth.

She was, in every sense, losing.

Tish waited, drowning in her disappointment. Neese looked flustered. Actually flustered. What kind of look was that for a High Roller? Something was off and she didn't like it. Perhaps, she reasoned, it was merely Neese's time. Theoretically, every High Roller would fall eventually, no matter how great they once were. Bice and Jean-Luc, for example. They were once among the elite and now were nothing but a crazy old man and an errand boy. Neese was losing it. Tish couldn't figure out why but it was obvious. Her time was here.

She pretended to give the Wheel another nudge and flipped the switch, then sighed wistful and waited for the inevitable result. It wasn't a pity, she decided. Just the way things were around here. Another great one was about to fall.

The Wheel slowed. The ball lolled. Thousands of heads turned with it as it went lazily around the core – once, twice, then downward, making a small, almost undetectable curve in its path to settle into a gold pocket.

For Beki, it was a confusing, but welcome relief. She reasoned that she had done something right and that Lady Luck was looking out for her. As part of her new-found persona she did not let her relief show and merely stood her ground while the crowd underneath chanted Neese's name. Her legs felt weak and blood was pounding in her ears. She muttered something vaguely incoherent, but it could be summarized as a prayer of thanks to Lady Luck.

For Tish, it was a miracle. She would not be picked by Neese as a handmaiden, but it would be because it never occurred to Beki to do so as opposed to the reason she assumed, which was that she had made the mistake of treating Neese like a commoner. She would spend a very long time mulling on this, sighing up to the black sky and writing poetry in the little notebook she kept in her locker. She would vow to learn from her mistakes and never to underestimate Neese Highwaters again.

IMMORTALITY 101: The Intro Course

33
STOPPER

The display screens flickered and turned off after Neese's triumphant round. They stayed dark for a few moments then turned back on, displaying a single line of scrolling white text.

Boxcat Pincher – disqualified on account of no-show. All bets null. No refund.

There was some grumbling, and a large portion of the crowd milled over to the bar. There was a time when they would have rioted, but time had taught them that rioting was just wasted effort. When it came to the High Rollers, there was no such thing as a refund. They knew it, but it never stopped them from betting. Therefore, it was their own fault. So, instead of waiting energy, they used the same effort a riot would have taken to pour drinks down their throats.

The text disappeared after five passes across the screen and was replaced by another.

Mojiha Jordan – disqualified on account of being a pervert. All bets null. No refund.

Another group broke off the dance floor and went to the bar, which was becoming increasingly congested. They joined the first group, toasted each other on their loss, traded stories of how the last time Mojiha was disqualified, it involved a pair of albino twins and a banister that could never be polished again.

A few minutes later that text disappeared, too, and a scrolling list showed the names of all the contestants who had lost or had been disqualified. All the people who had been too busy drinking, partying, and having a good time dreaming about the life they were going to buy with their winnings finally looked up and made note that they had lost. Then they either kept on having a good time or went to the bar. Either way, they effectively staved off the inevitable blues that would come crashing down later.

A small portion of the people was happy, however, since their bets on Gypsy and Kam were still good. They slapped each other on the back and continued to dream about the life they were going to buy with their winnings.

One man among them, Michigan Von Phant, desperately wished he'd bet more. It didn't occur to him until now that he could've really cleaned up if he'd just bet everything on Beki.

Geoffy was excited. It wasn't often that he got to see Gypsy in action, and her stopper technique got him downright jolly. He milled about the dance floor, throwing his weight around to get to anyone he could and brag about Gypsy's skills. More than once he threw his arm around the nearest stranger and asked, "So, that Gypsy, she's something, huh?" Since most people knew him as the only source of flowing alcohol, they nodded in agreement. Seeing that, he would punch them on the shoulder happily and tell them to come by the bar and get a free drink later.

He had no intention of seeing that promise through, but he liked to appear nice. In his current pleasant mood, he was even glad to hang around with Michigan.

Speaking of Michigan, he had lost track of the guy after he went into the bathroom. Geoffy hadn't realized this until he checked his watch and realized twenty minutes had passed. Usually he couldn't care less where Michigan wandered off to, but since he was feeling particularly happy, he decided to go check on his number ten customer (Michigan wasn't usually that high up on the list but what the hell, he was happy).

He went into the bathroom, expecting to see Michigan passed out on the floor, but he was nowhere in sight. There was, however, someone who had slipped off the toilet with his pants still on. Geoffy couldn't quite see his face, which was hidden by the stall. He tried the door, and found it locked. Part of his mind said the guy was dressed an awful lot like one of the contestants in the tournament but, since he was betting on Gypsy all the way, he decided it wasn't really his business.

When he came out, the tournament was going again, and apparently Neese had won against one of Sasha's cronies. He watched the screens for a bit, waiting for Gypsy's reappearance. She was playing against a commoner – in Geoffy's heart, Gypsy was anything but a commoner – who looked like a skinny, prepubescent teenager next to her. The red, flowing skirt and black corset she had donned for the occasion sent flutters through Geoffy's massive chest. She had even combed her hair back. Geoffy liked her hair however she wore it but, when she pushed it back, she looked especially fierce.

He watched her step up to the Wheel, his mouth hanging open, then he made sure to nudge a few people and mutter about how amazing she looked and how she was sure to win. If she won, he hoped, she could quit that fortune-telling business for a while and come live with him, make him her only lover and be a lovely companion waiting at home when he got off from the bar. Perhaps she would wait naked.

Gypsy strolled up to the Wheel. She looked at it, at her opponent, then at the Spin Doctor.

"I forfeit," she said, and walked out of the screen.

Beki gaped, along with everyone else who occupied the hall, as Gypsy walked out without looking back. Then, realizing that Neese would probably never gape at anyone with her mouth open, she closed her mouth and tried to look like she didn't give a damn. The Spin Doctor named Tish also looked surprised, but she recovered quickly. She cleared her throat and raised the list of contestants.

"Well," she said, and the two boys who accompanied her looked at each other and shrugged, "I suppose Gypsy Hoss is hereby disqualified on account of voluntary withdrawal."

IMMORTALITY 101: The Intro Course

The blond haired boy pulled out a device that very much resembled the fancy cell phone Beki's husband wanted for Christmas. He typed in a short message, which he had done several times in the past hour or so, and the screens in the Hall displayed a short message.

Gypsy Hoss – disqualified on account of voluntary withdrawal. All bets null. No refund.

Beki glanced across the room at the last contestant, who was the only person who did not turn at Gypsy's departure. Kam did not return her gaze. She was gazing straight ahead at the Wheel. Something about her demeanor made Beki uneasy. Her dark eyes were like cindering coals, hot and hard. In her face, Beki thought she could almost see some resemblance to Eric, but admitted to herself that it was probably just her imagination. She hated the idea of going up against her son, or someone who used to be her son in a past life. The situation was very strange and uncomfortable, and she was beginning to think the best way to deal with it was not to over think it.

Kam tilted her gaze in Beki's direction, and for a moment Beki thought she saw something bitter and cold in her dark eyes. Since her charade as Neese had begun, she had become oddly used to people giving her looks of distain among the sea of adoration, but Kam's cold gaze bothered her and though she tried not to let it show, Beki had to admit it was unnerving on many levels. Kam's eyes were filled with hate.

Tish folded up the sheet of paper and stuffed it into the pocket of her uniform. She looked at both contestants and addressed Beki. "Would you like to take a break, Miss Highwaters?" she asked with a polite smile, quite a change from the demeanor she wore when they competed against each other a few minutes ago. Beki hadn't taken the effort to figure out why the girl's mood was swinging back and forth and decided to write it off as some sort of personality disorder. Everyone in this place, she had long decided, had some sort of disorder.

"Miss Highwaters?"

"Yes? I mean, no." She tore herself away from Kam's cold gaze. "Let's get this over with."

Tish nodded. "Contestants to the Wheel, please."

Beki stepped up to the Wheel for the third time, with Kam standing across. They took the Wheel and readied themselves.

"Ready?"

"Wait," Beki said, and could almost feel the simultaneous shudder of surprise that went through the crowd below. She addressed Tish, whom she had singled out as the suggestible one. And rightly so, it seemed. Tish looked as if she might melt at the sound of Beki's voice. "I have a request."

"Y-yes," the girl stammered. "What is it, Miss Highwaters?"

"I'd like for this match to be in private."

"You want us to turn off the cameras?" Tish asked, looking crestfallen. "I'm so sorry, but we can't..."

"No, just leave the room," Beki said. "I don't feel comfortable with all of you watching this close. This is an important match. You wouldn't want any distractions to ruin the excitement, do you?"

The boys exchanged a look and shrugged. "I don't know," said Leonard.

"Sasha might get mad," said Mozart.

"She'd yell."

"We'd get in trouble."

"We hate getting in trouble."

"She makes us scrub stuff."

"We hate scrubbing."

"We're not clean people."

"We're pigs. It's true."

"Shut up!" Tish snapped. "I'm in charge."

"You're not," Leonard said.

"We'll get in trouble," Mozart said.

"I'll take responsibility," Tish said firmly. "I will take the punishment. You guys can get out of here and pretend you didn't see a thing. We'll give Miss Highwaters whatever privacy she needs." Turning, she grabbed the two boys by the collar and dragged them to the door. Mozart gave Beki a mock salute as he passed.

"She's a bit of a hot head," he said.

"Your number-one fan," Leonard chimed in.

"Don't let her down," they said together, right before Tish choked them off with a hard tug. Beki watched the door close behind them, looked up at the cameras, and turned back to the Wheel.

"You can't beat me," Kam said. Beki nodded in agreement.

"Yes, I know."

"You're just a Rounder. Rounders can't spin. You can't have had enough time to practice. Rounders are worthless in this game."

"Yes, so I've been told." Beki slid her hand over the Wheel. "I don't really care anymore. All anyone ever does ever since I got here is insult me. I'm a Rounder, I'm stupid, I'll never be Neese, blah, blah, blah. It's kind of annoying me." She moved the Wheel in a slow circle. "I just think it's kind of fun at this point, this whole game you guys play."

Kam narrowed her eyes in suspicion. She had thin eyes and narrowing them made her look tired. "What do you want?"

Beki continued to play with the Wheel. "What do you mean?"

"Your son is dead. What does it matter that you keep playing?"

"You know," Beki said, "I'm not sure. But you said I can't beat you anyway, right? So let's just play."

Beki and Kam's exchange went largely unheard as the gallery was not equipped with microphones. This was because Sasha valued her privacy and also because it wasn't necessary for the crowd to hear any exchanges that went on during the tournament. Any important announcements were made via scrolling texts across the screen, since broadcasting them through speakers would only add to the noise in the hall. There was a buzz, of course, when it became obvious that Neese and the commoner had been left alone and were carrying on some sort of conversation in private.

There was some speculation about the relationship between the two contestants. Most Rounders were not tracked so obsessively unless they were in the middle of doing something spectacular that involved large bets being placed on them. Neese's Round was closely followed simply because of who she was – High Rollers in the Round were always a high point of interest.

So naturally it was no surprise that Kameleon Hurley was recognized by many who followed Neese's career in the Round as the twin sister of Kameron Hurley, who was currently playing as Eric

Joseph Tempest, son of Rebecca Anne Tempest, the identity Neese had assumed in her 'recently terminated' Round. Someone ventured that this fact and the current events were related, but they did so while catching their drink on a round trip so it went unheard.

Kameron and Kameleon were both talented duelists. They were known in some circles as the "Wonder Twins", completely unrelated to the superhero duo of the same name in the Round. They also did not wear matching purple uniforms. They had won many duels, both together and individually. For commoners, they had a decent following of their own.

Beki didn't know any of this and wouldn't have cared if she did.

The music had stopped after Tish, Leonard, and Mozart left the gallery. The DJ, an avid fan of the Wonder Twins with a huge bet riding on Kameleon, had let the music drop as he stared fixedly at the nearest screen. The complaints were few, as the only people remaining on the dance floor were the ones with bets on Kam, and each was anxious to see his bet come one step closer to payoff. This match had set another unseen precedent, one of the many that had been set tonight. With both contestants standing at a payoff rate of fifteen-to-one and higher, the scent of greed and excitement infiltrated every nook and cranny of the hall. As far as anyone could remember, the highest payoff rate in history for a semi-finalist was seven-to-one.

Not to mention that, with the rumors and Neese's recent strange behavior, a loss could mean the fall of one of the most prominent High Rollers, and in a place where everyone lived to see someone else fail, no one wanted to miss it.

Kam began to spin. Her fingers worked even faster than before, moving the Wheel this way and that. She wasn't quite as nimble as Prescott, but her speed was astonishing nonetheless. Her entire body went into the motions and it was almost an acrobatic routine, a complex dance that moved with a flow that would have put the greatest dancers and gymnasts in the Round to shame. She never looked up at Beki, never wavered her gaze from the Wheel for even a split second. All of her concentration was focused like a laser beam.

Beki watched, since it was a great show and she doubted she'd get to see anything better once she went home.

IMMORTALITY 101: The Intro Course

Five minutes passed, during which the Wheel must have spun several thousand times. As many eyes watched, minds began to wonder why Neese wasn't doing anything. The crowd down below was preparing for something spectacular.

The Wheel was slowing now. Beki could almost follow the silver ball as it spun around the core. She waited.

Kam kept on spinning, putting so much force into the Wheel that Beki thought she could smell smoke coming from the axis. She wondered if the game would be declared a draw if the Wheel were to break and fall over before it stopped spinning.

She waited for the Wheel to slow to half speed.

She waited until she could almost see the shape of the ball.

She waited until the Wheel faced her just right.

Then she slammed her hand down on it the same way Gypsy had, and would have knocked it over had it not been bolted to the floor. The ball soared upward into the air.

Downstairs, a gasp could be heard, a combination of shock and awe.

For a split second she began to worry that she had hit the Wheel too hard, that the effort she had spent distracting Kam long enough for her to find and flip the switch underneath the Wheel before the match began would be all for naught. Then the ball took a tight arc and fell back down, bounced once, twice, struck the edge of the Wheel, and bounced back, slid momentarily against the surface, and arced into a gold pocket.

She silently thanked Lady Luck as the building came quite close to being uprooted by the explosive cheers.

She thanked Michigan, since he deserved it.

Then she thanked Jean-Luc, even if he was a royal prick.

"Too bad," she said to Kam as the Spin Doctors came into the gallery, Tish wearing the same look she used to see on TV, when some hopeless devotee was called before the evangelist to be saved.

34
ONE HUNDRED AND TWENTY

Stat arrived at the grand hall just in time to see the end of Beki and Kam's duel. The explosive shouts nearly drove him back out the door. Pressing his hands over his ears, he made his way through the crowd. Shockingly, in their ecstasy, few people remembered to avoid him as he shoved his way past writhing bodies.

Sasha had done a hell of a job with the hall. It couldn't be more luxurious or tacky. With the preliminaries over, the golden curtain had been drawn to hide the stage, leaving an enormous wall of gold that shimmered in the disco lights. Keeping his head down, Stat managed to wrench himself into a corner, where he stayed in the shadows and scanned the room. Most of the space, as well as the long bar, was filled with people. The flashing dance floor made it difficult to discern one shape from another, and he had a hard time picking out familiar voices over the noise.

He wanted to know what had been going on, but the only person who could explain it halfway decently was probably Michigan Von Phant, whom he'd never be able to find, not in this mess. Judging by the reaction of the crowd, he had missed quite an historical event. The young Spin Doctors behind the betting booths were busy tallying up the take. He made his way to the nearest one.

"How can I..." the young woman behind the booth looked up and started. "Oh!" she gasped, and quickly averted her eyes.

"What're the odds on Neese Highwaters?"

"We're not taking any more bets," the young woman said, then added timidly, "sir."

"I'm just asking what the odds are," Stat said impatiently.

"Fifty-to-one."

"Was that the last round before the finals?"

"Yes, sir." She gave him a look that said she would like nothing better than for him to take five steps back and fall into a hole. Just for kicks, he gave her a wink before backing off and took a second to enjoy the unnerved look on her face.

The monitors turned black – a momentary intermission before the finals. Someone noticed Stat and a ripple of silence moved through the crowd. Shaking his head, Stat turned back and pretended to concentrate on the booth. Within a few minutes, he figured, they'd forget about him and get back to their merry-making.

It didn't take a few minutes, however. Just as he dipped his head to avoid the Spin Doctor's uncomfortable gaze, the screens flickered on again. A new table appeared.

	Contestant	Payoff
1	Sasha B.C.	1.5-1
2	Neese Highwaters	99-1

Before the crowd could form a reaction, it disappeared and was replaced by a line of scrolling text in bold golden fonts.

FINALS TO BEGIN IN 00:30:00

The first second passed in silence. The next second there was a murmur. By the time there were twenty-nine minutes and fifty-seven seconds left until the final found, Stat looked up and was instantly knocked down by a barrage of bodies charging at the betting booth like stampeding animals. Someone nearly stepped on his hand and he quickly yanked his arms close to his body, crawling along the wall to get out of the way.

"Wow," someone said. Stat looked up to see Michigan standing over him. He scrambled to his feet. Behind him, mobs had formed around the betting booths. People shouted, waving their chips and tickets, trying to put the last of their chips in before the time was up.

Michigan clicked his tongue sadly. "They even knocked *you* down. Neese and Sasha are really powerful, aren't they?"

"I'm starting to regret showing up," Stat grumbled and dusted off his jacket. "And for freak's sake, stop staring at me like that."

Michigan shook his head. "Sorry. I'm drunk and you still look like her."

Stat gestured toward Neese's booth. "You're not betting on her?"

"I did."

"How much?"

"Fifty."

"Thousand?"

Michigan sighed. "Fifty-chip. At first I was just trying to save my money. Didn't think she'd reopen the bets. I mean, it's never been done before. Now I don't have anything else because I spent the rest of it on drinks."

"You're a loser."

"I know, right?" Michigan jerked a thumb over his shoulder at the bar. "But the bar's empty now. Let's grab good seats before the other losers start drinking again."

Kam left the gallery with more dignity than most of the other commoners. After the ball came to a complete stop, she seemed to freeze for a moment. Then, as her arms dropped slowly to her sides, she raised her eyes to Beki and gave her a shallow nod, as if accepting the result as inevitable. An hour ago Beki would have felt guilty about the victory, but as it was, she only felt a mix of relief and anxiety. The door closed behind Kam with a gentle click, and she was alone.

The video cameras overhead made a series of noises. Beki looked up just in time to see the little red power lights shut off one after another. The cameras purred to a stop when the door opened once more, this time revealing a small, familiar figure with whom she had become better acquainted than she would have liked in the last few hours. She and Sasha exchanged a knowing look. Sasha turned her chin slightly and addressed the figure behind her.

"Beat it, Jean-Luc," she said.

Jean-Luc nodded and drew the door closed behind her. Just before it closed fully, however, he looked in Beki's direction and winked. Beki had no idea how to take the wink, so she assumed it was some sort of compliment. The sound of the lock clicking into place was loud as echoing thunder.

"So," she said to Sasha. "I…"

"It seems you're pretty lucky," Sasha said, cutting her off. "For a Rounder, that is."

Beki let the insult roll off. "I thought so," she said with a composed smile.

Sasha removed a ruby-encrusted compact from a hidden pocket on her dress and checked her hair in the small mirror. She was still wearing the large golden dress, but the last time Beki had laid eyes on her, her meticulous outfit and hair were becoming disheveled. It seemed she had taken the last few rounds to put herself back together. Now, just in time for the finals, she was the picture of perfection once again.

"How did you beat Kam?"

"I don't think that's any of your business."

"Humor me," Sasha said, fixing the pink-and-white striped ribbons on her pigtails. "How did you do it? She's no slouch for a commoner." A single blue eye peeked over the edge of the compact. "Did Jean-Luc help you?"

Beki started to lie, but no words came to her immediately. Sasha chuckled at the strain her face must have showed as she tried to come up with something believable.

"I already know he rigged the Wheel for you," Sasha said, snapping the compact shut. "You have no secrets to keep from me. But the truth is, even rigged, the trigger is hard to hit for a Rounder. Since you won, you must have hit it, or gotten extremely lucky. But against someone with Kam's skills, I don't think luck alone would've done it for you. So tell me, how did you do it?"

Beki hesitated, causing Sasha to frown.

"The cameras are off," she said, pointing to the ceiling. "You've actually managed to catch my attention. I suggest you not waste it. Not many people – especially not Rounders – impress me enough to do that."

Beki scoffed. "You sure think a lot of yourself for someone who never hit puberty."

Sasha countered with a smirk. "I don't think you're in any place to be cocky right now."

They stared at each as the masses below pushed and shoved. Finally, Beki relented, not through being intimidated but because a stalemate would serve no purpose right now. "I hit the trigger before the game started," she said. "I knew she would spin immediately so the ball wouldn't go anywhere. Then I stopped it." She mimed the motion with her hand. "And from there she wouldn't be able to do anything but watch the ball go in, since she can't touch the Wheel once it's stopped."

Sasha clicked her tongue. "Not bad," she said. "For a Rounder. Though it's just like a Rounder to resort to something dirty like a Stopper."

"I learned it from watching Gypsy, who I find to be very skilled." She paused, then deliberately added, "and not to mention attractive compared to the rest of the stock around here."

The corner of Sasha's lip twitched, but her smiling mask did not break. Beki caught it and made a mental note of it. She had already resolved to play a very dirty game.

"I can't believe I'm being seen with you," Michigan said, casting a glance at the half-circle of empty space at their end of the bar that had been created by Stat's presence.

"Think about how I feel," Stat replied. "I have to be seen with *you*."

"Touché."

The countdown on the screens had just ticked past fifteen minutes. Michigan had fished in his pockets for any additional chips he might have had left and came up with nothing. Disappointed that he might have passed up the best chance he was going to get in a long time to clear his debts, he relented to his sad fate of keeping Stat company.

"You don't have to stay next to me, you know."

"I have nothing better to do." Michigan rubbed his temples. He was starting to get tired. "Tell me how you roughed up Snip."

"Again?"

"Come on. I like hearing about it." He paused. "Damn it. We're not friends, are we?"

IMMORTALITY 101: The Intro Course

"I don't think so."

"Good. I'd hate to think I was friends with you."

"Oh yeah? What about me? I'd have to be friends with..." Stat's words drifted off into the air. Michigan looked his way and saw that his newly found not-quite friend was looking up at the monitors, where a new chart had appeared underneath the countdown.

	Contestant	Tally
1	Sasha B.C.	$7,189,023
2	Neese Highwaters	$6,643,125

"That's just great," he heard Stat mutter. "She knows I'm here."

With a gesture from Sasha the Wheel was removed. Tish reappeared, followed by Leonard and Mozart. She held the door open for the boys as they hoisted the pool table inside, panting as they set it down in the center of the small gallery. After it was set, Tish stepped forward and pulled a deck of playing cards out of her pocket, which she laid in the center of the table. Then, after giving Beki a longing look, she departed with the boys and closed the door behind them.

Sasha bent over the pool table and reached into her sleeve, removing a large orange object, almost the size of her fist. Beki watched her roll it between her hands, then lay it down in the center. It was orange, chipped here and there, with more surfaces than she could count. She waited in silence as Sasha picked up the deck of cards and shuffled it in a manner that would have put the best dealer in Las Vegas to shame.

"Watch closely," she said to Beki. "This is how you play the game."

"The dice game is very simple."

"Is it?" Michigan asked, his eyes fixed on the screens. The tally for both contestants had topped eight million, but Sasha's was quickly approaching nine, with Beki trailing behind by almost seven hundred thousand. "I thought it'd be something really complicated and fancy. I mean, it's the final game. Everyone's going to be watching."

"A game doesn't have to be complicated to catch the eyes of many." Stat was drumming his fingers on the bar. Michigan was beginning to get annoyed at the rhythmic motion, but he reminded himself that, just because they were acting like pals at the moment, he should not forget that Stat still had good reason to kick his ass. "A simple game is understood by all, therefore experts and common men alike can watch and enjoy it." He looked up at the screens also, looking more agitated as Sasha's tally continued to grow. "But there's another layer to this game that's not known to everyone."

"There is?"

"Or so she tells me. It sounds impossible." Stat sighed. "But think about it, it's been ages since anyone around here tried to make sense of anything. Too much trouble. And once you stop trying to make sense of things or explain stuff, nothing's impossible."

"I think I'm too drunk to follow that. Could you repeat it?"

Stat waved him off. "Never mind. The point is, there's more than one game being played here, and judging by the way Sasha's doing things, she's thought it all out."

"The rules are just that simple," Sasha said, smirking at Beki's bewildered face as she dealt out five cards to each of them. You put down your chips, and you draw. Highest total rolls first."

"And whoever rolls highest wins; I got that." Beki couldn't tear her eyes from the die. There was something odd about it. Though it was perfectly symmetrical, it looked crooked, off-center, as if it was a puzzle piece meant to fit somewhere else. Two of the polar opposite sides, she noticed, were sunk in slightly. Sasha reached down and picked the die up by the sunken sides with two fingers, and with a start Beki remembered the hand of the Lady Luck statue in the Square.

"The highest roll is the winner," Sasha continued as if she didn't hear Beki's words. "There are one hundred and twenty sides to this die. It's much heavier than any dice you're used to. Usually I don't allow anyone to touch it. But hey," she shrugged, grinning, "it's a special occasion."

She tossed the die at Beki, who surprised herself by catching it in midair. Its weight startled her. She felt along its sides, looking at the little numbers. Though the surface felt like hard plastic to the touch, she was convinced the inside had to be solid metal. She looked up at Sasha, and saw that the girl was amused at the shock on her face.

Trying hard to hide her growing unease, she tossed the die back to Sasha.

"Let me give you a demonstration before I go on," Sasha said as she caught the die. With a twist of her wrist she sent the die spinning along the edges of the pool table. It rounded almost all the corners before rolling to the center and coming to a stop with a gentle wobble. A faded "120" was carved on the surface facing up.

"Did you see that?" Sasha asked as Beki swallowed thickly. "If that had been for real, I would've won. I always win."

"No way," Michigan said, shaking his head. He paused, and then shook it again. "That's insane. I mean, that's not possible, is it?"

"Is it?" Stat asked. The lines around the betting booths were growing short, with less than six minutes to go. The air in the hall had grown thick, saturated with the scent of anxiety. "Maybe it's not literally possible, but if the roll is based on skill, don't you think something like that could affect someone psychologically? It's something that'd be hard to get out of your head once it gets in, especially for a Rounder with so much riding on the line."

Michigan shook his head again. "Beki's smarter than that."

"Is she? How long has it been since you played a Round?"

"A while, I guess."

"Do you remember what it feels like to be in the Round? The exhilaration and anxiety that everything brings on? Worrying about dying, worrying your family will die, etc. etc. She's a *Rounder*. No matter how hard she tries, she can't get all that weight off her mind. And that's what Sasha's taking advantage of." Stat gestured at the screens. "I think I'm the only person she ever told her secret to. The fact that she's showing these tallies means she knows I'm here. She's saying, 'look, it's going to work. I'm going to show you I'm right.'"

"It's ironic," Sasha continued, "that something like this actually exists in this world. After all, when you have eternity and no risk of dying, there is no need for faith. And yet, here it is."

A moment ago, Beki was calm and determined to stay that way. Now, she could feel her heart pounding again. She crossed her arms and tried to look unfazed. "You're actually telling me," she said, "that this ugly die will roll higher for whoever has more bet on them?"

"That's just a theory, since there's no other way to measure faith around here." Sasha spun the die again, and it once again turned up 120. "Right now I can manipulate it because the game hasn't started. Once the game starts, the power of faith will kick in. The player who has more faith placed on their shoulders will win."

Leaving the die on the table, she strolled over to the bookshelf, where she moved a few dusty books aside to reveal a small screen. She blew some dust off its surface and turned it on. It flickered on, displayed a blue screen, then a chart appeared.

	Contestant	Pay-off	Tally
1	Sasha B.C.	1.5-1	$13,881,573
2	Neese Highwaters	99-1	$11,542,822

"Do you see?" Sasha said. "Even though you have fooled everyone into thinking you're a High Roller, even though Neese and I are supposedly similar in skill, and even though a bet on you would pay off much more than a bet on me, they are still betting on me more than you. This is because they have already lost so much in the previous rounds that they're taking the sure thing rather than the risk. Even the ones who believe you're Neese are betting on me, because the high pay-off ratio makes them nervous. By re-opening up the bets for the finals, I'm allowing them a second chance to make a safe bet. And by betting on me," she smirked. "Their faith is placed in me instead of you." She glanced at the die, then at Beki, who was beginning to feel faint. "Are you ready to play?"

IMMORTALITY 101: The Intro Course

35
ROLL

"Would you stop eating your knuckles?"

Michigan pulled his hand out of his mouth. He'd broken skin in several places and hadn't even noticed. Grumbling, he wiped his hand on his pants. "Easy for you to say. I owe Gypsy a life debt if she loses. A *life debt!* That's not even the worst, if Beki goes back and *breaks*. That Round she's playing could break her. I can't even..."

"Chill out," Stat said, shrugging. "I mean, if Sasha's theory is right, all that Rounder has to do is have more bets on her than Sasha, right?"

"Right," Michigan said sarcastically. "And she's only behind now by, oh, let's see, five million now! Everyone's so out of chips from the other rounds that even if I went around begging, they couldn't come up with five million."

"You don't have to beg."

"What? You think I fake being a pathetic loser to hide the fact that I'm actually filthy rich?"

"Well, no," Stat said, "but I do." He chuckled at Michigan's blanched face. "All you have to do is ask nicely."

"You have sixty seconds left," Sasha said. "Then all the cameras will come back on and the game will begin. Any last words?"

Beki thought long and hard. Though there were no clocks or watches in the room, she could almost hear the seconds ticking away. What they were counting down to, she could no longer predict.

"Ten seconds," Sasha announced smugly, as if victory was already in her grasp. Beki lifted her gaze and met the girl's eyes.

"I just hope," she said quietly, "that Stat has bet on *me* after everything I did to him."

"How the hell did you..."

Stat waved the ticket in front of Michigan's face to shut him up. "How I get my chips is none of your business," he replied, stuffing the ticket into Michigan's hands. The number of zeroes on it seemed unreal. Michigan couldn't stop staring it. "The point is I've got it and I'm using it. Can't you act a little more grateful?"

"I can. I mean, I *am*." Looking from the ticket to Stat, then back at the ticket again, Michigan tried once again to determine if Lady Luck had some sort of hand in this.

"I hope it's enough. There are still some people who haven't put in their bets, but I don't think I can come up with any more."

"I hope so too." Michigan held the ticket tightly, almost afraid it would blow away if he didn't clench it until his knuckles turned white. "But why? I mean, didn't you hook up with Sasha? Why are you betting on a Rounder instead of her?"

"Oh, lots of reasons," Stat said nonchalantly. Many eyes were turned their way. Just a few moments ago, a path had cleared to allow Stat to approach the betting booth, and hundreds of eyes grew wide as he laid down the chips. Now the word was passing and everyone had already begun to speculate what his reasons for betting on Neese were. "One reason is I want this to be finished and done with. If she loses she'll probably break down, and she probably won't want to leave, not without doing something about her son. Then I'll have to be the bad guy, manhandling a miserable woman and dragging her back to the Round. Despite what everyone says, I'm a pretty nice guy. Besides," he gestured at the packed hall, flashing dance floor, and monitors. "I said I was bored enough to watch this all play out, and you certainly didn't disappoint."

The die rolled off the back of Sasha's hand and she caught herself just in time to snatch it out of the air before it hit the ground. She started to open her mouth just as the video cameras clicked on with synchronized whirring sounds. The final round had begun. She cast her best poisonous glare at the Beki, who simply stood there, arms crossed and waiting.

Slowly, with considerable effort, Sasha forced her lips to close. The only thing worse than a lady losing composure was a lady losing composure in front of watchful eyes. Smiling stiffly, she set the die down in the middle of the pool table. The reverberation of music from down below had ceased, as did all conversation. In fact, she was certain, even the noise of thousands of people breathing had taken a pause.

"Turn over your cards," she said to the Rounder through clenched teeth, and together, they turned over their cards, their movements mirroring each other. Sasha kept herself from looking up at the woman pretending to be Neese.

"Are you lying?" she asked quietly as they turned over their third cards. The smile stayed on her face.

"I have nothing to lie about," the Rounder replied.

"Yes or no," Sasha said sharply.

"No."

They turned over the fourth card in their sets. Sasha's total was running high, which calmed her a bit. After all the cards were turned, she raised her head and tried to read the Rounder's face. But all the woman did was smile, and she longed to wipe that smile off her face.

"I will roll first."

"Be my guest."

Sasha picked up the die, gripping it in her hand tightly. She took a deep breath, and raised her hand. Below, a thousand observers drew breaths simultaneously.

She meant for, she told herself. She meant what she did for him. Maybe she kept him company. I will go to him after this, and make sure that he's never lonely again.

It was now or never. She rolled.

"Maybe he didn't bet on me," the Rounder said a split second before the die left her fingers. "Maybe I was too rough with him."

391

"She choked."

Michigan was so busy staring at the ticket that he hadn't even noticed the game starting. He leapt off of his seat, only to be pulled back down by Stat.

"Sit down," Stat said firmly as the large orange die spun out of Sasha's hand and onto the pool table. "Stay calm. This is good for your little Rounder girlfriend."

Michigan breathed a tiny sigh of relief. "For a second there I thought it was Beki who choked." He paused, looking at the screen closely, where the die was taking a flawless straight path along the sides of the pool table. "Wait, what do you mean she choked? Looks perfectly fine to me."

"I can tell."

"How?"

"The way she flicked her wrist. The angle was off. By maybe half a degree or so, but she recovered. The force of compensating spin might offset..." Stat turned to Michigan, who was staring at him blankly. "Never mind. Just watch."

As one, the audience tensed as the die began to slow.

"So if I had asked you earlier, would you have bought Beki out of her debt without this whole mess?"

As one, they looked down at their tickets, as if making sure they had bet on the right one, whoever that might be.

"No."

"Why not?"

As one, thousands of pairs of eyes widened as the die began to slow, spinning in place at the center of the pool table.

"How would that be fun for me?"

"I thought you were a nice guy."

As one, they gasped as the die came to a stop, with the topside reading one hundred and fifteen.

"I'm not *that* nice." Stat pointed at the screen. "See? What'd I tell you? She choked."

Sasha didn't move, wallowing in shock, surprise, and disappointment. Perhaps it was for the best, because it kept her from lunging at Beki when she picked up the die.

Beki was quite oblivious to the tension building all around her. She took a deep breath, looked up just long enough to see Sasha staring at the monitor on the bookcase, and rolled.

"You owe me," Stat yelled to Michigan over the explosion of cheers and shouts that erupted around them.

"What did you say?" Michigan shouted back.

"I said you owe me!" Stat pressed his back against the bar, making himself as flat as possible, but it didn't keep his toes from being stepped on as the crowd stampeded past them. "For goodness' sake! They're like animals, running to wherever the money is."

"What?"

"*You owe me!*"

Michigan took off his jacket and shoved it into Stat's hands. "Here. We're even."

Stat looked at the jacket, then back at Michigan, who was already pushing his way through the masses, and shrugged. "Alright," he said to himself.

IMMORTALITY 101: The Intro Course

SHUFFLE

IMMORTALITY 101: The Intro Course

Epilogue

THE CRESCENT

"So how did you do it?"

Beki was counting the chips over again. There were so many, more than Michigan thought he'd ever see, even if he had an eternity to earn them. He watched her slender fingers slide the chips into neat little piles.

"Lady Luck watched out for me," she said with a mischievous smile.

"No, seriously."

"I *am* serious."

Snaking his fingers across the table, Michigan picked up a thousand-chip. He had always thought that thousand-chips were nothing more than a legend, something the commoners talked about but never saw. He held it up to the light of the chandelier and studied it. Ironically, it was made of tin. "Stat was telling me all this crazy stuff," he said. "About that weird-looking die."

"Is it the same stuff Sasha told me?"

"Something about it working on faith?"

"Something like that." Beki put the last few piles into their respective piles. "Maybe that's how I won. I mean, I did wind up with more chips bet on me than her. Just by about a hundred though. I can't imagine it making that big a difference."

"Apparently it did. You rolled two higher than she did."

The video of the last match had already been immortalized on the network by the Snyperx. It was trimmed, polished, and matched to various musical numbers within an hour of the match's end. The focal point of almost every version was the die rolling that decisive one hundred and seventeen.

"Still, I'm surprised Sasha didn't roll higher, even if she did fumble." Michigan shook his head. "I'm surprised she fumbled at all, after all the trouble she went through."

"Yeah," Beki muttered under her breath. "I'm not proud of it."

"What?"

"Nothing." She stood. Neese's robe spilled over her form. Her hair was still tied up. Michigan dearly wished she would let it down. "What do we do with all these chips now?"

"We fix your life."

THE GALLERY

The hall was eerily silent. Here and there was the gentle clink and clack of the Spin Doctors' shoes. After a game, they became nothing more than glorified cleaning crews, as was the way things usually went. Some of them grumbled, but most knew it would do no good and simply kept their heads down as they picked up the mountains of empty glasses and bottles, piles of losing tickets, and cleaned up unidentifiable stains wherever they happened to be. There was a phantom echo, however, that lingered. As if the raucous aftermath of the game has left a permanent mark.

Tish went about her task with a smile on her face. For the first time since becoming Sasha's slave, she felt she saw hope. There was such a thing as miracles, and Neese Highwaters was the physical embodiment of it. She resolved with her tender heart to work harder than ever to be close to her goddess.

Leonard and Mozart took advantage of her good mood and directed her to scrub up the most mysterious of the stains.

"We found a guy in the bathroom." Tish looked up, still grinning.

"We thought you'd be interested."

"Might be Boxcat."

"He looks asleep."

"I bet..."

Footsteps and voices drifted off when a figure wearing a high-collar black jacket with red trim stepped into the hall. They followed him with their eyes until he disappeared up the back stairs.

398

"I like it," Leonard said.
"Better than the brown one," Mozart said.

Sasha sat at the top of the stairs. The hall, like her parlor, was dark and murky. She sat with her face buried in her hands.

Her meticulous hair had fallen apart. Ribbons littered the ground around her feet. Her dress, once light and airy as a cloud, now fell into a hopeless crumble, as if weighed down by the darkness. Her shoes lay at the door of the parlor. Her bare feet trembled as she wiped her face with her palm and wrists.

"Hey."

In the dark, she could barely make out his shape through the space between her fingers. "What do you want?" she asked.

"I wanted to see if you're okay."

"You came to laugh at me." She wrapped her arms around her knees and hid her face behind them. "They're all laughing at me, aren't they? I lost to a Rounder. I'm ruined."

She heard the shuffle of his clothes as he sat down next to her. Out of the corner of her eyes she could see the red trim on his jacket.

"Are you?" he asked her. "Looks to me like you pulled off the most memorable game in history. If we still had history books this game would go down in it. So you didn't win. You're the one who put it together. Whenever they talk about this game – which is going to be a pretty *long* time – they're be thinking of you."

"And her," she whispered bitterly.

He shrugged. "So what?"

Sasha tightened her grip around her knees. "They believed she would win. In the end, they believed in her. That's why I lost. I was about to win." Her fingers formed into fists. "It was that Michigan. I don't know how he did it. I don't know where he got those chips to bet, but…"

"From me."

Her head snapped up, swollen red eyes focused on him. Stat gave her a wan smile.

"He got the chips from me."

"You?"

"You're looking at me like I betrayed you."

399

"*You did!*" she shrieked, lunging at his face with her nails. He caught her wrists and pulled her forward firmly, her surprised face inches from him.

"I bet on her," he told her slowly. "I bet on her because I had faith that you could win whether I did or not. I didn't even believe all that mumbo-jumbo you were telling me about the die, but I still did it. I still don't believe it. I don't think you lost because I bet on her. You lost because of something else."

"Did you sleep with her?"

He blanched. "What?"

"That Rounder. Did you sleep with her?"

"Of course not. Why would you even think that?"

Sasha's eyes fell. Stat released her. Slowly, she drew herself back into a ball, arms wrapped around her knees.

"Did you want me to lose?" she asked.

"Yes. I believed you would win regardless, but I hoped you'd lose. I think I bet on her because some small part of me did think it would make a difference, even if the rest of me thought it was bull."

"Do you hate me that much?"

Stat shook his head. "No. I don't hate you." He paused with a sigh. "I love you. No matter how fucked up it is, I love you. In the end I guess everything I did was selfish. I let Michigan go through with his harebrained scheme, I came to this game hoping you'd lose, even going as far as betting everything I had. All just so I could knock you down to my level."

She turned to him. "Your level?"

He gave her a crooked smile. "I'm a stigma in this place. Now you are, too. It's not the same, of course, but it's something. I don't want to be paraded around by you like some trophy. If you love me, you'd have to sink low with me once in a while."

"I do love you."

"I know." Stat pushed himself off the stairs and slid his arms under Sasha's legs and shoulders, picking her up as if she weighed no more than a leaf. "Come on, you're going to catch a cold if you keep sitting out here like this."

She wrapped her arms around his neck and buried her face under his chin as he carried her into the parlor.

THE ROUND

Calisa and Ro didn't appear to have moved since their entrance a few days ago. Michigan gestured for Beki to walk past them without a word. Ro turned to look at them as they approached. Calisa remained still, her white arms draped loosely at her sides. Beki slowed her step.

"What are you doing?" Michigan called back.

Beki pointed at the metal mask covering Calisa's eyes. "This was Neese's idea, right?"

"Yeah, so?"

She bent and took the mask in both hands. It came away surprisingly easily. Calisa opened her eyes and gazed at Beki in shock and awe, blinking like a baby animal seeing light for the first time.

"Why?" she whispered.

"Because I felt like being nice." She dropped the mask on the floor. "Better enjoy it. When I come back I can't guarantee I'll be this nice again."

As Michigan led her away, Beki looked back to see Calisa raise her hands to her eyes, a million emotions playing on her face. Ro crawled over the table and wrapped her long arms around her sister as Calisa burst into tears.

"Did you steal the truck?"

"Yes."

They were parked a block away from her house. She could see lights on inside, and her car parked in the driveway. Jonathan was probably home, and must be worried sick. She would have to go inside and face him now. There were no more excuses. Looking down at herself, she realized she had no explanation for Neese's silver dress.

"The offer still stands," Michigan said. "You can still come back and stay with me."

"Your desperation is endearing." She shook her head. "But this is my life. I can't run. Especially after going to all that trouble to buy those black chips."

He pulled a carton of cigarettes out of his pocket. "One more for old time's sake?"

"Why not?" She let him light the cigarette for her. "When you go back, are you still going to obsess over Neese?"

IMMORTALITY 101: The Intro Course

Michigan shook his head. "Nah. I think I'll find a better hobby for myself." He paused in thought. "You know, we never did figure out what it was that made you win."

"Does it matter?"

"If it was really Lady Luck," Michigan said, taking a drag, "maybe I'll give this religion thing a go when I get back. I hear it's a riot."

In a hushed hospital room, a nurse received quite a surprise when the boy she was told would be vegetative for at least three months opened his eyes.

APPENDIX I

Excerpts from *IMMORTALITY 101*

CH 1 It Sucks (in its entirety)
It sucks.

CH 2 It Really Sucks (in its entirety)
In case you think I'm kidding, I'm not. It really sucks.

CH 3 Forgotten Stuff (excerpts)

* * *

So the idea is, when life is forever, nothing else is. I mean, take books, right? Nobody writes books any more. Why? Because once upon a time books were invented as a way to keep records and leave legacies, or so I've been told. I don't know. I don't remember. And that, my friend, is the problem. When you live forever, you don't think about leaving something behind. Why bother? You're going to be around forever to sing your own praises anyway, and what better way to get people to know you than to talk about yourself? Live. In action. Visual over paper. I bet some people don't even remember how to write any more. We don't need records. We don't need history.

* * *

We have no history. History is that thing that came before our time. This *is* our time. It will always be our time. And we have no future either, because the future becomes the past. For us, it's always the present.

* * *

There are some advantages to not trying to remember anything, though – everything can be forgotten. With enough time, absolutely anything, no matter how glorious or hideous, can disappear without a trace. It's like a vanishing act. Totally groovy.

CH 5 Death (in its entirety)
We're addicted to it. (See Ch VII Round)

CH 7 Round (Excerpts)
The Round is a game of Death. Seriously. No joke. It's amazing what comes out of the Round. I mean, no one here ever bothers to do anything anymore besides drink, shoot up, gamble, and screw each other in one form or another. But in between the fun we kind of just sit there and stare. But the Rounders, man oh man! Do they get busy! It's incredible what one can do when he's on the clock. It's like, "You got 80 years. Make something of yourself. And… go!" And off he goes.

* * *

If you haven't heard a Rounder talk, I suggest you do. It's hard to come across one since the law's always on the move (yea, you know who I'm talking about). But if you find any, just listen to them. They say such crazy things, and what's crazier, it makes you want to join them. It's more fun than listening to someone when they're high. High just gives you nonsense. Rounders give you really, really great nonsense.

* * *

The Round is so awesomely fun. Some people can't get enough of it. Why? Because having an end to a life makes it more enticing. It's sort of like being a daredevil. Play with death.

* * *

They have this thing called a commitment. (See Ch X Silly Thing)

***

I could go on and on and on about the Round. That's probably why this chapter is almost a hundred pages long now. I should stop. Save it for the next book, whenever I feel like it. But there's one more thing I want to talk about. Some people think that the Round is more than just an amazing game. They think it's some other universe or something. But these people are generally high and tend to be ignored. There are even some people who think the Round is a reflection of how we used to be, before we started, well, not dying. I don't believe that either. That's just reading too much into a simple game.

I think the Round is not complex at all. The game itself is, sure, but its purpose was not. It's an escape. Someone invented the basic idea at some point, maybe just a blank space one could walk in and out of. Then it started to involve more people, more ideas. Then people started to build more and more within the Round so the game would last longer and longer. Then the Round and this place started to bleed into each other. Languages, ideas, art, music, slang, habits, designs, positions, etc etc. It made life a little less dull. No one remembers who started it anymore. But it's growing.

Like a tumor, but a benign one.

***

Ninety-nine pages. Hmm… I'll even it out to a hundred.
Blah
Blah
Blah
Blah
Blah
Blah
Blah

CH 8 Hierarchy (excerpt)

***

It lasts forever, or at least seems to. Although no one needs to rule with an iron fist, since everyone's too doped up to rebel.

IMMORTALITY 101: The Intro Course

* * *

CH 10 Silly Thing (excerpts)
Jim and Bob meet. Jim and Bob fall in love. Jim and Bob live happily for many years. Jim and Bob die.

Jim and Bob meet. Jim loves Sue. Bob loves Jim. Bob kills Sue and winds up in jail. Jim marries Bill. Bob, Jim, and Bill live out their lives and die.

Jim and Bob meet. Jim finds out he is actually Bob's long-lost brother. Bob loves Jo. Jim helps Bob get Jo. Jo falls in love with Jim. Jim and Bob becomes estranged again. Jim and Bob meet against after many, many years, confess they still care about each other, and they all live until they die.

The ending's always the same. Jim and Bob die. Jim and Bob die. Jim and Bob die.

* * *

So why do the Rounders keep committing, vowing forever, knowing that death will part them eventually? Because, my friend, death *can* part them. Nothing's forever in the Round. Out here, when life is forever, nothing else is. I mean, who can *really* spend eternity with someone. Give it fifty, sixty years (in Round terms, that is), and it's bound to end. If you're lucky, it's a little longer than that, but just like everything else, you get bored with each other. Doesn't that suck? You bet.

* * *

So, this new trend lately... playing a Round partnered up with someone instead of solo. It's pretty cool.

* * *

CH 12 The High Rollers' Club (in its entirety)
They're a bunch of bitches. There, I said it. It's been a long time since a new one joined their ranks though. The incumbents are doing a good job of keeping out the new meat. Although if I have to guess, my money's on Calisa Wright.